THE
CONGRUENT
EMPEROR

Book Four of the Congruent Mage Series

The Congruent Mage Series

www.CongruentMage.com

The Xenotech Support Series

www.XenotechSupport.com

Dedication

To the talented authors of the Lawrenceville
Science Fiction and Fantasy Writers Group
for all their support and inspiration.

Cover and Map designs by Dan Paulson

ISBN-13: 978-0-9978319-5-5

Spiral Arm Press
1725 Carlington Court
Grayson, GA 30017

www.SpiralArmPress.com

Prologue

Eynon was a thousand feet above the Tempest Isles' great harbor, spinning so fast he felt like an empty cask caught in a whirlpool. His protective sphere of solidified sound was buffeted by driving rain and near hurricane-force winds, knocking him about and slamming him into the interior of his sphere so hard he couldn't summon the focus he needed to gate out. In the space of a heartbeat, the surface of his sphere turned red-orange and the temperature of the air inside it rose to nearly unbearable levels as he was blasted by well-coordinated jets of flame from seven obsidian-colored dragons.

Eynon involuntarily inhaled and sensed the hot air scald his lungs. He coughed and felt himself close to passing out. He tried to center his mind and find inner calm amidst the shrieking gale and gouts of dragonfire but failed when the fearsome snout of one of the black dragons crashed into his sphere at an angle, increasing its rotation and sending Eynon off on a completely new vector.

At least they've stopped breathing fire, thought Eynon. *Just my bad luck a Roma dragon flew through my cloud illusion and revealed my presence. So much for trying to 'see' with my bat ears. I didn't even hear it coming.*

A pair of dragons chose that moment to speed toward Eynon's sphere from opposite directions. They struck his protective bubble seconds apart, tossing him against one side of his sphere then the other in quick succession. He tumbled inside the sphere like a stone in a fast-cranked lapidary's polishing machine.

The twin collisions in close succession unexpectedly helped Eynon by stopping his sphere from spinning. He risked a deep breath of the air inside the sphere—it was slightly cooler now as the wind and rain worked in his favor instead of against him. Eynon tried to follow the steps for forming *ad hoc* gates Verro had taught him. *First, fully visualize your destination.*

He closed his eyes and took another breath, remembering the details of Laetícia's study in Nova Eboracum, the last place he'd been before embarking on what should have been a simple scouting expedition. Eynon had gotten as far as capturing the details of Laetícia's writing desk when every hair on his body stood out straight and his skin tingled like it was covered by ten thousand angry bees.

Bright lights flashed on his retinas *through* his closed eyelids and his ears were assaulted by booms of thunder louder than the great green dragon Viridáxés' roar. Opening his eyes, he caught the outlines of four purple-robed figures on flying disks circling his sphere. *Roma wizards,* Eynon realized. Sírénae Accipiter's wizards.

Tendrils of tight light encircled Eynon's refuge and sent it spinning again, costing him any chance of escaping through an *ad hoc* gate. He no longer hovered inside his sphere but lay slumped at its base, barely conscious. His body was tossed from side to side as the sphere turned, but Eynon was too dazed to do more than moan when he slid back to the bottom.

Massive fists of solidified sound from the Roma mages struck the top of his sphere like hammer blows from a blacksmith the size of a mountain. Eynon's body flew upward as if hurled by a catapult. His head struck the interior of his shield and the sphere winked out. No longer conscious, Eynon fell through the tempest toward the storm-tossed sea.

Chapter 1

A Scouting Expedition

Most of the senior dignitaries from the party celebrating the newly-signed Treaty of Friendship had shifted from the party's walled garden to Laetícia's study. That location, high in Laetícia's tower, provided more privacy for their continued discussion.

Eynon had been surprised to discover the walled garden was inside the grounds of the governor-general's palace. It was only a short walk to Laetícia's tower, and there were enough wizards to lift everyone who *wasn't* a wizard, so none of them had to climb the stairs.

Servants or slaves who *had* climbed all seven hundred steps delivered pitchers of wine and cider, plus beer made from sorghum *and* from barley malt. Eynon even saw a few large jugs of mead for the Bifurlanders. The servants placed several trays of sweet honey cakes and a few with dough rings covered in seeds on tables around the study. Eynon noticed Doethan smile when he saw the dough rings and tubs of soft white cheese appear. Chee was more intrigued by the small baskets of grapes and figs arrayed between the larger trays.

The study was crowded with kings, queens, nobles, and senior wizards, but there *was* room for everyone to sit. Extra seating had been provided to supplement the chairs and dining couches already present. After everyone collected a mug or goblet and a small plate of something to nibble on, the servants withdrew.

"How long do you think we have before they get here?" asked Nûd.

"I have no idea," said Háiddon. "I'm not a sailor."

"It will depend on the number of wizards they have who are capable of summoning wind," said Laetícia. "I can't see them having enough to support the entire fleet, so they'll travel only as fast as the natural winds will drive them."

"Yes, but how long is *that?*" asked Nûd.

"Two weeks, if we're lucky," said Laetícia.

"We could take on a thousand ships and hold our own with our five hundred," said King Bjarni of Bifurland. "Our longships against *two* thousand Ocean-going Roma ships is another matter."

"Tamloch's three hundred and fifty larger vessels will help," said Dârio.

"What about Dâron's fleet?" asked Eynon.

Duke Háiddon laughed. So did Dârio and Jenet. Fercha shook her head in disgust.

"You can ask Princess Gwýnnett about Dâron's fleet," said Duke Háiddon.

"Word about it probably didn't reach the Coombe," added Merry, "but Gwýnnett sold most of Dâron's fleet off to the major merchant families two years ago, when Queen Carys was in mourning and before Dârio could stop her. Most of Dâron's warships have been rebuilt to carry cargo now."

"That seems shortsighted," said Eynon. On Eynon's shoulder, Chee covered his big eyes with his front paws to illustrate Eynon's observation.

"Tell me about it," said Dârio. He saw that Fercha was about to launch into a tirade against Gwýnnett's actions but pushed his palms down to signal her that rehashing the past would be counterproductive.

"As Grand Admiral of Tamloch's fleet, I was certainly pleased by Gwýnnett's greed," said Sónnel. "I expect selling the fleet was part of her scheming with Túathal." The Grand Admiral shook his head sadly over the lost Dâron ships and pulled his shoulders back. His one remaining eye scanned everyone gathered in Laetícia's study. "We still need to know more about the emperor's invasion fleet," he said.

"Deposed emperor," said Quintillius.

Laetícia rolled her eyes at her husband. With the Siren Hawk's fleet on the way, it was a distinction without a difference.

"I told you I'd be glad to scout things out with Laetícia and report," said Eynon.

"I'm still not convinced that's a good idea," said Laetícia.

"I'll keep us hidden," said Eynon. "Don't worry."

"I'm not going to do anything *but* worry," said Merry. "Please take good care of him, Laetícia."

"I can take care of…" began Eynon.

"I will," Laetícia answered. "It has to be done. We need a full and accurate assessment of Sírénae's forces and I'm the best-equipped wizard we have to do that."

"Duke Néillen's a trained military commander," said Dârio. "Why can't he do it?"

"He doesn't share Laetícia's in-depth knowledge of Roma military organization," said Quintillius. "Her uncle Valens is the Tetrarch for the Southern Empire."

"I thought her parents herded goats," said Eynon.

"They do," said Laetícia. "Thousands of them. My extended family has one of the largest herds on the upper Nile—but my uncle Valens left as soon as he came of age. He always wanted a military career."

"Oh," said Eynon. He looked at Laetícia thoughtfully.

Merry smiled, despite her tension. Eynon was finally learning the wider world was more complicated than the Coombe.

"Why didn't your uncle warn us about the invasion?" asked Jenet.

"I've been asking myself the same question," said Laetícia.

"We haven't heard *anything* from anywhere in the Imperium for several days," said Quintillius.

"The Imperium?" asked Eynon.

"All four empires," Quintillius replied.

"The silence from across the Ocean is puzzling," said Laetícia, "I'll find out why soon, but for now Eynon and I had best be going." She nodded at Eynon. "Duke Néillen also has to be notified. I'll let him know we're coming."

"You *will* bring Néillen back, won't you?" asked Verro. "We don't want Sírénae's forces capturing him. He knows too much."

"That makes sense," said Laetícia. "And he did warn us about the invasion fleet. We owe him something for that."

"But he doesn't trust *you*," said Verro. "I'll join you when you contact Néillen to reassure him."

"People used to treachery…" began Dârio.

"…expect it from others," finished Nûd.

Laetícia nodded and left her study through the door to her library, followed by Verro. Fercha moved to talk quietly with Inthíra and distract her from Doethan and Rúth.

"I'm going to have a private conversation with Eynon," Merry announced. "I need to properly convince him not to take unnecessary risks."

Eynon thought about replying but saw the serious look on Merry's face. So did Chee. The little raconette jumped down from Eynon's shoulder and scampered over to situate himself on Princess Rúth's lap. Eynon waved to his familiar and allowed Merry to lead him up a spiral staircase to the roof. He didn't see the others smiling but was fairly sure they were. He pretended not to hear Jenet's comment as they departed.

"Properly?" she said, in a tone that suggested Merry's intentions were anything *but* proper.

* * * * *

"A little wind and rain won't deter me from my destiny," said Emperor Sírénae Accipiter, the Siren Hawk, from the deck of the *Seahawk,* the flagship of her vast fleet. She was almost yelling to be heard over the roaring gale and the percussive beat of the driving rain pounding on the hemisphere of solidified sound above her.

"Of course not, Your Imperial Majesty," said Magister Callidius, her most senior mage and the wizard casting the hemisphere. "A *lot* of wind and rain are a different story, however. You're too wise to risk the fleet and your soldiers by trying to sail west through this mess." He waved his hands at the storm raging around them.

The third person inside the protective dome spoke. "It's lucky for us that we could shelter in such a good harbor when the tempest struck," said Machaera, Sírénae's top military commander. She was young with a muscular physique and was sly enough—and skilled enough—to out-wrestle her own centurions in competitions.

"Luck had nothing to do with it," said gray-haired Admiral Pixo. "Storms are always a possibility when crossing the Ocean. I made sure our course took us near the Tempest Isles for just this eventuality."

"Now that we've finished congratulating ourselves," said Sírénae, "we face the bigger challenge of conquering Orluin once the storm passes."

"Will you want the entire fleet to sail to Nova Eboracum harbor?" asked the admiral.

Before the emperor could reply, Magister Callidus tapped his ear then interrupted. "One of our warders reports a visitor," said the mage. "A wizard scouting high above."

"You mean a spy," said Machaera. "From Queen Carys, Túathal, or Laetícia."

"It could be someone from Bifurland," said Admiral Pixo.

"Doubtful," said Sírénae. "I'd bet an *aureus* it's Laetícia."

Pixo grunted. He respected the Bifurlanders' sailing skills and sometimes allowed that to influence his perception of their capabilities in other areas.

"We'll have a conversation about the disposition of the fleet later," said the Emperor. She turned to Callidus. "For now, deal with our *visitor* and see that she's captured and brought here for interrogation."

"As you direct," Callidus replied. He stabilized the hemisphere keeping off the elements, walked through its wall, stepped on his flying disk, and sped upward. His personal protective sphere sparkled and shed raindrops.

"Your Imperial Majesty," said Machaera, nodding to Sírénae, "we still need to discuss stores. We only have enough food for..."

"I told you not to worry about that," said the emperor. *"Our* forces won't starve."

Machaera and Pixo exchanged a glance. They knew what Sírénae was implying. Hungry enemies couldn't put up much of a fight.

* * * * *

Eynon followed Laetícia through the *ad hoc* gate she'd made. It felt odd to *step* through a vertical gate rather than fly down through a horizontal one as Verro had taught him. Still, he appreciated that it wouldn't be wise to simply gate into the sky above the Tempest Isles' great harbor—and the high winds made that unwise in any case. He wasn't quite fast enough at putting up a protective shield of solidified sound and found his robes drenched by driving rain. Eynon smiled when he used Doethan's clothes-drying spell to remedy his soaked condition. He and Merry had both learned that spell at Doethan's tower on the Rhuthro on the day Eynon had first met Rowsch, Doethan's canine familiar. Eynon had teased Merry and shocked Doethan by using his solidified sound illusion magic to make it seem like the big dog had three heads, like the fierce beast in the old Athican stories.

Laetícia's gate had emerged outside a limestone cave where Duke Néillen was said to be less-than-patiently waiting. She'd told Eynon the cave was on top of a hill overlooking the harbor, but Eynon couldn't verify that with his own senses directly. The rain was so intense he could barely see Laetícia inside her own protective bubble five feet ahead of him.

Visibility wasn't improved by the debris being blown by the wind, either. Eynon thought he recognized palm tree fronds like big fern leaves spinning by, based on illustrations in Robin Goodfellow's *Peregrinations*. One was plastered to the outside of his shields for a few seconds before the gale carried it away. He could feel the rushing air try to lift him *and* his bubble off the ground and was pleased to enter the cave behind Laetícia and escape the inimical elements.

"I'm glad you came," said Duke Néillen when they reached him thirty feet inside the narrow opening in the limestone. Tamloch's former earl marshal was shivering and his pants and tunic were dripping. Water formed a dozen small puddles on the cave's floor around his feet.

That may explain why he's not calling Laetícia a traitor at present, thought Eynon. He saw Laetícia drop her shield and dropped his own, then used Doethan's clothes-drying spell on Néillen. The duke mouthed a silent *thank you* to Eynon, looking not only grateful but a good deal more comfortable.

"How could you see the emperor's fleet in this weather?" Eynon asked Néillen.

"It wasn't like this when they arrived," Néillen replied. "The rain and winds came sweeping in from the west after the fleet had already entered the harbor."

"Sírénae and Callidus know enough to keep a close watch on the weather ahead of their course," said Laetícia. "And Pixo would insist on it."

"Callidus?" asked Néillen.

"Pixo?" Eynon added.

"Callidus is Sírénae's top mage and Pixo commands her fleet," said Laetícia.

"Thanks for the explanation," said Néillen. "Why is she an emperor instead of an empress, by the way?"

"Would Jenet settle for being Dârio's earl marshalette?" asked Eynon.

"Of course not," said Néillen. He rubbed his chin. "The nobles in Tamloch will be getting quite an education in the months ahead."

"Knowing Jenet, I'm sure they will," said Eynon.

"The sooner they learn to treat women with respect, the longer they'll keep their titles," added Laetícia. "It won't be long until Tamloch recognizes women in the line of succession, I expect." She shook her head and water flew from the beads in her braids. "But we're not here to talk about breaking open closed minds with sledgehammers, Your Grace. We're here to scout out the units under Sírénae's command."

"Right," said Duke Néillen. "I can tell you more about what I saw. It's too bad you won't be able to see anything for yourself through the storm."

"There are often breaks in weather like this," said Laetícia. "With luck, we'll get a few minutes of calm between bands of rain. I won't need long to identify ships and legions. Sírénae *had* fifty legions under her command, but with only two thousand ships it sounds like many of them stayed loyal to the Imperium."

"Only a Roma would say, '*Only* two thousand ships,'" said Néillen. He frowned and spat on the cave's stone floor.

His true attitude toward Laetícia is coming through, thought Eynon. He moved toward the opening of the cave and tried to peer out using the same sort of goggles of solidified sound that helped him see at night. They didn't make much difference. The cold rain outside the entrance looked like a solid wall of water. Behind him, Laetícia and Néillen were still talking.

"...a red standard with a gold elephant," said the duke who had obviously been reciting a list. "And lots of black banners with white gryffons."

"Those are snow-gryffons, Sírénae's personal symbol," said Laetícia. "They're snow leopards with falcons' heads, claws and wings and native to the mountains at the eastern edge of the Empire. I can promise you they're every bit as vicious as she is."

"Orluin's gryffons are bad enough," said Duke Néillen.

"These are worse," said Laetícia. "She keeps one on a chain as a pet—and I *don't* like to think about what she feeds it."

"Understood," said Néillen. He continued his litany of flags from the invading fleet while Laetícia took in the details he shared about the invaders.

Eynon agreed with Duke Néillen about native Orluin gryffons. He'd had several run-ins with them and had even been in one of their nests in the mountains near Melyncárreg. That was closer to the savage lion-eagles than he ever wanted to be again.

He looked outside at the wall of rain and considered ways to see through it. A drop of white guano fell from the cave's ceiling and landed by his boot. Eynon looked up and saw dozens of dormant leathery-winged forms sleeping above him. Their presence reminded him that bats have no trouble flying at night. His little sister Braith said she could sometimes hear them squeaking at the limits of her hearing when thousands flew above the Coombe on warm summer nights.

It took Eynon several tries but he eventually hit on the proper combination of high-pitched tones and solidified sound *ears* to amplify the returning echoes. Outlines of images appeared on a new sort of echo-tracking goggles he crafted. They let Eynon see the world outside the cave in much the same way he'd sensed the shapes and contours of Tamloch's capital, Riyas, when he'd constructed a copy of that city to fool Túathal and Viridáxés the week before. Things looked a lot like the wisent illusion Merry had made earlier—collections of shapes forming objects without fine details.

Looking over his shoulder to confirm Laetícia and Néillen were still deep in conversation, Eynon pulled his flying disk off his back, set his feet in its leather straps, generated a protective sphere of solidified sound, and added his bat-ears to the outside of the sphere. Before launching himself up into the storm to reconnoiter, he remembered to cast the illusion of a small dark cloud around his protective sphere and flew out of the cave.

"Eynon!" shouted Laetícia. "Stop!"

Her words came too late to make a difference.

Chapter 2

Plans and Consequences

"If they weren't wizards, I'd have them beaten," said the Emperor. "How can four mages and seven dragons fail to capture one spy?"

I must stay calm, thought Magister Callidus, *even though she knows exactly what to do to make me angry.* He cleared his throat and lifted his arms to indicate the storm still raging around the protective bubble of solidified sound he maintained. "Visibility *is* limited, Your Imperial Majesty," said Callidus. "And my best wizards aren't on picket duty."

"See that your pickets are properly punished for their incompetence," said the emperor. "If checking the wards and keeping watch overhead is too much, we'll have to come up with even more unpleasant tasks for them."

"I have hulls that need to be stripped of barnacles," said Pixo. "Will that do?"

"Admirably, Admiral," said Sírénae. No one smiled, and the emperor frowned. "I will have words with our dragons too, once the bad weather passes."

"I'm sure they'll be *properly* cowed by your displeasure," said General Machaera. The corner of her mouth turned up and the emperor saw it.

"It's more that they *won't* be cowed," said Sírénae. "I'll cut their rations of red meat in half for a week."

"That's not much of a threat when there are whales and tuna for the taking in the Ocean," said Pixo.

"Then I'll have to determine a more effective threat," said the emperor. "Dragons need to know my commands must be obeyed."

"Yes, Your Imperial Majesty," said Magister Callidus.

"Stop that," said Sírénae. "You only use my full title when you think I'm wrong."

Callidus nodded and began to speak, but the emperor cut him off. "Your wizards are sure the spy wasn't Laetícia? I expected to see her spying on us personally."

"They assured me the intruder was a boy or young man," said Callidus. "They would have scooped him up if the dragons hadn't gotten in the way when they all dove to capture him simultaneously and collided. The dragons started fighting and their bodies blocked my mages from seeing the spy's fall."

"It's not like they could see that well in this weather anyway," added Admiral Pixo.

"I still don't like it," said Sírénae. "Laetícia must be around somewhere. She always was a hands-on spymaster. Extend the wards beyond the harbor, Callidus."

"I'll see to it immediately, Your Imperial Majesty."

"You disagree?" said the emperor.

Machaera jumped in before Callidus could answer. "You're going to cite the old saying about locking the stable doors after the horses have already been stolen, aren't you?"

"Precisely," Callidus replied.

"Have them do a sweep searching for unfamiliar magestones then," said the emperor. "That should be within the limits of their competence."

"As the emperor commands," said Magister Callidus.

"You were going to do that anyway, weren't you?" asked Sírénae.

"You know me well," Callidus replied.

"Can we get back to planning our invasion?" said Machaera. "I need to focus on what it's going to take to keep our army fed and ready to fight."

"They'll be fed if every ship in the fleet has to be pressed into fishing duty," said the emperor.

"What?" said Admiral Pixo. "My sailors are warriors, not hook baiters."

"And fish won't do us much good if the legions are inland," added General Machaera. "What's your plan?"

"That will depend on Quintillius—and Laetícia," said Sírénae.

"You mean on whether they decide to support you or oppose you?" asked Pixo.

"Precisely," said the emperor, imitating the way Callidus had said the same word earlier.

"I expect you've got plans that cover both possibilities?" said Machaera.

"I do," said Sírénae. "Let's adjourn to my cabin and talk further."

"I'll be glad not to worry about keeping our protective sphere in place," said Callidus. "I'm ready for a cup of strong wine."

"So am I," said Admiral Pixo.

"Watered wine for me," said Machaera. "I need to keep my head clear."

"And I need Thraxa back at my side," said Sírénae.

"It *is* close to her feeding time," said Magister Callidus. There were times when he was sorry he'd given the snow-gryffon egg to the emperor years ago but stroking the fur on the beast's hindquarters was one of the few things that could calm Sírénae when she was angry. *At least she wasn't unhappy about my pickets for too long,* thought the senior mage. *And it makes sense to use them to clean barnacles off hulls for Pixo. We should make that standard practice, unless the good admiral prefers to reserve scraping hulls as a punishment for his own people.*

* * * * *

"Fetch me more fish," Sírénae commanded one of her personal slaves, a young woman with short brown hair and a perpetually nervous expression like a mouse in a room full of batsnakes.

The woman kept her distance from Thraxa's sharp beak and snagged the empty ceramic bowl that had previously held a dozen fat fish half as long as her forearm. The snow-gryffon's nearest eye followed the woman's movements as the vicious beast seemed to consider the possibility of snapping out with her sharp hooked beak and feasting on human flesh, rather than the finned fare she had been fed so far on the fleet's voyage. The slave backed away, her eyes never leaving Thraxa's until she left the emperor's well-appointed cabin.

Sírénae ruffled Thraxa's feathered head with one hand and stroked the snow-gryffon's thick spotted-white fur with the other. "Does that meet with your approval, Machaera?"

"It does," said the general. "It covers us no matter what Quintillius and Laetícia decide to do. I'd prefer to attack somewhere in Tamloch as well."

"You know what I think," said Admiral Pixo, frowning. "I want to keep the fleet together."

"You don't have any subordinates you feel are competent to hold an independent command?" asked the emperor.

"It's not that," said Pixo. "I can keep in touch with whomever I select via communications rings. I just don't like splitting our forces, that's all. Once is bad enough. Twice would be asking for trouble."

"We're not some random band of adventurers searching for treasure in catacombs who need to worry about splitting their party," said Magister Callidus. He was midway in age between Pixo and Machaera and felt the older man was too cautious and the younger woman too headstrong. He was the same age as Sírénae and thought her plan was just right.

"I understand your positions," said Sírénae, turning her head to nod to each of them. "So does Thraxa—don't you my dear?"

The snow-gryffon stretched her back like a cat waking from a nap, then opened her beak and let out a blood-chilling shriek like a hawk trying to paralyze a rabbit with fear before striking.

I hate when the beast does that, thought Magister Callidus, *though I think Sírénae loves it. She enjoys our discomfort.*

Sírénae soothed her pet with both hands. "Any further comments or observations?" she asked.

A low-pitched voice whispered from the shadows. "Only one," it said.

"Ah, Umbrose," said the emperor. "I didn't hear you enter—not that I ever do." Sírénae beckoned to the dark corner of her suite where the voice was coming from. "Come into the light and enlighten us with your wisdom."

A small man wearing nondescript gray and black robes stepped forward and joined the others. They were all seated in chairs, not reclining on dining couches. Umbrose was of medium height, medium build, and appeared middle-aged with a face that could pass as anything from Gaulish to Egyptian or Parthian. Today, it was pock-marked with acne scars. Tomorrow he might have a jagged lightning scar on his forehead or a large wart on his unremarkable nose. He sat carefully, as if to avoid having a hidden weapon catch on his undertunic.

Callidus could sense the black onyx magestone Umbrose wore around his neck. *That man disturbs me more than the snow-gryffon,* thought the Magister. *I think Sírénae also enjoys our discomfort around* him.

"What have we failed to consider, Spymaster?" asked Machaera.

"The northern and southern Clan Landers' inclinations to ally with us," said Umbrose. "I won't have reports on their feelings for a few days."

"Assuming your spies' fast ships weren't lost in the storm," said Admiral Pixo.

"They weren't," said Umbrose. "I know how to train *my* students, unlike some."

Magister Callidus let the spymaster's attack slip by without acknowledging it. It was unfair that Umbrose—a mage whose skill Callidus admired, if not his character—got to cherry-pick his best people and impress them into Sírénae's secret service. The emperor needed spies *and* martial mages. Callidus wouldn't let the spymaster provoke him.

The young female slave brought in a fresh bowl of fish for Thraxa during the brief lull in the conversation. She kept her head down and left as quickly as she'd entered, keeping a worried eye on the snow-gryffon as she did.

"Your agents in Nova Eboracum kept us up to date on the alliance with Dâron, Tamloch, and Bifurland," Machaera remarked. "Couldn't one of them be sent to the northern Clan Lands, at least?"

"None of my agents in Nova Eboracum are wizards," said Umbrose. "The northern Clan Landers would kill any non-wizard I sent them before they'd listen to them."

"Such a pity," said Callidus, trying to sound like he meant it.

"Keep us posted on your agents' progress then," said the emperor.

"Dealing with Clan Landers is like trying to handle the blade of a two-edged sword. However you manage it, you'll be cut."

"Geography dictates that the Clan Landers—north *and* south— will be more trouble for Dâron and Tamloch than for *our* forces," said Admiral Pixo.

The old man sounds far too smug, thought Callidus. *He thinks maps are more important than leaders' wills or a stubborn people's long memories. The Clan Landers bear no love for the Roma.*

"It will take time for the fleet to reach the coast of Orluin," said Sírénae. "We can adjust our plans based on whatever intelligence Umbrose's agents are able to gather."

"There won't be much *intelligence* where Clan Landers are involved," said Machaera.

"In the time of Alexander, the Athicans considered your Macedonia ancestors to be barbarians," said Admiral Pixo. "Perhaps the Clan Landers have also grown more civilized over time."

"Not likely," said Umbrose.

Everyone gathered in the emperor's suite laughed. Thraxa shrieked. The rain continued to pound on the decks above.

Chapter 3

Depths of Foolishness

"Get on!" Laetícia ordered Néillen. "If Eynon's going to provide a distraction, the least I can do is benefit from it." She put her sandaled feet through the straps on her flying disk and directed Tamloch's former earl marshal to hold her belt and hang on.

"What's the lad trying to prove?" asked the duke.

"That he can take on the emperor's entire fleet and College of Wizards single-handedly," offered Laetícia. "He seemed too sensible to have a death wish."

"He's the one who froze the Brenavon and came up with the wisent stampede, right?" asked Duke Néillen.

"Correct," said Laetícia as she gained altitude, keeping her distance from the harbor.

"Maybe he *can* take on the emperor's forces by himself?"

"Not with seven dragons against him, too," said Laetícia. "Watch!"

Néillen gazed in horror as the young Dâron wizard—Eynon—was buffeted by dragons, blasted by wizards' lightning, roasted by dragonfire, and spun about by tendrils of tight light. The rain had paused for a few heartbeats, giving the duke a clear view of Eynon's fall and the dragons' pursuit. He noticed Laetícia move her arms, as if pushing against a wall and saw one of the dragons diving to capture Eynon slam into two others, leading to snarls and snapping jaws and dragon-on-dragon aggression rather than pursuit.

"Nice distraction with that push," said the duke. "It's a good thing Verro said he'd count hulls from underwater and help as needed."

"As if Merry would let him count once Eynon hit the water," said Laetícia.

"Merry?" asked Néillen.

"A talented young wizard and Eynon's lover," said Laetícia. "She helped build the Riyas illusion."

"Right," said Duke Néillen, gazing west. "The headstrong lad will be in good hands—now look."

For a moment they stared down, trying to see through the heavy rain. A powerful gust of wind drove the descending droplets horizontally, then the tempest stopped briefly as they entered a gap between lines of squalls.

"There's a break in the storm," said Néillen. "This is the best chance you'll get."

Laetícia observed the ships below, bobbing like so many apples in the tub of the harbor. No one had spotted them yet—the wizards and dragons had all their attention focused on Eynon and the place where he had hit the water. Minutes passed while Laetícia etched what she saw into her memory. Néillen noticed one of the dragons strike the water of the harbor some distance from where Eynon had fallen and emerge without anything to show for its effort.

"Time to go," said the duke. "They'll look our way any minute now."

"True enough," said Laetícia. "Hold tight!"

After they gated out a stroke of lightning slashed through the spot in the sky they'd just occupied.

* * * * *

"Do you have him?" asked Merry.

"I do," said Verro. "Are you maintaining our disguise?"

"I am," Merry answered. "If anyone can spot the seafloor through the storm, they'll see a copy of the coral reef below us instead of a ten-foot sphere of solidified sound. How's Eynon?"

"Battered, but breathing," replied Verro. "I'll dose him with a healing potion, then move our bubble out of the harbor so I can concentrate and *ad hoc* gate us back to Nova Eboracum."

Verro and Merry rode their own flying disks inside the bubble while Merry supported Eynon's unconscious body on his disk between herself and Verro. It took all her concentration to keep Eynon's flying disk in motion while disguising their location. *Not that anyone is likely to be looking in this weather,* she thought. *Then again, there are still wizards and dragons above us. What prompted Eynon to take on odds of eleven to one?*

"How much air do we have?" asked Merry as she watched Verro pour a healing potion into Eynon's mouth. Knots of tension left her shoulders when she saw Eynon swallow.

"As much as we need," said Verro.

"I thought we'd breathe it all up over time," said Merry.

"Not if you create a congruency linked to the surface," said Verro. "Or the surface somewhere it's not storming."

"If wizards can do that, how can we knock them out by putting small spheres of solidified sound around their heads?" Merry asked.

"It's difficult to think and work magic when you're out of air," said Verro. "I teach my students to keep their heads when someone tries to asphyxiate them and practice forming congruencies to fresh air until they can do it without thinking."

"Can I be your student," whispered Eynon. "I have a lot to learn."

"You certainly do," replied Verro. "I'll teach you more about forming all sorts of gates if you promise to be less of a fool in the future."

"He can't promise that," said Merry. She was smiling now that Eynon was talking and starting to recover. "For that matter, I know a Tamloch wizard who was foolish enough to fall in love with a mage from Dâron when he was just a few years older than Eynon."

"Look how that fellow turned out," said Eynon softly. He moved his head slowly from side to side as if confirming it was still attached to his neck.

"You have me there," said Verro. "There's no shortage of foolish wizards in need of instruction."

Merry and Verro laughed. Laughing was too painful for Eynon's recovering ribs, so he just smiled.

Their protective bubble of solidified sound was three fathoms down in the center of the Tempest Isle's great harbor. Most of Sírénae's fleet rode at anchor to the east. Verro began to move their bubble toward the northwest where a long cape curved in like a hook. It served as a breakwater preventing the worst of the storm's wind-whipped waves from reaching the inner harbor. Merry changed her illusions as they moved so the top of their bubble always matched what lay below them.

They were making steady progress away from the center of the harbor when Merry heard Eynon whisper. She let her illusions waver for a moment and cast the listening spell she'd learned from Doethan and taught to Eynon on their trip down the Rhuthro. "What did you say?" she asked, paying close attention.

"Emergency gate," whispered Eynon. "Don't need *ad hoc* gate. Get out sooner." His eyes closed as if his words took all his remaining strength.

"Did you hear him?" Merry asked Verro.

"I did," said Verro, "thus proving I'm as big a fool as he was. I don't need to focus on creating an *ad hoc* gate back to Laetícia's study. I can act on reflex and use my emergency gate to take us back to Riyas."

"When do we leave?" asked Merry.

"When can you take over maintaining the bubble?" asked Verro. "Remember, it's harder with the greater pressure from water, not air."

"I can drop our disguise and do it now," said Merry. "It's not likely they'll spot us immediately even if they are keeping watch through the storm."

"Which is doubtful," added Verro. "I'll take over control of Eynon's flying disk and pull him through my emergency gate after me. You'll need to be right behind us since I don't know how long I can keep it open."

"Right," said Merry. "Here goes." She generated a twelve-foot sphere of solidified sound around their ten-foot bubble and struggled for a few seconds, allowing her outer sphere to flex and almost touch the inner one before she figured out how to stiffen it. Merry straightened her shoulders and called to Verro. "I've got it. Let's go."

Tamloch's master mage descended to the base of the inner sphere and dispelled it, leaving him on his flying disk a foot above the remaining sphere with Eynon floating immediately above him and Merry now kneeling on her flying disk above Eynon. Merry heard the snap of Verro's emergency gate crackling into existence and smelled the hint of summer thunderstorm that accompanied it. She sensed rather than saw Verro and Eynon descending and lowered her flying disk until it touched Eynon's chest. Then Eynon fell through to join Verro on the other side of the gate and the hair on Merry's arms stood out from her body as she began to cross the circular interface as well.

Something massive struck her protective sphere of solidified sound before she was all the way through, momentarily breaking her concentration. She vaguely recognized the snout of a large black dragon reaching for her head, jaws wide, before she finished her transition, taking along a substantial quantity of seawater and leaving a frustrated Roma dragon flailing behind.

Chapter 4

King Lessons

"What should I be doing to help Dâron prepare for the emperor's invasion?" Nûd asked Duke Háiddon and Dârio. "For that matter," he said, turning to Quintillius, "are you with *her* or with *us?*"

"I'm definitely with *you*," replied Quintillius. "I'm also with the other tetrarchs leading the empire across the Ocean. The Siren Hawk and I go back many years. I didn't trust her then and I don't trust her now. She's no true emperor—she's been deposed and sent into exile. It's our bad luck she decided to come *here* with her fleet instead of retiring with a few trusted servants to the Isles of Palms or some other remote location."

"As for what you should do," said Duke Háiddon, "I'd advise waiting until we hear back from Laetícia and Eynon. The Dâron army is still mostly in one place, camped near the battlefield south of Brendinas after the Tamloch troops were returned to Riyas."

"Thank you for returning my soldiers," said Dârio. "Remarkably few of Tamloch's officers decided to object to their change in monarch."

"Why is it remarkable?" asked Duke Háiddon. "Given the way Túathal treated them, they'd accept a cow as king over his continued rule."

"Father!" protested Jenet with a smile.

Dârio laughed, before pursing his lips to produce a resonant bovine *moo*. He composed his face, assumed a serious expression, and said, "I'll choose to take that as a compliment rather than an insult."

"It was meant as one," said Háiddon with a grin.

"You're incorrigible," said Jenet. She poked her father in the ribs and he grunted.

"As I was trying to say to Dârio before I was interrupted," said Duke Háiddon with a mock-stern look at Jenet, "Tamloch's troops respect you and appreciate that you could have treated them much worse than you did. They've also developed a fondness for roast wisent."

Dârio ignored the duke's culinary comment and gave a serious answer. "I'd hoped to have most of the army stand down and return to their homes and farms," he said. "Now it looks like they'll need to remain in the field for months. At least that will give me a chance to see which nobles and officers are able to lead by example rather than command by fear."

"Without the emperor's pending arrival, you could have learned that from joint operations with my legions against the northern Clan Landers," said Quintillius.

"Fighting Clan Lands' irregulars will be far different from dealing with a former Roma emperor's disciplined legionnaires," added Jenet.

"We may yet end up doing *both,*" said Duke Háiddon.

Bonnie had been sitting quietly next to Nûd, enjoying his company and following the conversation. Everyone was surprised to hear her speak.

"What sort of person is Sírénae Accipiter?" she asked Quintillius.

"Excuse me?" asked the governor-general of Occidens Province. "What do you mean?"

"I live inside my head a lot, studying at the institute near Bhaile Pónaire," Bonnie replied. "I don't need much for my sort of magical research—just large slates and chalk, mostly." The young mage shifted awkwardly on her couch before continuing. "I mean, what I've found is that when I *do* have to ask one of the deans for something, I make sure to understand how they think first. Are they all about numbers and budgets, or are they more interested in what my work will do to advance our knowledge of wizardry? I've found I'm more likely to get what I need if I tailor my approach to the specific dean's personality."

Jenet looked at Bonnie with new eyes and nodded. She squeezed Dârio's hand and the two exchanged a knowing glance.

Nûd smiled at Bonnie and clapped his hands together. "Yes, Quintillius," he said. "Please tell us what sort of person the emperor is."

Quintillius didn't immediately reply. He stood unmoving, his eyes unfocused as if he was trying to review distant memories. When he finally spoke, it was in a voice much softer than usual.

"You may know that the Tetrarchy has a policy of transferring promising legion officers from one tetrarch's territory to another's in order to provide them with diverse experience serving across the breadth of the Imperium."

Heads nodded around Laetícia's study—even Doethan and Princess Rúth looked up, and they'd been snuggling in a corner paying more attention to each other than the general conversation. Inthíra, who had intentionally positioned herself where she couldn't see Doethan and the princess, leaned forward in her chair.

Quintillius cleared his throat, glanced around the room at the others, and began. "Like Laetícia, I came from the area farther up the Nile from Egypt, and initially served in the legions of the Southern Empire," he said. "When I reached the rank of *legate*..."

"The officer in charge of a legion," Jenet noted for Bonnie's benefit.

"I was transferred to serve under Emperor Sírénae in a similar role with one of her legions in Nárbo..."

"The capital of the Western Empire," said Jenet.

Bonnie made a face at Jenet and Duke Háiddon's daughter silently mouthed, "Sorry." Dârio tried to hold back a smile but was unsuccessful.

"What was it like serving under Sírénae?" asked Nûd.

"Unpleasant," said Quintillius. "On the surface, she treated the members of her senior team with respect, but she delighted in making us uncomfortable. I think it was a way for her to prove her superiority."

"Do tell," said Duke Háiddon.

"She kept assigning me personal slaves who wouldn't back off when I told them I wasn't interested in them as bed partners," Quintillius responded. "Two of them in succession said, 'Beds are optional, dominus. Your desk or dining couch would serve as well.' It was like they were reciting from a script."

"Maybe they were," said Jenet.

"When she sent me young male slaves and they used exactly the same language, I knew Sírénae was training them personally and throwing them at me," said Quintillius. "I had to keep my quarters locked so there wouldn't be naked slaves in my bed when I retired every evening."

"I can see how that would be annoying," said Nûd.

Bonnie looked over at Nûd and realized he was absolutely serious. She squeezed his hand.

"What was that for?" asked Nûd.

"Being sensible," Bonnie replied.

"Perhaps she thought you were lonely and was trying to provide you with companionship?" suggested Dârio.

Jenet gave Dârio a disapproving sidelong glance.

"Sírénae knew I was engaged to Laetícia," said Quintillius. "She was trying to make Laetícia doubt my commitment as a way of hurting Valens, her fellow emperor. The bed warmers were just one small part of her larger design."

"What was her plan?" asked Duke Háiddon.

"We didn't learn that for several years," said Quintillius. "She was determined to enlarge her territory by taking North Afarika from Valens and adding it to her empire. Sírénae sounded me out about being her viceroy for Mauretania..."

"Western North Afarika..." began Duke Háiddon. He stopped himself when he saw the expression on Jenet's face. Her *now you know where I got it from* look made them both smile.

"But she passed it off as a joke when I didn't rise to her bait," continued Quintillius. "Now, more than a decade later, her plans for taking territory from her fellow tetrarchs must have finally moved forward."

"How do you think her plans went?" asked Dârio, pretending not to notice Jenet and Háiddon's byplay.

"The fact that she's headed for Orluin now should answer that," said Nûd.

"She must have finally sent legions into Afarika and maybe into Roma Province itself," said Quintillius. "It's clear the remaining tetrarchs pushed her out. I'm surprised any of her legions followed her west."

"Sometimes even the most despicable individuals are capable of inspiring loyalty," offered Princess Rúth.

Dârio realized that Rúth was talking about her brother Túathal, the deposed king of Tamloch and the man Dârio had recently learned was his father.

A few paces away Nûd was thinking about the Roma—and slavery. He'd posed as Damon's servant for years, to the point where it hadn't truly been a pose much of the time, but he knew he was a free man. Dâron, Tamloch, and especially the Clan Lands had strong feelings against keeping slaves and it disturbed Nûd to hear Quintillius offhandedly refer to slaves as bed warmers.

The Bifurlanders are every bit as bad as the Roma, thought Nûd. *They beat their chests and crow about being free men and women, but still keep captives as thralls—which might as well be slavery by another name. I'll have to talk to Dârio privately and see what he thinks about slavery. Sírénae's invasion is our top priority, but afterward there will likely be other battles to liberate* all *of Orluin.*

"Where did your brain go?" Bonnie asked Nûd.

"Sorry," said Nûd. "I was thinking too many moves ahead."

"You're quiet as well," said Jenet as she put her arm around Dârio's waist.

"Sorry," echoed Dârio, not even realizing he'd repeated what Nûd had said. "I was thinking about my father."

"Don't do that," said Rúth. "I can promise you he never thought of you as a son to love, just a means to an end."

"And now *his* life has ended," said Dârio. "Perhaps it's for the best. It's unwise to stare at a basilisk."

Heads around the room nodded in agreement. A large *pop* and the arrival of two new people through an *ad hoc* gate in the center of the study provided a further distraction.

Quintillius bent down and greeted Laetícia with a hug and kiss. He noticed she was wet, and puddles of water were on the floor around Laetícia and Néillen, but he wasn't disconcerted. "Welcome back, my love!" he said. "What did you learn?"

Duke Háiddon stepped close to Duke Néillen and held his upper arm in a tight grip. Now that he'd temporarily returned from exile, the former earl marshal of Tamloch wouldn't be going anywhere.

Several voices jumped in all at once.

"Where's Eynon?" asked Nûd.

"And Merry?" asked Doethan.

"And *Verro?*" asked Fercha, striding to the center of the room.

"Eynon fought four wizards and seven dragons and lost," said Laetícia with a frown. "He fell into the sea. I have no idea about Merry, but Verro said he'd come along shortly to count hulls underwater."

"Merry talked Verro into gating her to the Tempest Isles so she could help Eynon," said Quintillius. "I'm sure they're fine. *What did you learn?*"

"The weather was terrible," said Laetícia, "but there *was* enough of a break in the storm for me to identify quite a few ships and unit banners."

"I saw some huge ships," added Néillen. "They must hold thousands of legionnaires."

"Some do," said Laetícia. "Some don't."

"If not people, what *do* they carry?" asked Jenet. "Dragons?"

"No," said Laetícia. "Elephants. Sírénae is invading with hundreds and hundreds of elephants."

Chapter 5

Not Far from Riyas

Merry and her flying disk landed hard on a rough stone floor. Half a second after the impact, gallons of seawater slammed down on her back, leaving her drenched and disoriented. She was in a large, dark, echoing space illuminated only by tiny glowing pinpricks high above. Before she could cast a light spell, she heard Verro's voice.

"Llachartús!" he commanded. A hundred bright spheres arrayed around the ceiling came to life, revealing they were in a dome-shaped cavern half the size of the great hall at Dâron's royal palace in Brendinas. Verro's word bounced around the space a dozen times before fading away. In the light, Merry could see Eynon slumped on his flying disk between her and Verro. His robes were soaked, and he wasn't moving.

Still kneeling, Merry leaned close and confirmed Eynon was breathing. She saw that his face was bruised and one of his arms was in an odd position. There was also a lump as big as her fist on the back of Eynon's head. Merry looked up at Verro. "How long will it take for the healing potion to work?" she asked.

"Not long," said Verro. "It's one of Uirsé's."

"Good," said Merry. She remembered how quickly Doethan's healing potion had helped her recover from a blow to the head when she and Eynon had traveled down the Rhuthro river. Uirsé's potions had an even better reputation. "Is it safe to hold him?" she asked. "Do you think his neck or spine were affected?"

"I don't think so," Verro replied. "He was talking and could move his arms and legs. Go ahead and hold him—it will probably help him recover faster."

The water from the harbor at the Tempest Isles hadn't pooled around them. Merry noticed that the floor of the cavern sloped away from the center, so the stone underfoot was only damp.

29

The runoff channeled into a shallow groove toward only one segment of the perimeter. She cast Doethan's clothes-drying spell on herself and Eynon, moved him off his flying disk, then sat next to him and cradled her lover's head and shoulders in her arms. Eynon moaned and his right arm flopped about oddly.

"We'll need to reset his shoulder," said Verro. "It's dislocated. A healing potion can't heal *that*."

Merry knew what to do. She'd seen many similar injuries when apple pickers fell from high branches. "I'll hold him tight," she said. "You reseat the joint." Merry slid Eynon off her lap and placed him flat on his back with his head resting on the fabric near the hem of her robes. She pressed her palms down on Eynon's right collarbone and left shoulder to keep his torso immobile.

Verro looked at Merry and nodded. He took Eynon's right hand and extended the young wizard's injured arm, pulling slowly and firmly. The arm resisted, so Verro created a sleeve of solidified sound around the arm and used it to increase his pull. Eynon moaned louder and his eyes flicked open.

Merry spoke soft words of comfort and held Eynon tightly as the Verro increased his traction. Then she heard a small popping sound and saw Eynon's pain decrease. "Nicely done," she told Verro.

"Thank you," Verro replied. "You'd be surprised how many apprentices fall from their flying disks and need this sort of repair."

"Can't they just catch themselves with constructs of solidified sound?" asked Merry.

"Not every wizard has your skills," said Verro. "Or Eynon's."

"I have a lot to learn about wizardry—and my fellow wizards," said Merry.

"Plenty of time for that," said Verro.

"Maybe," said Merry. "Or maybe not, given Sírénae Accipiter's invasion." She looked around the chamber. "Do you have something I could use as a sling? And a pillow?" she asked Verro.

"I do," said Verro. "I should have offered to get them without you needing to ask. I keep my supplies around the edges of the cavern so the center where my emergency gate opens stays clear. It wouldn't do to land on a chair or a table." He left Merry and Eynon and headed for the cavern's perimeter.

"Bring some blankets," Merry added.

"I'd planned to," said Verro, already twenty feet away.

Merry stayed by Eynon's side and gently stroked his hair. She noticed the lump on his head was shrinking. *Thank goodness for healing potions!* she thought.

Verro was back in minutes with a four-foot square tray of solidified sound piled high with various items floating behind him. He passed Merry a pillow, a wide linen sheet embroidered with small green quatrefoils, several white wool blankets, and the biggest thing on the tray, a thick bearskin rug as wide as Verro's outstretched arms and as long as Quintillius was tall. The governor-general of Occidens Province was the tallest man Merry had ever met—half a head taller than Verro—so that was saying something.

Together, Merry and Verro spread the rug out on the floor of the cavern and gently maneuvered Eynon onto one side of it. After Merry arranged the pillow under Eynon's head, Verro handed her a second pillow and a square of sturdy cloth for a sling.

"Thank you for the sling, but why the second pillow?" she asked.

"That one's for you," Verro replied. "I don't think you'll be leaving his side for several hours."

Merry nodded. "I expect you're right," she said. "That's why you brought the big bearskin and sheet, too?"

"I brought them because that's what I had," said Verro. "I've used this hideaway for trysts with Fercha from time to time. She loves the rug."

"I see," said Merry. "Where are we, by the way?"

"Not far from Riyas," said Verro. "We're in a cave several miles northwest of the city."

"Interesting," said Merry. She adjusted the sturdy fabric into a sling and used it to prevent Eynon's right arm from moving. Then she pulled the sheet over him, covered him with a blanket, and put the pillow Verro had given her next to Eynon on the bearskin rug. She smiled at Verro and sat on the pillow. "I appreciate your hospitality. Will you teach *me* how to make an emergency gate?"

"Shouldn't Fercha do that?" asked Verro.

"Fercha's not here. You are," said Merry.

"You need to select a refuge first," said Verro.

"There's a spot not far from Applegarth, in the mountains between the Coombe and the Rhuthro that should work," said Merry. "I'd have to confirm that something like a" —she patted the rug— "bear wasn't already in residence."

"Yes, I'll teach you if Fercha doesn't do it first," said Verro, "after you've confirmed your destination's suitability. Now, however, is not the time."

"True enough," said Merry. "I have another question, too."

"Just one?" asked Verro.

"For now," said Merry. "You used *Llach-ar-tús* to light this cavern, not *Llach-ar*. What's the difference between the two spells?" Merry paused while saying the words of command so spells wouldn't be triggered.

"Ah," said Verro. "That's easy. The second one is the generic spell to generate glow balls. The first is something special I designed to instruct preconfigured light spheres in the ceiling to illuminate."

"It's the difference between making a candle and simply lighting one?" asked Merry.

"A lot like that," said Verro. "I can show you how it works if you'd like."

"I would," said Merry, "but would prefer to learn it later. Right now, I wish I had a cup of warm cider and a honey cake. I feel like all the excitement in the last hour or two has drained my energy."

"I can help with that," said Verro, "but you'll have to settle for twice-baked travel cakes drizzled with honey instead of proper honey cakes. I'm so seldom here I don't bring in new supplies very often."

"Travel cakes would be fine," said Merry. "If Eynon wakes up I can dip them in cider since I expect his jaw won't be up for gnawing on them without soaking first."

"I'll bring two mugs and two plates of cakes with a small crock of honey," said Verro. "Use them as you see fit. Once I fetch them, I'll pop out and find out what Laetícia learned."

"If anything," said Merry.

"If anything," echoed Verro.

"How will I get out of here if I need to?" she asked.

"There's a narrow passageway leading outside near the spring," said Verro.

"There's a spring?" asked Merry.

"All the best refuges have running water," said Verro with a smile.

"I'll keep that detail in mind when I select my own," said Merry, smiling back.

"I'll return as soon as I can," said Verro. "Eynon needs rest, and from what I can see, so do you."

Merry nodded her agreement. Verro went to the edge of the cavern and returned with the plates of cakes and aromatic mugs of cider. The cakes looked like pieces of white bone the dimensions of her index finger and were probably as much of a challenge to chew.

"Don't forget us," she teased Verro as he inserted his boots into the leather straps on his flying disk.

"I won't," said Verro. "And if I do, Fercha knows how to find you."

"If she's not distracted by some new crisis," said Merry with a grin.

"Come now, how likely is *that?*" asked Verro, grinning back. He rose to the center of the cavern and disappeared with an audible *pop* as air rushed in to fill the space he'd formerly occupied.

The noise of Verro's departure must have reached Eynon's brain. He opened his eyes, looked at Merry, then sat up abruptly.

"Ow!" he said. He tried to feel his head with his right arm and realized he couldn't thanks to the sling. He used his left arm to rub his ribs.

Merry smiled at him and kissed his forehead.

"What happened to me?" Eynon asked tentatively as he took stock of his injuries. "I feel like I just went ten rounds with Viridáxés."

"Something like that," said Merry. "More like one round with seven smaller dragons."

"I remember now," said Eynon. "I left Laetícia and Néillen and tried to scout on my own."

"I wasn't there, but that sounds right," said Merry. "Verro and I saved you when you fell into the harbor. I think you fought Roma wizards, too."

"It feels like it," said Eynon with pain still in his voice. He rubbed his ribs again with his left arm. "How did *this* happen?" he asked, tilting his chin toward his right arm.

"I think you were thrown around inside your shields a lot," said Merry. "It was hard for me to tell trying to look up from underwater."

"I can imagine," said Eynon. "I was such a fool."

Merry kept smiling but didn't say anything. *He* had *been a fool,* she thought. *Taking on an unknown opponent with undetermined— but extensive—resources wasn't a wise move under any circumstances.*

"I got cocky," said Eynon, shaking his head slowly.

"Overconfident," said Merry, holding back what she really wanted to say.

"I was stupid," said Eynon. He looked over at Merry, expecting some supportive reply. Instead, she nodded.

"You were stupid," she said after a delay. She smiled to lessen the blow.

"I guess I deserve that," said Eynon. "I failed. There's so much I don't know."

"That's true for me, too," said Merry. "We can learn more about magic together."

Now it was Eynon's turn not to answer. He looked down at the bearskin rug and seemed to retreat inside his head. His jaw was tight, and his fists were clenched like he wanted to punch someone.

Merry could feel the uncharacteristic anger radiating from Eynon and knew he was directing that anger at himself. She'd never seen him like this before and wanted to do something to break the cycle before it went much farther. She formed a solidified sound illusion behind Eynon's back and admired her handiwork. It was an imitation of Chee, and Merry animated the illusion, so it climbed on Eynon's shoulder and kissed him on the forehead. Eynon opened his eyes, ready to tell Merry to stay away from him when he realized the kiss came from something looking like Chee, not from Merry.

"How did...?" Eynon began, his anger shifting to confusion. Taking advantage of Eynon's shift in mood, Merry leaned over and kissed Eynon on the lips. Confusion changed to surprise and then to pleasure as he forgot to be mad at himself and enjoyed the kiss.

He's still my farm boy, thought Merry. *Anger doesn't suit him.*

The two lingered over their kiss until Eynon felt lightheaded. He broke their connection and shifted his upper body down until his head was on his pillow. Merry warmed one of the mugs of cider with a tiny fireball and dipped one of the travel cakes in it to soften. Then she drizzled a bit of honey on the softened cake and inserted it into Eynon's mouth.

"Mmmm..." said Eynon.

"Feeling better?" asked Merry. "Is the healing potion making progress?"

"I had a healing potion?" asked Eynon. "That explains a lot."

"It does?" asked Merry.

"Yes," Eynon replied. "I hardly ache at all now."

"I remember that feeling," said Merry. "I felt much better on the Rhuthro after I had a healing potion. *Much* better."

"I remember, too," teased Eynon. They'd made love not long after. "Something still puzzles me," he said after opening his eyes and looking up at Merry.

"What's that?" asked Merry.

"How did you get to the Tempest Isles?" Eynon asked. "It's too far to fly."

"Verro said he'd been to the Tempest Isles before," replied Merry. "He did quite a bit of traveling after Tamloch and Dâron stopped being on good terms. I think it was to help him forget about Fercha for awhile."

"He crossed the Ocean?" asked Eynon.

"I think so," said Merry. "Maybe more than once. There wasn't much time to talk about it."

"I wonder why he didn't mention that in Laetícia's study?" asked Eynon.

"I expect Verro doesn't mention a lot of things he knows," said Merry. "I think that's wise of him."

"While I'm an open book," said Eynon. "Are you saying I should be more careful about what I say?"

Merry smiled and nodded. "And what you do," she said. "I need to follow that advice myself, so you're not the only one." She reclined next to Eynon on the bearskin and put her head on the second pillow beside his. She held his left hand with her right.

"I really need to learn more about wizardry," said Eynon. "I know how to do a few things with magic, but I don't really understand why it works or what sorts of things are possible."

"Verro and Fercha and Doethan and Inthíra are glad to teach us," said Merry.

"I know they are, and I appreciate that," said Eynon. "But I want to *read* more about wizardry and the theory of magic. Reading was the way I learned about the wider world back in the Coombe." He paused, remembering when he'd first met Nûd and Damon before continuing. "There were several shelves of books about wizardry and magical theory in the library at Melyncárreg."

"Then go read them," said Merry. "You've got at least a week before you have to help stop an invasion."

"I think I will," said Eynon. "Later. When did Verro say he was coming back?"

"Not for at least an hour, I expect," said Merry. "It will take him that long to answer everyone's questions."

"Good," said Eynon. "That should be sufficient for my purposes."

"Our purposes," said Merry. "Just be careful with your arm."

Chapter 6

The Narrow Passage

Merry woke up slowly but sensed something was wrong. It was dark and she was warm, nestled under a sheet and heavy blanket on top of the bearskin rug, but she couldn't sense her lover's presence. She reached out to touch Eynon only to discover he wasn't there.

"Llachartús," said Merry softly. The glow balls in the ceiling lit with a dim light, illuminating the cavern without hurting her eyes. When Eynon had asked her to make it less bright in the cavern so he could sleep, Merry had discovered the level of light the ceiling spheres produced varied by the volume of the word of command.

She sat up, shifted her head, and scanned the chamber. Unless Eynon was generating an illusion to hide himself, he wasn't there. "Llachartús!" Merry shouted, then blinked as the cavern was flooded with light as bright as midday. "Where *are* you?" she said, only a bit softer than the word of command. "Show yourself." She paused for the length of a breath. "It's not funny!"

Only echoes of her own voice answered her.

"When I catch up to him, I'm going to nail him into a cider barrel and toss it into the roughest rapids on the Rhuthro," Merry muttered to herself. "He's gated out and left me to wait for Verro to return and retrieve me like a misplaced sock." She stood and paced around the rug, hoping that Eynon would drop an illusion spell and say, "Surprise!"

That didn't happen, however. Merry triggered a listening spell and strained to hear any signs of another person. All she heard was a trickle of burbling water.

At least I know where Eynon's gone, she thought. *And I know there are gates from Riyas to Brendinas to Fercha's tower to Melyncárreg so it wouldn't take me long to join him there—if I decide I want to.*

Merry walked away from the center to the outer edge of the chamber and stomped around its perimeter. She saw the heavy wooden chests where she assumed Verro's emergency supplies of food and drink were kept and realized with a smile that a cube-shaped chest marked with a carved crescent-moon on the opposite side of the cavern held a small permanent congruency to who knows where for disposing of necessary bodily functions. A quarter of the way past the congruent *necessarium* was a small pool fed by a spring whose bubbling she'd detected earlier.

Where was that narrow passage Verro had mentioned? Merry wondered. A dark slash in the rock of the chamber was evident to the right of the pool filled by the spring. *Do I stay, or do I go?* Merry considered. *Verro could return any minute and I don't want to miss him, but I also want to know where this passage comes out.*

In the balance, her curiosity proved more compelling than her worry about missing Verro. To make sure Tamloch's master mage would know where she'd gone, Merry created an illuminated illusion—and bright red arrow as long as her arm pointing at the passageway. The words *Wait for Me* were written along its length in shining white letters. *Verro won't miss that,* she thought, smiling at his probable reaction when he returned and saw it. She hoped he *would* wait for her.

Planning ahead, in case her exploration of the passageway took longer than expected, she opened one of Verro's emergency rations chests and found extensive supplies, including a canvas bag with a long strap. It was filled with packages of twice-baked travel cakes. She kept three packages and removed the rest, replacing them with a small jug marked with a raised image of an apple that she assumed was cider. A thin bass-wood box proved to contain strips of jerky—beef, or perhaps venison—so she added it to the bag as well.

I'm ready for a two-day journey, Merry mused. *Longer, if I'm careful—though I hope it will be more like two hours than two days.* She grinned and shook her head, hoping she wasn't being as foolish as Eynon by leaving the cavern. With a shrug, she slipped the strap of the canvas bag over her shoulder. Then she retrieved her flying disk from the center of the cavern near the bearskin rug and settled it into its familiar spot on her back.

Merry wouldn't be *flying* along the passage. It was too narrow for that. She walked to the entrance to the passageway and used a variation of the standard light spell to create a glow ball. Merry directed the ball to hover above and a few feet ahead of her, ready to help illuminate her way when she entered the narrow cleft.

Merry turned sideways to fit through the opening. As it was, her flying disk scraped along the wall behind her. *Verro would have to hold his flying disk over his head to get through,* she thought. After a dozen feet, the passage opened up until it was wide enough for two people to walk side by side.

The extra room made Merry feel more comfortable. Her imagination had kept thinking the walls in the narrowest part of the passage were closing in on her. Being underground wasn't a problem—she'd loved exploring the caves in the mountains between the Rhuthro river and the Coombe back home. It was just the tight fit that made her nervous.

One of the caves she'd explored earlier would be a good candidate for *her* refuge after Verro or Fercha taught her how to create an emergency gate. *I might even tell Eynon about the caves near the Coombe in case he wants to use one of them,* she considered, *after I give him a piece of my mind for deserting me.*

Before she'd gone too far along the passage, Merry remembered the old Athican tale about the hero who used a ball of string to avoid being lost in a maze. She didn't have a ball of string, so every few feet she inscribed small arrows on the walls with beams of tight light. They should point her back to Verro's chamber if *she* got lost.

As she walked, Merry directed her glow ball upward, trying to determine the height of the ceiling. It seemed to be more than fifty feet above her and tapered like the upside-down blade of a knife. Her glow ball didn't disturb any bats and Merry was surprised by the lack of life in this section of the passageway, except for crusts of pale green lichen dotting the walls. Ahead, she could see the passage begin to curve up and narrow again. Merry set her shoulders and trudged onward, hoping the narrow section would soon open to the outside world and she'd find herself not *too* far from Riyas. *You can always turn around and go back,* said the sensible part of her. *Where's the fun in that?* replied her adventurous spirit.

Merry had reached a spot where the passage was almost as narrow as it had been initially, so she had to turn sideways again. Her glow ball didn't really help her see ahead—it just lit up the smooth, light-gray wall immediately in front of her eyes. The feeling that she might be crushed between the walls returned and her heart beat faster. It was somehow harder not knowing how long this narrow stretch would last. Finally, after several long minutes inching along, pressing her back against one wall to ensure she'd fit, the passage opened up and she could face forward again.

So much for unspooling string, thought Merry. *I didn't leave any arrows along* that *part of the passage.* She inscribed a larger arrow at this end, pointing back in the way she'd come. Now that she could see in front of her again, she saw that the passageway wasn't as smooth as it had been. To her left was a loosely formed jumble of rocks, while twenty feet farther along, the smooth floor of the passageway led steeply upward. Merry paused for a few minutes to calm her racing heart. She leaned back against one of the larger rocks on the left and took the jug of cider from the canvas bag.

Cider's familiar smell will help, Merry thought. *And so will a few sips. I wonder if it's hard cider? I expect so—it keeps better.* Merry knew a lot about cider. It was her family estate's most famous product. She hoped the jug contained high quality cider that hadn't turned to vinegar.

Merry pulled the cork on the small jug and was instantly reassured by the scent of apples filling the passage. Confident the contents hadn't turned, she put the mouth of the jug to her lips and drank. It *was* fermented, but not fortified. The drink strengthened her spirits.

Not bad, she thought. *Not Applegarth's Finest, but it will do.* She wiped her lips and decided to try the jerky. She wasn't sure what spices had been used to flavor it. Merry put the cork back in the jug and returned the jug to the canvas bag before pulling out the basswood box. When she lifted its lid, the rich, meaty aroma of the jerky joined the scent of cider, making the passageway seem much more homey. Dried wild garlic had certainly been used in its preparation.

Before Merry could sample the jerky, the ceiling of the passage was disturbed by the flapping of thousands of leathery wings as a cloud of bats swarmed past above. Thanks to her still-functioning listening spell, Merry's teeth began to ache from their squeaking at and above the limits of her hearing. Something had clearly disturbed them and sent them retreating in her direction. Then a series of deep barks like the baying of a huge hound formed a counterpoint to the bats' high-pitched noises.

What. Is. That? she asked, scanning the ceiling and seeing the reason for the bat's flight. In the light from her glow ball, Merry saw something like a furry flying carpet a yard long by half a yard wide swooping and diving in and out of the frightened bats. The baying was coming from a square canine head like a terrier's at one narrow end of the strange beast. A long, straight tail stuck out from the opposite end. The fur on the creature's torso and legs was various shades of gray, while thin gray-black membranes filled the spaces between its limbs, completing its rectangular profile.

A long howl from the furry flying-carpet creature's throat seemed to freeze a few bats in mid-flight, allowing the predator to snap its jaws around a bat and descend to the floor of the passage to consume its prey. When it landed a few feet away from Merry, it tucked its head into its chest and rolled its body into a ball, hiding the bat from view. It looked much like another gray rock on the floor and could have been one of the pile of them that Merry was leaning against.

Merry heard crunching sounds coming from inside the mock rock. After a few final muffled squeaks from the captured bat, the odd creature pulsed twice and went still. Not knowing whether or not the beast would attack her, Merry generated a shield of solidified sound in front of her and kept a close eye on the animate *rock* as she resumed removing a piece of jerky from the basswood box. The creature reacted as soon as it smelled the jerky. It pulsed again and unrolled itself from a ball back into its furry carpet form, slowly pulling itself along the floor until its terrier nose was pressed against Merry's shield. She could see that the beast had huge reflective silver eyes, large, triangular ears, and a round copper-colored nose like one of the small Roma coins called an ās attached to the end of its muzzle.

Thinking about the coin's name made Merry smile. When she was younger, she'd read an old tale in one of her father's books about a girl from Tyford visiting Nova Eboracum and buying a hard-boiled egg wrapped in sausage from a street vendor for an ās. The story was set more than a century ago during one of the rare times when Dâron and Occidens Province had been allies.

Merry had asked her father what an ās was, making it sound like another name for a donkey. Derry, her father, had laughed and gently explained that the name of the coin rhymed with *pace,* not *pass.* Merry's face had turned red and she'd laughed, too, before succumbing to a fit of giggling that only ended when Derry had hugged her, lifted her off the ground, and spun her three times. She was too big to lift and spin now. Merry put her pleasant memory aside and focused on the beast before her.

The carpet creature was using its nose to sniff and seemed to be drawn to the jerky. It licked the surface of Merry's shield with a long red tongue. She adjusted the permeability of her shield and pushed one end of the piece of jerky through it. The strange animal gently pulled the jerky out of her hands with its front teeth, curled back into its rock-imitating ball form, and pulsed several times.

Merry assumed it was chewing and swallowing the meat and her assumption proved correct when the beast returned to her shield to beg for more. This time, it didn't crawl across the floor like an undulating carpet. It stood on four legs and retracted the skin between those legs up against its body, so it looked more like a small dog than a shaggy carpet.

She offered the creature another piece of jerky, which was received with evident pleasure. This time, it *didn't* curl up into a ball, but chewed the meat while remaining in its dog conformation.

"Would you like to try some travel cake?" she asked the creature, speaking to it the way she would have spoken to Rowsch, her first magical mentor Doethan's canine familiar. The animal sat on its hindquarters and stared imploringly at Merry with its big eyes. "I'll take that as a *yes*," said Merry, glad to have an excuse to speak.

She took a packet of travel cakes from her canvas bag, opened it, and tossed one through the permeable section of her shield. The beast caught it in the air and lifted its head to shift the cake to its back teeth, which Merry saw were designed for crushing. She had to soak travel cakes before she could eat them, but the friendly-seeming animal crunched its cake easily, pulverizing it and swallowing the small fragments in seconds. A moment later, the beast was back at the edge of her shield, staring up into Merry's eyes.

Merry felt a strange sensation as their gazes locked. It was as if something *clicked* inside her head. She could see from the way the odd animal tilted its head that it felt something too. The beast bounded up toward her, more in affection than attack. Merry dropped her shield and caught the creature in her arms. "You're a *rockhound*," she announced, stroking the fur on its head. The beast's long tongue licked her face. "Aren't you amazing," she said, realizing that she'd finally found her familiar. *"Err-ruff!"* answered the animal.

"What should I call you?" Merry asked herself, musing. "Your nose looks like an ās coin, so I think I'll call you *Ace.*"

Her words made the animal's tail wag at high speed. It jumped from Merry's arms to her shoulders. The rockhound's shifting weight causing Merry to lose her balance and fall back hard against the loose pile of rocks. Like a trap door suddenly opening in the upper level of a barn to let down an avalanche of hay, the rock pile collapsed into a previously unseen opening in the side of the passageway, dropping the large stones, Merry, and her new familiar into the inky depths below.

Chapter 7

Melyncárreg

Does it ever get warm here? Eynon asked himself after he gated to Melyncárreg. He'd chosen the spot delineated by four tall alabaster pillars striped with blue spirals as his destination. It was where he'd first arrived at Melyncárreg when he'd accidentally fallen through a gate at Fercha's tower on the Rhuthro what seemed like half a lifetime ago—though it was really only a few whirlwind weeks. He saw the same pleasantly familiar white-topped mountains reaching for a crystal blue sky in the distance and smelled the same unpleasant scents he remembered from his previous visits. Dozens of plumes of sulphurous steam from hot springs and fields of mud pots rose like yellow-tinged smoke columns at the edges of his vision.

Through a stand of pines downslope to his right, Eynon saw the deeper blue of the wide lake where he'd practiced making fireballs with Damon, the previous master mage of Dâron and his first mentor in magic. He smiled, thinking about the chilly morning when Damon had met him at the very spot where he was standing now and escorted him to the imposing castle above the pair of falls on the Melyncárreg river.

There was still snow on the ground around him, but Eynon was pleased it was only four fingers deep instead of piled up in mounds as high as his arm was long. He realized the alabaster spiral pillars defining the gate were taller than he'd thought, now that much of the snow had melted. It was still quite cold, however. His breath condensed in front of him each time he exhaled, and he realized he was decidedly underdressed for the weather.

Eynon rubbed his hands together to warm them, then stopped and smiled. *I'm a wizard now,* he considered. *I can warm myself up.* He generated a sphere of solidified sound just big enough to hold him and his flying disk, then drew on his blue magestone to constrain his red magestone's usual tendency to go overboard regarding heat and fire. Seconds later, a tiny congruency to the place where his fireballs came from was filling the sphere with warmth. Eynon and the sphere floated aloft, sailed over the colorful canyon carved by the fast-running river, and flew toward the castle.

From the air, Eynon could see just how big Melyncárreg Castle truly was. It was bigger than the earl's fortress at Rhuthro Keep and held two towers inside its walls—Damon's broad and solid square one of dark gray granite and Princess Seren's tall, slim one made from white limestone decorated with a spiral of blue stones.

Fercha based her tower's design on her mother's, Eynon realized. The castle seemed much too large for its stated purpose of housing the library, feast hall, map room, and dormitory cells of the Academy, Damon's school for wizards. *Maybe Nûd can tell me why?* Eynon considered. *Damon would probably spin some improbable tale if I asked him,* he thought. *I wonder if Astrí—Princess Seren—would be willing to talk to me about the castle's history?*

Eynon circled the castle slowly and shook his head. *I'm trying to distract myself,* he thought. *I really shouldn't have left Merry back at Verro's refuge, especially without leaving a note.* He involuntarily cringed when he considered what Merry would have to say to him the next time she saw him. *Why did I leave like that?* he wondered. *She's figured out I'm angry at myself for being foolish back at the Tempest Isles. I don't like losing, and hate being seen as stupid even more.* Eynon made a growling noise deep in his throat like he was trying to dissuade a cat from drinking milk from his cup. In this case, however, he was growling at himself.

I'm falling back into old habits, he thought. *When I was younger and life got complicated, I'd find a hidden spot and disappear there with a book. I remember a clearing in a thick stand of pines on a hill near Haywall...* he mused. *That's where I read Robin Goodfellow's* Peregrinations *for the first time. I always felt better after reading a few chapters of a good book. Maybe I'll feel better—and less stupid— after I read a few books on the theory and practice of wizardry?*

The castle was immediately below Eynon now. There were no signs anyone was currently in residence—no smoke was rising from chimneys, for example. From what he'd overheard, Astrí had no interest in returning to Melyncárreg. She wanted to live in Riyas and Brendinas to be close to her future grandchildren.

Maybe she talked Damon into returning to the Great Falls? thought Eynon. *That spot near the Inland Seas is supposed to be romantic and goodness knows, Damon and Astrí—Master Mage Ealdamon and Princess Seren—must have lots of catching up to do after being apart for so long.*

Eynon laughed. He wasn't the only one who'd been stupid. Damon was probably the uncontested victor in that sort of competition after winning the heart of a princess, then driving her away. *At least that's what I* think *happened,* he considered. *I suppose the truth of the matter is more complicated.* He put the heel of his palm against his forehead, not sure if he was trying to fend off a headache or smack himself to create one.

Why does life have to be so confusing, he thought. *Things are simpler in books. Maybe that's why I want to spend time reading?* He stood straight on his flying disk and pulled his shoulders back, promising himself to be less foolish in the future. *Apologizing to Merry will be my top priority the next time I see her,* he resolved.

Feeling more at peace with himself, Eynon circled the west side of the castle's walls and landed in an abrupt hawk's dive, bouncing the bottom of his flying disk on the cobblestones outside the door to the castle's kitchens. *It won't be the same without Nûd and Damon teasing me,* thought Eynon. *And deceiving me,* said another part of his mind.

Eynon tugged on the door and was pleased to find it opened easily. *There's not much cause to lock doors when you're thousands of miles away from everyone,* he mused. After stepping inside, Eynon slung his flying disk over his shoulders and began to walk downstairs. It was cold enough to see his breath. Since he and Damon and Nûd had left, nobody was there to tend the fires in the kitchens' hearths below. He warmed himself with congruency-derived heat from his red magestone, keeping its power in check with his blue magestone.

When he reached the kitchen level, he started a small fire in one of the ovens, so he'd be able to proof some dough overnight. He was fine with providing his own heat, but the fire was comforting in a way a congruency couldn't match. Eynon inspected the kitchens' larders to see what he might turn into meals during his stay. He was beginning to get hungry from all the excitement earlier, even after the delicious food served at the party to celebrate signing the treaty.

There was plenty of smoked meat in the cold storage room and quite a few burlap sacks of legumes and root vegetables seemed unspoiled in a not quite so cold storeroom next door. He found another room filled with grain sacks and determined he could make pease porridge of a sort for dinner later, after they'd had a chance to soak. More poking around revealed a barrel of fine white flour that had clearly been imported from Brendinas. Nûd and Damon must have reserved it for special occasions. He hoped the flour would make good bread, unlike the inedible ale-cakes Nûd had served him when he'd first arrived in Melyncárreg.

Eynon explored further and found what he needed to prepare a simple dinner by putting three cups of lentils and two scoops of groats in a crock, adding water, covering the crock, and putting the vessel in the bread oven to simmer while he spent time in the library. He'd mix up dough from the white flour and have hot rolls and fried eggs for breakfast in the morning, if the chickens in the courtyard were still laying.

For the present, Eynon cut a few inches of sausage from a piece as long as a sword hanging from the ceiling in the cold storage room and claimed a small jug of cider from another storeroom. He didn't need a mug—it would just be one more thing to carry. Thus equipped, he made his way up the stairs leading to the upper floors of the castle—and the library.

That spacious room looked just as he'd remembered it. The library had a high vaulted ceiling and tall windows with east and west exposures. The inside wall held a fireplace with logs already set to be kindled. Floor-to-ceiling bookshelves filled every inch of wall space not occupied by the fireplace and the windows. Two rows of long tables finished with a dark stain sat in the center of

the room, ready for books to be placed upon them. Heavy wooden
chairs stained the same dark shade and padded with blue leather
seats and backs were at each table. Oil lamps rested atop the tables
at intervals, their glass chimneys blackened with soot.

Why does a school for wizards need oil lamps for light? Eynon
wondered. *For apprentices, like I was? For visiting non-wizard scholars?*
Now that he knew how to cast light spells, it seemed odd they were
needed. He took a deep breath. The library smelled like leather,
wood smoke, and old parchment. Eynon loved the scent more than
crushed wintergreen leaves and almost as much as fresh-baked bread.

Ignoring the shelves on the left filled with titles written in lan-
guages Eynon couldn't read, he moved to the back wall and the
shelves next to the spot where he'd found massive tomes on the
history of Dâron earlier. *Metamagical Themes* read the spine of one
book. *That sounds too advanced,* thought Eynon. His eyes slid to
the right and he took in the title of a book with a black cover even
thicker than the one before. *Principia Magica,* it read. Eynon pulled
it out and opened the front cover. It was so heavy he had to lean the
book against the shelf to support it. The title page said it had been
translated by scribes in Roma from an Athican original text written
by Aristotéles, one of the great early Athican mages and a pupil of
Plátōn the Great. Both teacher and student were counted among
the first wizards to understand and codify serious magic.

Eynon flipped ahead a few pages and tried to read the first chapter
in the *Principia*. He found the text so dense and the prose so obtuse
it might have still been written in Athican. He put it on the table
to come back to later.

Perhaps it would be better to start with a thinner volume, he considered. A book only as wide as his index finger and bound in red
leather caught his attention. The words stamped in gold leaf along
its spine read *On Wizardry.* Eynon plucked it from the shelf and
turned to sit at the nearest long table. He opened the cover and
smiled at the slim book's subtitle: *A Recipe Book of Magic.*

That's more like it, thought Eynon. *Or as Merry would say with a
teasing grin, "Now we're cooking!"*

He turned another page to the table of contents. Spells and types of magic were arranged in various categories, like Offensive Magic, Defensive Magic, Healing Magic, Gate Magic, Detection, Illusion, Communication, and Miscellaneous Magic. Most of the recipes listed were things he expected. Fireballs, lightning, shield shapes, healing potions, fertility prevention charms, and the like.

The Gate Magic category included fixed gates, temporary gates, and emergency gates but not wide gates like the ones Fercha had helped create. Detection recipes included the familiar listening spell Merry had taught him as well as ways to use solidified sound to see farther or see better at night that Eynon had already figured out for himself. Some of the entries under the Illusion category looked promising and would help him refine his constructs to make them more convincing.

When he saw the topic *How to Make Communications Rings* under the Communications category, Eynon resolved to work on that first. He wanted to craft a pair of rings and give one to Merry as a peace offering, so they could always stay in touch. He scanned along the items listed under the Miscellaneous Magic category and was pleased to see Doethan's clothes-drying spell, another recipe he'd already mastered.

Running his finger further down the page, he was pleased to see *How to Make a Flying Disk*. Eynon promised himself to look at that one right after he learned how to make communications rings. He had some ideas for using flying disks offensively—and also wanted to understand how the shards of Fercha's shattered flying disk had been so sharp. Sharper swords might be useful against the emperor's legions. *Making a Bottle that Never Runs Dry* was another topic that intrigued him. For that matter, every recipe in the book pulled him in and encouraged Eynon to explore it, especially the oddly named item under Offensive Magic named *Using Nothing as a Weapon*.

Eynon was so completely focused on the book that he ignored his surroundings. He reached out to grab the length of sausage he'd cut, bit off a piece, chewed, and swallowed without his conscious mind being aware of the action. Likewise, he removed the cork from the jug with his teeth, drank cider, and returned the cork to its original location without his eyes leaving the pages of *On Wizardry*.

An hour later, Eynon was surprised—twice. First was seeing a note at the end of the book indicating it was part of a series. There were two more volumes for Eynon to read. Second was hearing a man clear his throat behind Eynon's left shoulder. Suppressing a desire to levitate to the ceiling, Eynon turned and saw a man of medium height who looked to be the same age as his father. He was wearing weather-stained blue robes and his face was framed by a full brown beard just starting to go gray. His eyebrows danced as he spoke. They were bushy in a way that made him seem comfortable, not crazed. A large blue magestone in a gold setting hung on a heavy chain at his neck.

"Sorry to startle you," said the man. "I just stopped by to see if I could borrow a cup of honey."

Chapter 8

Reporting In

The leaders of three kingdoms and an imperial Roma province were still talking in Laetícia's study when Verro gated in to an empty area by the door to the stairway. Tamloch's master mage strode confidently into the center of the room. Heads turned to note Verro's arrival and Doethan spoke from a spot in a far corner where he was sitting with Princess Rúth.

"How's Merry?" the older wizard asked.

"And Eynon?" added Nûd.

"What kept you so long?" asked Fercha. She smiled at Verro to show she was concerned, not angry.

"Fine, fine, and various details," Verro answered, smiling back at Fercha and moving across the room to join everyone.

"That's not much of an answer," said Dârio.

"You sound like you're barely thirteen and trying to hide something from your parents," teased Jenet.

"Fine," said Verro. He paused to give the others time to glare at him, then continued. "You want details? I'll provide them."

Princess Rúth put her hand over her mouth to hide a laugh. She was quite familiar with her older brother's sense of humor. Chee bounded from Rúth's lap and rushed to Verro. The raconette climbed the wizard's back and settled in a spot on Verro's shoulder, chittering happily as if he could smell Eynon's scent on Verro's robes.

"About time," said the princess. She enjoyed watching her brother's reaction to Chee and loved keeping Verro off balance when she had the chance, which was seldom.

Duke Néillen marked the siblings' exchange, remembering King Túathal's more heavy-handed and less successful attempts at manipulation.

"Very well," said Verro as he reached up to rub the soft fur on Chee's belly. "Merry and I rescued Eynon when he fell into the harbor."

Heads nodded. Chee bobbed his head to imitate them.

Sónnel put his oar in. "Laetícia told us about his fall when she gave us details about the emperor's fleet. The lad is lucky you and Merry were there."

"I'm glad Merry insisted on coming," said Verro. "I poured a healing potion down Eynon's throat immediately, then used my emergency gate to transport both Merry and Eynon to my personal refuge."

Fercha gave Verro a sidelong glance and frowned slightly. His refuge had been *their* special place and she wasn't sure how she felt about Eynon and Merry spending time there. Then she smiled on the inside, remembering stolen hours with Verro on a bearskin rug.

"They were both exhausted, so I made them comfortable and told them to rest while I left to inform you they were both safe," added Verro.

Frowning more directly at Verro now, Fercha wished it was possible to send thoughts from her head to his. *They'd better not be sleeping on* our *rug!* Verro noticed Fercha's expression and shrugged, understanding her unspoken message. The corners of his mouth turned up and for a moment he looked like he had when they'd first met twenty-five years ago. They briefly embraced, glad to be together, and by silent mutual agreement determined to talk at a later point when they were alone.

"How's Eynon really?" asked Duke Háiddon. "Dâron will need its master mage in good health."

"Father," said Jenet sharply.

"Don't *father* me, daughter," said the duke. "I *am* interested in Eynon's welfare, but as earl marshal of Dâron I also have to worry about his combat effectiveness and strategic value."

"Yes, *father*," teased Jenet. "I understand and am glad you didn't say anything patronizing like, 'Now that you're Tamloch's earl marshal you'll have to start worrying about such things."

"The thought never crossed my mind," said Duke Háiddon. He was trying—and failing—to hide a grin underneath his serious expression.

"If you don't mind," inserted Nûd, "I want to know Eynon's status because he's my friend, not just my kingdom's master mage."

"There's good news about his *physical* condition," Verro replied. "The worst damage to his body is cracked ribs, a dislocated shoulder—which I've put back in place—and assorted bumps and bruises."

"Drop the other boot," said Queen Signý.

"What is it you're *not* saying?" asked King Bjarni.

"I'm concerned about Eynon's mental condition," Verro answered. "He's beginning to doubt himself."

"Is that a bad thing?" asked Inthíra, speaking up for the first time. "I'd think it would do him good to learn he isn't invincible."

"Maybe," said Verro.

"I understand your concern," said Doethan. "One of Eynon's strengths is that he doesn't know what's impossible."

"I remember that fireball of his above my fleet on the Brenavon," said King Bjarni, shaking his head and setting his long beard waving.

"I'm surprised he didn't sink every one of our ships," contributed Queen Signý.

"He froze the river when Damon couldn't," said Nûd. "And his constructs of solidified sound..." Nûd's voice trailed off.

"We all know the lad has exceptional magical talent," said Verro. "There's no question of that. My question is how will he react to finding he *does* have limits."

"Four Roma battle wizards and seven combat-trained dragons simultaneously," said Laetícia softly.

"That's an impressive limit," added Duke Néillen, nodding his head in admiration.

"I've lived near the Coombe for many years," said Doethan. "From what I've seen, people raised there are good at overcoming obstacles."

"Speaking of obstacles," said Duke Háiddon. "Can we let Eynon and Merry rest for a few hours and get back to the larger question of how *we* are going to overcome the rather challenging obstacle of Sírénae Accipiter, her fleet, and her legions?"

"That sounds sensible," said Jenet.

"We can ask Eynon what he's thinking after he's had a chance to rest," Nûd offered. "It's *fine* for us to speculate," he said, smiling at Verro, "but only Eynon knows his own mind."

"And Merry," said Doethan. "She'll likely know his thoughts better than he does."

A ripple of laughter circled Laetícia's study.

"You may be right," said Verro. "But they aren't joined at the hip—or the forehead." He picked up a dough ring spread with soft white cheese from a silver tray, broke it in half, and handed one portion to Chee, who accepted the treat enthusiastically. After taking a large bite, chewing and swallowing, Verro wiped a dot of cheese from the corner of his mouth and asked a question. "What's your current thinking on the best way to counter the emperor?"

"There are three major options," said Dârio.

"Assemble our united forces here in Nova Eboracum and meet whatever the emperor decides to throw at us head-on," said Quintillius. "Viridáxés would love the idea."

"I'm sure he would," muttered Fercha, remembering how much the great green dragon hated the Roma.

"The downside of that is Sírénae's greater mobility," said Quintillius. "If we concentrate our forces, she can sail elsewhere and hit us somewhere lightly defended."

"Unfortunately," said Duke Háiddon. His forehead was creased with concentration—or worry.

"Second," said Grand Admiral Sónnel in the silence following Duke Háiddon's single word. "We do everything we can to stop their fleet before they can reach Orluin. With Tamloch's fleet and the Bifurland longships, we can do them a lot of damage at sea."

Verro moved his hand in a circular motion, encouraging someone to provide the third option.

Nûd looked left and right, then revealed what was clearly the choice he favored. "I think we should evacuate our cities, abandon our lands and let the emperor take them without a fight."

Duke Háiddon looked at Nûd and nodded but said nothing. Others' reactions were louder and more negative.

"That's absurd," said Quintillius. "Why should we surrender our cities?"

"Are you a coward that you'd have us run before our enemy without striking a blow?" asked Bjarni. He jumped to his feet and stared daggers at Nûd until Signý put a hand on his arm and he sat down again, still glaring.

Jenet looked at her father and noted his thoughtful expression, so she held her tongue—at least for the moment.

Dârio did speak, calmly. "You've obviously thought this through, cousin," he said to Nûd. "Why should we do what you recommend?"

"Before I go into detail, I need to ask Quintillius and Laetícia a few questions," Nûd replied. "Is it likely that Sírénae's forces can be resupplied from one of the four empires?"

"By magic?" asked Laetícia.

"Or by sea?" added Grand Admiral Sónnel.

"Either," said Nûd. "They can't have infinite stores even in the holds of large ships. Sailors, legionnaires, and elephants have to eat. *Are* they limited by the food they've brought with them?"

Quintillius turned his head toward Laetícia and lowered his chin. Laetícia provided Nûd with an answer.

"I haven't had confirmation from my uncle Valens, but I'd find it hard to believe that Sírénae still has many allies anywhere across the Ocean. My guess is all those still loyal to her are with her fleet."

"That's what I expected," said Nûd. "In all probability, Sírénae plans to commandeer supplies from *us* and make our citizens her slaves. It's still early spring in Orluin. She'd have to take our supplies to feed her troops, since it will be several months until there's anything ready to be harvested."

"I see where you're going," said Duke Háiddon. "What if we leave and take all our food and drink with us. They can't enslave our people if they aren't in easy reach."

"And their supplies will run out quickly without our provisions to appropriate," added Jenet.

"You're missing something," said Grand Admiral Sónnel.

"And I know what it is," said King Bjarni. "Fish."

"Precisely," said the admiral. "The emperor's sailors could catch enough cod at the banks off the coast of Bifurland to keep them going until their first crops came in."

"Not if Zûrafiérix and Viridáxés caved in their hulls below the waterline or fouled their nets," said Nûd. "Zûra would support that effort if we didn't let Sírénae's sailors drown."

"Wait," said Fercha. "We're forgetting her elephants."

"I didn't forget them," said Nûd. "I was counting on them to eat shoots and leaves before they matured. The elephants will be competing with legionnaires and cavalry horses for edibles. There were cavalry horses with the fleet, weren't there?"

Laetícia nodded. "There were enough horse transport vessels to carry twenty *equites,*" she answered. Inthíra raised an eyebrow. "About six thousand mounted cavalry troops," Laetícia clarified. "Not a large percentage of the emperor's forces, but enough for quick raids and scouting."

"Wizards do more of the scouting these days," said Doethan. "At least on this side of the ocean."

"A mounted warrior can still spot things from horseback that a wizard high above on a flying disk might miss," said Laetícia.

Duke Néillen cleared his throat and the others looked in his direction. "True enough," he said, "but you're overlooking the obvious."

"What's that?" asked Duke Háiddon. He bore little love for Tamloch's former earl marshal.

"You've said that Sírénae has a brilliant military mind. You've told us she's won battle after battle in the four empires of the Roma," said Néillen. "You also said she's a hawk who makes Túathal seem like a sparrow."

"Get to the point," said Dârio.

"I'm trying to," said Duke Néillen. "Túathal's mind was twisted like a snake coiled around a rat. He always had reasons for what he did—at least until the end when madness took him."

"You're making me mad by not speaking plainly," said Dârio.

Jenet put a hand on Dârio's arm. "Let him talk," she said.

"What if Sírénae's elephants aren't traveling with her fleet just to supplement the combat strength of her legions?" Duke Néillen asked.

"I see where you're going," said Princess Rúth from her spot in a corner next to Doethan. Heads swiveled to look at her instead of Néillen. "What if the elephants are a portable larder?"

Néillen bowed to the princess and smiled. "My very thought," he said. "Elephants can forage in forests and be butchered as necessary to sustain the emperor's legions. You can feed a lot of soldiers with an elephant."

"My proposed option isn't completely without value," said Nûd. "If we can disrupt their attempts at large-scale fishing, it could still work."

"I have some thoughts about how to handle Sírénae's elephants," offered Queen Signý. "Bjarni and I will confer with Fercha to see if they're feasible," she continued.

"I'm glad to talk when you're ready," said Fercha. She turned to the others. "You're all overlooking a few important considerations. It won't take long for the emperor's mages to hear about Eynon's trick with the stampeding wisents."

"There are plenty of wisents in Dâron now for them to capture for that matter," said Jenet.

"Plus a few miscellaneous flathorns," said Dârio, earning a poke in the ribs from his earl marshal.

"As you say," said Jenet. The corners of her mouth turned up and she raised an eyebrow. "We can round them up and send them back, but how long do you think it would be before Sírénae's wizards discover there are lots more wisents to the west. It shouldn't take *that* long for them to figure out a way to gate them here to feed the emperor's soldiers and slaves?"

"Not long," said Fercha. "Once you know wide gates can be made, it wouldn't be hard to work out the magic needed to create them."

"Especially if one of Sírénae's spies watched one being constructed," said Laetícia.

"You think she's got agents in Nova Eboracum who watched the wide sea gate being built to transport the Bifurland longships from the Brenavon," said Nûd.

"I know she does," said Laetícia.

Chee hopped down from Verro's shoulder and landed on the table with the tray of dough rings. He appropriated a dough ring and a small crock of soft white cheese and disappeared under the table. None of the humans in Laetícia's study even noticed.

"It may well be possible to starve the Siren Hawk's invaders," said Princess Rúth. "You're a resourceful group of leaders who could figure out ways to sabotage their food supply, I'm sure."

"But?" asked Jenet.

"But the larger problem is how to evacuate our largest cities and strip them of supplies in only a week," answered the princess. "I can see the wisdom in avoiding a direct confrontation with a superior foe, but moving several hundred thousand people out of harm's way would be a major logistical challenge."

"My grandfather Ealdamon would have an epigram to cover that situation," said Nûd. He paused and smiled at them.

"Speak, Your Majesty," said Jenet. "Tell us what it would be."

Nûd stood and assumed a pose that copied a statue of an Athican orator. "Nothing speeds people up as much as the prospect of enslavement if they dawdle."

"Let's get on with it, then," said Quintillius. "We have a lot to do and very little time to do it."

Chapter 9

What Lies Below

Falling is always disorienting and falling in the dark even more so. Luckily, Merry's glow ball fell with her, remaining a few feet above her head, giving her an excellent view of a dozen rocks the size of blackseed melons descending above her. Concerned with the damage the rocks would do if she didn't protect herself—and worried about additional damage when she eventually hit bottom—Merry took two actions simultaneously. First, she threw up a sphere of solidified sound around her body, and second, she directed her flying disk to hover, holding up her back flat while her head and lower torso hung down.

The heavy stones in her field of vision struck the shield, knocking it left and right before bouncing off. Merry had time to take a breath before she heard them land below with a *squish,* rather than the expected clatter of rocks hitting rock.

Ace was barking and seemed concerned for Merry's welfare. He'd jumped off her lap as soon as she'd started to fall, and his yelps echoed around the space like they were in some sort of underground amphitheater. Merry shifted her flying disk so she was hanging by its straps and looked down. The light from her glow ball wasn't enough to illuminate more than a dozen feet around her, so she issued an intensifying word of command and it suddenly grew brighter, revealing the space she'd fallen into. It was a large cavern as tall as a castle tower and as broad around as the circular stadium she'd recently seen in Nova Eboracum before the signing ceremony. The cavern's floor was covered in something bumpy, white, and carpet-like that Merry couldn't identify.

She slowly sent her flying disk lower until she was only a few feet above the cavern's floor. The white carpet was now clearly identifiable as acres of snow-colored mushrooms. Merry inhaled. Her nose took in a not-unpleasant musky smell that the mushrooms must be releasing. Ace circled Merry twice and landed near where one of the falling stones had crushed some of the white fungi. A long red tongue extended from the rockhound's mouth and curled around some of the pieces of mushrooms broken by the stones, pulling them inside like a frog snatching flies out of the air. Ace swallowed, barked, and smiled up at Merry.

"Good boy," said Merry. "How do they taste? Are they delicious?"

The rockhound's tail flicked back and forth, dislodging more mushrooms from what seemed to be several inches of fine soil lining the bottom of the cavern. Ace captured one of the loosened mushrooms the same way he'd done earlier and rose to Merry's height, extending his tongue to present it to her. Merry accepted the gift but didn't try to eat it. Ace barked.

"Maybe later," Merry replied. "After I've had a chance to check it for toxins."

"Arf! Arf! Rrrruff!" Ace replied.

Merry brought her flying disk down until she could stand on top of one of the largest stones—more of a boulder, really—that had fallen with her. She was reluctant to step on the mushrooms even though Ace seemed to think they were not only innocuous but tasty. She looked up to see if the ceiling of the cavern was covered in nesting bats but was relieved to find it was largely bare rock. Eating mushrooms fertilized from above by bat guano was not appealing.

She heard running water and saw a waterfall no taller than Eynon's wiry six-foot-two some distance away to the left at one end of the cavern. Merry could trace the path of a stream that meandered its way through the cavern from the waterfall to some unseen exit far to the right. *The stream must provide nutrients for the mushrooms when it floods,* she thought. *This place is really big,* Merry realized as her senses finally took in the cavern's dimensions. *It's almost as big as Viridáxés or Zûrafiérix,* she determined.

Merry's curiosity got the better of her and she extinguished her glow ball by clenching her fist and speaking a word of command. After her eyes adjusted to the dark, she sensed a pink glow from the cavern's walls and rounded ceiling. "Magestones, Ace," she said. "The rocks around this cavern are rich in magestones."

"Yip!" said Ace in apparent agreement. The rockhound joined Merry on her flying disk and curled into a rock-shaped gray ball at her feet. She dropped the mushroom Ace had given her near her familiar and the stem and cap disappeared inside Ace's ball-like form.

"What do you think, boy?" asked Merry. "Will the walls be smooth or more *interesting?*" she mused, more to herself than to the rockhound. She restored her bright glow ball and guided her flying disk from the boulder near the center to a spot close to the walls. Merry smiled. There *was* a pattern imprinted into the cavern wall before her. It was scales—tens of thousands of scales—*dragon* scales.

Hah! thought Merry. There *were* other great dragons, but from the apparent age of this cavern, its former resident must have left long ago. *There were legends of great dragons in ancient days,* Merry considered. *But it's strange to have one this size go unmentioned in the histories. Could there be dragons in Orluin that hadn't been brought across the Ocean on the First Ships?*

Ace launched himself from Merry's flying disk and hovered at her eye level without doing anything to maintain his altitude. *How?* Merry asked herself, then chuckled when she realized the obvious answer. *Rockhounds must have internal congruencies to fly like dragons,* she decided. *I wonder if Ace can breathe fire? Maybe he can roast the bats he catches before he eats them?*

Her new familiar was flitting back and forth, encouraging Merry to move toward the end of the cavern away from the waterfall where she assumed the stream made its exit. "Just a minute," said Merry. "I'll follow you, but I want to test these mushrooms first."

"Arf!" barked Ace. He retrieved a large specimen of mushroom from the cavern floor and brought it back to drop it in Merry's outstretched hand. She ignored the drool and wiped the white-capped fungus off on her new sky-blue robes. She thought back to the single lesson Fercha had given her on detecting poisons.

"Anyone dealing with Gwýnnett or Túathal should learn how to detect poisons," Fercha had said. "I hope you won't have cause to use such spells, but they may save your life someday."

"Especially if I'm ever out in the woods collecting truffles and morels," Merry had answered. "I don't want to mistake Autumn Skullcaps and Deadly Whitecaps for their benign cousins." At the time, she'd considered that prospect more likely than worrying about someone trying to poison her deliberately. Then she'd met Dârio's mother, Princess Gwýnnett, and knew her earlier opinion had been naïve.

Ace flew off and returned with a brown-capped mushroom from closer to the waterfall. Merry wiped it off as well and put it next to the first mushroom in her right palm while she tried to remember the steps in the spell Fercha had shown her. In theory, it was simple. Push a wall of tuned solidified sound through the samples and look for flashes of angry reds and oranges from the items being tested that were supposed to indicate the strength of the poison. Fercha had warned Merry that the spell wouldn't detect metals like arsenic or lead, but it did do well at marking organic poisons.

What was the pattern again? Merry mused, pushing her tongue against her lower teeth. Then she remembered. Solidified sound for detection spells was halfway between physical shields and illusion magic. She took a quick breath and generated a vertical plane of solidified sound two feet in front of her and parallel to her torso.

Merry slowly extended her left hand, palm still open, and carefully watched the white and dark-capped mushrooms as they intersected with the plane. No sparks of red or orange appeared around Ace's gifts, though flashes of red glinted from the walls. *Good,* thought Merry. *Verro will be pleased his refuge will provide a new source of food for the people of Riyas—assuming the citizens of Tamloch like mushrooms.*

"Arf! Arf! Arf!" barked Ace again. He had returned to his earlier attempt to get Merry to follow him out of the cavern. This time, Merry directed her flying disk to follow the rockhound as he flew away from the waterfall and toward a wide dark space the light from her glow ball had not yet illuminated.

It must be a large opening if it's how a great dragon left the cavern, she realized. To Merry's surprise, it *wasn't* a large opening. Once her light spell lit up the other end of the cavern, she saw what *had* been a large opening was now blocked by thousands of rocks and boulders, some bigger than Merry was tall. For that matter, some were bigger than *Quintillius* was tall. Most were too big for her to move, even with magical assistance. The pile of boulders reached all the way to the ceiling. *That explains why there aren't any bats in the cavern,* thought Merry.

Ace had landed at the spot where the stream intersected with the wall of stone. The water flowed between two medium-sized rocks and had made a channel of sorts beneath them, its current carrying gravel and sand along with it. The rockhound flew high up and descended quickly to land on top of the left-hand rock with the full weight of its modest mass. The rock shifted in the gravel below, and Merry understood what Ace intended before the rockhound had to bark again.

"Let me see what I can do," said Merry. She created a fulcrum and long lever from solidified sound, thinking of Eynon's creative constructs as she did so. The fulcrum was triangle shaped, like the tip of a dragon's tail and the lever was a cylinder with two flattened ends. The short end of the cylinder went under the left-hand rock and the long end stuck high in the air ten yards farther back into the cavern. Merry rose until she was above the far end of the lever and brought her flying disk down on the flat part of the cylindrical rod, pushing with a weight greater than the rockhound's.

The left-hand rock popped up like a cork from a jug of cider left fermenting too long. It struck the ceiling of the cavern then fell back down on the pile with a clatter and rolled a few feet toward her. An opening next to the stream large enough for Merry to crawl through was revealed in the space behind where the rock had been. She sent her glow ball into the opening and saw the wall of boulders ended after a dozen feet.

Ace scampered up and down the narrow passage beside the stream, encouraging Merry to follow him. *It's easier for Ace to fit through than me, but I don't have much choice,* she thought. Merry put her flying disk on her back, got on her hands and knees, and crawled through the opening and the passageway beyond.

As she approached the far end, beyond the wall, she detected a scent far more unpleasant than the musty smell of mushrooms. Her nose was assailed by a pungent stench that made her want to turn around and retrace her path. It was familiar, but she couldn't place it. Ace bumped against her backside like a moth hitting a lamp, butting her with his head several times in succession as if encouraging her to move forward.

"I'm moving, I'm moving," said Merry softly. Only a few feet of passage remained. She generated a protective shield of solidified sound close to her body, crawled the last few feet, and stood up in a much more modestly-sized cave shaped like an egg on its side. She was emerging from one end of the oval while sunlight streamed into the space from the opposite end, casting shadows halfway into the cave.

Ace flew out of the passageway and hovered over her head. Merry wasn't sure, but she thought her new familiar was on edge about something—she just didn't know what. Then she did. One of the shadows near her moved—and growled. A great bear with a short snout rose on its hind legs, its head nearly touching the cave's ceiling. The beast was a foot taller than Eynon and bigger around than Tibbo, the innkeeper at the Blue Whale tavern in Riyas, though its matted fur hung on its body like an ill-fitting cloak. *The bear is just waking up from its winter sleep,* thought Merry with the part of her brain that wasn't terrified.

The huge animal blinked in the light from Merry's glow ball, opened its fierce mouth, and *roared.* Saliva dripped from its jaw and its eyes were a bright gold color from the glow ball's reflection. It marked Merry as an intruder in its den, took two steps forward and swiped at her with paws the size of dinner plates. Sharp claws glistened white as they extended to rake her flesh.

Merry's back was to the rock wall, so she couldn't retreat. Her flying disk was still on her shoulders so she couldn't lift herself out of reach—and besides, the ceiling of the cave was too low for that mode of escape. The bear's blows landed left-right-left on Merry's shield, battering her from side to side like a dog shaking a child's doll.

Now I know how Eynon must have felt fighting seven dragons, thought Merry. *I'm sure I can figure out how to get past this justifiably grumpy bear if I just have a moment to think!*

Ace provided the distraction Merry needed. Her familiar swooped above the bear and descended on its head, covering the beast's eyes with his carpet-like body and staying well above the giant's snapping jaws. The blows from the bear's paws stopped briefly and Merry fell back to her hands and knees, strengthening her shield above her as she crawled past the bear toward the sunlight at the far end of the cavern. When she was well out of reach of the bear's long arms, Merry stood and ran until she burst out of the cave's dark mouth into a warm spring day on a rocky hillside.

Merry quickly pulled her flying disk from her shoulders, boarded it, and lifted herself twenty feet in the air. She smiled when Ace zoomed out of the cave's entrance a few seconds later and rose to hover beside her.

"Thanks for your help," she said, tossing the rockhound a travel cake.

Ace expertly snatched the twice-baked cake from the air and barked after swallowing it whole. Below them, the bear was lumbering out of the cave, gazing up at them, and bellowing its displeasure.

"Go back to sleep," she said to the beast. "We didn't mean to wake you." She looked down at Ace, who'd just landed beside her on her flying disk and was clearly hoping for another travel cake or a piece of dried meat. Merry scratched her familiar's head and he rubbed it against her knee affectionately.

"Arf!" said the rockhound.

"Arf indeed," Merry replied. "Now let's see if we can find someone who can tell us the way to Riyas."

Chapter 10

Meet the Neighbors

Eynon's manners overrode his incredulity. "That shouldn't be a problem," he told the bearded older wizard in weather-stained blue robes who'd surprised him. "There are several crocks of honey in the kitchen's storerooms."

"Excellent," said the wizard. "My wife and I are making dried apple and raisin tarts. They're so much better with honey instead of maple syrup."

"I agree," said Eynon. "Maple syrup is *too* sweet and overwhelms the flavor of the fruit…"

"While honey enhances it," completed the new arrival. He smiled down at Eynon and waited for the younger wizard's mind to catch up with his senses.

A moment later, Eynon popped up from his chair in the Melyncárreg Castle's library and turned to face his unexpected visitor. "Excuse me," he said, "but who *are* you? I'm Eynon of Haywall, by the way. From the Coombe. That's in western Dâron."

"Call me Rōlin," said the older wizard. "My wife and I have a small steading thirty-five leagues south of here."

"Damon and Nûd intimated that there weren't any other humans within a thousand miles of here," said Eynon. He knew he looked like a deer staring at a lantern but couldn't help himself.

"There's your first mistake, young man," said the visitor. "You should never believe everything Ealdamon tells you. He's fond of making things up."

Eynon nodded his head slowly. He knew Damon and Nûd hadn't been telling him the complete truth and the implication that they'd been misleading him about more than Nûd's parentage was starting to sink in.

Rōlin continued speaking after realizing Eynon was still processing his previous words. "Did Ealdamon or Nûd actually *say* that no one lived nearby, or did they simply allow you to believe that?" Rōlin asked.

"The latter," said Eynon, finally regaining control of his tongue. He smiled at Rōlin. "Not that more than a hundred miles is nearby—at least not how we reckon distance in the Coombe."

"Here in the western mountains our standards are different," said Rōlin. "Anyone within a hundred and fifty leagues is a neighbor west of the great river."

"But *I* live west of the great river!" exclaimed Eynon.

"Not the Moravon," said Rōlin. "The Mormoráfon, the great mother river that drains the center of the continent."

Eynon thought back to his brief time down the hall in the Map Room. He'd been focused on the impressive distance from Melyncárreg to Brendinas, but he vaguely recalled a wide blue line snaking its way from north to south in the center of the map.

"I see," said Eynon. He resolved to visit the Map Room again at his earliest opportunity. "How did you know I was here, by the way?"

"I didn't," said Rōlin. "I have an arrangement with Damon and Nûd. I can pop in and borrow this and that from their storerooms and in return I'll bring them fresh fruit and vegetables from my greenhouses—not that they'd know what to do with them. Neither one of them can make a palatable pie or a simple salad."

"Agreed," said Eynon. "After tasting what Nûd had prepared, I had to do the cooking in order to have anything worth eating."

"Damon is an even worse a cook than Nûd," Rōlin added. "And Nûd's ale-cakes aren't fit food for pigs."

"Very true," said Eynon. He looked at Rōlin. "Does the air smell like sulphur where you live?"

"Not at all," said the older wizard. "It smells like pine trees."

"That alone is a big advantage for *your* cooking, I'm sure," said Eynon. He continued to look at the older wizard then realized he'd been impolitely staring at Rōlin's full brown beard. *My mind must be playing tricks on me,* Eynon noted. *I thought I saw eyes in his beard, staring back at me.*

Rōlin followed Eynon's gaze and began to laugh a full-bodied laugh that made his chest shake. He put his hand behind his beard and pulled out a chittering gray squirrel with sparkling eyes who'd been hiding beneath it. "This is Lléwys," said Rōlin. "He's my traveling companion," the wizard continued. The squirrel burrowed back into the older wizard's beard. "And a bit shy," Rōlin added.

"Pleased to meet you, Lléwys," said Eynon. He extended his hand close to Rōlin's beard and the squirrel's head poked through bushy brown whiskers to sniff, then lick Eynon's fingers. "Does he eat meat?" asked Eynon. "He seems to like the taste of sausage."

"Lléwys will eat anything," said Rōlin. He stroked the top of the squirrel's head with the edge of his hand, making Eynon wish he had Chee with him.

I wonder if Chee and Lléwys would get along, he considered. Eynon turned back to the table where he'd been reading and cut half an inch of sausage off for Lléwys. When he offered it to the squirrel it was gratefully received. Lléwys took the morsel and retreated back inside the curtain of Rōlin's whiskers to consume it in relative privacy.

"Would you like some sausage too?" Eynon asked Rōlin.

"No thank you," said the older wizard. "I don't want to spoil my lunch."

"Lunch?" protested Eynon. He'd had lunch of a sort after the signing ceremony back in Nova Eboracum. Then he remembered things seemed to be earlier in Melyncárreg. From the position of the sun streaming through the library's windows, it was only a bit past local noon. "Of course," said Eynon, making a quick recovery. "Lunch. Let's get you some honey for your apple-raisin tarts right away. It's a long trip if you're flying thirty-five leagues."

"Flying?" replied Rōlin. "I'm not *flying* all the way back to Travelers' Rest. That would take far too long."

"Then how..." Eynon began, before closing his mouth. He really should have known better. *Maybe the healing potion still has work to do on my brain,* he thought.

"You haven't been a wizard very long, have you?" asked Rōlin.

"No sir," said Eynon. "Not even a month yet."

"Then don't worry about it," said Rōlin. "I expect you'll get the hang of wizardry eventually."

Eynon didn't mention that he was about to be confirmed as the Master Mage of Dâron. Some intuition told him Rōlin would confirm Damon had lied to him about the responsibilities of his new position. It had happened far too fast and seemed far too good to be true.

Rōlin continued. "The gate to my home is in the Map Room. You've seen the Map Room, haven't you?"

"Yes, sir," Eynon replied. "That big map of Orluin taking up a full wall is beautiful."

"It certainly is," said Rōlin. "Why don't you come with me and have lunch with us? I'm sure Peregrína would love to meet someone fond of maps."

"Peregrína is your wife?" asked Eynon.

"She is, and has been for more than two decades," said Rōlin. "She's also my partner, my collaborator, and my favorite traveling companion—no offense to you, Lléwys."

The squirrel squeaked from under Rōlin's beard but didn't show himself.

Eynon didn't bother asking what project or projects Rōlin and Peregrína collaborated on. He was sufficiently intrigued by a chance to learn more about Melyncárreg's history and find out what else Damon and Nûd hadn't told him—or the ways they had deliberately deceived him.

"Thank you for your kind invitation," said Eynon, smiling at the older wizard. "I'd enjoy joining you for lunch at your home and meeting your wife. I've always liked to be on good terms with my neighbors, however geography defines them."

Eynon and Rōlin shared a grin at that comment. "Let me put the book I was reading back on the shelf," Eynon continued. "Then we can head down to the kitchen to get some honey."

"What are you reading?" asked Rōlin.

On Wizardry..." began Eynon.

"...A Recipe Book of Magic," Rōlin completed. "That looks like volume one."

"It is," said Eynon. "I found it fascinating—and quite clear to read."

"Indeed," said Rōlin. "I'm glad you like it."

"Very much so," said Eynon. "I love to cook, and cooking up magic seems quite intuitive."

"As it should be," said Rōlin. "But it seldom is if you read most of the musty tomes in Damon's library. For the longest time books on magic were deliberate exercises in soporific obfuscation. The authors of this series decided to write something easier to understand—a basic cookbook for magic. The Academy wasn't very happy about it."

"They were against writing clearly?" asked Eynon.

"Exactly," said Rōlin. "For centuries, the formal study of wizardry was meant to be difficult. Wizards had to learn Athican to read books about magic"—the older wizard waved to the shelves filled with volumes whose spines were stamped with characters he couldn't read—"then when such books came to be written in the vernacular, scholars of wizardry still wrote them using the tortuous grammatical constructions and circumlocutions of Athican."

"Really?" said Eynon, lifting both eyebrows.

"Take that book you've got out. The thick one with the black cover—*Principia Magica*," said Rōlin, pointing at a heavy tome on the table. "I recognize it from *my* student days studying in this very room."

Eynon put his hand on the book Rōlin referred to.

"Open it to any random page and read a paragraph," the older wizard requested. "Any paragraph will do."

"Yes, sir," said Eynon. "I tried that earlier and found it completely impenetrable."

"Of course you did," said Rōlin. "There aren't more than a dozen wizards who can make sense of such texts these days." He rubbed his chin and added, "Most of them are at the Institute at Bhaile Pónaire or in the Valley of Towers. Give it a try anyway."

Eynon had heard of Bhaile Pónaire. That was where Nûd's new friend Bonnie was from, but he hadn't heard of the Valley of Towers. He'd have to remember to find out what he could about it.

Rōlin waved a hand at *Principia Magica,* encouraging Eynon, who opened the book and read.

"The Contradictory Function at the heart of Shield Magic begins with argument p, where p is any proposition expressed as solidified sound, along with the proposition which is the contradictory of p, that is, the proposition asserting that p is not true. This is denoted by ^p. Thus ^p is the contradictory function with p as argument and means the negation of the proposition p. It will also be referred to as the proposition not-p. Thus ~p means not-p, which means the negation of p and the negation of attacks."

Eynon looked over at Rōlin. "Do I have to go on?"

"No," said Rōlin. "There's not much point, is there? What do *you* think it means?"

"I can't really tell," said Eynon. "It feels logical, but irrational at the same time. Perhaps it means wizards' shields are the negation of something?"

"Not exactly," said Rōlin, "but I don't understand it well myself. I'm more of a pragmatic mage than a scholar."

"I think I am too," said Eynon, "though I like *On Wizardry* well enough and can learn from it. I'm going to read the other two volumes later today."

"Good for you," said Rōlin. "Let's get that honey. I'll let Peregrína know we're having company."

* * * * *

Rōlin and Peregrína's sprawling home was made from massive cut logs and its kitchen was simultaneously cozy and spacious. Eynon sat scraping his plate at a long trestle table with his hosts. They were watching him eat and smiling.

"That was delicious," said Eynon. "I'd never had such big trout before. And the salad with cider vinegar dressing was excellent. How do you get such huge fish? And fresh lettuce in April?"

"Trout grow large in mountain lakes," said Rōlin.

"There are lots of flies and beetles for them to eat," added Peregrína, a thin woman with wavy brown hair, a merry smile, and graceful fingers. Her oval blue magestone was in a delicate setting on the back of her right hand, held in place by an openwork glove made from small links of fine silver. "The lettuce comes from our greenhouses," she continued. "I'll show them to you after dessert."

"I look forward to a tour," said Eynon. "I'm sure my family would like to know how to grow food year 'round."

"It's easier when you can provide light and heat with wizardry," said Rōlin.

"Maybe I can build one for my village back home," said Eynon. "People get tired of carrots and turnips and parsnips and rutabagas by the spring equinox."

"No doubt," said Peregrína. "I hear you like my map."

"Your map?" asked Eynon.

"The big one I painted on the long wall of the map room in the Castle," Peregrína replied. "The one that shows all of Orluin from the Ocean to the Far West Sea."

"*You* painted that?" asked Eynon. "It's beautiful, impressive, and somewhat overwhelming for a person who hadn't been more than thirty miles from home before he left on his wander year. How did you get all the details you needed to draw it?"

"We flew back and forth across the continent," said Rōlin.

"And I made sketches before drawing the full-scale maps," said Peregrína.

"The whole continent?" asked Eynon. "That must have taken decades."

"About fifty years," said Rōlin. "My parents started the job. We're moving on to the southern continent next year."

"There's a southern continent?" asked Eynon.

"And quite a few islands in between," contributed Peregrína. "I can show you my preliminary drawings."

"I'd love to see them," said Eynon.

"You might also like to see *our* map room," said Rōlin.

"You have a map room?" said Eynon.

"To show off my wife's cartographical creations," said Rōlin.

"We can show it to you after the greenhouses," said Peregrína.

Eynon began to stand up from his chair at the rustic birchwood dining table. "I'll bring the tarts from the oven."

"Sit," said Rōlin. "You're our guest. And the tarts are made with your honey."

"Damon's castle's honey," said Eynon, lowering himself back down.

"Damon's castle?" said Peregrína, her voice rising. "Rōlin's great-grandfather built that castle with the money he made from his book."

"What?" asked Eynon. "I thought Damon built it for Princess Seren when they left Brendinas so she could learn magic. Nûd said they turned it into a school for wizards later."

"I told you not to believe everything Damon and Nûd told you," said Rōlin. "My great-grandfather welcomed Damon and Seren into his castle many years ago. He even let them build their own towers inside the keep. Years later, he decided to move south into Three Mountains Valley where the air doesn't stink, and the water doesn't taste like sulphur."

"The fishing is better in the lake here, too," said Peregrína.

"You do have a wonderful view of snow-topped peaks," said Eynon. "But I'm still confused. Who was your great-grandfather?"

"I thought you knew," said Rōlin.

"Everybody knows Rōlin's great-grandfather," said Peregrína. "He wrote *Peregrinations.* My family named *me* for the book.*"*

"Your great-grandfather is Robin Goodfellow?" said Eynon. His eyes felt like they'd grown six sizes too large for his head.

"Of course," said Rōlin. "And we're following in his footsteps. *The Atlas of Orluin* is almost ready for publication."

Chapter 11

Merry's Return

"Why didn't you come to get me?" asked Merry, her tone indicating her displeasure. "I had to use the back door to your refuge and your eight-foot growling door guard nearly knocked my head off."

"My *what?*" asked Verro. "I don't have a door guard for my refuge. The passage I told you about opens up into a small cave with its mouth hidden by a solidified sound illusion."

"The cave I discovered belonged to a giant bear with a muzzle that looked like someone slammed a shield into it," Merry insisted.

"A short-faced bear?" said Verro in surprise. "They can be vicious when you surprise them."

"So I noticed," said Merry.

"I'm glad you escaped unharmed," said Verro as they flew south above one of Nova Eboracum's broad avenues. The street was lined with tall, thick-walled apartment buildings. It was filled with wagons, ox-carts, chariots, and thousands of people who all seemed to be in a hurry.

They were making good time heading for Laetícia's tower from the park where Verro had *ad hoc* gated in. He smiled down at Ace, who looked like a small dog at present. He was sitting on his haunches on Merry's flying disk with his mouth open, drinking in the fast-moving air from their flight. After a few minutes, Verro realized the dog wasn't really a dog. "It looks like you've made a new friend," he said. He tentatively extended his hand to pet Merry's familiar.

Ace sniffed Verro's offered hand and looked up at Merry. She nodded her approval. The rockhound extended his long tongue and licked Verro from the middle of his forearm to his fingertips. Verro quickly pulled his hand back and wiped the drool off his arm with the hem of his robes.

"Enthusiastic, isn't he?" Verro offered.

"Arf!" said Ace. His tail smacked out five quick beats on the surface of Merry's flying disk.

"Ace is full of energy," said Merry.

"Ace?" asked Verro. Then he grinned. "Oh. Because of his bright copper nose."

"Exactly," said Merry, grinning back.

"I took my time returning for you because I didn't want to disturb you and Eynon," said Verro. "You were both tired and if you weren't sleeping, I certainly didn't want to *interrupt* anything." Verro winked conspiratorially at Merry but she didn't smile. "Besides, once Eynon was feeling better I thought he could generate an *ad hoc* gate and transport both of you directly to Laetícia's study. Where *is* Eynon, by the way?"

"That's part of the problem," said Merry. "He left while I was asleep."

"Do you know where he went?" asked Verro.

"I have my suspicions," said Merry. "He was really upset about what happened at the Tempest Isles."

"So I'd noticed," said Verro. He smiled at Merry. "You were resourceful to get out of my refuge and find a way to contact me."

"Thanks," said Merry. "Once I got past the short-faced bear and out of the cave system, I flew to the nearest farm and asked how to find Riyas. The farmer was surprised to see a blue-robed Dâron wizard, but she pointed me in the right direction. It only took me an hour to fly there—I have a good sense of the city from the illusions I had to generate."

"I remember," said Verro. "How did you find a wizard who knew how to contact me?"

"That was simple," Merry replied. "I remembered the inn where my brother had worked, the Blue Whale. Tannis and Tibbo were still running the place and as I expected, all ten of the wizards who'd gotten drunk in the fish-drying shed down in Arthábben were there."

"Were they drunk?" asked Verro. He didn't seem too pleased with that prospect.

"Just a little," said Merry. "Tibbo helped me identify the one most likely to be able to contact you."

"Chéadólta," said Verro.

"I think that's the name he gave," said Merry. "He used his communications ring to reach you. You gated to Riyas, and now you've brought us back to Nova Eboracum." She looked at Verro's green robes flapping in the wind and caught his eye. "Come to think of it, why didn't you gate directly into Laetícia's study?"

"I was embarrassed," said Verro. "I was supposed to protect you and Eynon and I forgot about you in the midst of planning how to deal with the emperor's invasion." He shrugged his shoulders and turned his palms out. "Sorry. I thought I could convince you not to point out my oversight."

"Apology accepted," said Merry. "I won't mention being forgotten if you give me more lessons on how to generate *ad hoc* gates. Maybe if I keep trying, I can figure it out."

"I'd be glad to," said Verro. "But I make no promises. Forming *ad hoc* gates is a rare talent."

Merry nodded. *Trying will be good enough for now,* she thought. "I've also got some big news to share about something I discovered," she said.

"Do tell," said Verro.

"It's better to tell everyone at once," said Merry.

"You won't have to wait long to do it," said Verro. "There's Laetícia's tower. We're here."

* * * * *

"Hello everyone," said Merry as she bustled in from the landing. Ace was at her heels and Verro trailed behind them. She spotted Doethan and Princess Rúth on a small sofa in a corner. Chee was curled up on Rúth's lap with his head hanging over the arm of the sofa. "Doethan," she called in a stage whisper. "I need you to teach me how to make communications rings as soon as possible."

"Certainly," said her old friend. "After dinner tonight?"

"That will do," said Merry. She turned her head and caught the eye of Occidens Province's spymaster. "Laetícia," she continued, "can you join Verro in helping me try to master making *ad hoc* gates? I hate not being able to gate where I need to—and I'm not thrilled with Eynon being able to do it when I can't."

"If it's important to you," said Laetícia, "we can try."

"Good," said Merry.

"Arf! Arf!" barked Ace. He left Merry's side and trotted over to Doethan, Rúth and Chee. The rockhound's tongue flicked out to lick one of Chee's exposed ears and the raconette seemed to shoot three feet into the air, his involuntary reaction accompanied by a plaintive, wailing *cheeeeeee!!!* Ace kept barking and Chee bounded from Rúth's lap once he'd come back down, seeking safety by hanging from an unlit torch in a nearby wall sconce. Ace jumped, extended the flying membranes between his legs, and hovered in front of Chee, trying to lick the raconette again while Chee dodged left and right, attempting to evade the enthusiastic rockhound's tongue.

"A new sort of magical creature," said Queen Signý, clapping her hands in delight.

"I've never seen anything like him," added King Bjarni. "He looks like a flying carpet!"

"Like I read to the children from the tales told in the eastern end of the empire," said Quintillius.

"I don't think those carpets were alive," said Laetícia.

"This flying carpet *is* alive and needs to learn some manners," said Doethan. He addressed the situation by creating a sphere of solidified sound around Ace and slowly moving the sphere and its occupant back to where Merry was standing.

"Thank you," said Merry, nodding at Doethan. She restrained Ace with a leash of tight light and signaled to Doethan that he could cancel his sphere. Dârio removed a tidbit of steak from a skewer and tossed it to Ace. The rockhound settled down to chew his treat and Nûd knelt beside Merry's familiar, stroking the gray fur on his back. After Ace finished eating, he curled into his ball-form and seemed like a gray stone from the city walls left on the floor of Laetícia's study by a careless decorator.

"That was exciting," said Fercha. "I'm glad to see you've finally found your familiar."

"It's more like he found me," replied Merry.

"As is often the case," added Inthíra with a smile.

Merry didn't remember Inthíra having a familiar and wondered if she spoke from experience.

"You poor thing," said Jenet as she walked over to the wall sconce Chee gripped nervously. The raconette was trembling and his eyes seemed even bigger than usual. Jenet stroked Chee's back and enticed the raconette into her arms for a reassuring hug. Chee held her close and eyed the ball of gray fur on the floor of Laetícia's study as if he expected it to hatch into an angry dragon. "There there," said Jenet reassuringly. "I'll protect you."

"*Chi-chee,*" said Chee in a tiny voice.

"Where's Eynon?" asked Nûd from his place on the floor. "I expected the two of you to return together."

"So did I," said Merry. "Eynon's dealing with a case of self-doubt after what happened at the Tempest Isles. He *ad hoc* gated out while I was asleep and left me."

"I don't relish being Eynon when the two of you meet again," said Quintillius with a smile.

Laetícia shot her husband a look that was easy to interpret. *Let the young people work things out for themselves.*

Quin nodded to Laetícia and put his hand in front of his mouth.

Duke Háiddon quickly jumped in. "Do you have any guesses where Eynon may have gone?" he asked.

"Yes," said Merry. "But I'm going to give him time to get past his feelings of inadequacy first. He's such an optimistic person that his good sense should overwhelm any negative thinking quickly."

"He shouldn't feel *that* inadequate," said Duke Néillen. "Simply keeping his shields up against the attack he faced was impressive."

"You can tell him so when he returns," said Merry.

"Gladly," said Néillen.

"I also want to give myself a few days to be less angry at him for leaving me at Verro's refuge," Merry continued.

"That's perfectly understandable," said Fercha. "I'm no stranger to being angry at the ones I love."

Verro looked left and right as if trying to find Damon and Seren, then flashed a quick smile at Fercha.

Merry sighed. She poured herself a goblet of red wine from a tall jug, put a small wedge of cheese and three figs on a plate, and sat on the edge of an unoccupied dining couch. Her eyes scanned the room to confirm she had everyone's attention. "I've got big news to share," she announced.

"So do we," said Dârio.

"I'm going first," said Merry.

Dârio nodded.

Merry told the story of waking up alone on a bearskin rug in Verro's refuge. She described leaving through the narrow passage, meeting Ace, and her fall into the much larger cavern filled with mushrooms.

"Were they edible?" asked Doethan.

"They didn't spark when I tested them for poisons," said Merry.

"I'm glad you remembered the spell I'd shown you," said Fercha. She moved to stand beside Verro and encouraged him to join her on another couch.

"I don't know about things like lead and arsenic," said Merry, "but Ace seems to think the mushrooms are tasty. I didn't try them, I just tested them."

"Ace?" asked Bonnie, who'd joined Nûd kneeling next to Merry's familiar. "Why Ace? What sort of name is that for a rock-dog?"

"I call him a rock*hound,*" said Merry. "Because Doethan's familiar Rowsch is a hound. Offer him another piece of meat and you'll see why I gave him that name."

"Do you want another treat, boy?" asked Bonnie. She stood and retrieved a skewer of beef from a table. After sliding it off the thin piece of wood she waved it above the rock-shaped rockhound. He promptly unrolled his body, revealing his silver eyes and round, copper-colored nose.

Ace allowed Bonnie to drop a morsel of beef into his mouth.

Laetícia laughed. "His nose looks like a shiny ās coin," she said. "Is he good with children? I expect mine would love him—and Chee for that matter."

"I don't know how Ace will react to children," said Merry. "He seems to eat bats, and maybe that's why he was so interested in Chee."

"He'd better not try to eat my new little friend," said Princess Rúth. "If he tries, I'll have Doethan turn him into a frog."

"Wizards can't actually do that," said Doethan, returning to sit with the princess. "We just *threaten* to do so."

"His tongue is like a frog's already," said Duke Néillen.

Merry grinned and generated a solidified sound illusion around Ace, making the rockhound look like a frog the size of a cauldron. "Will this do?" she asked.

Ace shot out his long red tongue and captured a skewer of spiced beef from a platter on the edge of a nearby table. His teeth crunched the small sliver of wood threaded through the roasted meat. His tongue, and Merry's illusion, made him look very frog-like indeed. Everyone laughed.

"What's your big news?" asked Merry.

Dârio replied. "We've decided we're not going to fight the emperor," he said. "We're going to evacuate our cities and take our stores with us, so Sírénae's only choice is to leave Orluin or starve."

"I think you're overlooking something," said Merry.

"What's that?" asked Duke Háiddon.

"The way Dâron defeated Tamloch on the battlefield south of Brendinas," said Merry.

"Oh," said Nûd, now standing next to Bonnie, who seemed to be petting a big frog. "There are several more large herds of wisents near Melyncárreg. They'd help the emperor's soldiers make it through until the harvest."

"I told them that already," said Jenet as she rubbed Chee's belly.

"And I raised a similar point about codfish off the coast of Bifurland," said King Bjarni. "It was suggested Viridáxés and Zûrafiérix could sabotage the imperial fishing boats' nets."

"Maybe that would work," said Merry, though she had her doubts. "We'd have to prevent the invaders from learning about our dragons, wide gates—and Melyncárreg."

"With tens of thousands of wisents still in Dâron and all the soldiers' tales of the stampede through the Tamloch army, I don't think it will take them long to figure it out," said Verro.

"That's true enough," said Quintillius, shaking his head. "Does anyone have a better idea?"

"I might," said Merry. "Remember how Eynon convinced King Bjarni and Queen Signý to ally with Dâron?"

"He bribed them with gold," said Nûd.

"I'd prefer to think of it as a substantial payment for switching sides," said King Bjarni, smiling.

Merry nodded at Bjarni and turned to Laetícia. "If we gave Sírénae enough gold, could she use it to buy her way back onto the Tetrarchy and leave Orluin?" she asked.

"I don't think so," said Laetícia, the beads on her braided hair clacking softly. "I doubt they'd take her back under any circumstances."

Chapter 12

Take a Message

Magister Callidus was pleased the storm had now passed the main fleet as it lay at anchor in the Tempest Isles' great harbor. The sky to the west was a crystalline blue, dotted with puffs of white, and the air smelled like fresh-washed wizards' robes dried in the sun of Roma's capital province.

For all he appreciated the improvement in the weather, he was dreading what would come next—getting the fleet underway and the prospect of war with the kingdoms of Orluin. Sírénae favored armed conflict over peaceful negotiations, and as her chief magister he was often at the tip of her spear. *Or the magical bolt from her crossbow?* he mused. *It's much the same either way.*

Callidus knew Admiral Pixo was at the second sheltered harbor eight miles to the east, confirming the status of the smaller fleet that had ridden out the storm there. From his vantage point looking down on the dock from the stern deck of the *Seahawk,* the emperor's flagship, he could see—and *hear*—General Machaera shouting orders to a contingent of legionnaires who were poking pachyderms with pilums to encourage them back onto their transports. The elephants had done an excellent job of consuming all the leaves that had been blown off trees and palms in the storm.

Two hundred elephants might do as much damage to vegetation as a storm, for that matter, thought Magister Callidus. He noted that the few hundred inhabitants of the Tempest Isles were absent. *Given a choice, I'd prefer to be somewhere else, too,* he noted. *I expect they would have been enslaved and their stores seized if they hadn't gone into hiding.*

Movement in the sky to the north caught his eye. Callidus could see the fleet's seven black dragons wheeling and diving, catching fish, dolphins and, he hoped, a black-and-white sea wolf or two for their dinners.

Callidus had developed a friendship with Xaxidiánus, the senior-most dragon, after they'd worked together on a campaign subduing rebellious tribes in the mountains between northern Hispania and southern Gallia three years ago. He'd been impressed by the dragon's measured ferocity when it was needed to overawe the rebels.

The magister smiled, remembering that Xaxidiánus liked sheep much more than fish. There had been plenty of sheep for him to eat on their last campaign together. *There should be sheep for him in Orluin as well,* Callidus considered. He'd heard there was good sheep country west of the Moravon in Dâron and in the low mountains of western Tamloch.

Following Sírénae's orders, Callidus had seen to the punishment of the wizards who had been unable to capture the youth who'd come to spy on them earlier. They'd be assisting Pixo's cleanup crews making the fleet ready to depart. That wasn't pleasant duty.

Xaxidiánus had let out a firedrake's rumbling laugh when Callidus had informed him that the emperor was similarly displeased with the dragons' inability to capture the spy. His scaly friend's reply, saying he'd pass that message on to the others, sounded like the universal temporizing phrase, *I'll take that under advisement.*

Callidus understood why Xaxidiánus had that reaction. Sírénae could have most people executed with a snap of her fingers, but she needed the dragons more than they needed her. The only hold she had over the fleet's dragons was control of their eggs—and the threat of the dragons' retribution if she harmed those eggs kept things in balance.

Imperial dragons were trained in loyalty and obedience from the time they hatched, which allowed Sírénae to command them under most circumstances, but not to punish the dragons for their failures, or at least not punish them excessively.

I wonder what it would be like to be a dragon? Callidus mused. *Perhaps Xaxidiánus wonders what it would be like to be a magister?* The wizard laughed. *There's a lot of truth to that old maxim about greener pastures and fences,* he thought. Unfortunately, the grass in his personal pasture was sparse and eaten down to the roots. Sírénae liked it that way. Overly ambitious subordinates were promptly beaten down—and Callidus had risen as far as an imperial mage could rise. The royal robes of emperors were as forbidden to wizards as king's crowns were in the kingdoms of Orluin.

A thin young slave with unkempt hair, bare feet, and a tattered tunic came running across the ship's deck toward him, her feet slapping the wooden boards. Callidus knew why she sought him.

"She wants to see me," he said before the slave could catch her breath.

"Yes... good... magister..." said the girl, getting her words out slowly.

"Her cabin?" asked Callidus.

"The... foredeck..." said the slave, pointing to the opposite end of the ship.

"Thank you for the message," said Callidus. He pulled an almond crusted with sesame seeds from a twist of waxed cloth in his belt pouch and tossed it to the slave, then took his flying disk off his shoulders and put his feet in its straps. The *Seahawk* was nearly three hundred feet from stern to bow and Sírénae didn't like to be kept waiting.

*   *   *   *   *

Thraxa, the emperor's ill-tempered snow-gryffon, was perched at the very prow of the ship. Sírénae was standing a few feet behind her pet on the foredeck. She waved Callidus down beside her when she saw him approach. "Good," she said. "You're here. It took you long enough. I should have that slave whipped for dawdling. It will help keep all of them in line."

"She was out of breath from running the length of the ship to relay your command," said Callidus.

"You don't know how to ensure obedience in slaves," said Sírénae. "It takes a firm hand."

"I'm more used to working with wizards," said Callidus, hoping he could distract Sírénae from the girl who'd brought him her message. He braced himself. Sírénae liked to lash out at everyone around her when she was in a bad mood, and he expected it would be his turn soon enough.

"Wizards need a firm hand, too," said Sírénae.

"But they do better work when given wine, not vinegar," said Callidus, pressing his luck. To his surprise, the emperor smiled.

"Maybe so," she said. "But not too *much* wine." She paused to look west toward distant Orluin, then turned her head back to her senior mage.

Callidus nodded and risked a small smile. "How can I be of assistance this afternoon?" he asked.

"I have a mission for you," said Sírénae. She smiled again, showing teeth and making Callidus worry about what *sort* of mission it would be.

"And?" asked Callidus, expecting her to go on, which she did.

"It will take us another week to reach the shores of Orluin," said Sírénae. "Assuming the winds are favorable."

Callidus nodded again.

"I want to know if Quintillius and Laetícia will be with me or against me when the fleet arrives," said the emperor. "And I don't want to wait seven days to find out."

"I see," said Callidus, though he really didn't. He didn't know of any gates to Nova Eboracum, or anywhere else in Orluin, and neither did the wizards reporting to him. It was also much too far for a magister to travel on a flying disk. *Maybe Umbrose the spymaster or one of his wizards knows of a gate?* he considered.

"I want you to ride Xaxidiánus and fly to Nova Eboracum," she said. "Deliver a communications ring to Quintillius and stay to observe their end of the conversation when I speak to them. Afterward, you can assure them that I mean what I say."

"What *do* you plan to say, my emperor?" asked Magister Callidus.

"Join me or die," said Sírénae.

"I thought that might be the message," Callidus replied. His smile couldn't match the emperor's more feral one.

"Tell them about the overwhelming power of my fleet and legions," said Sírénae. "They must know already, but I doubt their recent scouting expedition is aware of the division of the fleet anchored at the other end of the island. Say nothing of those ships and soldiers."

"Yes, Your Imperial Majesty," said Callidus.

"What?" asked Sírénae. "You're calling me *imperial majesty* again. What's your objection this time?"

Callidus wiped his forehead with his sleeve. "I don't understand, Sírénae," he said. "Valens was always your greatest rival among the other tetrarchs. He's Laetícia's uncle and a distant cousin of Quintillius. They're loyal to the empire. What makes you think they'd ever fight *with* you?"

Sírénae slid her hands back and forth against each other as if ready to sample a particularly tasty dish. "That's right," she said. "I never told you about the special prisoner Pixo's sailors captured on a ship they boarded near the Isles of Dogs."

"A special prisoner?" echoed Magister Callidus. He hated it when Sírénae kept secrets from him. *How can I properly advise her without all the relevant information?* "Who might that be?" he said.

"Does the name Valentius mean anything to you?" asked Sírénae.

"Emperor Valens' eldest son?" asked Callidus. The young man was in his early twenties and already building a reputation as an able military commander in battles with the desert tribes in west Afarika. Callidus understood Valens was grooming Valentius to be his eventual successor. The Tetrarchy was theoretically *not* intended to be hereditary, but practice and theory often differed.

"When I inform them Valentius will be executed if they don't join me, I expect we'll have new allies," said Sírénae.

Callidus rubbed his chin. "You may be right," he said. "Valens may authorize them to take your side and help you gain control of all of Orluin as a price worth paying for the life of his son."

"And doing so will decrease Valens' influence over the other tetrarchs," said Sírénae.

"Since the proper thing for a Roma father and general to do would be accept his son's death as the price of honor," said Callidus.

"Precisely," said Sírénae.

"On the other hand, the complete conquest of all Orluin has been an imperial goal since Occidens Province was first established," Callidus noted. "Perhaps Valens' star would rise if he agreed to

Quintillius supporting our fleet in conquering Dâron, Tamloch, and Bifurland."

The emperor frowned. "I expected better insight from you," she said. "It's one thing to add Orluin to the empire controlled by the tetrarchs. It's another thing completely to make Orluin my *personal* empire." Sírénae laughed but didn't smile. "The best I'm hoping for is to delay Quintillius and Laetícia's alliance with the native kingdoms against us."

"Put that way," said Callidus, "of course." He rubbed his chin and nodded. "Quintillius and Laetícia have never had any affection for you."

"Nor I for them," said Sírénae. "Or for Valens." She rubbed her palms together then extended one hand in a gesture of dismissal.

"I'll leave at once," said Magister Callidus. "I just have to alert Xaxidiánus, retrieve a pair of communications rings, and pack a few things for the trip."

"Off with you, then," she said, tossing a scrap of meat to Thraxa. The snow-gryffon swiveled her cruel raptor's head and fixed Callidus with one baleful eye before he turned and departed.

Chapter 13

Rings and Arrows

Discussions in Laetícia's tower continued, but in several smaller groups rather than a single large one. Laetícia saw Merry pull Fercha and Verro over to Doethan and Princess Rúth's corner, taking care to keep Ace and Chee separated in the process. King Bjarni and Queen Signý were talking to Quintillius and Duke Háiddon in the center of the study, while Duke Néillen listened in. Jenet and Dârio were near the room's tall windows talking to Nûd, while Bonnie and Inthíra were next to an inner wall exchanging notes about esoteric forms of magic taught at Tamloch's Institute in Bhaile Pónaire and Dâron's Valley of Towers.

Laetícia caught her husband's arm and pulled him away from his conversation.

"I'm going to pop over to our bedroom and try to contact Valens," she said softly. "We didn't get any warning about Sírénae's armada, and I want to know why."

"Good idea," said Quintillius, leaning down to whisper near her ear. "He should have told you weeks ago, before they set sail."

"I want to know who's stepped up to be the new emperor of the west as well," Laetícia replied. "And what burden Sírénae added to the mule's back that finally made the other tetrarchs decide to exile her."

Quintillius nodded. "Gather as much information as you can, and don't worry. I'll play the dutiful host and make sure our guests are well cared for." He hugged Laetícia's shoulders before turning back to rejoin the discussion he'd left a few moments earlier. "Duke Háiddon," he said. "Where in Dâron do you recommend relocating a third of the population of Nova Eboracum and all their supplies?"

"I'd suggest the caverns below the forests along the north branch of the Moravon..." began the Duke.

Laetícia smiled at Quin, appreciating their partnership over the past decade. She could trust Quintillius in matters military while she did her part to provide the intelligence reports needed to respond to threats effectively. She felt like Sírénae's unexpected arrival was a personal affront to her skills and resolved to work twice as hard in the future to ensure such a thing never happened again.

Leaving her study through its main door, she stepped out onto the landing, nodded to the guards, created an *ad hoc* gate to the bedroom she shared with Quintillius, and stepped through.

"Mater!" shouted almost eight-year-old Primus from his position on top of the long bed Laetícia and Quintillius shared.

"We're playing Imperial Invasion," said Seconda, who was sitting next to her brother, holding their younger sister's shoulders as if they were a ship's wheel. "Your bed is our flagship," she continued. "It's bigger than ours."

"I'm helping steer," said Tertia, smiling as only a bright nearly four-year-old can smile.

"Where is Noskóma?" asked Laetícia, inquiring after the children's combination nursemaid and teacher, a no-nonsense woman whose mother had filled a similar role caring for Laetícia and her siblings back in Afarika.

"We asked her to get us more dough rings," said Primus. "She told us to behave ourselves and play quietly in our rooms while she went into the city to find some."

"And that's why the three of you are *here?*" asked Laetícia, trying hard not to smile. She was regretting she'd only given her children one dough ring each earlier.

"I told you," said six-year-old Seconda. "Your bed is bigger."

Laetícia expected Seconda was the one to initiate the children's move into her bedroom and onto her bed. She was the most impulsive and adventurous of her three children, while Primus was more measured and thoughtful in his actions.

"Fireball!" said Tertia, holding an imaginary sphere.

It was too soon to tell about her younger daughter's temperament, but from the way Tertia delighted in pretending to work magic,

Laetícia was confident the girl would be a wizard when she was older. She let a smile show when Primus added a comment.

"We heard it was a big invasion fleet," he said. "You're standing in the Ocean and not aboard the flagship. Be careful you don't drown."

"I can swim," said Laetícia, "and you three miscreants can leave. I need to ring Uncle Valens."

"Can we stay please, Mater?" asked Seconda. "I'd like to say hello."

"Stay?" said Tertia, making it sound halfway between a statement and a question.

Primus was about to speak, but Laetícia held up her hand to silence him.

"Sorry," she said. "This is business, not pleasure. I have to find out what's happening back in the Imperium."

"You mean you want to find out why Uncle Valens didn't warn you about Sírénae Accipiter's fleet," said Primus. He sounded very grown up and so much like his father Laetícia had to clamp her lips tightly together not to smile.

"Exactly," said Laetícia. "Now get back to your rooms as quick as rabbits—and don't spoil your dinner eating dough rings."

"Yes, Mater," came a trio of high-pitched voices. Her son and daughters were grinning like dough rings were likely to *be* their dinners. The children gave her individual hugs from their positions on top of her bed, then jumped down to the carpet and made splashing noises as they gleefully *swam* over to the bedroom door and departed.

Laetícia allowed herself a moment for silent laughter, then removed a ring from her right hand. She took a deep breath, centered her mind to reach out across the Ocean to Valens, and spoke the words to trigger the ring's spell. Three familiar tones chimed. The gold band expanded until it was two feet in diameter, revealing the familiar face of a large, gray-haired woman wearing a serious expression.

"Tembóku!" said Laetícia. "Has something happened to Valens?"

"Yes, child," said the gray-haired woman. Tembóku was a very senior Southern Empire wizard who had been present at Laetícia's birth, coming of age ceremony, and wedding. She had also been Laetícia's first instructor in magic. "Valens couldn't answer for himself. He's still in a coma."

"Still?" asked Laetícia. "What happened?"

"He was poisoned a month ago," said Tembóku, shaking her head slowly. In the past she'd worn long beaded braids, inspiring Laetícia to do the same. Now her hair was shorter than a lamb's wool a week after shearing.

"How?" asked Laetícia.

"An arrow struck his heel," said Tembóku. "He was inspecting the site of a skirmish with bandits outside Khartúmis when a stray arrow rose up from the field and struck him."

"Did you find the wizard controlling the arrow?" asked Laetícia.

"Hekíma found him," said Tembóku, referring to another wizard Laetícia knew well. "After extensive *encouragement* he confessed to being sent by Sírénae to kill Valens."

"And that was the final straw?" asked Laetícia.

"It was," said Tembóku. "Flavia and Phraátēs acted immediately to expel Sírénae from the Tetrarchy. They'd been wanting to for some time, given her provocations and attempts to take more territory along the Northern Sea and Valens' western holdings."

Laetícia had met Valens' counterparts, the emperors of the northern and eastern empires, at various official functions over the years. She was surprised they'd waited so long to take action against Sírénae, but now her major concern was for the health of her uncle.

"How is Valens?" she asked. "The poison must have been quite serious if it hasn't responded to standard healing potions."

"It was," Tembóku replied. "I expect that snake, Magister Umbrose, worked long and hard to come up with such an insidious attack. The poison had two parts. One was the essence of a virulent fever from the far south that liquefies a person's organs, causing terrible pain. The other was an accelerant that forces the fever to do its work in minutes, not days."

"That's horrifying," said Laetícia. Her fingers went white from her tight grip on the circle of the communications ring.

"Hekíma and I were there when it happened," said Tembóku. "We gave Valens potion after potion, just to stabilize him. Valens only began to heal after I had *ad hoc* gated south and retrieved a special herb from the tribes who have skill in fighting the fever."

"My uncle is lucky you were there," said Laetícia.

"We'll see how lucky he is when he comes out of his coma," said Tembóku. "His internal organs have been rebuilding themselves all this time and we don't know if his brain has been affected by the fever."

"Now I understand why I didn't receive any warning about Sírénae's fleet," said Laetícia.

"Things have been a bit chaotic on this side of the Ocean," replied Tembóku with a wry smile. "Forgive me that I didn't think to warn you myself. My attention was focused elsewhere."

"As it should have been," said Laetícia. Her voice went softer. "What do you think will happen to my uncle?" she asked.

"He'll live," said Tembóku. "He's past the worst of it and should wake on his own in a week or two. I just don't know how much of my friend will be there when he does."

Laetícia nodded. Fevers of that sort often burned out minds, not just bodies. "Who now rules the Southern Empire?" she asked.

"Valentius has been summoned from the Isles of Dogs," said Tembóku. "He should be back to hold his father's place soon. In the meantime, General Sénnex manages the Southern Empire."

"He's a good choice," said Laetícia. *Flavia and Phraátēs wouldn't be threatened by a man over eighty years old. And besides,* thought Laetícia, *the Northern and Eastern emperors would be too busy trying to sort out the succession in the now vacant Western Empire to spare much concern for the leadership of the largely stable Southern Empire.*

"I thought so," said Tembóku. "In fact, I suggested it. Sénnex is glad to fill in until Valentius arrives." Tembóku put her hand to her forehead and lowered it before continuing. "I should tell you," she said. "I heard seven of Sírénae's dragons left with her."

"We know," said Laetícia. "We were warned about her fleet by someone on the Tempest Isles, so I had a chance to discover more details about Sírénae's forces. She's also got two hundred elephants."

"So *that's* what happened to them," said Tembóku. "Valens was shipping them to Roma for a fête in the Flavian Ampitheatre. Sírénae must have intercepted their transports."

"Apparently so," replied Laetícia.

"I'll tell you a secret about those elephants," said Tembóku. She leaned close to the communications ring's interface and whispered something to her former student.

Laetícia smiled. "That's good to know," she said. "I hope it will surprise Sírénae when she tries to use them in battle."

"I wish I could be there to see it," said Tembóku.

"I wish *Valens* could be there to see it," Laetícia responded.

"We can hope," said Tembóku. "Though I doubt he'd be up for a voyage across the Ocean even if he comes out of his coma soon."

"That reminds me," said Laetícia. "One of the Dâron wizards has learned how to make wide gates stable. Such a gate was used to transport a herd of wisents across most of a continent."

"So they might work across the Ocean?" asked Tembóku. "Tell me more."

Laetícia shared the details of building wide gates using powdered magestone-encrusted boundaries. The older mage looked thoughtful. "If they work over long distances, we could send an army to help you defeat Sírénae."

"Perhaps," said Laetícia. "We're also considering abandoning the province and Nova Eboracum so that Sírénae finds nothing to eat and no one to enslave when she arrives. We might want to send some of our people to you for temporary sanctuary."

"If that becomes necessary, I'm sure Valentius would authorize the project on this end," said Tembóku. "We'll need to test things out and confirm whether gates across the Ocean—of any size—are feasible."

"I will ring you back later to work out the details," said Laetícia. "We'll have to find somewhere private for the test—and do it soon."

"There's a place outside one of Valens' hunting preserves that would work well, I think," said Tembóku. "I'll set Hekíma the task of finding enough powdered magestones. No, wait. Valentius said he'd bring back magestones from the lava fields on the slopes of the Old Man Mountain on Canis Magnus. We can use *them.*"

"Good," said Laetícia, remembering when she'd flown above the clouds to the top of the tall, snow-capped peak in the center of Big Dog Island on a previous Ocean crossing. There were huge deposits of obsidian below it and on its steep slopes. "I hope he arrives soon."

"So do I," said Tembóku. Her image began to waver on the other side of the interface.

"We should at least make a conventional gate..." began Laetícia, but the ring's connection had closed. It shrank from hoop-sized to ring-size and she caught it in one palm before returning it to her finger. "Well, that explains a lot," she said out loud, considering her conversation. She hoped her uncle would soon make a full recovery and reminded herself to repay Sírénae in kind for her actions. Then she laughed, remembering what Tembóku had told her about the elephants.

On top of everything else, she thought, *I'll have to find a trumpeter.*

Chapter 14

Rings and Recipes

Eynon's smile was as bright as a wizard lamp as he beamed at Rōlin and Peregrína. "I'd love to see *The Atlas of Orluin*," said Eynon. "Does it show the Coombe?"

"I don't remember," said Rōlin. "Do you recall, my dear?"

"An enclosed mountain valley on the western border of Dâron," Peregrína replied with her brows knit in concentration. "Part of the baron of Caercadel's lands if I remember correctly."

"The baronial seat is Caercadel," said Eynon. "The barony is Cadelluin."

"Of course," said Peregrína. "My apologies. I drew that part of the atlas more than a decade ago. Are you from Brynhill—or Wherrel near that quarry?"

"Haywall, good lady," Eynon answered. "It's east of Brynhill. We keep dairy cows there."

"It sounds like a lovely place to grow up," said Peregrína.

"Why don't you skip the greenhouses for now and show Eynon the Coombe in the *Atlas?*" Rōlin suggested. "He'll enjoy it and you can refresh your memory."

"An excellent idea, husband," said Peregrína. "You can take the tarts out of the oven so they'll cool, then join us."

Lléwys, Rōlin's squirrel familiar, lifted his head from the edge of the table when he heard Peregrína mention the tarts. He zipped over to sit on Rōlin's shoulder, where he could supervise the process and, Eynon assumed, ensure he got a few morsels. Watching Lléwys made Eynon miss Chee and further regret heading west without telling Merry or retrieving his raconette friend.

Rōlin didn't notice Eynon's reflective expression. "As you wish," he told his wife. The corners of his mouth turned up and he bobbed his head toward Peregrína affectionately.

"Come along then," said Peregrína. "The *Atlas* is close at hand, and we don't want the tarts to get *too* cool."

Eynon followed Peregrína as she led him down a hallway to another portion of the house, a large white-painted room with tall ceilings, two desks, and four long tables. Two-by-three-foot sheets of paper covered with beautifully drawn and colored maps filled all the room's available horizontal surfaces, and the left-hand walls held framed maps of various larger sizes. The right-hand wall was a copy of the map of the continent of Orluin Eynon had seen in the map room back in Melyncárreg.

Or perhaps this is the original and the one in Melyncárreg is the copy, Eynon realized.

Peregrína guided Eynon to one of the desks and invited him to sit down. She stepped over to a long table and sorted through what proved to be several layers of paper until she found the particular sheet she was looking for and brought it to Eynon. "Look, but don't touch," she admonished. "The oil on your fingers can damage the ink."

Eynon nodded and put his hands on his lap below the table so he wouldn't reach out inadvertently. A beautifully drawn map of the Coombe was spread out on the desk in front of him. Its scale was large enough to take in the entire enclosed valley from Liamston in the north to the lands below Caercadel in the south. It took in the quarry west of Wherrel where he, Nûd, and Merry had found the great green dragon Viridáxés and the course of the upper Rhuthro river encompassing Merry's family's barony.

The mountains were shaded with deft pen strokes to indicate their relative heights, and towns were marked with circles whose sizes varied based on what Eynon assumed were their populations. Caercadel's circle was larger than Haywall's anyway, and a small tower like the shah-mat castle piece was drawn beside it.

"The little towers are baronial seats?" Eynon asked.

"Yes," said Peregrína. "Towers for earls and dukes are larger, and wizards' towers have conical tops above their crenellations," she added.

"Even if a particular wizard's tower has a flat roof?" asked Eynon, thinking of Doethan and Fercha's homes.

"It's a symbol, not a representation of what's actually there," Peregrína replied.

"That makes sense," said Eynon. "It's good enough to know a wizard lives in one place and a baron in another." He looked more closely at the page on the desk. "A crossed pick and shovel in a circle marks a quarry?" Eynon asked.

"Correct," said Peregrína. "Without the circle, it's a mine."

Eynon nodded. His eyes followed the blue line of the Rhuthro as it flowed from its source in the southern Coombe until it left the map near the upper right corner. "The little waves on the river are rapids?" he asked, thinking about the challenges he'd had traveling down that river with Merry not so long ago. He'd nearly drowned on that trip, which would have brought a quick end to his wander year.

"Yes, they're rapids," said Peregrína. "Remind me to show you the map of the Great Falls to the north when we have more time. There are two falls, really. One is shaped like a horseshoe and the other is straight."

"I'd like to see that," said Eynon.

"The map, or the falls themselves?" interjected Rōlin's voice behind Eynon, who turned around to note his arrival.

"Both," Eynon replied.

Rōlin and Peregrína laughed and Eynon joined them.

"There are two lovely inns by the Great Falls," said Peregrína.

"One on the Dâron side and one on the Tamloch side," said Rōlin.

"The view from the Tamloch side is nicer," said Peregrína.

"Not that we spent much time out of our room," teased Rōlin.

Eynon hid a smile when he saw Peregrína blush. His hosts reminded him of slightly older versions of his parents. They knew exactly what to say to each other to provoke specific reactions.

"That was more than thirty years ago," Peregrína responded after giving Rōlin a look that had as many layers as the sheets of maps stacked on the tables.

"But I still remember it fondly," said Rōlin. "The apple-honey tarts are cooling. We should enjoy them while they're still a bit warm."

"Thanks for reminding us," said Peregrína. "We'd best get back to the kitchen," she said, retrieving the map from the desk in front of Eynon and putting it back where she'd found it. "You've clearly left Lléwys watching the tarts and we know how that's likely to turn out if we're not back soon."

"He likes nut tarts more than apple," said Rōlin with a smile.

"Still," said Peregrína, smiling back.

Eynon was disappointed not to have more time in the map room, but he got up to follow the older couple.

"Don't look like you've eaten a green persimmon," said Rōlin. "We're neighbors. You'll have more time to look at maps while we're working through the recipe book for magic."

"What?" asked Eynon as he trailed behind Rōlin and Peregrína.

"We don't have to if you're not interested," said Rōlin.

"I'm *very* interested," Eynon replied.

"Good," said Peregrína. "Neither one of us is happy about Damon's training methods. Sending his would-be apprentices out into basilisk territory seems needlessly cruel."

"We can start your first lesson using *On Wizardry: A Recipe Book of Magic* after dessert," said Rōlin.

"And you're welcome to spend the night, so we can continue your lessons in the morning," added Peregrína.

"That would be wonderful," said Eynon. "I'll *ad hoc* gate up to Melyncárreg for the bread I was proofing and come right back."

* * * * *

Eynon had returned from Melyncárreg with a covered bowl filled with rising dough. Rōlin helped him put it in a proofing niche next to their own oven and Eynon hoped brief exposure to cold wouldn't affect the bread's likelihood of rising when they baked it in the morning. *I wonder if I can add bubbles to dough with magic if it seems too dense?* thought Eynon. Then he smiled at himself. *I hope I'm not too dense to learn magic from books instead of one-on-one instruction.* He surveyed the kitchen and noticed Lléwys was asleep on the sill of the window above the sink after eating half his body weight in apple tart. *Chee would do that, too,* he mused.

"Do you want to work through *On Wizardry* here in the kitchen or in one of our studies?" asked Peregrína.

"If you don't mind, I like the idea of learning from *A Recipe Book of Magic* in a kitchen," said Eynon. "I love to cook and feel at home in kitchens."

"Good," said Rōlin. "Peregrína and I love to cook, too."

"Are you going to tell him, or should I?" asked Peregrína.

"Tell me what?" asked Eynon.

"We're very pleased you like *On Wizardry,*" said Rōlin.

"Because we wrote it," said Peregrína with a wide grin.

"All three volumes," added Rōlin, keeping his face perfectly serious.

"Here in this very kitchen," said Peregrína. She stepped close to Rōlin and put her arm around his waist, then tickling him until he laughed. Rōlin moved his arm around her shoulders and she stopped tickling. Together, they beamed at Eynon. He smiled back and clapped his hands.

"How wonderful!" said Eynon.

"We didn't want young wizards to have to plow through those obtuse Athican mathemagical texts," said Rōlin.

"Recipes made a perfect analogy for wizardry," said Peregrína. "Like recipes, there's room for creativity. It's not a matter of following a set formula to the letter."

"Though some recipes are less open to experimentation," said Rōlin.

"Like making bread?" suggested Eynon. "Too much salt or a spoiled starter will lead to poor results?"

"That's a good analogy," said Peregrína. "On the other hand, you can add almost anything to honey cakes—berries, raisins, chopped apples—and create something tasty."

"That makes sense," said Eynon. "Can we start with communications rings? I need to make a set, so I can give one to Merry."

"She's someone special?" asked Rōlin.

"Very," said Eynon. "We're going to get married someday. She's Fercha's apprentice—and was Doethan's."

"Two good teachers," said Peregrína. "I'm surprised she didn't come to Melyncárreg with you."

"It's a long story," said Eynon, looking at the floor.

"It always is," observed Rōlin. "Let's get started."

The three of them cleared off the kitchen table, putting the crockery dishes and such into a deep sink on an outside wall. Rōlin retrieved a leather sheet made from a pair of stitched-together wisent hides and unrolled it to cover the top of the table with assistance from Eynon. Peregrína produced a birchwood book stand and a well-used copy of the first volume of *On Wizardry* from shelves on the far side of the room. She turned the book to the recipe for communications rings and positioned it carefully in the stand so the steps in the process would be easy to read.

"Where should I start?" asked Eynon after Rōlin waved him into position in front of the book stand.

"Where do you usually start when following a recipe?" replied Peregrína, using the tactic so common with wizards of answering a question with another question.

"With the list of ingredients," said Eynon. "At least when it's not a recipe I've made before."

"The same is true with more complex magic," said Rōlin. "What does this recipe call for?"

"Half an ounce of gold, a pig's bladder, and a pinch of powdered magestone," said Eynon. He looked at his hosts and frowned. "I have more than enough gold, but I don't have a pig's bladder or any magestone powder."

"You don't cook from recipes very often, do you?" asked Peregrína. Before Eynon could reply, she continued. "If you did, you'd know to read the *entire* recipe before attempting it. Why don't you read the whole thing and see if that provides any answers?"

"Yes, good lady," said Eynon. He reviewed the list of ingredients and read through all the steps twice, then looked up and smiled. "I can substitute a sphere of solidified sound for the pig's bladder," he said.

"Indeed," said Rōlin. "Its function is to provide the pair of rings with the ability to expand."

Peregrína crossed to what looked like a rack of spices some distance from the prep area near the sink. She returned with a small clear-glass phial and put it on the table near the book and book stand. "Here's the powdered magestone you'll need," she said. "I collected it up in Melyncárreg. You'll only need a little."

"Thank you," said Eynon, accepting the phial and giving Peregrína a small bow.

"I'm sure you've noticed it also calls for a small crucible to melt the gold," said Rōlin. "I'll fetch ours for you."

"I don't think I'll need it," said Eynon. "I figured out how to heat gold inside a sphere of solidified sound when I was making my artifact."

"I'd like to see that," said Rōlin. "I'm always glad to learn new magical techniques."

"Heating gold and silver is why we have the leather cover," said Peregrína. "I got tired of having molten metal burning the tabletop."

Eynon remembered inadvertently coating the ceiling of Damon's studio with gold when an earthquake had startled him while making his artifact. He resolved to be *very* careful heating gold in Rōlin and Peregrína's kitchen.

Rōlin went to the shelf where his wife had found the book stand and brought over a small block of dark gray soapstone. Eynon saw it had a deep circular impression incised into it.

"Here's our ring mold," said Rōlin. "There's no need for you to carve your own."

"I appreciate it," said Eynon, giving Rōlin the same sort of small bow he'd given Peregrína. "It looks like it's twice as thick as a normal ring—and the recipe says I have to bisect the thick ring to make two connected rings."

"Correct," said Rōlin.

"I think I can make my own mold from solidified sound as well," said Eynon. "It will cool faster and I can add an apple design to these rings. Merry likes apples."

"It would be best if you followed the standard recipe the first time before experimenting," said Rōlin. "Crawl, walk, run, fly."

Peregrína laughed. "Oh, let Eynon experiment," she said. "He seems ready to run or even fly. The worst that can happen is that the rings won't be congruent."

"As you say, my dear," said Rōlin. "Give it a try, Eynon. If it works, we can put your recipe in the *fourth* volume of *On Wizardry.*"

"Just be sure to make the designs identical on both parts of the initial ring," added Peregrína. "The congruency between them won't form if you don't."

"Good advice," said Eynon. He reached into his pouch and removed the ball of gold left over from making the setting for his magestone. It was heavy—at least ten ounces—and he'd only need half an ounce for making the communications rings. There would still be plenty of gold left over.

Rōlin and Peregrína took a few steps back from the table. Rōlin created a transparent shield of solidified sound in front of both of them. Eynon expected they'd seen lots of mishaps from students learning magic. He resolved not to give them any reason to regret inviting him into their home.

Melt half an ounce of gold, said the recipe. Eynon tossed the ball of gold into the air and cut off a small snip of it with a plane of solidified sound. He put the larger piece back in his pouch and surrounded the smaller one with a sphere of solidified sound, adding heat until the yellow metal turned liquid and began to bubble.

Add a pinch of powdered magestone, the recipe continued. Eynon picked up the phial that Peregrína had left on the table for him. Through its clear sides he could see flecks of blue, green, purple, and black. There were even a few bits of red in the mixture. He took a generous pinch, opened the top of the sphere holding the gold, and let the magestone powder sift down between his fingers where it was soon distributed into the mixture by the churning bubbles.

Freeze the pig's bladder and dip it in the gold mixture until it is fully coated. Giving himself a silent admonishment not to get cocky—like he had at the Tempest Isles—Eynon formed a small sphere of solidified sound inside the larger one where the melted gold bubbled. That sphere was the substitute for the frozen pig's bladder called for by the recipe. He slowly expanded both the inner and outer spheres of solidified sound until the inner one was two feet in diameter.

That's the size most communications rings expand to, he considered.

Then a loud sound like thunder combined with hail on a slate roof disturbed his concentration. Both spheres expanded from two feet to eight feet wide before Eynon could regain his focus. He was lucky the kitchen had high ceilings.

"What is that *noise*?" asked Eynon as the disconcerting booming and drumming continued.

"Noise?" asked Rōlin.

"I think he means the elk herd," said Peregrína. "We hardly notice them now. Some wolves or night-hunting gryffons must have frightened them. Our house is between two of their ranges."

"It could be worse," said Rōlin.

"Yes," said Peregrína. "It could be wisents. They bump the house logs from time to time when *they* pass through."

"Let me know if you expect any migrating wisents tonight, please," said Eynon. I'm going to try to finish making these rings."

"Of course," said Peregrína.

"From now on we're definitely going to use spheres of solidified sound for heating metal instead of crucibles," said Rōlin. "That's very clever. Are you ready to pour?"

"Unless I'm interrupted by a thousand migrating dragons," said Eynon. He tried to blot out the sound of the elk herd and shrank the spheres down from eight feet to just a few inches and dispelled the inner sphere. It had done its work—perhaps a bit too well.

"A thousand migrating dragons," said Rōlin softly behind him.

"Wouldn't *that* be something," whispered Peregrína.

Pour the gold and powdered magestone mixture into your prepared mold. Eynon mentally scolded himself for not crafting his mold first. He held the sphere with the molten gold under tight control while visualizing a thick band decorated with a double row of apples. It was easier than he'd expected to keep the sphere with the gold *and* the solidified sound mold in his head simultaneously. Perhaps after all the illusions he'd generated to build a duplicate of Riyas, Tamloch's capital, he was getting better at creating and maintaining complex constructs.

Eynon created a narrow tube leading from the sphere with the molten gold to the construct forming the ring mold. Bright liquid flowed down the tube and exactly filled the mold, leaving no gold remaining in the solidified sound crucible.

Prime the spell with three chimes

"Three chimes?" asked Eynon.

"Of course," said Rōlin. "Communications rings always have three chimes. It's tradition."

Peregrína held three narrow metal tubes strung on wires above her head and tapped each of them in turn with a small mallet, making clear, bell-like tones. The gold in the mold vibrated sympathetically, soaking up the sound.

Bind the thick ring as one with a word or phrase of command.

"Síarad â chi!" he said in a firm voice, binding a trigger phrase that had popped unbidden into his mind. Three notes, exact duplicates of the chimes, echoed inside the kitchen, signifying the linkage was successful.

Bisect the thick ring before it cools completely.

Eynon dispelled the crucible and held his hand out to sense the heat level in the mold. It was cooling rapidly, so he didn't need to remove heat from it with wizardry. The recipe said the next step should be done while the thick ring was still warm, so he stopped maintaining the mold construct and smiled at the way the decorative apple design appeared. The upper and lower parts of the ring were identical. Eynon neatly cut the thick ring horizontally into two equal parts. He caught both in his outstretched palm.

Behind him, Eynon heard Rōlin and Peregrína clapping.

"Well done," said Rōlin. "That was impressive, young man."

"I knew I was right to encourage him to experiment," said Peregrína. Eynon could sense her smile without turning around. "I've never seen decorated communications rings before. They're always plain bands."

"There may be a good reason for the lack of decoration on communications rings," said Rōlin. "We have to confirm this pair work properly first before we get too excited."

Eynon rotated to face his hosts and extended the hand that held the rings. "Can we test them, then?" he asked. "Or do we need to let them sit a bit and finish cooking, like a pork roast taken from the oven?"

Peregrína laughed. "No need to wait," she said. "The recipe is complete."

"They will either work or they won't," said Rōlin. "I'll take one out on the back porch and we'll see what happens."

"Couldn't you just go to the far end of the kitchen?" asked Eynon.

Rōlin laughed this time. "You've clearly never used two communications rings in the same room before," he said. "Sounds from one ring are picked up by another and the noise level quickly gets unbearable." He reached for one of the rings, holding it between his thumb and forefinger, and went through the sturdy door leading out of the kitchen.

"Mind the wolves," said Peregrína to Rōlin's departing back. They couldn't hear his answer.

Shortly, the ring still resting on Eynon's palm began to vibrate and three familiar tones sounded. He tugged on the ring and it expanded—then kept on expanding until it was eight feet in diameter. Eynon and Peregrína could see Rōlin standing at the far end of the back porch, illuminated by a small glow ball.

"That's interesting," said Rōlin from the other side of the interface, which didn't have the same familiar shimmer as the communications rings Eynon had seen before. A moth that had been flitting around Rōlin's glow ball crossed the interface and circled a wizard lamp in the kitchen. Rōlin stepped through the interface, collapsing the ring behind him as he came, and shook Eynon's hand.

"Well done, young man," said Rōlin. "Most impressive."

"We're definitely going to need to add a new recipe," said Peregrína.

Chapter 15

Night Flight

Magister Callidus was bored as they flew through the dark, but he couldn't sleep. He glanced at his compass again, confirmed they were still flying northwest, and wondered if Xaxidiánus was bored as well. Given the fact he was riding on the dragon's back, he might as well ask him. It would help to pass the time.

"Is this as dull for you as it is for me?" asked Callidus. He had to amplify his voice with magic so it would carry over the rush of wind from their passage and be heard through the protective wedge of solidified sound around his body.

"I think not," rumbled Xaxidiánus. "I have never been to Orluin and am looking forward to exploring somewhere new."

"You don't think one land is much like another?" asked Callidus.

"Of course not, and neither do you," said Xaxidiánus. "I remember how much you talked about the beautiful scenery in Princess Pyréne's Mountains three years ago when we were putting down those rebellious shepherds. After we'd won our victory, I was basking in a high meadow beside a waterfall deep in the mountains and you were going on about how you'd never seen a place more lovely."

"You have me there, my friend," replied Callidus. "That was a moment of weakness when I'd suppressed my natural cynicism and highly cultivated sense of ennui."

"That must be it," said Xaxidiánus.

Callidus could feel the vibrations of the dragon's laughter through the leather of his saddle and its fleece padding.

"Are dragons *ever* bored?" asked Callidus after a dozen of the dragon's powerful wing beats.

"Have you ever owned a cat?" asked Xaxidiánus.

"What's that got to do with being bored?" asked Magister Callidus. "Or the price of fresh lavender in the trading markets of Narbo, for that matter?"

"Answer the question," insisted the dragon.

"Yes," said Callidus. "I once owned a cat, though the matter of who owned whom remained open for debate."

"As with all felines," said Xaxidiánus. "Sírénae thinks *she* owns her dragons, but—well—that's a different topic."

More draconic laughter vibrated up from below Callidus.

"Does this diversion have a point?" asked the mage.

"It does," said Xaxidiánus. "Dragons, like cats, are predators. We know how to conserve our energy, then pounce when prey is at hand and it's time to attack."

Now Callidus laughed.

"What?" asked Xaxidiánus.

"I'm picturing a dragon attacking a mouse."

"Small dragons fresh from their shells eat rats," noted Xaxidiánus. He sounded a bit affronted that Callidus would laugh at a mental image of *any* dragon. Xaxidiánus and his kind took great care to protect their dignity.

"Are you trying to say that dragons are never bored because they sleep instead?" asked Callidus.

"Say 'nap' rather," said Xaxidiánus. "Sleeping makes it sound like dragons are lazy."

"But they are, aren't they?" asked Magister Callidus, knowing it would provoke a reaction.

Xaxidiánus made a deep, angry rumbling growl like far off rolls of thunder.

"Present company excepted," said Callidus quickly.

The rumbling growl changed to draconic laughter.

"Of course they are," said Xaxidiánus. *"We* are. Dragons' internal congruencies help us fly, breathe fire, and regulate our temperatures, but we still need a lot of food to keep our hides and hearts together. If we didn't rest most of the time, we'd need to spend all day hunting."

"And there are only so many fish in the sea," said Callidus.

"Or sheep on the hillsides," said Xaxidiánus, snapping his jaw closed for punctuation.

Callidus could imagine the look on the imperial dragon's face as Xaxidiánus considered consuming a few fat ewes, plus a well-fed goat or two for extra flavor. The magister rubbed his eyes. He was getting sleepy, so he opened a small hole in the wedge of solidified sound in front of him to let in a blast of cold air. It swirled around his face and made the tops of his ears cold before he closed the opening. After a few minutes and consideration of just how much he could trust the discretion of Xaxidiánus, he spoke.

"I think I'm tired, my friend," said Callidus. "Not just tired right now, tired in general." He put his warm hands on his ears, then pulled them down. "I've worked side by side with Sírénae, helping her for more than three decades, from before she had her first legion, and I'm not looking forward to the struggle ahead."

"I see," said Xaxidiánus. "You'd hoped to retire when she stepped down as a tetrarch?"

"Only in my dreams," said Callidus. "I'd considered building an isolated tower in the mountains where I could spend my last years. I wanted to put it in that meadow by the waterfall you'd mentioned but knew it would never happen. Sírénae would never step down or retire. She was and still is determined to hold the reins of all four of the Imperium's empires in her hands."

"But it turned out the other three tetrarchs had something to say about her ambitions?" asked Xaxidiánus. His deep voice trailed off, encouraging Callidus to say more.

"Rule of the entire Imperium hasn't been in one person's hands since the days of Antonia Ferox," said Magister Callidus. "And she had the wisdom to split it in two."

"Then it was further split into three and four empires," said Xaxidiánus. "I listened to my tutors when I was small. Twenty years from now, maybe a unified Orluin under Roma rule will be the fifth division and there will be *five* emperors?"

"A pentarchy?" said Magister Callidus. "I'm too old to deal with *that*. I've helped Sírénae stabilize the west, cemented her hold on the Green Isle, and led her wizards against invaders from Northland in their dragonships."

"Dragonships, hah!" snorted Xaxidiánus. "One dragon smaller than I am could burn a hundred of their ships."

"I know, my friend," said Callidus. "But we needed *our* black dragons to counter their gold dragons. And that was before the treaty the tetrarchs signed with the king of Nordland, allowing his kingdom's continued independence in return for annual tributes of fish, furs, amber, slaves, and soldiers."

"True," said the dragon, as if lamenting a lost opportunity. "The Nordlanders are nearly as tall as Valens' Southern Empire warriors and make impressive imperial guards in Byzantium, from what I hear. Not that it's easy for me to tell one human from another."

"If you expect me to believe that, you'll have to try harder," said Callidus, chuckling. Dragons were skilled at feigning ignorance when it worked to their advantage.

"I'm one of the largest dragons in all four empires," said Xaxidiánus, blowing steam from his nostrils to emphasize his words. "I can fight off gold dragons *and* destroy dragonships at the same time. I'm almost sorry the Nordlanders signed the treaty."

"You'll soon have a chance to prove yourself against the dragons of Dâron, Tamloch, Bifurland, and Occidens Province," said Magister Callidus. "Though I haven't heard word about dragons anywhere on this side of the Ocean except for Bifurland's golds, and they're supposed to be no bigger than horses."

"Nordland wouldn't allow eggs out of their kingdom until twenty years ago," said Xaxidiánus.

"Something about a dispute over a Bifurlander settlement on the north shore of the Smoking Isle?" asked Callidus.

"Yes," said Xaxidiánus. "The Bifurlanders settled there without permission, then traveled overland to steal a clutch of eggs from a Nordland settlement where they were warming."

"Humans are always seeking advantage over other humans," said Callidus.

"The same can be said for dragons," responded Xaxidiánus. "It's one reason why we work well together."

"Except when you're trying to *eat* us," teased the magister, referring to an incident in an isolated mountain valley three years ago.

"Those were *wild* dragons," said Xaxidiánus.

"I doubt their victims' orphaned children would care about that distinction," teased Callidus. He leaned back in his saddle and followed the steady rhythm of his huge black mount's wing beats. "How are you holding up?" he asked.

"Fine," said Xaxidiánus. "We're more than halfway now and should reach the coast of Orluin before dawn."

"If you need a rest or a snack, let me know," said Callidus. "I can hover if you spot a pod of sea wolves."

"Perhaps later," said the dragon. Dragons could easily dive into the water, then launch themselves back skyward with their prey, but the acrobatics involved wouldn't be comfortable for passengers.

Callidus yawned.

"Rest your eyes," said the dragon. "I can keep our course by the stars for a few hours. You'll need to be at your best when you meet with Quintillius and Laetícia."

"Thank you, my friend," said the magister. "I'm weary and need to store up my energy for one last fight."

"You have more than one fight left in you," said Xaxidiánus.

"I hope so," said Callidus. He leaned against his high saddle back and tried to sleep as Xaxidiánus flew on.

* * * * *

Back in her cabin on the *Seahawk,* Sírénae slowly removed a silver thimble from her ear, leaned forward, and smiled, showing teeth like twin rows of pearls. Magister Umbrose's listening device embedded in the dragon saddle on the broad back of Xaxidiánus had worked well and revealed what she had expected.

Her snow-gryffon shifted position at her feet, sensing Sírénae's movement. The emperor ruffled Thraxa's feathers and removed a mouse from a box holding half a dozen, delivered by a slave an hour ago. It squeaked in protest as Sírénae held it upside down by its tail then went permanently silent after it was tossed to the snow-gryffon.

Thraxa caught the mouse in midair, swallowed it whole, and screeched her pleasure. She rubbed against the emperor's leg, smoothing the mostly-white feathers on her raptor's head flat again.

Callidus is getting old and tired, thought Sírénae. *But he was still loyal to me, as much as any of my subordinates are truly loyal. He's weak, and insufficiently ruthless for my taste, but we make an effective combination. I provide the hard mailed fist and Callidus the soft silk glove. If I needed to sacrifice him in the coming struggle it would be unfortunate, though trading a valued minister for an enemy monarch is often the price of victory in shah-mat or my imperial calculations.*

She fed Thraxa another mouse then put the tips of her fingers together in contemplation. *Umbrose won't do as a replacement—he's too valuable in his current role and prefers working behind the scenes. I'll have to see if one of the wizards working for Callidus can be groomed for the job or consider an ambitious mage from Orluin as a candidate to take his position.*

There was sure to be someone *suitable.*

Chapter 16

Ad Hoc Gate Lessons

"Blast!" shouted Merry. "Why can't I do it?" She was pacing across Laetícia's study like a caged gryffon. Passing a tall table, she snatched a honey cake from a tray and angrily—if unthinkingly—devoured it.

"Have patience," said Laetícia, who was leaning against the edge of her desk in the center of the room. She'd informed everyone about the news from across the Ocean hours ago and now almost all of the people who'd been in her study earlier had left for their beds.

"Not everyone can create *ad hoc* gates," said Verro. He was standing next to high windows near the door to the balcony.

"Eynon can. You can. Laetícia can. Damon can. *That one* can," Merry replied, nodding toward the silent, amber-robed and hooded Bifurland wizard who was also observing and supposedly assisting at Queen Signý's request. "Why can't I?" Merry continued, sounding much more than usual like her chronological age of nearly sixteen.

Even Ace has abandoned me, Merry's mind protested. Her familiar had flown out when Verro had opened the balcony door earlier. She didn't spare a moment's concern for any bats above Nova Eboracum he might catch and consume.

Merry smacked her fist into her palm with such intensity that she narrowed her eyes and frowned in pain. Like the tip of a whip cracking, the sound of the blow echoed off the room's plaster walls. No one spoke for a dozen heartbeats.

The Bifurland wizard stepped close to Merry and put a comforting hand on her arm. Merry could see the wizard smiling, deep in the shadows of the amber hood. Slowly, the hand that wasn't on Merry's arm moved up and down in the same rhythm as the motion of the Bifurland wizard's chest.

"You're telling me to breathe," said Merry. "Center my thoughts and control my breathing?"

The amber-robed wizard nodded, dropping the hand that had been resting on Merry's arm.

Merry closed her eyes, took a few slow breaths, and reopened them. "I'm sorry I got angry," she said calmly. Merry nodded at Verro and Laetícia in apology, receiving reciprocal nods of acceptance.

"Have another honey cake," said Laetícia. She offered Merry the tray. "You've been working at this for an hour and the sweetness will help restore your body's balance."

"Mens sana in corpore sano," said Verro.

"A healthy mind in a healthy body," said Merry, smiling now. She took another honey cake from the tray, eating this one slowly and savoring its flavor.

"Just so," said Laetícia. She continued to hold the tray out to Merry, but the young mage demurred.

"No more right now," said Merry. "I'm feeling much better, thank you."

Laetícia offered the tray to the others, but both declined. She returned it to the table and the amber-robed Bifurland wizard resumed moving an arm up and down.

"Breathe, and try again," offered Verro. "Fix your destination firmly in mind and don't force it."

Merry walked over to stand by the balcony door near Verro. He gave her a reassuring smile and joined Laetícia at her desk to give Merry plenty of space. Merry smiled back at him.

"Here goes," she said. "Wish me luck!"

Before attempting an *ad hoc* gate again, Merry tried to relieve the tension that gripped her body in the wake of her previous failures. She lifted both arms above her head and moved them like the blades of a windmill through a few rotations. Then she tilted left and right at the waist, stretching her muscles and vertebrae. Her neck was next. Merry moved her chin one direction and another, moving her head like a pestle grinding spices in a mortar.

Almost there, she thought.

Merry leaned forward and relaxed her shoulders, then shook her hands out at the end of her loosely-held arms like a dog coming in from the rain.

With all these physical preparations completed, Merry stood straight, closed her eyes, and began to take deep, measured breaths.

The Bifurland wizard silently stepped to the far side of the study near the door to the landing.

Laetícia and Verro were both startled when they heard a pair of *pops*. One moment Merry was near the door to the balcony, the next she was standing in front of the Bifurland wizard. An eye blink later she had returned to her original position.

Merry opened her eyes and frowned. "It still didn't work," she said, shaking her head.

"Yes," said Laetícia. "It did. You gated across the room and back."

"I did?" said Merry, turning the statement into an incredulous question.

The Bifurland wizard clapped softly. Verro and Laetícia joined in.

"All three of us saw you," said Verro. Laetícia and the Bifurland wizard nodded in agreement.

"But I was trying to gate to the top of Fercha's tower," Merry protested. "Why didn't I go there?"

"What was the last thing you saw before you closed your eyes?" asked Laetícia.

"The other side of the..." Merry began. "Oh," she said. "I went to the last place I'd seen."

"That seems likely," Verro confirmed. "Stand next to our amber-robed friend and see if you can gate across the room in the other direction."

"I can do that," said Merry. She had a large grin on her face as if someone had just hand-delivered her very own copy of *The Venerable History of Dâron from the First Ships.*

Merry crossed the room and positioned herself beside the Bifurland wizard, who gave her a small bow of encouragement.

Laetícia moved her hands in a circular *get on with it* motion and Verro said, "Focus on your destination."

Merry didn't roll her eyes at his repeated instruction but wanted to. Instead, she followed his advice, looked across the room at the high windows beside the balcony door, and kept her eyes open when she tried to form a gate.

Only *one* pop sounded this time. Merry found herself looking out the windows on the room's opposite wall. Before her were the mostly dark streets of Nova Eboracum near Laetícia's tower, some dimly lit by the glow of wizard lamps, others by flickering torches. She turned to see smiles on Verro and Laetícia's faces and heard more gentle applause from the Bifurland wizard.

"I really did it," said Merry. "I can make *ad hoc* gates!"

"Congratulations," said Verro.

"Well done," said Laetícia. "You can try longer distances in the morning."

"I can't wait that long," said Merry, smiling. She closed her eyes and her chest rose and feel as she slowly inhaled and exhaled. After a dozen breaths the smile on her face turned to a frown. "I can't gate to the top of Fercha's tower."

"There could be a number of reasons for that," said Verro. "The space where you want to gate could already be occupied by something else, for example."

"Fercha is here in the Governor-General's palace," said Merry. "Who could be standing on top of her tower?"

"Foresters watching for fires?" Verro suggested.

"At this time of night?" Merry protested.

"Fires are easier to see in the dark," said Verro.

"Try somewhere else," Laetícia offered. "There's got to be somewhere truly special for you."

Merry considered Laetícia's words. *There was the kitchen at her home in Applegarth and the bench on the street of the jewelers in Tyford where she liked to sit with a book. She could visualize them easily. Or maybe Farnam's cabin on the Rhuthro where she and Eynon had spent a pleasant night? No, other travelers might be using it. Applegarth seemed like her best choice.*

"There is," said Merry. "There's no place like home."

"I'm surprised you didn't try going there first, instead of Fercha's tower," said Verro.

"You wouldn't be, if you knew my parents lied to me about my brother being dead," said Merry.

"Oh," said Verro. "Salder does seem very much alive now. It was touch and go for a bit, but Uirsé is back to feeling quite fond of him."

Uirsé was one of Verro's talented protégés with outstanding skills in healing magic. She was five years older than Merry, about the same age as Salder.

"I'm glad for them," said Merry. "But I'm still angry at my parents— and less than happy with my brother for not telling me, too."

"Spies often have to make hard choices," said Laetícia. "Don't stay angry at your family *too* long."

"I won't," said Merry. "But even after spending time with them before the signing ceremony this morning, we're still in rapids, not calm water."

"Understood," said Laetícia. "Perhaps another location would be better?"

"No," said Merry. "Going home will be fine. My parents are on their way to Brendinas to shop and visit with old friends. Applegarth should be empty."

"Which should make it easier for you to stay calm when you focus on gating there," said Laetícia.

"I hope so," said Merry. She closed her eyes and let her breathing slow again, visualizing her mother at the fire cooking porridge for breakfast and her father positioning a glass of milk beside Merry's bowl. She tried to form an *ad hoc* gate, but again, nothing happened. Merry frowned. She opened her eyes and made three quick jumps around Laetícia's study—*pop, pop, pop*—then returned to her original position near the balcony. "Blast!" she repeated.

"Still not working?" asked Verro.

Merry glared at him.

"Obviously not," said Laetícia. "Why don't you get some sleep and try again in the morning?"

"I don't think I *can* sleep," said Merry. "It's so frustrating."

The Bifurland wizard clapped three times, distracting Merry and attracting the others' attention. Above one outstretched hand a glow ball appeared, then disappeared three times in succession.

"Turn out the lights, tonight's training session is over?" asked Verro with a hopeful tinge to his voice.

"I think our friend means Merry may not be accounting for the lack of light in her visualizations," said Laetícia.

The amber-robed wizard gave Laetícia a slight bow.

"Of course," said Verro, nodding at Laetícia. "It's second nature for us now, but a destination will look quite different in the dark than it does in daylight. Visualizations don't have to be precise. They're more symbolic than exact, especially if you've made an *ad hoc* gate to the same place before, but I can see how not accounting for darkness could get in the way of Merry forming *ad hoc* gates to places she can't see directly."

"I can picture the kitchen at Applegarth at night as well as when the sun's in the sky," said Merry. She put her tongue behind her lower teeth and focused, trying to form an *ad hoc* gate home, but again nothing happened. "Blast, blast, blast! Thunder and lightning! Rot and mold! I'm going to bed."

After her final declaration Merry strode to the door from Laetícia's study to the landing. Verro held back a grin. He could almost sense the metaphorical storm clouds above Merry's head. Merry had her hand on the door's handle and was about to open it when her demeanor drastically changed. She turned around wearing a sheepish smile. "I'm sorry for acting like a child," she said. "Please forgive me."

"Certainly," said Verro.

"Errare humanum est," said Laetícia. "To err is human."

"I've made a year's worth of errors in the last few hours, I expect," said Merry. She laughed at herself, not holding back.

The amber-robed Bifurland wizard laughed too, surprising them all.

Merry turned her head toward the door to the landing then looked back at Laetícia. "There's just one thing," said Merry. "I really *do* want to go to bed, but I don't know where you want me to sleep. Where are your guest quarters?"

"I'll take you there myself," said Laetícia. She moved to stand beside Merry at the outer door and turned back to Verro and the Bifurland wizard. "I'm sure you both can show yourselves out."

Two soft *pops* sounded behind them as Laetícia and Merry stepped out onto the landing.

Chapter 17

Nocturnal Conversations

Dârio and Jenet were on their sides in a large, comfortable Roma-style bed with their heads propped up on pillows so they could talk easily while maintaining contact between as many square inches of their bodies as possible. They were still in the warm afterglow of the sort of sensuous lovemaking couples can only share when they're tired but want the reassurance of physical as well as emotional connection before sleep.

Jenet saw Dârio's eyelids flutter down then snap up a few times. She was having trouble keeping her eyes open herself. They didn't *need* to stay awake but chose to because they both treasured time for pillow talk.

"How is the king of Tamloch feeling this evening?" asked Jenet.

"The king of Tamloch is feeling wonderful, thank you, though he's still trying to get used to the fact he's switched kingdoms," Dârio replied.

"I thought it was very kind of Quintillius and Laetícia to put us in rooms decorated in green and gold to help remind you of your new position," Jenet teased.

"You look every bit as good in green and gold as you did in dark blue and sky blue," said Dârio, teasing back. Their bed's richly embroidered coverlet was the color of new spring leaves. He slid a few inches of the fine fabric off Jenet's shoulder, revealing only Jenet below. "Of course, my favorite ensemble is the one you're wearing now," he added.

Jenet's eyes opened wide in feigned shock. "Your Majesty!" she exclaimed. "I thought you valued me for my strategic mind!"

"That, and other intangible qualities, Earl Marshal," said Dârio.

Jenet pressed close against him beneath the silk sheets. "Do I feel intangible to you, my king?" she asked.

Dârio ran a hand along Jenet's side, then moved it lower.

"You feel quite tangible to me," he said.

"Does that make me a tangible threat to king and kingdom?" asked Jenet.

"That depends on what you have in mind," said Dârio.

"Sadly," said Jenet, "I want to talk about logistics—where in Tamloch we're going to put a third of the population of Nova Eboracum and their stores."

"In that case, you're definitely a threat," said Dârio. "I need my sleep."

"So do I," said Jenet. "I was thinking we could resettle fifty thousand Roma refugees north of the Great Falls. The land is good there, and it's underpopulated."

"We can ask Fercha for help setting up a wide gate to handle that phase of the evacuation," suggested Dârio. "She can work with Mafuta and that tall wizard Eynon's sister is sweet on."

"Felix," said Jenet. "We're also going to need to pull everyone and all our stored food out of Riyas and other population centers," said Jenet. "I've been looking over the records, and..."

* * * * *

"Good night," said Nûd as he stood next to Bonnie holding hands outside the door to her guest room.

"Good night to you," said Bonnie, smiling up at him.

"It's been a delight to see so much of you lately," said Nûd. "Thanks for accepting my invitation to the signing ceremony."

"I was glad to," said Bonnie. "Spending time with you is nearly as much fun as non-Euclidean geometry."

"You prefer mathematics to me?" asked Nûd. He made a feigned hurt face at Bonnie and she made one back at him that was even more exaggerated and made Nûd laugh. Bonnie began laughing, too.

"I've been studying numbers since I could count," said Bonnie after she'd collected herself. "We've only known each other a few days, but you're growing on me."

"Is your affection increasing in an arithmetic, geometric, or exponential progression?" asked Nûd, keeping his face perfectly serious this time.

"Exponential," said Bonnie without pausing to consider her answer. "Definitely exponential."

"More power to that kind of thinking," said Nûd. He put his arms around her and gave Bonnie a hug which was welcomed and reciprocated.

"That's one of the reasons I like you," said Bonnie. "You make me laugh—and appreciate mathematics."

"Forgive me if I seem awkward at times," said Nûd. "I like you a lot, and I haven't had much experience talking to women. I spent most of my life in an isolated castle two thousand miles west of here."

"You don't seem awkward to me at all," Bonnie replied. "Then again, I spend most of *my* time at the Institute surrounded by gray-haired wizards with robes covered in chalk dust. Most of the young people there are so caught up in their mathemagical theorems they don't realize I'm a woman."

"Not that you're not caught up in *your* theorems, too," teased Nûd.

"Yes, of course," said Bonnie. "But then I went off to war and served as a spy for the Tamloch fleet. I met a dashing young man on wyvern-back and everything changed."

"You thought I was dashing?" asked Nûd.

"I still do," said Bonnie, squeezing Nûd's hand. "For that matter, I wouldn't mind it a bit if we spent a few minutes kissing."

"Purely as an experiment to see if you like it?" asked Nûd.

"I *know* I like it," said Bonnie. "Uirsé and I tried kissing each other when we were younger. It was pleasant enough, but I'd like to see if kissing a man is different."

"Any man?" asked Nûd. "I can recruit one for you if you'd like."

"No need to bother," said Bonnie. "You'll do."

"Good to know," said Nûd. "Do you want to start standing here in the hall?"

"If there's a couch in my room that might be more comfortable," said Bonnie.

She disengaged from her embrace with Nûd and reached for the door handle. Smiling to herself, Bonnie opened the door a few inches and peered into the room, which was lit by a single dim wizard's lamp. "Good," she said, stepping inside and reaching out to take Nûd's hand. "There *is* a couch."

"If not, we would have figured *something* out," said Nûd, glancing over at the bed across from the couch. "There's so much I want to learn about non-Euclidean geometries."

"Of course there is," said Bonnie. "Or is that just one of your angles to get closer to me?" She sat near the middle of the well-padded couch, and Nûd joined her.

"You are acute, woman," teased Nûd as he gently grasped Bonnie's hand again.

She pulled her hand away and wagged her finger under Nûd's nose. "That was a *triple* pun," she said. "I like it. Did you set me up for it?"

"Maybe a little," said Nûd. "I really *am* interested in non-Euclidean geometries." He smiled as he stretched his arm around Bonnie's shoulders.

Bonnie leaned against Nûd's chest and sighed. "Later," she said. "I want to find out if I like kissing men first."

* * * * *

On another hall in the guest wing of the Governor-General's palace, Doethan and Princess Rúth were talking outside *her* door. Chee had wrapped himself around Rúth's shoulders like a stole. From his regular breathing, the raconette was asleep.

"Are you sure you want me to come in?" asked Doethan.

"Why wouldn't I?" asked Rúth. She took the older wizard's hands in hers. "We've waited so many years."

Doethan started to reply. "Yes, but you're a Tamloch princess— *the* Tamloch princess—and I'm just..."

"A wise and powerful wizard selected to lead Dâron's Conclave..." broke in the Rúth. "I've heard stories about your exploits. You were the victor in a formal wizard's duel for leadership of the Conclave over that disgusting *Bigblig* wizard loyal to Princess Gwýnnett— that blasted, useless, grasping..."

"It didn't happen quite that way," said Doethan, cutting short Rúth's list of insults. "*Hibblig* was right where I wanted him, and I would have soon bested him if Ealdamon hadn't shown up."

"I'm sure that's true," said Rúth. "You *are* a worthy mage and a worthy man, and I love you. I know you love me."

"With all my mind and heart," said Doethan softly.

"Then stop worrying about our different ranks and take me to bed," said Rúth. "You know the only reason I couldn't marry you twenty years ago was because Túathal didn't want any other potential heirs. He was completely focused on his cuckoo's egg scheme with Dârio so he could rule both Dâron *and* Tamloch."

"Well..." began Doethan.

"Túathal is dead," said Rúth, "and good riddance to him even if he was my brother. Dârio is king of Tamloch now and he has no interest in using his forty-two-year-old aunt as a pawn to cement an alliance with Dâron, the Roma, or Bifurland. Given the signing ceremony this morning, there already *is* an alliance uniting all Orluin."

"And not a moment too soon, now that Sírénae Accipiter's fleet is on the way," said Doethan, speaking quickly.

"I think it's good the three kingdoms and Occidens Province came together *before* they knew about the emperor's arrival, don't you?" asked Rúth.

"Very much so..." said Doethan.

"So, as I was saying, there's no reason why you shouldn't join me inside and marry me tomorrow if you're still interested," said Rúth.

"Tomorrow?" asked Doethan.

"Do you want to wait *another* twenty years to do it?" replied Rúth.

Doethan was smiling but looked dazed and more than a bit surprised. "Won't it take time to plan a big royal wedding?" he asked. "You'll want it in the Great Hall of the royal palace in Riyas, and..."

"And nothing," said Rúth. "We can declare our vows and confirm our marriage right after breakfast. Nothing is stopping us. We can do it here in the Governor-General's palace with all our friends as witnesses. That would be more than grand enough for me, and no doubt less of a burden for you."

"Marrying you could never be a burden," said Doethan. He grinned at Rúth. She opened her mouth to speak but changed her mind and kissed Doethan firmly on the lips instead. Chee, curled around Rúth's neck, stirred but didn't wake.

"Come inside," said Rúth. "We can find Eynon's familiar a nice soft cushion to rest on, so he won't get in our way."

"Can you make love to me with a raconette watching?" asked Doethan, enjoying the way Rúth's expression changed when he teased her.

"I doubt he'd be interested in what we'd be doing, but if Chee does decide to watch, he's welcome to and might learn something," said Rúth. "I certainly expect to."

"And I as well," said Doethan. He paused and looked thoughtful for a moment.

"What is it?" asked Rúth.

"Chee made me think about Eynon," said Doethan. "I'm sorry he won't be there for our wedding."

"Merry will be, and she'll tell him everything about it," Rúth replied. "What's going on between them now? It doesn't make sense to me."

"Eynon just learned a hard lesson and needs to work certain things out for himself," said Doethan. "He's trying to spare Merry pain—"

"—and in the process is causing her more," said Rúth. "They're both so smart—and so foolish. Young love is hard."

"We're ones to talk," said Doethan. "I should have flown into your rooms in Riyas and eloped with you when *we* were young."

"Starting a war between Dâron and Tamloch in the process," said Rúth.

Doethan shook his head slowly. "Not that a war wouldn't have begun in a year or two under some other pretext anyway."

"Dâron's Old King managed to stretch the periods of peace out to decades, not years," said Rúth.

"With a great deal of help from Queen Carys," added Doethan.

"So perhaps we *could* have wed without armies called to the field?" asked Rúth.

"Probably not," said Doethan. "Abducting a princess is an extreme provocation."

"Even if the abductor marries her?" asked Rúth.

"I think that makes it worse," said Doethan.

Chee stretched and repositioned himself on Rúth's shoulders without waking up. He made soft *chee-chee-chee* sounds as if chasing a bug, then went quiet again.

Doethan and Rúth looked at each other and realized they were still standing in the hall.

"Are you as nervous as I am?" asked Rúth.

"Probably," said Doethan. "Maybe more so."

"I doubt it," said Rúth. "Let's both put our hands on the door handle."

"I've got it," said Doethan. He released a small construct of solidified sound that pressed down on the handle then gently pushed on the door until it stood open before them. "After you, my princess," he said.

"Both at the same time," said Rúth, taking Doethan's hand.

Together, they crossed the threshold.

* * * * *

Fercha was reading in bed. The book she held was a treatise on the history of the Roma empire she'd borrowed from the Governor-General's extensive library. She had flipped to the chapters describing when the third and fourth empires were subdivided from the Imperium's dominions. Because each of the individual emperors wanted to control the Italic peninsula and the city of Roma herself, a series of compromises—and bloody battles—had resulted in a solution that kept all four tetrarchs equally dissatisfied.

It had been agreed that the Apennine peninsula and the city of Roma would not belong to any tetrarch's holdings. Instead, magnificent villas for the tetrarchs to reside in during quarterly meetings would be built around the huge palace of the Caesars and its gigantic dome. The palace itself would henceforth be the home of the Imperial Museum. For many centuries, until the Tax Revolt of Emperor Carloman, it would also house the central bureaucracy that coordinated collecting taxes across the Imperium.

Fercha smiled, thinking of the fierce reputation for honesty and diligence earned by the men and women of Caesar's palace, renowned even in Dâron and Tamloch. She looked up when Verro gated in.

"Did your lessons go well?" Fercha asked.

"Better than I expected," said Verro.

"What happened?" Fercha asked.

"Merry made *ad hoc* gates," said Verro.

Fercha stood up, put her book down, rushed to Verro's side, and hugged him. "How marvelous," she said. "I knew my apprentice was something special."

"She's certainly that," said Verro. "She threw a tantrum like a two-year-old when her *ad hoc* gate attempts kept failing."

"But you got her past it?" asked Fercha. "You must have—you're a marvelous teacher, I'm sure."

"It wasn't all me," said Verro. "Laetícia did her part, and that strange *person* in amber-robes, one of those three odd wizards from Bifurland, really helped get Merry on track."

"How fascinating," said Fercha. "That one never speaks. I think it's to seem more mysterious."

"All three of them make me uncomfortable," said Verro, "but the one who joined us showed Merry how to focus and center herself better than Laetícia and I could."

"Do you think the Bifurland wizard could help teach *me* how to make *ad hoc* gates?" asked Fercha.

"You could ask," said Verro.

"Maybe I will," said Fercha. "In the morning. For now, I'm glad you didn't get back too late."

"Too late for what?" asked Verro. He winked at Fercha and she raised her eyebrows.

"I think you know," Fercha replied. She climbed back into bed, closed her book, and smiled.

* * * * *

"I will *finally* have a chance to fight the Roma it seems," said Viridáxés. The great green dragon rubbed his massive back against a rock formation near the shore of Bucket Island off Tamloch's southern coast.

Zûrafiérix, an equally large blue dragon, was mostly submerged in the shallow water nearby. She'd just returned from a hunting expedition and had shoved a small whale above the tide line nearby. She cleared her throat with a rumbling cough that released a deluge of seawater. "So it appears," she said. "Maybe we were meant to wake in time to face this challenge."

"Laetícia said they have seven black dragons with their fleet," shared Viridáxés. His eyes spun with excitement.

"Are they as big as we are?" asked Zûrafiérix.

"About a quarter our size," answered Viridáxés. "At least that was Laetícia's impression, or so I heard. They could be twice as big, and I'd still *smash* them."

"Did Laetícia say we needed to keep our existence a secret and coordinate closely with their efforts?" asked Zûrafiérix after submerging then rising to blow jets of water from her nostrils.

"She, uh, may have," said Viridáxés reluctantly.

"I thought so," said Zûrafiérix. "If you listen to me and do as I say, I'll promise you a great many opportunities to attack the Roma."

"But I want to smash them *now*," said Viridáxés.

"How long until the emperor's fleet gets to Orluin?" asked Zûrafiérix.

"A week," said Viridáxés, "or thereabouts."

"Then we'll have enough time to do what needs to be done," said Zûrafiérix.

"What's that?" asked Viridáxés.

"Lay a clutch of eggs in case anything happens to either one of us," Zûrafiérix responded.

"How can I help?" asked Viridáxés.

* * * * *

Merry thanked Laetícia for personally showing her to her guest room. When she was inside and had heard the *pop* that signified her host's departure, Merry made a series of *ad hoc* gates and jumped from one side of the room to the other, bouncing around with a dozen soft *pops* of her own. She was still frustrated but forming the *ad hoc* gates to places she could see seemed easy—it was just jumping to places she *couldn't* see that was problematic.

Holding her hands high above her head and shaking them, Merry silently screamed. Then she realized she had a better option. She created two spheres of solidified sound around her body, then sucked the air out between them using a congruency linked to high above her. Now insulated from others around her, she screamed again without holding back. When her throat started to hurt, she stopped and let out a few more frustrations.

"Blast you, Eynon, why aren't *you* here to help me!" shouted Merry. Then she laughed at herself. *Why aren't I out in Melyncárreg helping Eynon work through* his *challenges?* She balled her hands into fists and lowered them to waist level. *Because he doesn't want my help,* she thought. *He's ashamed of his failures—but now I've got a failure of my own to share. We can learn how to overcome our failings together.*

Merry felt more optimistic now. She'd ask Verro to take her to Fercha's tower in the morning and she could step through the gate to Melyncárreg at the base of the tower and reunite with Eynon. She really missed him. After removing her clothes and washing up, she was about to pull back the sheets and comforter when she heard something solid *thunk* against the window of her guest room. The expensive glass window was only latched closed and she was able to open it easily.

Ace flew in and shifted from his flying carpet form to his nearly spherical gray-boulder shape, dropping like a stone ball into the center of the bed.

Merry climbed in beside her familiar, wrapped her arms around the rockhound, and was asleep before she'd taken a dozen breaths.

Chapter 18

Landfall

"Wake up, my friend," said Xaxidiánus. The dragon sounded less energetic than he had when they'd departed from the Tempest Isles for Nova Eboracum. "I can see the lighthouse that marks the harbor."

"Are we there yet?" asked Magister Callidus after a yawn.

"Stop sounding like a child," teased Xaxidiánus. "That's what I just said."

"It's still dark," Callidus protested.

"The beating of my wings is like a hurricane, and my power is beyond compare," Xaxidiánus intoned in a booming voice.

"Yes, yes," said Callidus. "That's straight from my collection of dragon's boasts. You stole it from the great wurm who knocked down the outer wall of Troy in the old stories."

"I'm tired and couldn't be more original," said Xaxidiánus.

Callidus could imagine the dragon's toothy smile.

"There was a tail wind and I made good time, but now I need to rest," Xaxidiánus continued.

"Maybe you can nap on a beach near the lighthouse," said Magister Callidus. "I'm more rested and can keep watch."

"That would be appreciated, my friend," said the dragon. Xaxidiánus circled the tall copper statue of a woman in long wizard robes holding a book of magic in one hand and a huge, torch-shaped wizard lamp in the other. The statue had marked the entrance to the harbor at Nova Eboracum for generations and was known as the New Colossus, since it replaced a similar statue that had collapsed fifteen hundred years earlier.

Callidus admired the skill of the long-dead mage who'd managed to prevent the copper from turning green over the years as so many statues in Roma's empire across the Ocean had done. "There's a broad stretch of sand south of the statue," he informed his scaly comrade. "That seems to be a likely spot."

"And not a moment too soon," said Xaxidiánus. His landing was due to be more of a controlled fall than a graceful decent.

Sensing his friend's stamina was at its end, Callidus disengaged from the straps holding him in his saddle, stepped onto his flying disk, and floated above as Xaxidiánus thudded down, throwing curtains of sand in all directions.

"Are you unharmed?" asked Callidus.

The dragon's rumbling snores were his only answer.

"You earned your rest, my friend," said Magister Callidus softly. "Seven hundred miles of flying in one night is a praise-worthy accomplishment. The emperor will be pleased. I certainly am."

Callidus walked up the hill—more of a hump in the dunes than a true elevation—and examined the copper colossus. As he'd expected, it ran without need for a lighthouse keeper. If it had belonged to Sírénae, she would have used it as a punishment posting for a subordinate who'd displeased her. It seemed Quintillius didn't share her philosophy, or perhaps it was too early, and the keeper was still sleeping, though Callidus hadn't noticed any sort of dwelling nearby.

The light from the torch had partially ruined his night vision, but he could see a dark smudge on the northern horizon that must be the capital of Occidens Province. He and Xaxidiánus would make their appearance a few hours after dawn, flying high above Nova Eboracum to make their presence known. He'd inform any wizard scouts coming to investigate that he and the dragon were emissaries from the emperor with important news for the Governor-General. With luck, all would go well, and he'd get a few good meals and some sleep in a real bed before he had to return to Sírénae's fleet.

He considered retrieving some traveling rations from a bag attached to the dragon's saddle, but decided it was wiser to follow the old adage and *let sleeping dragons lie.* In a spur-of-the-moment bit of whimsy, he rose to the statue's head and sat cross-legged on his flying disk in a hollow of curls on top. As he rose, he smiled to see a beautifully orna-mented headband worked in fine detail. The sculptor had included a smaller wizard lamp behind an oval of purple-tinted glass nearly as tall as he was to mark the guardian wizard statue's magestone.

He wondered if the artist in metal who had crafted this marvelous statue had made any pieces displayed on the other side of the Ocean. If so, he wasn't aware of them, and work like this was something that would have come to his attention. Callidus reminded himself to find out the name of the sculptor after Sírénae's conquest of Orluin was complete.

He fingered the communications ring on his index finger, the one linked to the ring he'd given Sírénae before he'd left. Magister Callidus hoped everything would go well during his audience with Quintillius and Laetícia in the morning. Somehow, given the blunt words of the emperor's message, he wasn't optimistic.

Chapter 19

Rúth and Doethan

Doethan awoke with music in his ears. At first, he thought it was birdsong outside the window, but as his mind became more coherent, he realized it was Rúth singing from the bathing room attached to her suite. It was the height of Roma decadence to have a room for bathing *and* a private necessarium attached to a guest room, but his beloved was a royal princess and therefore certainly deserved such luxury. As he listened, Doethan could hear splashing water providing a counterpoint for Rúth's song.

A long, contented sigh of pleasure interrupted the singing.

"Good morning," he said tentatively.

"You're up!" said Rúth, sounding far more alert than Doethan on what must be less rest. "It's about time, sleepyhead. Come in and scrub my back. I didn't invite in any servants, so you'll have to do."

"Ummm, yes, dear?" answered Doethan, not quite sure about all this. He was still getting used to Rúth being *with* him instead of just loved from afar. "Hurry it up, slowpoke," Rúth said. "You need a good wash after last night, too, and I can scrub your back when you've finished scrubbing mine."

"Yes, dear!" said Doethan with more enthusiasm now that the reality of the situation penetrated his brain. *Rúth and I are getting married in a few hours!* he thought, almost tasting his joy. He made his way to the bathing room, appreciating the genius of the Roma's hypocaust that kept the tiles warm beneath his feet and fed the warm water in the large oval tub where his beloved Rúth was—for want of a better word—frolicking. She tossed a spray of droplets from her fingertips with a wave of her hand.

Doethan stepped into the opposite end of the tub, savoring the temperature of the water and the excellent company—and scenery—his soon-to-be wife provided. Rúth took both his hands in hers and pulled herself to closer toward him, dropping her hands and twisting as she slid until her hips were between his legs and her back was directly in front of him.

"There are sponges on the ledge behind you," said Rúth. "Be thorough when you scrub my back. I'll let you know if you don't measure up to my servants."

"I hear and obey, my princess," said Doethan playfully.

"I love it when you say that," said Rúth.

"My princess?" asked Doethan.

"Obey," replied Rúth. "I haven't had a man willing to obey my orders for a long time—except during the battle of Riyas, of course."

"That wasn't a battle," said Doethan. It was a wizard's duel writ large."

"With dragons," added Rúth.

"True enough," said Doethan as he found a sponge and began scrubbing. "Speaking of dragons, I wonder how Viridáxés and Zûrafiérix are managing up north on Bucket Island?"

"They're also a pair of newlyweds, aren't they?" answered Rúth. "I expect he's driving her crazy."

"I'll try not to do the same," said Doethan.

"Thank you," said Rúth. She didn't say anything as Doethan applied pressure to her shoulder blades with the sponge. After he'd finished both and moved to her lower back, she spoke. "Do dragons actually marry?"

Doethan laughed. "I don't think so. They mate."

"We mated last night," said Rúth.

"Twice," said Doethan.

"And we'll mate again this morning before we marry," Rúth asserted.

Doethan lowered his chin then raised it back again.

"I hope you're nodding," said Rúth.

"I am, my dear, I am," he said, repeating his gesture while moving the sponge in circular motions at the small of Rúth's back.

The next hour passed quickly, and soon Rúth and Doethan were leaning back against the pillows of their bed holding hands. Doethan couldn't stop smiling. He could hear splashing sounds and gleeful raconette cries from the bathing room where Chee had decided to swim in the tub they'd recently abandoned.

"I need to get back to Riyas soon to organize the city's evacuation," said Rúth. "After our wedding, of course," she added. "I'll have to contact Laetícia once I'm dressed to enlist her assistance with the nuptials."

"Don't hurry to dress on my account," said Doethan.

"I think I'm going to like having a husband," said Rúth reflectively.

"And I a wife," said Doethan.

"Will you be joining me in Riyas, husband-to-be?"

"I expect so," said Doethan, "but there's something I have to do first."

"What could possibly keep you away from your beloved bride so soon after your wedding?" asked Rúth.

"A crew of street urchins I met when I gated up to Nova Eboracum the day before the Battle of Riyas," said Doethan. "I told you about the dough rings."

"Yes, but not about any street urchins," said Rúth. "Tell me more."

Doethan recounted the story of the young thief who tried to steal his bag of dough rings. The thief went by the name of Távi and appeared to be the leader of a small band of similar young opportunists. He hadn't been able to tell if Távi was a boy or a girl, and it didn't seem proper to ask.

He'd given Távi food and money to get food for the others as well. Doethan knew they made their way by their wits on the streets of Nova Eboracum and was afraid the children might be left behind during a general evacuation of the city.

"That sounds exactly like something you'd do," said Rúth. "I'm glad you're going to ensure those feral children are safe. You can join me in Riyas later."

"I wouldn't call them feral," said Doethan. "They are quite civilized. It's the Roma State with its bundled sticks and axe that imposes the slavery they fear and pushes them into the shadows."

"It sounds like we'll have another war to wage against slavery in Orluin once we defeat the emperor," said Rúth.

"*If* we defeat the emperor," said Doethan.

"Don't forget the thralls in Bifurland," said Rúth.

"They're not quite the same as Roma slaves," said Doethan. "Thralls' children are free."

"Perhaps," said Rúth. "It's still subjugating one group of people to another—which reminds me, I need to start planting seeds in Dârio's mind to include women in Tamloch's line of succession, like they do in Dâron. Jenet will support me."

"You want to be queen, my love?" asked Doethan.

"Of course not," said Rúth. "But I wouldn't mind seeing my yet-to-be-conceived niece on the throne someday."

"Sounds good to me," said Doethan. "Much as I hate to get out of bed, we have to. We've got a wedding to plan."

"That we do," said Rúth after kissing Doethan's lips with enough passion to make him want to postpone the wedding by a few hours. She grinned at the man she'd loved for over two decades.

"I guess we'd best get to it," said Doethan.

* * * * *

"I agree," said Princess Rúth. "Your husband's audience chamber will be a much better place for the wedding than the informal dining room near the kitchen."

The room was rectangular with a raised dais at one short end opposite the main doors. The left-hand long wall was white plaster adorned with colorful Athican-style frescoes, and the right side of the room held tall clear-glass windows leading to a balcony that looked out over the palace gardens two stories below.

"I knew you'd like it," said Laetícia. She gave Rúth a hug and looked up to smile at Chee clambering around in the chamber's intricately carved and interlocked rafters. "The ceiling is much prettier here."

"Chee agrees," said Rúth. "And the frescoes are perfect for a wedding."

"I'll second that," said Doethan. "Who doesn't like depictions of near-naked young men and women cavorting around the country-side in spring?"

"Is that what they call it in Dâron?" asked Laetícia. "Cavorting? Here in Nova Eboracum it's—"

"—not really important," said Rúth. "I just like them. Did you get word back from the people we wanted to join us?"

"I did," said Laetícia. "Everyone's coming, except Eynon of course. Nobody knows how to reach him."

"I've got to give that young man another communications ring," said Doethan. "There's no reason for Eynon to be out of touch. I'd really like to have him at the wedding."

"So would I," said Rúth. "He and Merry make quite a couple."

"Speaking of Merry," said Laetícia, "I passed along your invitation to her personally. She wanted to gate to Melyncárreg right away to find Eynon, but I talked her into waiting a bit so she could attend the wedding. She said she'd go for a flight first to clear her head and join us soon."

"She probably just wants a look at the wizards playing qua-qua," said Doethan, who had seen formations of purple and white-robed wizards weaving about overhead earlier.

"That's not a match," said Laetícia. "It's just a practice session."

"I don't think that would matter to Merry," said Doethan.

"She's missing Eynon and looking for distractions," offered Rúth.

"I think she's practicing her *ad hoc* gating skills," said Laetícia.

"You and Verro succeeded?" asked Doethan. His voice rose and a broad smile lit his face.

"Sort of," said Laetícia. "She can *ad hoc* gate to anywhere she can see."

"Line-of-sight *ad hoc* gating?" said Doethan. "Never heard of it."

"Merry's not pleased she can't form true *ad hoc* gates," added Laetícia. "She's frustrated with herself and that's not helping her get better at what she *can* do."

"Maybe you should speak to her, dear," said Princess Rúth, touching Doethan's arm. "She was your apprentice first, before Fercha, from what you've said."

"Merry needs to work things out for herself," said Doethan firmly. "She's a sensible young woman—most of the time. Besides, I want to stay with you until the ceremony."

Rúth hugged Doethan while Laetícia smiled at them, remembering her own wedding. Chee cried *chee-chee-chee* from the rafters above.

"Well then," said Laetícia, "I'll get all the items you'll need for the ceremony. I'm pleased you asked me to play a role in the process beyond providing the site."

"And your children, too," said Doethan. "I hope they're willing."

"Willing?" Laetícia responded. "They jumped up and down on their beds when I told them."

"Good," said Doethan. "Rúth and I will return to her suite and get out of your way."

"Planning to do some *cavorting?*" teased Laetícia.

"Maybe," said Rúth. The corner of her mouth turned up in a smile.

"So soon?" replied Doethan in mock protest. "I'm not eighteen anymore."

"I'll inspire you," said Rúth.

Chapter 20
A Long-Delayed Wedding

Laetícia was pleased with the job she'd done making Doethan and Rúth's impromptu wedding special. Almost everyone the happy couple wanted to attend was there.

Dârio and Jenet looked impressive in new green and gold ensembles. Nûd and Bonnie stood beside them, an equally well-matched pair. *There will be more weddings in the near future,* Laetícia suspected. She admired Nûd's sky blue and dark tunic, which harmonized nicely with Bonnie's soft leaf-green wizard's robes.

King Bjarni and Queen Signý were present, wearing fur-trimmed cloth-of-gold robes of state. The person who served as their equivalent of a master mage stood a few steps behind them. Sigrun, Bjarni and Signý's young daughter, and her best friend Rannveigr were in a corner of the room next to the balcony windows, stroking Rocky. The large black wyvern had insisted on joining Nûd in the audience chamber, and Laetícia saw no reason not to welcome him.

Thank goodness the double doors leading out to the balcony were wide enough for the wyvern to fit through when he pulled his wings in tight, she thought. *Although it could have been worse. The bride and groom could have wanted Viridáxés and Zûrafiérix to attend as well.*

Duke Háiddon was next to Duke Néillen, making sure the former earl marshal of Tamloch didn't attempt any mischief or try to escape. Fercha and Verro were holding hands. Laetícia assumed they were remembering their own quickly organized wedding more than two decades earlier.

Mafuta and Felix, Occidens Province wizards, were sending up small sparkling balls of colored light to enhance the chamber's festive air. Near Laetícia, Quintillius was leaning down to talk to Grand Admiral Sónnel of Tamloch, who stood at least a foot shorter than he did.

Inthíra was there, hiding behind Rocky. She wore a wistful expression but was distracting herself by creating illusions of late spring flowers around the audience chamber, since just a few optimistic daffodils and crocuses were blooming in the palace gardens.

Merry—and Eynon—were the only invited guests missing.

Laetícia was particularly pleased to find a skilled trumpet player, whose musical abilities would be helpful for the wedding—and who might prove useful in a future confrontation with the emperor as well. She had also recruited a harpist, two flute players, and a potbellied man with a large round drum from the musicians' hall in the city. All but the trumpet player were providing a low-volume sort of music that made a pleasant background for conversation.

The trumpet player was standing by the main entrance to the chamber. She waved to Laetícia and received a confirming nod in reply. The trumpeter put her instrument to her lips and began a rousing fanfare.

Conversations in the audience chamber stopped. Guests spontaneously arranged themselves into a semicircle facing the doors in the back of the room. When the doors opened, Tertia and Seconda were the first to enter. They carried branches of apple and cherry trees in bloom and shook hundreds of pink and white blossoms onto the narrow carpet leading to the dais. The guests parted to give them room and most wore smiles as they watched the children—particularly little Tertia—concentrate on performing their tasks well. Primus followed his sisters. He carried himself like a proud young warrior and held a silver tray with items needed for the ceremony.

Another trumpet fanfare signaled it was time for Doethan and Rúth to enter. They didn't just step into the room, they seemed to skip, their hearts so light and filled with long-thwarted joy that Laetícia wondered if their feet were actually touching the carpeted floor.

The other musicians joined the trumpet player to expand on her theme as the happy couple made their way to the dais where Primus and his sisters were standing. Sigrun and Rannveigr left Rocky to stand in front of Bifurland's king and queen, where they'd have a better view.

Rocky carefully stepped behind Nûd and Bonnie, keeping his wings furled to take up less space. Chee jumped down from a rafter and sat on Rocky's head, watching every action around him intently.

When Doethan and Rúth ascended the steps to the top of the dais, Fercha and Verro joined them, Verro standing next to his sister and Fercha finding a spot near Doethan. Their four faces shared smiles. Then the music stopped and Doethan took Rúth's hand.

"Rúth," he said, "My love. I've waited half my life for this moment. I've loved you since the first time I saw you at court in Brendinas when you were a shy girl and I was a new-made mage from the hinterlands of Dâron. Be my wife now, at last, and make my long-deferred dreams come true."

"Doethan," said Rúth. "My love. The one person at court so long ago who saw me as a young woman, not a princess or a pawn, who always knows what to say to make me smile, be my husband now and make *my* dreams come true." She turned to Doethan and put her free hand on top of their joined hands. Doethan added his free hand as well.

Verro removed a long green ribbon from the sleeve of his robe and held it up so everyone could see. He loosely wrapped it around Doethan and Rúth's interlocked hands.

"This green ribbon signifies my love and support for this con-nection. It further represents the love of the people of Tamloch for their princess and her husband. May you have many years of hap-piness together." He bowed and Doethan and Rúth nodded their thanks.

Nûd joined the group on the dais next, looking a bit awkward, but still regal. He took a long blue ribbon from his belt and held it up, then wrapped it loosely around the couple's hands.

"Doethan is a respected wizard in Dâron," he said. "I am proud to have him in Dâron's Conclave and to count him as a friend and a fitting match for my new-found aunt. This blue ribbon signifies my love and support for their union and the warm welcome Doethan and Rúth will always have in Dâron." Nûd stepped down to rejoin Bonnie.

Laetícia noticed the Tamloch scholar-wizard squeeze Nûd's hand and smile up at him. She revised her internal odds on which royal wedding she'd be attending next.

Sigrun left her parents and cousin and came to the dais. She held a gold ribbon above her head for everyone to see and spoke in a crisp, clear voice. "My mother and father tell me it is customary for young people to serve as witnesses at weddings," she said. "We are able to keep memories alive across the years." She draped the shimmering length of what she held over the couple's hands.

"This gold ribbon signifies the love and support of the people of Bifurland for this union," she said, looking at her parents for confirmation. They nodded and smiled, so Sigrun continued. "It also signifies that I like Doethan and Rúth a lot because Rocky likes Doethan and Chee likes Rúth. Rocky and Chee are excellent judges of character—at least *I* think so."

Everyone laughed. Sigrun returned to her family and her cousin. She'd improvised, but did so sincerely, creating a memory that would never fade across decades.

Laetícia herself joined Rúth and Doethan next. She gently tied a purple ribbon around the colorful trio of ribbons already there.

"This purple ribbon signifies the love and support of the people of Occidens Province for this marriage," she began. "Quintillius and I are *very* pleased to provide a place where this delightful ceremony could be held and look forward to welcoming Doethan and Rúth here at the Governor-General's palace whenever they'd like to visit, even if Doethan *doesn't* have an entry token."

Doethan grinned and Rúth looked at him. He winked back. Laetícia was sure Rúth would get the referenced story from Doethan shortly.

"He also brings dough rings!" said Tertia with a voice like a tiny flute that pierced the silence. The little girl realized what she'd done, dropped her branch of cherry blossoms, and put her hand over her mouth. Laetícia was trying so hard not to laugh that she couldn't spare any time to be angry.

"Speaking of rings," said Doethan. "It is not customary in Dâron for couples to exchange rings. We feel that people own themselves and are not anyone's property." He smiled at Rúth and blinked away tears. "However," he said, "I do have a ring of a different sort to give my beloved." He turned to Fercha.

"These rings?" said his friend with a grin. Fercha produced two plain gold bands from her belt pouch and held them out in her palm.

"Could we have a little help here?" asked Rúth, looking down at her hands bound fast to Doethan's.

"Of course," said Laetícia. She carefully unwrapped the four ribbons and passed them to her husband. They'd be used to seal the wedding scroll all the guests would be signing to mark the ceremony. "Joined, but not bound," she said, using words commonly used on such occasions, though weddings seldom featured ribbons from three kingdoms and a Roma province.

Doethan took the pair of rings from Fercha and gave one to Rúth, saying, "I made this communications ring with my own hands, so we will always be able to talk to each other, even when we're separated. Please accept it as a token of my love and abiding affection. I plan to use these rings to ensure I can always tell you I love you every day for the rest of our lives."

Rúth was smiling and tears of joy were streaming down her face. "I will gladly accept your gift and employ its magic for the same good purpose," she said.

"You can also use your ring to tell me you'll be late for dinner," teased Doethan.

"That's just another way of saying, 'I love you,'" said Rúth. "Now let's finish the ceremony."

The guests clapped and cheered. Laetícia beckoned Primus to join them with his tray.

Rúth found a knife and a loaf of fine white bread among the items Primus carried. She cut a small slice from the loaf and shared it with Doethan. He ate half of it and Rúth ate the rest. "This bread represents the home and life we plan to build together," she said.

"May you never know want," said the guests in unison.

Doethan took a pinch of salt from a silver salver on the tray. He touched it to Rúth's tongue and then his own. "This salt reminds us to savor our lives," he said, "and also to taste everything life offers with more intensity, sharing our tears of pain and joy."

"May you live life in all its fullness—together," came the guests' reply.

"We don't have to do this next part if you don't want to," said Rúth.

"I want to," Doethan replied. He deftly pricked Rúth's finger with a silver pin he'd dipped in a small bowl of winter wine, then did the same to his own finger. Two tiny drops of blood appeared, and they touched them together."

"Shared minds, shared hearts, shared blood," they recited.

Tertia spoke, her tiny little girl's voice carrying in the silence. "Are they married now?" she asked.

"Almost," said Laetícia. She heard a *pop* and turned to see Merry appearing next to her on the dais. Her face looked like she was ready to explode with news.

"Wait!" said Doethan.

"Not a word," Rúth commanded.

"I thee wed," said Doethan.

"I thee wed," said Rúth.

"I thee wed," they both said together. Then they embraced.

"Now they're married," Laetícia told her younger daughter. "What's so important?" she asked Merry.

"An ambassador from the emperor is here on a big black dragon," Merry replied. "He wants to talk to you and Quintillius." She pointed toward the balcony, where an older purple-robed wizard hovered on dragonback above the palace gardens.

"Is *that* all?" asked Laetícia.

Chapter 21

Breakfast Conversations

"Breakfast was delicious," said Eynon. "I especially loved the red-wine-cheese omelet. It turned my eggs pink."

"Rōlin learned how to make that cheese across the Ocean," said Peregrína. "When he visited Narbo, the capital of the Western Empire."

"You start with a rich red wine and boil it to make it thick," said Rōlin. "When it cools, stir it into a sharp yellow cheese and mix it in with the blade of a flat knife so the wine-color swirls through instead of blending."

Eynon nodded because he'd just bitten into a thick slice of hot buttered bread.

"Let the cheese age for a few months so the flavors merge, then enjoy the result," Rōlin continued.

"I'll have to try making some myself," said Eynon. He was thinking about sharing Rōlin's recipe with his parents and the people of Haywall. They made lots of cheese from their excess milk and red-wine-cheese might count double or even triple when it came time to pay their taxes to the baron. *Of course there's the challenge of finding a source of red wine,* Eynon mused. He took another bite of bread and wiped excess butter off his lips with the back of his hand.

"Thank you for the excellent bread," said Peregrína. "It's very light and fluffy."

"I added bubbles of air using tiny spheres of solidified sound," said Eynon. "I didn't want my loaves to fall flat."

"Another recipe for a future book?" teased Rōlin.

"A future *cookbook,*" said Peregrína.

"Not if you need solidified sound to make it," Rōlin responded.

"Volume Four of *On Wizardry* it is," said Peregrína with a smile. "What shall we work on after breakfast?" She slid a platter of bacon and sausages toward Eynon, but he shook his head.

"Offensive and defensive magic," Eynon replied once he'd swallowed. He told them what had happened to him above the Tempest Isles.

"It was only a matter of time before the other tetrarchs had Sírénae killed or exiled," said Rōlin.

"I'm surprised it took this long," added Peregrína. "She had a way of looking at you like she was a hawk and you were a mouse. And that snow-gryffon of hers..."

"Thraxa," said Rōlin.

"Yes," said Peregrína. "Thraxa looks at visitors in Sírénae's court like they're her next meal. It's intimidating."

"I think that's the point," said Rōlin.

"Of course, dear," said Peregrína. "But you'll have to admit it's off-putting for invited guests."

"You've met the Siren Hawk? The emperor of the West?" asked Eynon.

"We've had that dubious honor," said Rōlin. "We needed to buy precision surveying tools from a workshop in eastern Gaul and Sírénae insisted on meeting us before she would give us permission to do so."

"Do you know how hard it is to make a surveying chain that won't get shorter or longer with changes in temperature?" asked Peregrína.

"That's not the point here," said Rōlin. "Sírénae gave us permission, but only if we gave her a copy of the *Atlas of Orluin* when we finished it."

"Do you know how much work goes into making a copy of the *Atlas,* Eynon?" asked Peregrína.

"A lot," Rōlin interjected before Eynon could reply. "I think Sírénae knew even then that she might have to sail west if she miscalculated the resolve of the other tetrarchs."

"I'm glad we didn't finish the *Atlas* and send her a copy before it happened," added Peregrína.

Eynon listened to the exchange of comments made by Rōlin and Peregrína and tried not to smile. The two sounded a lot like his parents, even to the point of finishing each other's sentences. It was like watching two children tossing a ball back and forth as they spoke.

"What about learning offensive and defensive magic?" he asked. "Where do you think I should start?"

"Hmmm..." said Rōlin.

"Are you thinking what I'm thinking?" asked Peregrína.

"I expect so," said Rōlin. "We're going to teach you a few of our unpublished recipes—like the *Mule.*"

"And the *Hedgehog,*" said Peregrína.

"Can you generate illusions?" asked Rōlin.

Peregrína laughed. "Haven't you realized yet?" she said. "Eynon is the one who created the illusion of Riyas we heard about so that huge green dragon controlled by Túathal didn't destroy the city."

"Really?" said Rōlin. "That was impressive work."

"I had lots of help," said Eynon.

"I'm sure you still carried a lot of the load," said Peregrína. Then a thought crossed her mind and she changed the subject. "Is it true little Nûd is king of Dâron now? He used to come here to visit us and eat at this very table when he was small."

"It's true," said Eynon. "He's not little now and is taller and broader-built than I am."

"We know," said Peregrína with a smile. "But he'll always be 'little Nûd' to us."

Rōlin nodded, then got back on topic. "Since you *are* good with solidified sound illusions," he said, "we can teach you the *Locusts.*"

"Ooo!" said Peregrína. "That's a good one."

"Are you both warrior wizards?" Eynon asked. "You don't come across that way."

"We're not," said Peregrína, "but we *are* collectors and have traveled widely."

"We also have to protect ourselves when we're surveying," said Rōlin. "From magical creatures, wild animals, and two-legged humans."

"Sometimes the magical creatures have two legs," said Peregrína. "Remember those eight-foot kickbirds with serrated beaks in the western desert."

"I don't think Eynon will need to deal with *them,*" said Rōlin. "We know more magical techniques than we've had cause to use," he said, "and my father and grandfather collected even more. I suspect many of them are unknown to Sírénae and her wizards, so they will at least surprise them."

"Are any of these techniques useful against dragons?" asked Eynon. "There are seven black dragons between fifty and sixty feet long with the emperor's fleet."

"Ah," said Peregrína. "For that you'll need to learn the *Skunk.*"

"And find a supply of dragonsbane," said Rōlin.

"Where is it found?" asked Eynon, who wondered just what *dragonsbane* was.

"In the Caverns of Jewels," said Peregrína.

"Are the caverns close by?" Eynon asked.

"They're not far at all," said Rōlin. "Only four hundred miles to the east."

"It should only take you half a day to fly there," said Peregrína. "I'll pack lunch and dinner for you."

"The *Skunk* is a simple spell," said Rōlin, "but you must have dragonsbane before starting the recipe. We have everything else you'll need here."

"Just be sure to come back in one piece," said Peregrína.

"Right," said Eynon. He didn't really hear her implied warning. Instead, he was busy reminding himself to recalibrate what it meant to be *close by* here in the west. *Four hundred miles is the distance from Haywall to Nova Eboracum! At least it's a good day for flying.*

Chapter 22

The Quest for Dragonsbane

Eynon didn't start his journey to the Cave of Jewels for another hour. Rōlin had explained what dragonsbane was and how to collect it. While not exactly a pleasant prospect, it didn't sound too onerous for a boy raised in a dairying village who'd grown up cleaning cow stalls. His host had also given him a bag holding two dozen hollow clay spheres with carved wooden stoppers. They were the size of unshelled walnuts and designated as containers for the dragonsbane once Eynon found it.

Peregrína brought Eynon a cloth bag containing bread, cheese, sausage, dried fruit, and a water skin. "At least you won't have to fly back, since you can make *ad hoc* gates," she said. "I saw you gate to Melyncárreg to get your bread without using the fixed gate Rōlin's grandfather created."

"It's too bad I can't immediately gate *to* the Cave of Jewels," said Eynon. He grinned at his hostess.

"Gates don't work that way, even *ad hoc* ones," said Peregrína. She pulled a square of folded white linen from somewhere in her robes and handed it to Eynon. "This should help you get there expeditiously," she said.

Eynon unfolded the square and saw it was a carefully drawn map showing the course he should take to get from Rōlin and Peregrína's home in their beautiful mountain valley to the Cave of Jewels. A few landmarks were noted, but not many.

"Keep heading east and fly for five hours or so until you get to more mountains," said Peregrína. "There's an outcrop of white granite northeast of the cave that can serve as a landmark," she added.

"My father enlarged the entrance and marked it with a dolmen," said Rōlin. "Look for two stone uprights twice your height topped with a stone lintel."

"Like the old henge back in the White Isle I saw illustrated in *Peregrinations?"* asked Eynon.

"Exactly," replied Rōlin.

"My grandmother's first cousin *drew* that illustration," said Peregrína.

"How wonderful," said Eynon.

"Drawing skills run in my family," said Peregrína proudly.

Eynon smiled. "I have a question," he said. "You've told me where to find dragonsbane, but I have no idea *why* it's found in the Cave of Jewels. I've met two colossal dragons and have fought seven medium-sized ones, but I can't see why they'd want to poke into narrow caves?"

"That's because you're unfamiliar with the wild dragons of western Orluin," said Rōlin. "They're smaller than piglets when they hatch and often seek caves for shelter."

"Primarily to get away from other dragons," said Peregrína. "The older ones are short-tempered and have no patience for the newly hatched."

"I see," said Eynon, though he really didn't. The thought of wild dragons growing up without the civilizing influences of human beings was frightening. *Then again, if Viridáxés is a typical example,* Eynon considered, *dragons could be quite fierce even if they'd had a long association with humans.* Then he got it. "It's like male bears killing sows' cubs so they can mate with them sooner," he said.

"Not exactly," said Rōlin. "Bears aren't intelligent at the level dragons are, and dragons aren't particularly maternal once their eggs hatch."

"I think it's just nature at work," said Peregrína. "There can't be too many dragons, or they'd all starve."

"So they're short-tempered to keep their own numbers down?" asked Eynon.

"Maybe," said Peregrína. "No one really knows, and wild dragons don't welcome humans, except as unexpected meals."

"I'll keep that in mind," said Eynon.

Rōlin spoke up. "Dragonsbane works on wyverns too, by the way. Gryffons seem unaffected."

"That's too bad," said Eynon. "I could have used something to keep gryffons away a week ago."

"That sounds like another good story," said Peregrína.

"I can tell you that one when I get back," said Eynon. He checked the angle of the sun and saw the morning was passing quickly. "I guess I'd better get going. Wish me luck."

He climbed on his flying disk and headed east into the sky with Peregrína's map fluttering in his hands.

"Goodbye," shouted Rōlin as he waved farewell from the ground.

"Safe travels," said Peregrína, waving as well. "We did warn him he might meet wild dragons on his trip, didn't we?" she asked her husband.

"Not explicitly," he said. "Only by implication. He should be fine if he doesn't stray too far north of the course you drew him."

"What if he's attacked?" asked Peregrína. "We didn't teach him the *Skunk* recipe yet."

"He's a capable young man," said Rōlin. "Given the recipe's name, I'm sure he'll figure it out."

"Only if he's on his way back and already has a supply of dragons-bane," said Peregrína.

"There is that," said Rōlin. "Though if the dragons don't eat him, it will certainly boost his confidence."

"Wait," said Peregrina. "Eynon can *ad hoc* gate back. Nevermind. What could wrong?"

* * * * *

Eynon hadn't heard his hosts' conversation and flew on with a smile on his face. He was on a quest, of the sort he'd read about in books. *The Quest for Dragonsbane sounds like a good title for a book,* he thought, though in most books *Dragonsbane* would be a magic sword instead of what Rōlin had told him to collect. A sword would be far more impressive.

According to Peregrína's map, the Cave of Jewels was located in a hilly area some distance to the east. The first part of his trip, how-ever, would take him over high mountains. Eynon created a sphere of solidified sound around himself and his flying disk to protect him from the cold winds at higher elevations, then adapted it into a wedge shape with its point in front of him so he could cut through the air more efficiently. Below him, the rough terrain shifted from hardwoods to pine forests to moss and lichen and finally to bare rock and snow.

He started to feel a bit light-headed and figured it must be because the air got thinner the higher he went. *It's like fog back in the Coombe,* Eynon mused. *Thick in the valley's floor but wisps near the summits.* The mountains back home were barely hills compared to these, however. The ones around him seemed almost purple in the morning sun.

How majestic, he thought. *Purple mountains' majesty has a nice ring to it. I'll have to show them to Merry next chance I get.* Eynon smiled, then frowned, remembering Merry was likely to be angry at him when they met again. "I can be an idiot," he said to himself, stating one of the mildest things he expected Merry to say.

After crossing a snow-capped summit, the vegetation below him repeated in the opposite order. When he'd been flying for an hour, he reached a broad landscape of gently rolling hills and flat plains covered with tall green grass and segmented by swift-flowing blue streams coming down from the mountains. "I'll bet *their* water is cold," he said, then realized there was no one nearby to hear him. *Spending time with Rōlin and Peregrína has spoiled me,* he realized. *I don't even have Rocky or Chee to talk to now.*

Ahead, Eynon saw what looked like a dark roiling sea amid the grass. He checked Peregrína's map, trying to figure out how he had missed such an important landmark. Then he realized the cloud he'd taken for mist above a lake was actually dust raised by tens of thousands of wisents slowly making their way northwest. This assemblage far outnumbered the herds of wisents he'd seen near Melyncárreg, one of which he'd sent charging through a wide gate into Tamloch's army.

Eynon wondered about Peregrína's theory about dragons not having enough to eat to support a larger population and frowned. *How long would it take a thousand dragons to eat this herd if each one ate a wisent a day? Maybe Peregrína's idea still makes sense. I'm much happier with the notion that there are only hundreds of dragons in the West instead of thousands.*

A few dozen wisents split off from the herd and milled about wildly. Eynon generated lenses of solidified sound to help him see at a distance and saw what had caused the new pattern. The biggest cat Eynon had ever seen, with dark and light tan stripes to blend into the grass and two tremendously long incisors, was pursuing a wisent calf. *No!* thought Eynon. *Not one big cat. Seven of them. Hunting in a pack like wolves.* He slowed to watch the chase play out.

The calf's mother interposed her body between the calf and the long-tooth, kicking the feline in the ribs as she passed. The attacker tumbled and didn't get up, while a few big bulls and cows charged the other six cats and scattered them. They flowed away into the tall grass—to try again later, Eynon assumed—and at last the first cat got to its feet and staggered toward where the others had disappeared.

Interesting, thought Eynon. *Wisents don't have carnivores' teeth or claws, but they do have sharp hooves and a lot of weight to throw around. Nothing in Orluin could handle the Roma dragons like the wisents dealt with the cats, except Viridáxés and Zûrafiérix—and we have to keep them in reserve to surprise Sírénae.* Eynon didn't know any good ways to counter the emperor's dragons—or elephants, for that matter—but he was sure he'd come up with something if he thought hard enough. *Pit traps might work against the elephants,* he considered, noting that he'd never *seen* an elephant, except in Robin Goodfellow's *Peregrinations.*

Eynon kept up a steady pace as he flew on, fighting a strong wind from the south that came sweeping across the plains and pushing him farther and farther north under what felt like a vast blue dome from horizon to horizon. It was an exceptionally big sky. Nothing back in the Coombe or the rest of Dâron was anything like it. It made Eynon feel both great and small at the same time. Peregrína's map said there were mountains ahead. They'd block the winds and give him a chance to tack south to find the Cave of Jewels.

Off to his left, Eynon saw a flock of odd-looking buzzards circling. *I wonder what's dying?* he mused, triggering his distance lenses again. He saw a huge beast—near death—far below. It was eight times the size of a bull wisent and covered in red-brown hair so thick it made a bear in winter look naked. Great curved white horns of some sort came from its head. *No, those are tusks, like a boar's,* he realized. *Or like the long-toothed cat's dagger-like incisors but bent into half a circle.*

Is that a mammoth? Eynon wondered. He'd heard there were mammoths in Bifurland, but never realized their range extended this far west.

Eynon looked back at the buzzards with his augmented eyes and realized they weren't *buzzards* at all. They were dragons. It was difficult to judge how large they were, since they were so far away, but it didn't matter to Eynon. He had no interest in tangling with even one dragon, let alone two dozen of them, until he'd learned more from Rōlin and Peregrína. Eynon generated an illusion around himself that made him look like an innocuous cloud and tried to inconspicuously float past the dragons before he was noticed.

It proved to be too little, too late, however. One of the dragons was winging its way toward Eynon and closing rapidly. As it neared, Eynon could see its hide was a mottled brown and its wings were black. It was quite a bit larger than Rocky, while smaller than the emperor's black dragons who'd attacked him at the Tempest Isles.

Departing at speed seemed to be the wisest course, so Eynon dropped his cloud illusion, sharpened the point of his wedge of solidified sound, and applied as much of the energy from his blue and red magestones as he could muster to make a hasty exit.

Unfortunately, the curious mottled dragon followed—and was gaining on him.

Chapter 23

Imperial Ultimatum

Laetícia had just finished saying, "Is that all?" when Merry shouted.

"What do you mean, '*Is that all?*'" she said, her eyes wide and her face turning red. "There's a dragon in your garden with a mage sent from Sírénae."

"We've been expecting them," said Quintillius.

"We know how Sírénae's mind works," added Laetícia. "I'd appreciate it if you'd help Magister Callidus in, Merry. You can practice your line-of-sight gating."

"I'll step out on the balcony and alert the palace guards not to attack Xaxidiánus," said Quintillius. He called back to the trumpeter. "Tell the cooks to bring a fat ewe for the dragon," said the Governor-General.

"Roasted or live?" the trumpeter responded.

"Live," said Quintillius over one shoulder. "I expect the big fellow is starving after such a long flight."

The trumpeter departed, accompanied by the other musicians, who needed no encouragement.

Merry disappeared with a *pop* then reappeared a few moments later with another *pop* and a tall older mage in purple robes standing on the back of her flying disk.

"Magister Callidus, good to see you," said Laetícia as she helped Merry's passenger step down. "You must be tired after such a long flight."

"Good to see you and your husband as well," said the magister. "I'm not *that* tired. I napped on our flight and Xaxidiánus had some rest out by the harbor colossus."

"It is a restful spot, isn't it?" said Laetícia. "I go there from time to time to watch the waves roll in across the Ocean."

By this time, Merry had realized things wouldn't be happening the way she expected. She tamped down her temper and stepped up to hug Doethan and Rúth on the dais. "Congratulations," she said softly. "I'm so sorry I missed the ceremony."

"You'll have to make up for it by babysitting for us," said Rúth with only a hint of a smile.

"What?" said Merry.

"*What?*" said Doethan, much louder.

"At some point," Rúth clarified.

Merry laughed and Doethan hugged his new bride. "Is this how it's going to be?" he asked when he stepped back.

"Probably," said Rúth. She squeezed his hand and kissed him lightly on the cheek. "Even with a late start, I expect we'll have a *productive* partnership."

"Yes, my love," answered Doethan.

Quintillius walked back into the audience chamber through the same double doors to the balcony Rocky had used to enter. Behind him, the large, scaly black head of Xaxidiánus followed, like the nose of a bear entering a tent in search of food.

"You might as well attend the conference," Quintillius told the dragon. "I know Sírénae will insist on a complete report and you don't want to tell her you couldn't attend."

"You're very kind," said Xaxidiánus.

The other guests at the wedding had moved to the wall with the frescoes when they'd seen Xaxidiánus appear outside the balcony windows. Nûd spoke first.

"Are we welcome at this conference or is it for Roma only?" he asked.

"Of course, you're welcome," said Quintillius, "though I'm sure Sírénae would prefer it to be more private. I have nothing to hide from my allies."

"Allies?" asked Xaxidiánus.

"The kingdoms of Orluin and Occidens Province have signed a treaty of alliance against our mutual enemies," said Laetícia.

"Just yesterday morning," said Quintillius.

"That's going to make the upcoming discussion rather awkward," said Magister Callidus.

"Because Sírénae is going to invite Occidens Province to join her—or be destroyed," said Laetícia.

"That will be her message," said Magister Callidus. "With a few extra incentives. Support her conquest, or *Occidens Provinciae delenda est.*"

"Does she mean us, Mater?" asked Primus. He'd put down his tray and was holding his younger sisters' hands. "The province must be destroyed? It's our home."

"He means all of Orluin must be destroyed, or subjugated to Sírénae's will," said Verro, looking at Callidus and Xaxidiánus in turn. He turned to Dârio and nodded, receiving a nod in return. "Tamloch stands against the Siren Hawk."

"As does Dâron," said Nûd.

"And Bifurland," said Bjarni and Signý in unison.

"We'll make it unanimous, right my husband?" asked Laetícia.

"We will," said Quintillius.

"You really should listen to what Sírénae has to say before you decide," said Magister Callidus. "I'd hate to see all you fine people in chains."

"And I have *no* interest in flying back to the imperial fleet without following the emperor's instructions," said Xaxidiánus. "I wouldn't like seeing Magister Callidus fed to Thraxa."

"Who's Thraxa?" asked Tertia.

"Take your sisters to their play room," Laetícia ordered Primus. "Your father and I will be up to see you as soon as we can get free."

"Yes, Mater," said Primus. Seconda went willingly but Tertia wanted to stay. Primus had to tug her out of the audience chamber, crying.

"She might be a senior magister someday," Laetícia whispered to Quintillius.

"Or an emperor," he replied.

"Shall we begin?" asked Magister Callidus. "And for the record, I would prefer *not* to be dinner for a snow-gryffon."

"There are better ways to go, I'm sure," said Duke Háiddon.

"We should all stand on the dais," said Princess Rúth. "Shorter people—like me and Doethan and Merry—in front. Inthíra, come join us." Rúth waved to Inthíra and the talented wizard reluctantly joined them on the floor. Rúth organized the people of medium height on the first step and tall ones, like Nûd and Dârio and Verro and Felix on the top level. Rocky, with Chee still on his head, stood in back, while Laetícia and Quintillius were on either side of Magister Callidus.

"Could you angle the interface so she can see me?" asked Xaxidiánus. "At least my left is my good side."

"I'll try," said the magister.

"There's no end to the vanity of dragons," Nûd whispered to Bonnie.

"Is that from Ealdamon's *Epigrams?*" she asked.

"It's in the second volume," said Nûd. "If my grandfather ever publishes it."

"Everyone be quiet," ordered Princess Rúth in a tone that was instantly obeyed.

Magister Callidus took a ring from his finger, spoke an obscure phrase, and tugged on its edges. Three tones sounded and the ring expanded, showing a shimmering interface. Sírénae's stern, hawk-like face looked out at them. General Machaera and Admiral Pixo were behind her and Thraxa sat on her haunches to the emperor's right with Sírénae's hand stroking her feathers.

"What's this?" said Sírénae. "I wanted a *private* conference. Remove these non-Roma immediately."

"You'll talk to all of us or none of us," said Quintillius, his voice as hard and cutting as a spear point. "Say what you have to say and accept the consequences."

"Hah!" said Sírénae. "You and yours will need to accept the consequences if you reject my offer."

"Which is?" said Quintillius.

"Join me and rule whichever newly conquered kingdom you prefer as your new province as my viceroy," said Sírénae. "Reject me and your heads will be on pikes and your children will be my personal slaves for as long as they live—which I don't expect will be long."

"I'd prefer the odds of challenging you on the battlefield," said Quintillius.

"We outnumber you ten to one," said Sírénae. "And I have war elephants and dragons."

"I have allies who will stand with me against you," said Quintillius.

"We'd still outnumber all your forces combined by five to one," Sírénae replied. "You can't win against those odds. Join me and live. I will make the same offer to your allies. Become part of my new empire of Orluin and I will give you land and wealth and power as my vassals. Stand against me and you'll end up in chains—or with your heads displayed atop the walls of Nova Eboracum."

"We've heard your offer," said Quintillius. He looked over his shoulder and spoke. "Should we accept and join the Siren Hawk's empire of the west, my friends?"

"No!" came their united response.

"You have your answer," said Quintillius. "These lands are ours. Try and take them."

"I will," said Sírénae. "You can be assured of that." She smiled a knowing smile that made Quintillius concerned about what she would say next. "Laetícia," said the emperor. "You can tell Valens— if he ever recovers—that I have his son Valentius. Since you and Quintillius won't be joining me, I'll be sending him back to his father, one piece at a time." Sírénae stroked Thraxa's feathers and the snow-gryffon snapped her sharp beak. "Think on that," said the emperor. "And don't be too long about it."

The ring's interface went black, and the hoop of gold shrank back to a size that would fit on a finger. Magister Callidus put it on his left hand. He looked around the room, wondering if someone would decide to punish the messenger.

Xaxidiánus snorted and withdrew to the palace courtyard. He was bloodthirsty and loyal to his emperor, but even he disapproved of some of Sírénae's tactics.

Quintillius glared at Callidus and took a measured breath. His face turned fierce, and solemn, like one of the Afarican masks carved from ebony on the walls of his study. He regarded his allies and saw similar resolve in their faces. They were in this together. Laetícia put her hand on her husband's arm. No one spoke.

Then someone knocked on the doors to the audience chamber. A young cook with a dirty face stuck his head into the room.

"Who wanted the sheep?" he asked.

Chapter 24

The Cave of Jewels

Eynon looked over his shoulder and confirmed only a single dragon was following him. The rest still circled the dying mammoth. *Good,* thought Eynon. *Maybe I can handle one dragon—without using a fireball that would draw the attention of every dragon, wyvern, and gryffon for ten leagues.*

He tried various aerial maneuvers to increase the distance between him and his pursuer, swerving first left, then right. The mottled dragon followed his moves with ease and even gained a little. Eynon tried swooping up, but that course change caused him to lose airspeed while the dragon behind him grew still closer. He felt like a rabbit chased by a scaly, sixty-foot greyhound.

There was one more direction to try—Eynon could dive. He risked a second look over his shoulder. The mottled dragon was only a few feet behind him. He'd need the perfect place to pull off what he wanted to accomplish.

Ahead, Eynon spotted the range of hills he'd remembered from Peregrina's map. These were quite unlike the purple snowcapped mountains he'd flown over earlier. They were more like the mountains surrounding the Coombe back home. He could understand why such elevations wouldn't count as mountains by western standards.

The hills were directly below him now. They were covered with dark green pines so tightly clustered they looked almost black. The Cave of Jewels was southwest of a taller hill that should be easily visible because of an exposed white granite outcrop. He saw something white glint amid the dark pines on a hill ahead of him and steered in that direction. When Eynon was high above it, he dove for the exposed granite, confident the dragon behind him would follow.

Eynon had planned to do a quick change of vector and pop his flying disk straight up out of the way while the dragon struck the rock at high speed. He'd never tried anything like it on a flying disk and wasn't sure it would work. Then a voice inside his head told him he was being an idiot. The voice used Merry's exact intonation, and Eynon slapped his forehead. His brain was not-so-gently reminding him he was a powerful wizard and could use an *ad hoc* gate to escape.

Inches from the rounded upper surface of the granite, Eynon gated up a hundred feet vertically. The dragon wasn't able to stop *its* dive, however. It slammed into the stone snout-first, sending granite chips shooting off in all directions. Stunned, the mottled dragon's body hit the outcrop with equal force, generating more shards of rock in a great arc. Slowly, the dragon's great bulk slid down the curve of the granite extrusion, leaving a thin trail of red behind.

From his position high above, Eynon saw holes in the rock had been chiseled out by the impact of the dragon's skull and front claws leaving a caricature of a face carved on the white granite. He could see his former pursuer was still breathing, and its wingtips were flicking, so it wasn't dead, just stunned. *Dragons are such magnificent creatures that I wouldn't want to end one's life,* thought Eynon. *I'd better leave for the Cave of Jewels before it wakes up.*

After consulting Peregrína's map, Eynon set a course to the west and south, scanning the ground for any sign of the dolmen that marked the cave's entrance. It was only a few minutes before he saw the standing stones and heavy crosspiece. *How would they have ever been able to lift such heavy stones in the days before the Athican philosophers discovered magic?* he wondered. *Ropes and pulleys are fine for raising hay bales, but not for stone slabs as heavy as a dozen milk cows.*

Ancient construction methods weren't his current focus, however. Eynon landed in front of the dolmen and stowed his flying disk on his back. The bag of hollow, walnut-sized clay balls Rōlin had given him clacked together on his belt. Eynon observed his surroundings carefully and committed them to memory so he could *ad hoc* gate back easily if need be. The cave's entrance was between the standing stones. Eynon smiled when he saw that someone—probably Rōlin's father—had carved "Cave of Jewels" into the dolmen's lintel.

I'm glad I'm in the right place, thought Eynon. *I'd hate to enter the Cave of Snakes or the Cave of Spiders by mistake.* He triggered a glow ball, adjusted its brightness, and stepped inside.

The cave's mouth had a smooth floor and sides as if it had once been a river channel. When he was twenty feet past the entrance, Eynon realized the stretch of tunnel he'd just traversed had been smoothed by magic, not water. The true surface of the cave floor was before him. It was rough and marked by small pocks where pools of acidic water had eaten away the limestone. The surface was easier to walk on than the wizardry-smoothed floor, so Eynon continued forward and down, as the path he followed led deeper into the hill.

There were large, colorful beetles and other unusual bugs in evidence, crawling on the tunnel's wet walls. He was startled by a trio of segmented worm-like things half as long as his arm with hundreds of legs and mandibles that looked strong enough to chew through rock, marching up toward the ceiling in single file. *I'll stay away from them,* he told himself. Three dozen steps farther in and down, the tunnel he followed opened up into a vast cavern with long, tapered spikes of stone hanging down from the ceiling, rising up from the floor, and joining together to form thick pillars.

Eynon had heard about a small cave south of Caercadel back in the Coombe. A few of his cousins had been in it and said it was nothing special, so he had no idea caves could be so beautiful. The spikes and pillars were marbled with colors as if someone had melted a broadleaf forest in fall and poured the results over rocks. He stood, turning his head this way and that, trying to take in all the details of the cavern around him.

Then Eynon noticed someone had scratched a message on a large flat rock next to the path. An arrow pointed ahead, and the words above it read, "This way to the jewels." Eynon squared his shoulders and resolved he would return to the cavern with Merry someday to show *her* how pretty it was. He headed in the direction the arrow indicated. The path made a hairpin turn two hundred paces later and began a sharp descent. The creepy-crawly multi-legged creatures on the walls were getting bigger, but they didn't like the light from Eynon's glow ball and scurried away to avoid him.

Eynon's path continued farther and farther down, deeper into the roots of the hill, until it came to an end at a pool of some sort of gooey white paste. Eynon inhaled. The pool smelled as subtle as birch bark and as sharp as wild mint. He saw more dots of the white aromatic goo on the walls above the pool, like droppings on the floor of a dovecote.

Another message was scratched into the wall to his right. "See the jewels in darkness," it read. Eynon had come this far. He'd take the advice of the person who'd written the message. With a quick hand gesture, he dispelled his glow ball. Then he closed his eyes, so they would adapt to the darkness faster.

When Eynon opened his eyes, the ceiling was glowing. Uncountable tiny disks in dozens of colors, seemingly drawn from an overachieving rainbow, were densely packed in an intricate mosaic. They formed a pattern that Eynon's mind *wanted* to see even though he was confident the arrangement was random. He stared up at the disks and tried to determine what they were. *Could they be colored precious stones?* he wondered. *True jewels? Magestones? It doesn't seem likely.* Eynon generated distance-viewing lenses again and examined the ceiling in more detail.

The disks weren't rubies, sapphires, diamonds or emeralds—they were the colorful wing cases of beetles like the ones he'd seen when he'd first entered. Cold white and yellow light like the glow of fireflies filtered through the beetles' translucent wing cases to create the range of colors above him. The pool below was also glowing. He heard a soft *plop* in the goo in front of him and saw ripples circling out from where something had landed. Eynon watched the ceiling and saw a beetle release a tiny drop from the rear of its abdomen. He followed the drop until it hit the pool and created more ripples. *The pool must be filled with dragonsbane,* Eynon realized.

He called up another glow ball, unhooked the bag of hollow clay balls from his belt, and was about to kneel to fill them from the pool when he had another *you're-an-idiot* moment. He remained standing and created a ladle of solidified sound to scoop goo from the pool and direct it into each of the two dozen clay balls in turn. The process didn't take long and the level of dragonsbane in the pool didn't seem lower. *Good*, thought Eynon. *I might need more some day.*

Eynon had accomplished his quest but wasn't ready to leave. He refastened the bag of clay balls to his belt, leaned back, and snuffed out his glow ball for one last look at the cave's jeweled ceiling. He stood for perhaps a quarter hour, entranced by the pattern that wasn't really a pattern. From time to time, beetles would shift position in a dance with a purpose Eynon's mind couldn't fathom. He only knew he could watch the *jewels* for hours.

A strange tickling sensation brought Eynon back to reality with a start and more than a touch of panic. Something hard and sharp bit into his elbow. When he generated a new glow ball, Eynon saw that at least seven of the thick, segmented, multi-legged creatures were crawling on him and one was locked on to his right arm. *This isn't good,* he thought. *Not good at all!*

Chapter 25

The Streets of Nova Eboracum

"Tired of me already, my husband?" teased Princess Rúth as she watched Doethan dress. Chee had crawled into bed next to Rúth, enjoying the warm spot Doethan had recently vacated.

"Not at all, my love," Doethan replied. "It will take a few years for that." He fended off a pillow Rúth threw at him from her position in the bed. "You and your brother are returning to Riyas today to get plans started for the evacuation," Doethan continued. "While you're busy in Tamloch, I thought I'd find Merry and recruit her to help me connect with Távi and those street urchins I told you about."

"The ones you fed?" asked Rúth.

"The dough-ring man's brother-in-law fed them," said Doethan. "I just supplied the coin."

"Cold cash?" teased Rúth.

"It wasn't cold until after I enchanted it," Doethan replied.

"You always did have a soft heart," said Rúth, giving her new husband a tender smile. "Guard your purse and your person," she continued. "I've heard that the streets of Nova Eboracum are far from safe."

"I'll be fine," said Doethan. "I'm worried that Távi and the other street children won't be. I don't think they'll evacuate with the rest of the population. They're too afraid of being enslaved."

"With good reason, I expect," said Rúth. "For all that the Roma say they're civilized, slavery is barbaric. People aren't *things* to be owned."

"We can do something about it after we deal with the emperor," said Doethan.

"We can," said Princess Rúth. "And we will."

Doethan adjusted the folds of his robes, slipped on his boots, and crossed to Rúth on the bed they'd shared. He leaned down and kissed her firmly.

"I'm glad we stand together on that," he said.

"You're standing," said Rúth. "I'm still in bed. I didn't get a lot of rest last night."

"I found making up for lost time invigorating," said Doethan. He stroked Rúth's hair. She extended her hand and pointed toward the door.

"Go," said Rúth. "I'll join you at breakfast if you're still there after I take a leisurely bath."

"Yes, m'love," said Doethan. "Best of luck figuring out where to relocate the population of Riyas."

"Thank you, dear," said Rúth. "I expect Merry's caves will help."

"Especially if the mushrooms prove edible," said Doethan.

"Don't keep Merry too long," added Rúth. "Verro said he'd need her help locating the caverns beneath his emergency sanctum."

"I'll try," said Doethan. "Távi and the urchins are as skittish as newborn colts. They'll bolt if I don't handle this delicately."

"What do you hope to accomplish?" asked Rúth.

"Ensuring that gang of rapscallions stays safe when the emperor arrives," said Doethan. "I'd planned to offer them sanctuary in Tamloch—or Dâron, if they preferred. Assuming they'd be welcome in Tamloch?"

"Of course they would," said Rúth. "Children should be loved and protected."

"Even runaway slaves?" asked Doethan with a smile.

"Especially runaway slaves, if they really *are* slaves," Rúth replied. "Tamloch and Dâron and even the Clan Lands were founded by people from the White Isle and the Green who had no interest in being Roma slaves. It would be hypocritical for us not to welcome them."

"I knew there was a reason I loved you," said Doethan.

Rúth pulled Doethan's hand close to her mouth and pretended to bite his index finger. He didn't move his hand, but kept it there, enjoying her touch.

"Mmmmm," said Rúth.

"What are you thinking?" asked Doethan.

"I'm thinking I love hearing your voice. I love making plans with you. I love the way we can tease each other," said Rúth. "And I very much love being your partner." Her eyes twinkled, and she smiled up at Doethan.

"What can I say in reply except I agree in every particular," said Doethan. He rubbed his free hand beneath his eyes and straightened. "Now I've got to head for breakfast and find Merry. If you're not too slow in the bath, maybe you'll see us before we leave."

Chee perked up at the second mention of food and bounded from the pillow beside Princess Rúth to Doethan's shoulder. Doethan ignored the raconette to focus on his wife.

"Maybe," said Rúth. She slowly kissed each of Doethan's fingertips and released his hand, then smiled at his departing back as he left the room.

* * * * *

Breakfast was being served in a larger room than the one where Quintillius, Laetícia, and their children normally had their first meal. This room was long and narrow. It was filled with a wooden table big enough to seat more than twenty people comfortably. Doethan and Laetícia were the only ones currently seated there, however. They were enjoying hard-boiled quail eggs and toast.

Chee was stretched out in the middle of the table on his back. He was spinning an apple in all four paws and taking dainty nips from it at intervals, ignoring the conversations around him. Ace was above Chee in the rafters. He seemed to be stalking and eating *something,* but Doethan didn't want to think too hard on what his prey might be.

Merry held a thick slice of fine white manchet bread topped with butter and honey. She was forming *ad hoc* gates from one end of the room to the other every time she took a bite of bread.

Pop. Pop. Pop. The sounds were distracting, but Doethan was more amused than annoyed. He glanced at Laetícia and they shared a smile whose meaning was easy to translate. *Ah, youth!*

"Any luck gating to places you can't see?" Doethan asked Merry when her latest leap brought her to his end of the table.

"Not yet," said Merry. She licked a drop of honeyed butter from her upper lip. "I'm still trying." Two *pops* sounded.

"I have a thought," said Laetícia. "Emergency gates are like special *ad hoc* gates. They take you to a safe and familiar place. Maybe if I teach you how to make an emergency gate, it can help you extend the range of your line-of-sight gates?"

"That's worth a try," said Merry. She'd finished the bread, so she found a few slices of crisp bacon on a tray and repeated her previous maneuvers, this time with the accompanying sound for each jump being *crunch pop*.

Chee noticed the bacon as well. Without dropping his apple, he scooted down the table, snatched up a piece, and threw it toward the ceiling. Ace caught it before it began to descend and perched on a rafter to consume it.

"Have you decided where you want your emergency sanctum?" asked Doethan, after taking a moment to smile at the two familiars' antics.

"I think so," said Merry. "I was considering one of those—"

Doethan held up his hand to stop her. "Don't tell anyone," he said. "Not even me. Emergency gate locations are supposed to be secret."

"Oh," said Merry. She looked thoughtful for a moment and *crunched* without *popping*. "That makes sense. I feel honored that Verro let me learn the location of *his* sanctum."

"You should," said Laetícia. "He'll probably have to pick a new location for his emergency gate now. Especially since you've found those huge caves nearby, which means soon half of Tamloch will know its general position."

"Right," said Merry. "I'll need to do some scouting to confirm my own future sanctum's location, so I expect we'll have to put that project on hold for a while." She pointed the last remaining piece of bacon at Laetícia. "Unless you can gate me out to Fercha's tower or the quarry west of the Coombe?"

"I can probably spare the time for that later this afternoon," said Laetícia. "Once Quin and I work out the details of our evacuation, we have competent administrators who can move things forward without our personal supervision."

"The strength of Roma lies not in its legions but in its clerks," said Doethan, repeating an old maxim.

"There's more truth to that than most realize," said Laetícia with a grin. "What are you up to today?"

"I thought I'd find that merchant with the pole and buy more dough rings," Doethan replied. He didn't know how Laetícia would respond to him trying to rescue lost children from the streets of the provincial capital.

"Bring some back for my chicks," said Laetícia, accepting his answer. "And for me. I'd enjoy one for lunch."

"It would be my pleasure," said Doethan. Merry was at the far end of the table, so he called to her. "Please come with me," he said.

Crunch. Pop.

"For dough rings?" asked Merry, now standing beside him.

"For practice using your line-of-sight *ad hoc* gates to attack and defend," said Doethan. "I don't know of any other wizards with that capability, so your opponents won't expect it."

"If you need a good spot for training, there's a big park in the center of the island," said Laetícia. "We often use it for teaching skills to new wizards."

"I'll keep that in mind," said Doethan. "Are you coming with us, Chee?" he asked the raconette. The cute little beast might help attract and hold the interest of Távi and the other children.

"Chee!" said Chee. He threw his apple core at Doethan, but Merry popped in between them and intercepted it, wagging the core by its stem.

"Nice try, little buddy," said Merry. "Will you be riding on me or on Doethan?"

The raconette answered by launching himself at Merry's shoulders. She surprised him by popping out to the other end of the room, then jumping back in time to catch Chee before he hit the floor. "Chee," said Eynon's familiar, his voice and his eyes making it clear he wasn't pleased with how Merry had tricked him. The raconette frowned and reluctantly crawled up from Merry's arms to her shoulder.

Ace glided down from the ceiling in his flying carpet form and stood on Merry's flying disk in his small dog shape. He looked quizzically up at Chee with his long tongue lolling out. The raconette stared down, now more curious about Merry's familiar than afraid of him.

"Thank you for breakfast," said Doethan.

"Yes," said Merry. "Breakfast was delicious—and thank you for taking me west later."

"You're both welcome," said Laetícia. "Now off you go—and be sure to get some dough rings with seeds."

* * * * *

Doethan, Merry, Chee and Ace didn't have any trouble finding Távi and the other beggar-children. The dough-ring merchant had been selling his circular wares on the same street where Doethan had encountered him earlier. He'd been more than glad to sell his entire stock to the wizard and distributed the rings into six net bags holding a dozen rings each, three plain, three with seeds. Chee and Ace both got dough rings of their own. Chee preferred seeds, while Ace chose plain with a clearly understandable sniff of the appropriate bag.

The merchant requested payment in enchanted coins and Doethan was glad to comply. Merry watched Doethan connect a coin to a small congruency that channeled cold, following his movements carefully, while Chee and Ace chewed their rings, curled up together at Merry's feet.

Merry and Doethan stared at the two familiars and smiled but didn't say anything. They were pleased Chee and Ace were getting along.

"You try it," said Doethan after a few minutes.

"I'd be glad to," said Merry. The merchant handed Merry a small copper coin. After a single false start, she enchanted the coin to such a low temperature that it left a circular burn on Merry's palm before she inserted it into a dough ring, so it could be handled.

Doethan showed Merry how to identify the temperatures on the opposite sides of heat-and-cold spectrum congruencies and Merry was able to link another coin to chilly, but not bitterly cold temperatures.

"You can use Merry's first coin to turn water to ice," Doethan told the merchant. "That should prove valuable to you and your sister."

"Very much so, good wizards," said the merchant. "A thousand thanks to you and your apprentice." He bowed five times, took the enchanted coins, and left—Doethan assumed—for the bakery in the back of his brother-in-law's taverna.

Merry rubbed the frozen circle of skin on her palm and jumped when Ace's long tongue shot out and licked it for her. A few seconds later, the pain was much less intense. "Isn't *that* interesting?" she mused.

"What?" asked Doethan.

"Ace's tongue made my burn less painful," she replied.

"Maybe his tongue secretes something to numb what he catches for dinner before he eats it?" Doethan offered.

"Maybe," said Merry. She ruffled the fuzzy gray fur of Ace's head with one hand and scratched Chee's chin with the other. Both animals made contented sounds until Merry stopped.

"I'm glad they're getting along now," said Doethan.

"All it took was dough rings," said Merry. She grinned at Doethan then looked more serious. "How are we going to find your urchins?" she asked.

"We don't need to," Doethan replied. "They've found us. Hello, Távi."

Merry was surprised to see a young person of indeterminate age and gender step out from the shadows of one of the nearby buildings.

"Hello, your wizardness," Távi replied. "Will you be sharing some of those dough rings? The young ones are hungry."

"I'm sure they're always hungry," said Doethan. He held out a bag of plain dough rings and nodded to Merry to offer one with seeds.

"That's very kind, good wizards," said Távi. "You'll make a lot of younglings happy with your gifts." Távi clutched the bags and stared at Ace and Chee. "That's the strangest dog and the smallest raccoon I've ever seen. I see a lot of dogs and masked bandits when we scrounge for food that others have tossed away, and I've never seen anything like these two."

Ace trotted over to sniff Távi's legs while Chee came close and seemed to debate whether either of Távi's shoulders was wide enough to risk a jump before deciding they weren't.

"That's because they're not dogs or raccoons," said Merry in a voice that she'd use for talking to one of the children back at her father's barony. "I call Ace a rockhound and Chee is an animal from western Dâron called a raconette. I expect they're related to raccoons, but they're much cuter."

Merry's familiar blinked up at Távi. "I see why you call him Ace from his copper nose," said the youth. "But why is the little one Chee?"

"Chee," said the raconette as if on cue. He extended a paw.

Távi laughed and shook it gently. "That taught me!" Smoothing a tunic that was thin and patched but clean, Távi grew serious. "I doubt you came here just to buy me and me mates a meal, not that we didn't appreciate your gift earlier. It's been a long time since any of us have had hot stew. But nobody does nothin' for nothing. What brings you back to our territory?"

"We've come to warn you," said Doethan.

"The emperor's huge invasion fleet is on its way to Nova Eboracum harbor and the city will soon be evacuated," blurted Merry.

Doethan resolved to have the conversation about *loose lips* with Merry as soon as he could manage it.

"Doesn't worry us none," said Távi. "That rumor's made it up and down the White Way already and we're not worried. We can hide from the emperor the same way we hide from the O.P. bulls."

"O.P. bulls?" Merry asked Doethan.

"You mean the Occidens Province constables, I expect?" Doethan asked Távi.

"That's right in one, your wizardness," Távi replied. "When the emperor comes, we'll steal silently away and hide where no one can find us."

"In the cisterns?" asked Doethan.

"And the bigger sewers," said Távi. "We'll be cloaked in the *Cloaca Maxima*. We won't be found there."

"What will you eat?" asked Merry.

"Whatever we can find," said Távi. "Just like we do now."

"I came to offer you a better option," said Doethan. "I married a Tamloch princess yesterday."

"A bit late for an old man like you to take a wife, isn't it?" asked Távi.

"It is, but that's not my point," said Doethan, smiling at Távi. "My bride has offered you and yours permanent refuge from the emperor in Tamloch. They don't believe in slavery there."

"That's a kindness," said Távi, "but me and mine are going to stay here where we know our way around. Nova Eboracum is our home, even if our piece of the city is humble."

"I thought you might say that," said Doethan. He held out a plain gold band—a communications ring—to Távi. The youth tied the bags of dough rings to a rope belt and stared at Doethan's offering.

"What's this for?" Távi asked. "Nothing good comes of taking rich gifts from strange men, and you certainly count as strange, no matter how nice you seem."

"That's wise thinking," said Doethan. "This isn't a gift. It's a loan. If you give it back to me when I ask, I'll give you five gold aurums. That's far more than you'd be able to sell it for yourself."

"True enough," said Távi. His eyes focused on the ring.

"This is a communications ring," said Doethan. "It will let us stay in touch in case you ever decide to take me up on my offer to escape to Tamloch. You can also keep me posted on the emperor's doings once she arrives in the capital."

Távi relaxed. "I see," said the youth. "There *is* something you want from me. The wizard in the tower asks us for information now and again, too. The one with the braids and beads."

Merry smiled. Laetícia had tentacles everywhere.

"Find us somewhere private and I'll show you how the ring works," said Doethan.

Távi led Doethan and Merry and their menagerie into an alley and received instructions in making the communications ring work.

"You're good folk for foreigners," said Távi after slipping the ring on a thong that disappeared beneath tunic folds. "We'll keep you informed, though I hope it doesn't get so bad we need to leave the city."

"So do I," said Doethan. He turned to Merry. "Time to go, my one-time apprentice. Let's gain some altitude so we can spot that park Laetícia mentioned and see if you can *ad hoc* gate me there along with you."

"Come on, fellas," said Merry. She placed her flying disk on the cobblestones and Chee and Ace joined her when she stepped aboard. "Bye, Távi," she said as she and Doethan ascended then flew away.

"Isn't that something," said Távi to several other urchins who'd materialized from the alley's shadows. "It's odd though—the wizard in the tower pays us for our trouble."

"Not very much," said one of the smaller children.

"You're right about that," said Távi. "And dough rings will do for payment of a sort. Who's hungry?"

Chapter 26

Return to Sender

Magister Callidus thanked Quintillius for the dinner Occidens Province's governor-general had provided and for the comfortable bed and bath the senior wizard had enjoyed after his meal. Quintillius had been a gracious host, or as gracious as possible, given that Callidus was kept locked in his rooms overnight, but the magister had been released before dawn. The Governor-General's slaves and servants had fed him breakfast and given him bottles of wine and bags with sausage, cheese, bread, and dried fruit for his return trip to Sírénae and the invasion fleet.

Callidus rose on his flying disk then descended to settle into his saddle on the broad back of Xaxidiánus, who was taking up a large percentage of the palace gardens. The magister buckled himself in with thick leather straps, looked down, and addressed Quintillius. "Let me know if you change your mind," said the magister. "I don't want to be your enemy."

"Your so-called emperor does, however," said Quintillius. "Be sure to tell the Siren Hawk that Orluin stands united against her—and so do all the empires of the Imperium."

"You've heard word from across the Ocean?" asked Magister Callidus. "Who did you talk to? What did they say?"

"Sírénae can find that out for herself," said Quintillius, staring up at Callidus.

The magister nodded. His questions had been worth a try.

"Thank you for the sheep," said Xaxidiánus. "Mutton was a welcome change from fish."

"You're welcome," said Quintillius. "Our quarrel is not with you, but with the one you serve. You'd both be welcome in Occidens Province if *you* decide to change your loyalties back to the true Roma empire instead of your false emperor."

"Noted," said the dragon. "I hope I won't have to kill you."

Quintillius shook his head slowly. "Go then," said the Governor-General. "I hope I won't have to order *your* death."

Xaxidiánus unfurled his glossy, obsidian-colored wings, stretching them out before his departure.

"Wait!" said Quintillius.

"What?" asked Xaxidiánus. "You've decided to surrender after all?"

"I doubt that's the reason," said Magister Callidus.

"You'd be right," said Quintillius. He squared his shoulders and somehow seemed to stand even taller than his considerable height. "Answer me this. Why is Sírénae attacking Orluin instead of establishing her new empire in the undeveloped lands to the south of Dâron? She would find plenty of land there, and she wouldn't have to fight for it."

A rumble of laughter came from the massive lungs of Xaxidiánus.

"You've answered your own question," said Magister Callidus. "Sírénae *wants* to fight for her new lands. She wants to humble her enemies and make new slaves. I'd advise you to make peace with the emperor now, so you don't become a slave yourself."

"Let her try to enslave Orluin," said Quintillius. "I promise you she will fail." He frowned at Callidus and Xaxidiánus. "Your so-called emperor has overreached herself once already to be removed from the Tetrarchy. She will do so again when she tries to conquer Orluin. I guarantee it."

"We're talking in circles," said Xaxidiánus. "I have a long flight ahead and had best get on with it."

"I won't wish you safe travels," said Quintillius. "If I could control the weather, I'd wish for a dozen hurricanes to slam Sírénae's fleet."

"The beating of my wings is like a hurricane," said Xaxidiánus accompanied by more rumbles from his chest.

Callidus laughed as well at the standard example of dragon bravado. He shouted down to Quintillius. "I think he means you should stand back, since he's about to take off."

Quin stepped a few paces away from the black dragon and stood in front of a pair of doors leading back into the palace from the garden. Wind swirled, tossing mulch and dead leaves in spirals as

Xaxidiánus ascended. Quintillius watched the dragon until he disappeared over the eastern horizon.

* * * * *

"Did you get some rest?" Callidus asked Xaxidiánus after the coast of Orluin was only a thin dark line behind them.

"I did," said the dragon. "I was directed to a warm, sandy beach and slept undisturbed."

"At least there was no way to lock *you* in a room," said Callidus.

"You were a prisoner?" asked Xaxidiánus.

"My windows were barred, and my door was locked, but it was a comfortable prison, at least," said the magister. "My bed was soft, my blankets were thick, and my bathwater was hot."

"I'm glad you got some rest, my friend," said the dragon.

"And two good meals," said Magister Callidus. "Did you learn anything helpful?"

"Beyond Quintillius thinks he can order my death?" asked Xaxidiánus. "I don't understand how he's confident he could kill a dragon."

"Large ballista bolts, perhaps?" suggested Callidus. "We'll have to send you and your dragons out with wizards on your backs to provide shields."

"That's a good idea," said Xaxidiánus. "But I don't think that's what he meant. He sounded too sure he could give such an order and expect it to be carried out successfully."

"That is puzzling," said Callidus. "Considering there aren't any dragons in Orluin."

"Hmmm..." said Xaxidiánus, as his musing turned into a hum deep inside him.

"Did you hear something?" asked the magister.

"The servants who brought my second and third ewes were talking to each other," said Xaxidiánus. "I heard them say, 'He's not as big as the other ones.'"

"Interesting," said Callidus. "Are you sure they were referring to other dragons?"

"No," said Xaxidiánus. "Though it seemed that way from the context of their conversation. I don't understand it. I'm the biggest dragon in all the lands of the Imperium. I don't see how there *could* be larger dragons?"

"I don't either," said Callidus. "I don't think we need to bother Sírénae with unsupported rumors, do you?"

"Not when they call into question my status as the world's largest dragon," answered Xaxidiánus. "What do a couple of ignorant servants know, anyway?"

They flew on together in silence for several minutes before Callidus spoke again.

"What do you make of that comment Quintillius made about the entire Imperium being united against Sírénae?" asked the magister. "Do you think he's really heard from someone across the Ocean?"

"I expect he has," said the dragon. "Though even if he hasn't it would be a safe assumption. After her failed attempt—Umbrose's failed attempt—to assassinate Valens, it's clear that the empires of the North, South, East, and West, along with the city of Roma itself, would be against her."

Callidus was quiet for a few seconds. He often wondered if he'd made the right decision by staying with Sírénae and expected Xaxidiánus had similar thoughts, despite the emperor's control of his eggs.

"I was surprised by the way they reacted to hearing we held Valentius captive," said the magister. "I expected hot rage, not cold anger."

"Yes," said Xaxidiánus. "I saw their faces from the garden. You should warn Sírénae to expect a rescue attempt, if I read the humans' expressions correctly."

"I'll be sure to share that observation with her," said Callidus. "And I'll add more mages to the guard around Valentius, too."

"You could take some wizards from the contingent guarding my eggs," offered Xaxidiánus.

"Sírénae would remove my head for even suggesting such a thing," said Callidus. He rubbed his neck and sighed.

"Don't worry, old friend," said the dragon. "I'd recover your head and retain it as a keepsake."

"Somehow I don't find that even the least bit reassuring," said Callidus.

Chapter 27

Raven and Dragon

When he'd been younger, another boy in Haywall had dropped a centipede down the back of Eynon's tunic. Eynon hated having hundreds of tiny legs crawling down his spine then and hated having hundreds of much larger legs pressing spiked feet into his flesh even more now. The legs weren't the worst part, however. The sharp pincers embedded in the exposed flesh behind his right wrist were. They felt like hawk's talons digging into his skin, and Eynon could feel waves of pain radiating up his arm.

Don't panic, he told himself. A second pair of megapede pincers latched on beside the first. Part of Eynon's brain was signaling him that panic was indeed an appropriate response, but he pushed it down. Centering his thoughts, he generated forceps of solidified sound and mirrored spheres to help him see his back. One by one, he used the forceps to pick the multileggers off his robes and toss them off into the darkness, where he heard them scuttle away. That maneuver didn't help with the pair of segmented creatures already attached, however.

Channeling some of his fear, he shook his right arm like a wet dog and dislodged the lower legs of the two most aggressive multileggers, leaving them hanging by their jaws from his wrist. Using a sharp plane of solidified sound, he separated the megapedes' heads from their trailing body segments. The disconnected segments rolled on their backs and curled into spirals on the cave's floor with their angled legs kicking spasmodically.

The strong-jawed megapede heads remained attached to Eynon's wrist and seemed even more committed to staying there without their additional segments. Eynon could feel himself losing sensation in the affected wrist and wondered if the multileggers secreted some sort of natural anesthesia to dull the minds of their prey. He didn't need encouragement to breathe faster to push through any sort of soporific venom the creatures' jaws had injected.

Eynon wasn't really sure how to proceed. He knew that you could get ticks to release by holding them underwater or carefully putting a candle flame beneath them, but the megapedes' heads were far larger than any tick Eynon had ever encountered. Eynon remembered there were pools of water farther back up his path in the caverns, but he could try applying flame immediately. He focused, drawing on his blue magestone for control, and created a tiny blue-white flame just above his left index finger. With slow precision, he moved the flame just below one of the latched-on heads.

That proved to be a mistake, however. The pincers gripped his wrist still more tightly, if that was possible. Eynon nearly screamed. *I must be wrong about any anesthetic effect,* he thought. He lashed out with another plane of solidified sound and bisected one of the megapede heads. To his surprise, not only did the rear portion of the head fall off, the jaws on the front portion released and both halves fell to join the rear segments on the stone floor.

Eynon looked at the detached segment with the now-released pincers and realized there were structures in place in the creature's head that snapped those pointed mouth-parts into flesh and locked them there. When he'd cut the first head in half, he'd released the structures and unlocked the jaws. After a deep breath, he bisected the second head and watched it fall as well.

His right wrist looked like it had been bitten—twice—by a very large batsnake. All four punctures were bleeding. Eynon ripped a length of fabric from his undertunic and bound his wrist then collected all four head segments in another twist of fabric he put in his belt pouch so he could show them to Rōlin and Peregrína later.

Maybe they can spare a healing potion? thought Eynon. *Or maybe they can show me the recipe for making one myself.* Eynon's brain began to spin in spirals like the detached megapede segments. *I may have to rethink the nature of the megapedes' venom,* he considered. He blinked several times and yawned, inhaling the birch bark and wild mint scent of the pool of dragonsbane.

Can't sleep here, a still-functioning part of Eynon's mind determined. He summoned what focus he could and formed an *ad hoc* gate to the last place he'd committed to memory.

* * * * *

Eynon woke up with his right wrist throbbing and something sharp hopping about on his chest. He opened his eyes slowly and saw the biggest raven he'd ever seen staring at him. The bird was nearly the size of an eagle and it regarded Eynon curiously, then began pecking at the top of his robes.

"What are you doing?" he asked, not sufficiently coherent to realize the raven couldn't answer. He shook his head and saw that the big bird was trying to work his red magestone in its gold setting out from the folds of his robes. Eynon started to sit up but fell back. The raven walked a few inches along Eynon's chest to his collarbone and leaned its head—and sharp beak—directly above Eynon's eyes. "They're *my* eyes, not yours," said Eynon.

"Ca-caw!" said the raven. It turned around so its tail feathers tickled Eynon's nose and returned to pecking at his red magestone and its shiny setting.

Shaking his head to clear it, Eynon drew on the power of his red magestone and formed a sphere of solidified sound around the raven, then lifted the sphere six feet above his chest. Using his left arm, not his right, he levered himself up and managed to stand. A quick look around confirmed his location. Eynon had gated back to the dolmen marking the entrance to the Cave of Jewels.

"I guess I should be glad you're the only thing to find me," he told the raven. "A bear or a cougar would have been more of a challenge— to say nothing of that dragon who'd been chasing me."

The raven regarded Eynon from inside its spherical prison. It tried to climb the sphere's smooth walls but slipped back to the bottom of the sphere after every attempt. Eynon didn't like the raven's expression. It felt like the raven had gone from regarding him as a convenient perch for stealing a sparkling treasure to viewing him as a major annoyance. "Ca-ca-ca-*caw!*" Eynon heard as the raven pecked angrily at the invisible bubble of force that held it.

"Sorry, bird," said Eynon. "I want to keep my magestones *and* my eyes for the present, and if I read things right, you think they should be yours."

"Caw!" said the raven in confirmation.

Eynon extended his right arm and examined his wrist. The skin where the megapedes had bitten him was hot, red, and puffy. He tried to rotate his wrist and found the joint stiff and slow to move. *I really need a healing potion,* he thought. *I hope Rōlin and Peregrína have one made already.*

The angle of the sun told Eynon he hadn't been asleep for very long. Something nagged at the back of his brain. He'd been hurt—but so had the dragon who'd been chasing him. He'd better check on the mottled brown dragon with the black wings to see if it had recovered.

Eynon pulled his flying disk from his back with his left hand, boarded it, and set off toward the granite outcrop where he'd left the dragon. It would be enough to confirm his scaly pursuer was no longer there, but if for some reason it had a more serious injury, Eynon resolved to do what he could to assist. If the dragon decided to attack him, it would also provide Eynon with an opportunity for testing his newly acquired supply of dragonsbane.

I have no idea how dragonsbane works, he considered. *Does it repel dragons like a skunk's spray, or act like catnip does on cats?* The thought of a dragon the size of a Bifurland longship rolling around on the ground like a house cat that was *high* made him smile. Eynon headed off toward the granite outcrop where he'd left the dragon, distractedly carrying the raven in the sphere of solidified sound along for the ride.

Eynon approached the granite outcrop carefully—though less so than he would have if his mind wasn't muddled by the venom from the megapedes. He laughed when he saw the simplified human face the dragon's collision with the mountainside had created but was pleased to see the dragon was no longer collapsed at the bottom of the outcrop's steep slope. He descended to check for signs of blood, which would have indicated his former pursuer had more severe injuries, but saw only boulders and mounds of scree at the base.

Good, thought Eynon. *I can go back to Rōlin and Peregrína's home.* He was about to trigger an ad hoc gate when a shadow loomed above him—the mottled brown dragon with black wings. The creature came to earth a dozen yards in front of Eynon. Its landing sent dust and small rocks into the air, but it made no threatening move.

"Come with me," said the dragon as it extended its head closer to Eynon. "The boss wants to meet you."

Chapter 28

Dragons' Tower

"The boss?" asked Eynon, somewhat startled. It was disconcerting to have a dragon's snout so close to his face.

"That's what I said," the dragon rumbled. "Follow me—or hop on if you don't want to fly yourself."

"I'll fly, thanks," said Eynon. He was curious. The only dragons he'd dealt with before had been Viridáxés and Zûrafiérix, and they'd been bigger than wizards' towers. The prospect of meeting the leader of a weyr of wild western dragons intrigued Eynon. Part of his brain also realized his sense of caution was diminished by the megapedes' venom, but that part wasn't strong enough to convince him not to follow along.

The mottled brown dragon with black wings seemed polite, thought Eynon. He noticed, a bit late, that some of its scales seemed damaged from its collision with the granite outcrop. Eynon was glad the dragon didn't seem to hold a grudge—or perhaps its loyalty to orders from its boss overrode the dragon's personal desire for payback. *Good enough,* Eynon considered.

"You may want to reconsider," said the dragon. "It's more than thirty leagues to our destination."

"Just fly," said Eynon. "I'll keep up." He found a spot above and behind the dragon where the wind from its wide wings didn't interfere with Eynon's own flight. He watched the dark, fir-clad hills speed by below and saw high plains ahead as they traveled northwest and into territory Eynon hadn't seen on his trip *to* the Cave of Jewels. The clay spheres filled with dragonsbane rattled in their net bags on his belt.

Eynon made a megaphone of solidified sound and shouted to his guide. "Where are we going?"

"To the Dragons' Tower," said the mottled brown dragon, as if that was all the explanation Eynon could possibly need.

"What's that?" asked Eynon, unwilling to stop probing for details.

"You'll know it when you see it," said the dragon, who proved easy to follow despite his conversational evasions.

Eynon's right wrist continued to throb and his head was beginning to ache, too. His mind felt fuzzy, but he pushed through it and tried to get more information. "Do you have a name?" he asked. "My name is Eynon."

"Brünedíxés," said the dragon, snapping his jaws shut when he'd finished speaking.

Getting more from the dragon would be like pulling teeth, Eynon determined. *Long, scimitar-like teeth at that.* "There were a lot of dragons circling above that mammoth," he noted. "Were they part of your weyr?"

"Not *my* weyr," said Brünedíxés. "The boss's weyr."

"Oh," said Eynon. "Where's the boss's weyr?"

"I told you," said Brünedíxés. "The Dragons' Tower."

Eynon nodded then realized Brünedíxés wouldn't be able to see his gesture. "I'm sorry," he said. "My head's not very clear at the moment."

"Caw!" said the raven inside the sphere of solidified sound that was trailing Eynon. He turned, surprised to realize the raven was still there.

"Should I set you free?" asked Eynon. "I didn't mean to keep you captive for so long."

"Ca-Caw!" exclaimed the bird. It pecked at the sphere and gave Eynon a look that made him feel like more of an idiot than a sharp word from Merry could.

Eynon dispelled the sphere with a gesture and expected the now-released raven to fly off, but instead it kept up with his speedy passage, circled his head, and landed in front of his feet on the leading edge of his flying disk. "Don't peck my feet!" said Eynon. He cut off a small slice of sausage from the bag Peregrína had given him and dropped it next to the raven as a peace offering.

The raven looked up and tilted its head to regard him with one eye, snatched up the sausage in its beak, and turned back to watch Brünedíxés.

Put in my place by a raven, thought Eynon. After the bird ate the sausage, it hopped from the front edge of Eynon's flying disk to his right shoulder. It didn't seem to weigh more than Chee. *Hollow bones,* Eynon realized with a smile. He readied a small shield of solidified sound to protect his eyes in case that proved necessary and leaned forward into the wind.

Man, bird, and dragon flew on for nearly an hour before Eynon spotted something odd on the horizon. "What's that strange-looking mountain?" Eynon asked Brünedíxés. He had to shout to ensure he was heard.

"That's our destination—the Dragons' Tower," Brünedíxés answered. "We should be there soon."

Steering by instinct, Eynon's full attention focused on the unusual mountain—if it was a mountain. It looked like the stump of a tree tall enough to reach the Moon, and Eynon judged it to be nine hundred or perhaps a thousand feet tall. Its sides were vertical, except where they tapered out slightly near the base.

From their current distance, it seemed to be made of great uprights, cut lumber posts with sharp angles. Eynon thought it looked like it was made of stone pillars ripsawed and glued together into a weathered, integrated structure. The tower's summit was flat, or appeared so, and the entire formation was all the more impressive because it rose up from an otherwise featureless plain.

Brünedíxés adjusted his course to head directly toward the tower.

Eynon copied his maneuver. *I may have a chance to find out more details about the strange tower soon,* he realized.

Brünedíxés angled upward as they approached until they were above the tower's summit. Eynon was amazed to see that the top of the tower wasn't flat but formed a deep bowl. Inside the bowl was a writhing mass—of dragons.

It's more like a nest of huge snakes than the well-ordered collection of dragons I imagined a weyr must be, thought Eynon. *Then again,* he considered, *stories aren't always right.*

Most of the dragons had hides of muted colors that matched the browns and tans of the surrounding landscape. Several bore bright yellow and black patterns, like immense yellowjackets, and a few seemed almost metallic, with shining scales in steel, copper, brass, and bronze.

The largest dragon by far within the bowl or the nest or the weyr was the color of rusty iron, with ochre and sienna wings and a vast tapered head like a spear point. Perhaps a third of the size of Viridáxés and Zûrafiérix, Eynon was confident *this* dragon was the one Brünedíxés considered the *boss*.

When his scaly guide dove into the twisting collection of dragons in the bowl at the top of the Dragons' Tower, Eynon decided not to follow Brünedíxés. He gently touched down on a wide, flat ledge of rock that circled the bowl. Its surface seemed made of thousands of uneven stone hexagons. Eynon balanced his flying disk on top of one of the taller hexagons and glanced over his shoulder, confirming that the view of the land around him was indeed spectacular. His attention immediately returned to the bowl, however.

The massive head of the rust-colored dragon was now just a dozen feet from Eynon. Its snout sported hundreds of red-stained teeth as long as broadswords, and Eynon noticed what he thought might be part of a mammoth's furry ear stuck between two of them. The great dragon's chest rumbled and Eynon prepared a protective sphere of solidified sound in case the *boss* tried to eat him in one bite.

"I'm so glad you could come," said the rust-colored dragon in a deep, cultured voice. "We don't have visitors here very often."

Eynon exhaled and relaxed slightly. In his experience, which was limited, visitors were seldom eaten. He summoned his courage and spoke. "I am honored to visit, O Great One. My name is Eynon of Haywall."

"Kârkingórēx at your service, young wizard," said the rust-colored dragon. "I am responsible for the dragons of the tower."

"He's the boss," said Brünedíxés from below. His words were repeated by a dozen other dragons farther down in the bowl.

"As they say," noted Kârkingórēx, "I ride herd on these wild wyrms and try to teach them manners. If that makes me their boss, then so be it."

"I was afraid you might eat me," blurted Eynon in a moment of candor.

"Some of these dragons might have," said Kârkingórēx, "without my civilizing influences. Take particular care with the yellow and black ones."

"I will," said Eynon, thinking he'd planned to do that even before the warning. "I take it you're not a wild western dragon?"

"Certainly not," said Kârkingórēx. "My egg was brought across the Ocean by the wizards of the First Ships. After I hatched, I was given an education by the First Mages and placed in a cavern full of magestones in Tamloch to grow."

"Fascinating," said Eynon. "I think I've met two of your clutch mates."

"Really?" asked Kârkingórēx. "Which ones?"

"Viridáxés and Zûrafiérix," answered Eynon. "He's green and she's blue."

"I know them well," said Kârkingórēx. "Viridáxés was a hot head, but Zûrafiérix..." The rust-colored dragon's voice trailed off as if he was reliving ancient memories.

"Zûrafiérix is quite wise," said Eynon.

"And quite lovely," said Kârkingórēx. "Of course, they were both light gray when we shared lessons together."

"Buried dragons must soak up the color of the magestones around them," said Eynon.

"That seems to be true for me, at least," said Kârkingórēx.

"And for Viridáxés and Zûrafiérix," Eynon replied.

"I would love to see them again," said Kârkingórēx. "Zûrafiérix the Fair, especially."

"They're far to the east on an island off the southern coast of Tamloch," said Eynon. "I expect they'd be pleased to see you."

"I'll have to consider a trip there," said Kârkingórēx. "If I can figure out how to ensure that my *associates* don't eat an entire wisent herd—or each other—in my absence."

"Best of luck with your travel plans, then," said Eynon.

"Thank you, Eynon," said Kârkingórēx. He paused and put the tip of a front claw to his jaw and tapped it twice. "I'm being a poor host," he said. "What brings you to the vicinity of the Dragon's Tower?"

Eynon thought it unwise to mention dragonsbane, so he told the truth, in a limited fashion. "Rōlin and Peregrína said I should see the Cave of Jewels," he said. "They said it was spectacularly beautiful, and they were right."

"If you say so," said Kârkingórēx. "I stuck my head inside the entrance once and nearly choked, it smelled *so* bad."

"I'm sorry," said Eynon. "The crystals and spikes and pillars are amazing."

"I'll take your word for it," said Kârkingórēx. "I should have guessed you know the cartographers. I visit them from time to time and they read to me."

"You enjoy books?" asked Eynon.

"In principle," said Kârkingórēx. "They're so much smaller than I am, I can't read the fine print myself."

"That's understandable," said Eynon. "I wish I had a book with me. I'd be glad to read to you."

"Perhaps you can stop back later and do so," said Kârkingórēx. "I love history books."

"So do I," said Eynon. "I'll be glad to bring one to read to you once I learn to be a better wizard and stop a Roma invasion."

"The Roma are invading?" said Kârkingórēx. His huge spear-point head bobbed up and down. "That changes things. Now I'll have to visit Viridáxés and Zûrafiérix to find out what they plan to do about it. Stopping the Roma from gaining a foothold in Orluin is important."

"Things are more complicated in that regard than you might think," said Eynon. "You'll want to talk to Rōlin and Peregrína, so they can bring you up to date on the current situation."

"I shall!" said Kârkingórēx. "I'm *so* glad you stopped by. I wish I had more visitors like you."

"It was a pleasure meeting you as well," said Eynon. "Unfortunately, I have to get back to my studies. I have a lot more magic to learn."

"Give my best to the cartographers," said Kârkingórēx. "Let them know I'll be stopping by soon."

"I will," said Eynon.

"Caw!" said the raven.

"And if you need to contact me, just tell the bird," said Kârkingórēx. "She has a particular talent for getting messages to me quickly."

"Ca-Caw!" the raven confirmed.

"Th-thanks?" said Eynon, looking at the bird from the corner of his eye and wondering what special magic *she* might have.

"Fly safely and swiftly," said Kârkingórēx.

"You, too," said Eynon. "Goodbye!"

Eynon lifted his flying disk from its hexagonal stone perch and headed west into the sun. He made tinted lenses from solidified sound to protect his eyes. Soon, the Dragons' Tower was only visible as a dot on the eastern horizon behind him.

"Do you have a name?" Eynon asked the raven. "Or should I just call you Bird?"

"Corvi," said the raven.

"I thought it would be something memorable," said Eynon. "It's a pleasure to meet you, too, Corvi."

"Ca-Caw!" Corvi replied.

Eynon was pleased with another key piece of information he'd learned from Kârkingórēx. Dragons didn't like the smell of dragonsbane. That made Peregrína's mention of a *Skunk* spell self-explanatory. His right arm was still painful, though meeting the big rust-colored dragon had distracted him from his injury for a while. He didn't relish the hours of flight time remaining to return to Rōlin and Peregrína's.

Corvi made a clicking sound with her beak that sounded like *pop!*

Eynon slapped his forehead with his left hand, called himself an idiot, and *ad-hoc*-gated back to the cartographers' home in the valley south of Melyncárreg.

Chapter 29

Practice in the Park

Merry and Doethan flew north up the center of Insula Montes, away from Nova Eboracum at the island's southern tip. The land below them grew more varied, with hills and outcrops of gray granite poking out through the forests of oak, pine, and tulip trees that covered much of the surface. A few miles north of the city walls, Merry spotted a long, wide plot of cleared ground marked by a small blue lake, huge domes of pale stone, and a few dozen tall trees crowned with spring-green leaves. They were mostly oaks and had massive trunks that extended a hundred feet or more into the air. To her eye, Merry thought the trees must be at least a century and a half old. They were every bit as big as the largest trees on her father's estates back in the Rhuthro Valley.

Before the two wizards could touch down inside the cleared boundaries of the park, Ace jumped from Merry's flying disk and glided toward a towering oak. He was spotted by bushy-tailed squirrels who dove deeper into the oak's leafy canopy. Temporarily thwarted, Ace circled on currents of air warmed by the open parkland and looked for squirrels foolish enough to show their small black noses. Chee leaped off just before Doethan and Merry landed. He scampered to the oak Ace was circling and started climbing.

"Looks like the boys will be enjoying themselves," said Merry.

"But maybe not the squirrels," Doethan replied. He kept his feet in the leather straps of his flying disk, so Merry did likewise. "I want to see you use your unique talent for line-of-sight *ad hoc* gate-making. I've never known another wizard who could do it."

"Maybe I'm like Eynon," said Merry. "I didn't know I *couldn't* do it, so I did it."

"That could be it," said Doethan. "I certainly tried forming *ad hoc* gates when I was learning wizardry but couldn't do more than form an emergency gate."

"Which I still need to do," said Merry.

"Later," said Doethan.

"You said you wanted to help me learn how to use my line-of-sight *ad hoc* gate-making skills for attack and defense," said Merry. "Where do I start?"

"First, tell me your best forms of offensive magic," said Doethan. "You've learned a lot since you were *my* apprentice—of a sort—and I want to know what you've got to work with."

"I can throw fireballs," Merry answered, "though they're lightning bugs next to Eynon's house fires."

Doethan nodded and motioned her to continue. Eynon's red magestone helped him form spectacularly powerful fireballs.

"I can also create lightning bolts, blasts of cold, and missiles made from solidified sound."

"Good," said Doethan. "All those spells are useful offensively."

"Maybe," said Merry. "I don't tend to use them very often. My favorite attack magic is tight light."

"Fercha must have shown you that," said Doethan. "I never had a chance to earlier."

"She said I had a knack for it," said Merry. "You're good, too. I watched you use tight-light beams when you dueled with Hibblig."

"They're subtle—good for when you need a kitchen knife, not a battle axe," said Doethan.

"Not that you were all that subtle using them against Hibblig," Merry teased.

"I saw you spin Hibblig and pin him to the ceiling of the Conclave's Great Hall after the duel," said Doethan. "Fercha's right. You do have a special talent for tight light."

"Thank you," said Merry. "How will that help me leverage my line-of-sight *ad hoc* gate-making skills?"

"By keeping your opponents off balance, of course," said Doethan. "Most wizards don't use spheres of solidified sound for protection. They prefer hemispheres, so they can send spells back against their enemies more easily. You can jump behind them and attack faster than they can respond and reset their shields."

"Maybe," said Merry.

"Let's give it a try," said Doethan. "Gate up to the top of that out-crop and shoot beams of tight light at my shield. Then pop behind me and tap the back of my head—gently if you please. I'll see if I can switch my defensive shields fast enough to avoid being tapped."

"That sounds like fun," said Merry. She rose a few feet, then Doethan heard a *pop* and saw Merry standing on top of a tall granite dome on the left. He waved, and she waved back. Then Doethan heard Merry shout in alarm. "Ahhhh!" she cried, tossing something that looked like a thick black rope from the top of the dome. As it began to fall, Ace zoomed to catch it and started to consume the snake even before he joined Merry on top of the rocky, gray extrusion.

"Are you safe?" said Doethan, making a cone of solidified sound to help amplify his words.

Pop! Merry appeared by his side and answered. "I'm fine," she said. "I wasn't expecting the top of the dome to be occupied. It wasn't a shake-tail, or one of the other venomous snakes, so I was never in any danger. It just startled me."

"Ace seems happy you found him something for lunch," said Doethan.

"He's a good boy," said Merry. "Let's try this again." *Pop!*

Doethan saw Merry was back on top of the dome. He created a hemispherical shield in front of him that protected him from the ball of lightning Merry tossed his way. He also generated a few small spheres of solidified sound for a special purpose and sent them on a roundabout course toward the outcrop. A moment later, Doethan was not surprised when he felt a gentle tap on the back of his head from a bar of tight light sent from Merry's fingertips. She had followed Doethan's instructions and gated behind him.

"Nicely done," said Doethan, turning around and smiling at Merry. "Try it again and see if you can do it faster."

"Glad to," said Merry. She *popped* back to the top of the outcrop and was about to throw another ball of lightning at Doethan when a dozen granite pebbles Doethan had transported in bubbles of solidified sound collided with her back and neck.

"Got you!" said Doethan.

"Hey! That stings!" Merry protested. She *popped* back to stand next to Doethan.

"I hope that will make the lesson stick in your mind," said Doethan. "Never assume your opponent is stupid," he said.

"And expect the unexpected," said Merry. "Right. I should have known better."

"Yes," said Doethan. "You should." He grinned at her. "Again, please."

"Yes, good wizard," said Merry. She *popped* back to the top of her outcrop and was successfully able to tag Doethan with beams of tight light three out of four times.

Ace had finished eating the snake Merry had startled and had returned to circling the big oak Chee had climbed. From inside the canopy of new spring leaves, Merry and Doethan heard a loud *Cheeeee!* and saw several branches shaking. A dozen squirrels jumped down from the tree and shot toward a second large tree nearby. Ace caught one of them in his jaws and swallowed all of it except the squirrel's bushy tail, which was left on the grass like an oversized caterpillar. Chee jumped down from the first tree and capered over to Doethan, who gave him a dough ring.

"You're as bad as Rowsch chasing muskrats," said Doethan, wagging a finger at Chee. The raconette waved his dough ring at the wizard and bit off an inch of the ring's circumference.

Pop!

"Are we done now?" asked Merry from beside Doethan.

"Let's do a few more," Doethan replied. "Remember to think in three dimensions. You can gate *up* as easily as *over*. That could be helpful for defense, not just offense."

"Good advice," said Merry.

Pop!

Doethan looked for Merry back on top of the granite outcrop, then remembered too late to look up. Ten spears of tight light formed a stockade around him before he had a chance to generate a shield.

"Well done," said Doethan. "Dispel these and we'll see how you can use your line-of-sight *ad hoc* gates for defense."

"Right," said Merry as Ace glided down to land beside Chee and the wizards. Ace looked at Doethan, begging with his reflective silver eyes.

"You can have a dough ring, too," said Doethan. He removed one from a bag and tossed it high in the air. Ace caught it before it began to descend, then settled beside Chee to eat it.

"You're spoiling them," said Merry.

"True," said Doethan. "But they're both so cute."

"The squirrels probably don't think so," teased Merry. She prepared to gate to the far end of the park, but Doethan stopped her.

"Wait!" he said. "Can you take someone with you when you *ad hoc* gate?"

"I don't know," said Merry. "Do you want me to take you with me?"

"I was thinking you could take Ace or Chee," said Doethan.

Merry picked up Chee and held him in her arms. The raconette didn't mind. He even offered Merry a bite of his dough ring, but she declined. "Here goes," she said. *Pop!* A beat later she and Chee were on top of the granite outcrop. Chee waved, then climbed on Merry's shoulder so she could wave, too. *Pop!* Merry was back beside Doethan.

"Good to know you *can* take others with you," said Doethan. "Let's see if you can transport Ace riding on your flying disk, not just Chee in your arms.

Merry began to call to Ace, but the rockhound was already trotting over to her. He stood next to Merry on her flying disk in his terrier form. "One more time," said Merry. *Pop!* Merry, Chee *and* Ace were on top of the outcrop. She *popped* back, took Doethan's arm, and *ad hoc* gated the wizard to the rock and back as well before he could protest.

"Interesting," said Doethan. "We can test the limits of what you're able to transport later. For now, Ace and Chee can stay with me and I'll try various offensive spells against you. You should be able to gate out of the way if you see them coming."

"I have a different idea," said Merry. "Try and hit me!" She disappeared and reappeared at the far end of the park.

Doethan threw a ball of lightning at her, but Merry *popped* to random spots around the park faster than he could take proper aim. After several misses, Merry stopped gating and stood still back on top of the granite dome. Knowing the rock wouldn't burn, Doethan tossed a fireball at Merry's stationary figure. To his surprise, the fireball passed right through Merry's form and he felt fingers tapping on his shoulder.

"Always expect the unexpected," he said, turning around to smile at Merry. "You generated an illusion that you were standing there and gated behind me."

"Correct," said Merry. "You taught me well. And the hiss of your fireball hid my *pop* when I gated next to you."

"I'd say Inthíra taught you well, at least where illusion-magic is concerned," said Doethan. He was grinning and gave Merry a hug. Ace and Chee crowded in to join the two wizards.

"Have we practiced enough for now?" asked Merry.

"I believe we have," said Doethan. "The next step is dealing with multiple foes, and we'll need to recruit some help for that."

Merry looked down at Ace, who had finished his dough ring in a single gulp, and Chee who was licking seeds from his dough ring off his tiny fingers. "I don't know about you," she said to Doethan, "but *I'm* hungry. Let's get some lunch."

"We can fly to the governor-general's palace," said Doethan. "Laetícia will see that we're fed."

"I have a better idea," said Merry as she encouraged Chee and Ace to join her on her flying disk again. "Let's see if Távi's crew can help us find the taverna run by the dough-ring man's brother-in-law. I want to see how he's using my coin and would love a mug of *cold* cider."

Chapter 30

A Raven at the Door

Tap. Tap-tap. Tap-tap-tap.

"Is someone at the back door, Peregrína?" asked Rōlin.

"I'll see," his wife answered. She walked down the hallway from their shared studio to the kitchen and opened the small door-within-a-door to see who was there but couldn't see anyone. The tapping repeated, but from the area of her shins, so Peregrína opened the door to see a big black raven poised to peck again. Sprawled on the three stairs leading up to the back porch behind the bird was Eynon. She thought their new young friend was unconscious. "Rōlin!" shouted Peregrína. "Come quickly! Eynon's hurt."

Rōlin's rapid footsteps preceded his arrival, and together the two older wizards carried Eynon inside and gently placed him in the bed he'd used the previous night. They saw his wrist was swelled to the size of a brain apple, the light green or bright yellow fruit that grew on bow-wood trees.

Peregrína noticed the pair of pincher marks. "Giant fire ants?" she suggested.

Rōlin inspected the twist of cloth hanging out of Eynon's pouch and saw the decapitated heads of big multileggers. "Megapedes," he said. "I'll get a healing potion."

"Better run," said Peregrína. "He's left this untreated far too long."

Rōlin's answer was the sound of his quickly receding footsteps.

"Caw!" said the raven, who—unnoticed—had followed the wizards to the bedroom.

Peregrína removed Eynon's belt, belt pouch, and the attached net bag of clay balls filled with dragonsbane and put them on the chest at the foot of the bed. Then she slid Eynon's new blue wizard's robes and undertunic off over his head, taking care not to put pressure on his right wrist. Peregrína tossed the clothes on the chest, where Rōlin could magically launder them later. Eynon was still wearing his small clothes.

After gently easing Eynon under the bed covers, Peregrína stared more closely at his puffy right wrist. She didn't like the look of it, so she generated a torus of solidified sound big enough to go around his wrist, then opened a congruency inside the donut-shaped ring that linked to chilled arctic seas. The torus promptly filled with frigid water. Peregrína removed a tiny bit of heat and the water turned to ice inside the ring, keeping Eynon's wrist cold and preventing it from swelling larger from the megapedes' bites.

Eynon tossed his head and moaned softly from the strange new sensation. "Dragons," Peregrína thought she heard him say. *"So many* dragons..."

"I think he found the Dragons' Tower," Peregrína told Rōlin when her husband walked into the bedroom a moment later. He was carrying not one, but *three* bottles of healing potion.

"He's lucky Kârkingórēx was in a good mood," said Rōlin.

"Because he's alive?" asked Peregrína.

"Precisely," said Rōlin. "There are days when that old wyrm would just as soon eat you as talk to you."

"C-c-c-caw!" affirmed the raven, who had moved to perch on the bed's headboard.

"You don't think he told Kârkingórēx about the other two great dragons, do you?" asked Peregrína. She held Eynon's head up and poured a bottle of healing potion down his throat.

"I hope not," said Rōlin. He moistened a cloth with healing potion from the second bottle, dispelled the ring of ice, and bathed the young wizard's wrist. "A hundred wild dragons could cause immense damage back in the settled part of the continent."

"Caw! *Click click click!* Caw!" said the raven. Its vocalizations sounded like laughter.

"I guess we have an answer to that," said Peregrína. "Didn't anyone teach that boy to let sleeping dragons lie?"

"I doubt Kârkingórēx, Brünedíxés, and the other dragons at the tower were sleeping when Eynon found them," said Rōlin.

Peregrína took the cloth from her husband and continued to rub healing potion directly into Eynon's wrist. She could already see substantial improvement. The swelling had decreased significantly and Eynon's hand, wrist, and forearm no longer felt quite so warm to the touch. *My ice ring helped with that,* she thought.

Rōlin watched Peregrína work. "Looks like we caught it in time," he said.

"Eynon's wrist is healing, at any rate," said Peregrína. "We don't know what the megapedes' venom did to his mind."

"True enough," said Rōlin. "My father's journals noted strange reactions in some people who'd been bitten. I never talked with him about it directly, but the account I read said the woman bitten by megapedes compared it to the way she felt after eating cactus buds."

"Who *does* that sort of thing?" protested Peregrína. "You'd never catch *me* eating cactus buds." She frowned and continued bathing Eynon's wrist. "We'll have to keep a close watch on the lad for a few days, I expect," she said. "We don't want him sending fireballs at things that aren't really there."

"Agreed," said Rōlin. "Wizards who live in log houses shouldn't throw fireballs. At least not inside." The corners of his mouth rose in a grin.

Peregrína turned to smile at her husband. "That sounds like one of Ealdamon's," she said. "Are you planning your own book of epigrams?"

"No, thank you," said Rōlin. "I've already got plenty of pots on the fire—and you know quite well we've got to finish the *Atlas* before we take on anything new."

"Of course, my love," said Peregrína. "I'm just teasing you."

"I would never have guessed," said Rōlin, teasing right back.

Peregrína gave him an exasperated look that she'd perfected over the decades. Then she noticed the third bottle of healing potion on the nightstand where her husband had left it. "Why *three* healing potions?" she asked.

"I wasn't sure how many we'd need, so I brought all we had," said Rōlin.

"Ouch," said Peregrína. "I hadn't realized we were that low. I'll make more tonight if you'll cook dinner. Eynon will likely be hungry enough to eat a wisent once he wakes up."

"I'd be glad to," said Rōlin. "Does a menu of pronghorn sausages, eggs scrambled with scallions, and toasted bread with freshly churned butter sound good to you?"

"It does," said Peregrína. "It sounds as much like breakfast as dinner, but that combination has healing properties of its own."

"Which is why I suggested it," said Rōlin. "There are leftover apple tarts with honey, too, if the boy still has corners of his stomach left to fill."

"I wouldn't mind seconds on apple tarts myself," said Peregrína.

"We can split one," said Rōlin. He smiled at Peregrína tenderly. "How's he doing?" Rōlin asked.

Peregrína put her wrist on Eynon's forehead and reported. "He doesn't have a fever, and the swelling from his elbow to his finger-tips has nearly disappeared," she replied. "I think it's safe to let him sleep on his own for an hour while we do our chores."

"Speaking of chores," said Rōlin. He tossed Eynon's wizard's robes and undertunic in the air and caught them in a sphere of solidified sound.

Peregrína stopped him with a hand on his forearm. "Don't mix whites and colored clothes," she insisted.

"You don't think Eynon would prefer a light blue undertunic to a white one?" asked Rōlin.

"No," said Peregrína. "I don't."

Rōlin gestured and Eynon's robes and undertunic were suddenly separated into two different spheres. Peregrína watched as her husband filled the spheres with water and a slurry of pumice powder he found from congruencies to who-knows-where. The older wizard agitated the liquids in the spheres, then allowed it to drain out through new congruencies in the bottom, only to be replaced by several spheres full of clean water that also drained away. Rōlin put his palms together and pulled them apart to shoulder width, transforming the sphere into a cylinder that he sent spinning with a flick of his wrist, driving out still more water. Finally, Rōlin added heat to the cylinder and let it continue to rotate until the residual water on Eynon's robes, small clothes, and undertunic had evaporated.

Peregrína clapped softly. "I really love watching you do that," she said.

"Because I was so clever to come up with the technique?" asked Rōlin.

"No," said Peregrína. "Because *you're* the one doing it, not me."

"Good partners know each other's strengths and weaknesses," said Rōlin.

"Another epigram," teased Peregrína. "Ealdamon will have a worthy competitor soon, I'm sure."

"I think the boy is more likely to be competition for Damon," said Rōlin. "At least if he's the one we heard about?"

"How many young wizards with *red* magestones do you think there are in Orluin?" asked Peregrína. "He's also got *Fercha's* magestone. I recognize the setting."

"I'll bet there's a story there," said Rōlin. He caught the now-dry wizard robes and folded them, after dispelling the first of his laundry bubbles.

"I'm sure," said Peregrína as she watched her husband dispel his second laundry bubble, fold Eynon's now-clean undertunic, and put it on top of the young wizard's robes. "Though I expect Damon has also talked the lad into being his replacement. Maybe he can tell us at dinner." Peregrína stood and hugged Rōlin. "I'll get started on those healing potions—you get started on dinner. Take your time. I'll be making several potions, and that's not a quick process."

"Don't worry, my dear," said Rōlin. "It will take a while for me to make the bread. I'm going to try Eynon's trick and add tiny spheres of solidified sound to the dough to make it light and airy."

"Ca-caw!" croaked the raven. "Ca-caw!"

"I'll save a fresh hen's egg for you, good bird," said Rōlin. "Will that do? I don't want you telling Kârkingórēx I was a poor host."

The raven dipped its beak, imitating a human nod.

"Please keep an eye on Eynon and let us know if he wakes," said Peregrína. "I'll be brewing up potions."

On the bed, Eynon's head shifted left and right. The others could hear him muttering words like *Mule, Hedgehog, Locusts,* and *Skunk.*

"I think we're going to have to teach the lad more spells after dinner," said Rōlin. "He's talking about them in his sleep."

"We can teach him in the morning," said Peregrína. "Now get cooking!"

Chapter 31

Aboard the Seahawk

"And that's how things went when Magister Callidus delivered my ultimatum to Quintillius," said Sírénae from the tall, throne-like chair in her cabin on the *Seahawk* as she met with her senior staff. "All the rulers in Orluin were also there, and they've decided to fight instead of surrender." Thraxa screeched and Sírénae smoothed the feathers on the snow-gryffon's head.

"How could they possibly hope to stand against us with their ten legions against our forty?" asked General Machaera. "Even with support from Dâron and Tamloch's armies?"

"Don't forget the Bifurland fleet," said Admiral Pixo. "Their ships are small, but they're fast, and their warriors are a terror when they board, or so I'm told."

"My agents report the Bifurlanders only have five hundred longships," said Umbrose, the emperor's spymaster. "I doubt they'll offer much resistance to our two-thousand-vessel fleet."

"I'd rather overestimate than underestimate my opponents," said the admiral. "History has too many examples of larger fleets being defeated by smaller ones for me to think otherwise."

"We admire your prudence, Admiral Pixo," said Sírénae. "We also don't doubt your initiative in taking battle to the enemy. That's one reason why I've given you responsibility for a key part of my overall plan."

"Thank you, Your Imperial Majesty," said Pixo. He nodded, knowing Sírénae would tell him what she had in mind in her own good time.

"What about the Clan Lands?" asked the emperor, looking at Umbrose.

"One of my agents in Riyas found a pair of mages in a tavern. One of them had a communications ring linked to a ring worn by one of the clan chiefs in the southern Clan Lands," said Umbrose.

"The Clan Landers there are *very* angry with Dâron after some sort of recent major disaster, and the clan chief promised to lead thousands of his clan members against western Dâron."

"Excellent," said Sírénae. "Pixo, your forces will have to strip central and western Dâron of its stored food and drink before they arrive. We'll be vulnerable until we secure what we need to last through until the harvest."

"Forty legions in the field require a lot of food," said General Machaera.

Sírénae gave Machaera a look as sharp as the point of Thraxa's beak. "You don't need to remind me of the importance of logistics, General," said the emperor. "I was leading armies before you learned to hold a sword."

"Of course, Your Imperial Majesty," said Machaera. She didn't lower her eyes. It didn't pay to show weakness in front of the emperor, and she wasn't about to start doing so now.

"I'll speak with you later about a suitable commander to lead the ground forces detached with Pixo's inland strike force," said Sírénae.

"You mean to send part of the fleet up the Moravon?" asked Pixo. "Then take Tyford before moving into the good farmland east and west of the river?"

"Precisely," said Sírénae. "I thought you'd see the value of such a strike. The majority of Dâron's army is still assembled near Brendinas, ready to counter our invasion from the Ocean or up the Brenavon." She glanced at Umbrose for confirmation, and her spymaster inclined his chin by an inch.

"I have the perfect woman for the job," said General Machaera. "Like Pixo here, she shows a lot of initiative, while still having good judgment."

"Érikka Belisaria?" asked Sírénae. One corner of her mouth turned up and she raised an eyebrow.

"You knew my answer before you asked," said Machaera.

"Of course," Sírénae replied. "She'll do nicely—won't she, Pixo?"

"We've worked well together in the past," said the admiral. "During the most recent pacification of northern Catalania for example. She's an able commander."

"Good," said Sírénae. "We're agreed."

"When do Callidus and Xaxidiánus return?" asked General Machaera.

"Probably by dinner time," the emperor replied.

"That should work," said Machaera. "I need to coordinate with Callidus on which contingent of his battle mages will go with Pixo and Belisaria."

"There's no need for that," said Sírénae. "Take the thirteenth cohort."

"I... see..." said Machaera slowly. The thirteenth cohort of battle wizards was where Callidus concentrated his mages who were too green or too lazy to be useful, treating it as both a dumping ground and a reserve force only to be used to guard already-defeated opponents. "As you wish, Your Imperial Majesty."

Sírénae smiled at Machaera's discomfort. "We'll do what we can to keep Dâron's best wizards in the eastern part of the kingdom," said the emperor. "Belisaria shouldn't face much opposition from the local free wizards and hedge wizards."

"We can hope," said Machaera reluctantly. It seemed like Callidus had managed to get on Sírénae's bad side—not that disappointing the emperor was difficult to accomplish. "Will I get any dragons?" she asked.

"No," said Sírénae. "I'm saving the dragons for scouting work and to overawe the citizens of Nova Eboracum. The provincials will be easier to subdue if they can clearly see that our forces are overwhelmingly superior."

"That makes sense," said General Machaera. "Can you at least spare some elephants?"

"I think not," said Sírénae. "Elephants can be nearly as intimidating as dragons, especially when you face them on the field."

"Very well," said Machaera. "Belisaria will make the best of whatever forces are put at her disposal."

"I'm counting on that," said Sírénae. The emperor turned to Pixo. "You'll take the fleet that was at the Tempest Isles' eastern harbor."

"The one we don't think Laetícia's spy observed?" asked the admiral.

"Precisely," said Sírénae. "When our main fleet sails into Nova Eboracum, I don't want Laetícia thinking we even *have* a second fleet."

"What about locals observing our fleet moving up the Moravon?" asked Admiral Pixo. "How can we stop them from getting word back to Brendinas?"

"By killing them all," said Sírénae. "Or enslaving them, if you can do so without tying up your own troops. They're not Roma, after all."

"I'll have some of my agents accompany your forces," said Umbrose from a shadowed corner of the cabin. "They'll cast illusions and take *other measures* to help ensure your upstream progress goes unseen."

"That should help," said Pixo. He was glad his sailors could focus on their jobs instead of killing farmers and townspeople. Machaera would make sure there were plenty of archers in the troops assigned to Belisaria. Umbrose's stealthy spy-wizards would only have to deal with observers out of bow range.

"Let me know when you learn more about the intentions of the northern Clan Landers," Sírénae instructed Umbrose. "Perhaps the southern clan chief you've reached has a way of contacting someone in the north."

"I'd planned to explore that later today," said Umbrose. "The southern Clan Lands wizard in Riyas who's serving as our go-between is being cautious about how much he's helping us. My agent has been instructed to provide him with a well-paying position on my staff if he can help us in other ways—like connecting to northern Clan Lands' leaders."

"Make sure he knows the compensation will be *very* generous," said Sírénae. "And if he's sufficiently skilled, there may be a larger role for him on *my* staff as well. Make the same offer to the other wizard with him."

"As you instruct," said Umbrose. "I'll pass the word and keep you informed."

"Do you have any idea who these wizards might be?" asked Sírénae.

"Yes," said Umbrose. "But I don't want to say more until I have additional information. The stories my agent heard when he got to Riyas a few days ago are hard to believe and I need to confirm them."

"Don't wait too long," said Sírénae. "We don't want any surprises."

"Except for our enemies," Umbrose replied.

Everyone nodded, even Thraxa.

Machaera and Pixo carefully avoided looking at each other, but both shared the same thought. They were very glad they weren't Magister Callidus.

Chapter 32

Big Plans

Merry and Doethan had left an hour earlier with Chee and Ace. Now nearly every place at the large rectangular breakfast table in the governor-general's palace was filled.

"Would you like more ham?" asked Quintillius. Steam was still rising from the platter he held by its edges.

"One slice was enough for me," said Jenet from a few seats down.

"I'll have another," said Dârio.

"So will I," echoed Nûd.

The two royal cousins looked at each other across the table and laughed as they both tried to spear the same slice from the platter Quin offered. Nûd lifted his knife and shifted its tip to snare a different slice, so they could both enjoy one.

"I'd like another *libum* cake, if there are any left," said Bonnie. "We seldom have anything sweet on the menu at the Institute."

"You're sweet," said Nûd as he turned to focus his attention on the talented scholar-wizard, whose face promptly turned the same color as the ham.

"Stop that," she said, though everyone could see she didn't mean it. Bonnie mock-frowned at Nûd, then grinned and kissed his cheek, making it Nûd's turn to blush.

"There are plenty of *libum* cakes left," said Laetícia, jumping in to offer a distraction. She passed Bonnie a plate with six of the honey-soaked cakes made from white flour and thick, soft cheese.

"Thank you," said Bonnie. She selected two of the cakes before passing the plate around the table.

Jenet took a *libum* cake and bit off a piece, licking honey from her lips.

Dârio noticed and pretended to ignore how sensuous Jenet's gesture appeared. He wasn't convincing.

Duke Néillen smirked and Duke Háiddon elbowed his ribs. "Behave, or you'll eat in the dungeons," growled Duke Háiddon.

"Sorry," said Duke Néillen. He painted a neutral expression on his face and reached for a slice of ham for himself.

Verro and Fercha exchanged glances and smiled, remembering their own youthful courtship. Fercha popped a hard-boiled quail's egg into her mouth, then washed it down with a swallow of watered wine. Picking up another quail egg from Fercha's plate, Verro guided it toward Fercha's mouth. She accepted his offering and had more watered wine before collecting a *libum* cake of her own and feeding Verro half of it.

Inthíra sat beside Grand Admiral Sónnel and across from Princess Rúth at the far end of the table. Mafuta, the Roma wizard, was present as well. There was an empty chair for Felix, her young colleague. He was out in the garden delivering breakfast to Rocky. The big black wyvern was getting an entire smoked ham all for himself. King Bjarni and Queen Signý were seated beyond Mafuta drinking beer and mead, respectively. They'd been the last to arrive at breakfast, but there'd been no shortage of food for them, thanks to all the dishes prepared by the talented cooks at the governor-general's palace.

Laetícia was pleased to see Princess Rúth and Inthíra talking without Inthíra's expression showing hints of pain. Perhaps Doethan and Rúth's marriage the previous morning had finally convinced Inthíra to let her hopes for a relationship with Doethan go? Laetícia began to run through the list of unmarried older wizards in Occidens Province but stopped when Quintillius tapped the edge of his goblet with his knife. The *ding ding* of metal on metal drew everyone's attention.

"We have a big decision to make," Quintillius began. "What are the best ways to use our dragons?"

"That is a *big* decision," joked Sónnel.

"And it's not really ours to make," said Nûd. "Zûrafiérix and Viridáxés will do what *they* think is right, not what we tell them."

"Of course," said Quintillius. "But we can suggest a recommended course of action and encourage them to follow it."

"You'll have a better chance of Zûra doing what we ask than Viridáxés," said Dârio.

"Unless it's attack the Roma," Nûd replied.

"I'd be happier if you said, 'Attack the emperor,'" said Quintillius.

"Though I expect Viridáxés has a short memory when it comes to remembering we're all on the same side," said Laetícia.

"That *is* why we wanted to make sure both of them were present for the treaty-signing ceremony," said Duke Háiddon.

"And even if Viridáxés isn't interested in doing the wisest thing strategically," said Dârio.

"If we can convince Zûrafiérix, *she* will convince Viridáxés," said Jenet.

"I hope you can agree on what's best better than the faculty at the Institute can decide who's going to be Dean," offered Bonnie. "It's just a job that takes them away from their research, but they fuss over it like chickens after the same bug."

"Now that we've been put in our places," said Quintillius, smiling at Bonnie, "let me sketch out our options, as I see them." Quin paused until he saw he had everyone's attention. "First, we keep the existence of Zûrafiérix and Viridáxés a secret, using them primarily against the emperor's fleet from undersea and against any fishing boats Sírénae sends out to help feed her troops."

"That was my idea," said Nûd. "It avoids direct confrontations between our dragons and the emperor's seven black wyrms. Zûra and Dáx might be injured if all seven attacked them at once."

Quinn nodded at Nûd, then held up two fingers. "Second," he said, "we can use them as the vanguard of an all-out attack on Sírénae's fleet before it reaches the shores of Orluin."

"Hadn't we agreed not to try a full-scale attack?" asked Jenet. "The odds are too high against us."

"Not if we can sink enough of their ships while they're still on their way," said Grand Admiral Sónnel. "With help from our dragons and all the mages of three kingdoms and Occidens Province, I expect we could reduce the emperor's forces by half."

"Killing tens of thousands of Roma in the process," said Princess Rúth.

"It's them or us," said Duke Néillen. "Why can't our dragons sink *every* ship in their fleet?"

"I can answer that," said Verro. "I worked on the estimates with Grand Admiral Sónnel. The emperor has at least as many mages as we do combined, and they're better trained—at least in battle magic."

"How effective can battle mages be at stopping dragons the size of Viridáxés and Zûrafiérix?" asked Duke Néillen.

"I can think of at least three ways to stop them," Verro replied.

"So can I," said Laetícia.

"I wonder if they're the same three ways?" asked King Bjarni.

"We'll have to see what *our* master mage thinks might work," added Queen Signý.

"My point is we could only stop half of Sírénae's invasion fleet," said Grand Admiral Sónnel. "With twenty legions remaining, she would still substantially outnumber our united forces."

"Don't forget *her* dragons and elephants," said Dârio.

"They may be less of a problem than we think," said Laetícia. She smiled as she remembered what Tembóku had told her and why she needed a trumpeter.

"I may have something to help deal with elephants, too," said King Bjarni. "We'll need assistance from Fercha on a wide gate to make it work, though."

"A *very* wide gate," added Queen Signý.

"I'm intrigued," said Dârio.

"So am I," said Nûd.

"My initial gate-making will be focused on supporting the evacuation of eastern Orluin," said Fercha. "It's going to take a tremendous amount of work to get everyone to safety *and* take all their stores with them."

"Of course, that will have to be your top priority," said Laetícia. "Mafuta and Felix can help, but you'll need to show more wizards how to build wide gates if we're going to move everyone out of harm's way quickly."

"Inthíra can help me identify good candidates in Dâron," said Fercha.

"I can do the same in Tamloch, with help from Bonnie to pick people from the Institute in Bhaile Pónaire," said Verro.

"Glad to assist," said Bonnie. "There are several who want to do real-world wizardry, not just sketch out calculations on slates."

"Good," said Laetícia. "Mafuta can select appropriate Occidens Province wizards."

The older, gray-haired wizard nodded and stared at Laetícia. "Are you going to ask Fercha?"

Occidens Province's senior magister nodded, setting the beads in her tight braids clacking. "Yes," Laetícia replied. "Could you stay after the meeting is over, Fercha? Mafuta and I have something gate-related we want to discuss with you."

"I think I can guess what you want to talk about," Fercha replied. "There's no reason, at least in theory, why it shouldn't work."

"It would simplify things if it did," Laetícia replied. "We can test it tonight, if you think you'll have time."

"I'll make time," said Fercha. "This is too important."

Quintillius spoke. "If you don't mind postponing your mysterious future plans, we still have decisions to make."

"Of course, Governor-General," teased Laetícia. "My sincere apologies for taking things off track."

"See that you don't do it again," said Quintillius sternly. Then he smiled and handed Laetícia a *libum* cake. "Coming back to the matter of how best to use our dragons," Quin continued. "We've discussed using them for a full-scale attack and using them for stealth attacks against the emperor's fishing vessels." He scanned the room, looking for anyone interested in adding more. "What other options do we have, my friends?"

"Holding them in reserve until we can spring their existence on Sírénae when she least expects it," offered Dârio.

"Aren't you forgetting that the entire population of Riyas has seen these dragons?" asked Princess Rúth.

"To say nothing of the armies of Dâron and Tamloch," said Duke Háiddon.

"It can be equally effective if Sírénae knows our dragons exist but doesn't know where they are and when they might appear," said Jenet. "That would likely make her more cautious, father."

"You're right, daughter," said Duke Háiddon. "There's nothing like having the pupil school the teacher."

Jenet smiled and Dârio squeezed her hand. Her father nodded, acknowledging the wisdom in Jenet's words.

"I'm for the options that don't include a full-scale attack," said Princess Rúth. "I don't want us to drown twenty legions' worth of soldiers if we can avoid it."

"Better to have them leave Orluin by choice because they're starving," said Inthíra.

"Assuming they *don't* find the food and supplies they'll need," said Quintillius.

"It will be our job to ensure they don't," said Nûd.

Heads around the table nodded.

"Are we agreed, then?" asked the governor-general.

"Assuming Viridáxés goes along," said Dârio.

"Let me talk to Zûrafiérix first," said Nûd. "*She* can convince Viridáxés."

"You're appointed as our Emissary to Dragons then," said Quintillius. "It's too bad the master mage of Dâron isn't available to *ad hoc* gate you to Bucket Island."

"I'll take him," said Verro. "It's the least I can do for my new-found nephew."

"I'm coming, too," said Bonnie. "I want to examine the dragons' congruencies and try to figure out how they can support their own weight."

"So long as you don't make them mad in the process," said Verro.

"I'll try not to," said Bonnie.

"Try hard," said Verro. "We can leave in an hour."

"Let's talk more first," said Laetícia.

"Jenet and I will see to the logistical details for the mass evacuation and determine who will be in charge of what," said Duke Háiddon. "Along with you, of course, Quin."

Quintillius nodded and Laetícia cleared her throat. "There's one more critical item beyond all that," she said. "Master Callidus told us when he presented Sírénae's ultimatum."

"Valentius," said Mafuta. Her voice was intense, and her eyes looked like they held thunderstorms.

"Exactly," said Laetícia. "We have to rescue him."

"How are we going to do that?" asked Inthíra.

"I'm putting a small group of wizards together," said Laetícia. "I'd like you to be one of them, Inthíra. Your skills with illusions would be very helpful."

"Gladly," said Inthíra. "I'll do whatever I can to support the rescue."

"Thank you," said Laetícia. She called to Felix, who was walking in from the garden. Sigrun and Rannveigr were following behind him like a pair of ducklings. "I need you to step forward as well, young wizard."

"What have I been volunteered for?" asked Felix.

"A dangerous mission," said Jenet.

"With slim odds of success," said Bonnie with a smile.

"To pull off a daring rescue," Mafuta added.

"Sign me up," said Felix. "I'm too young to have any sense of my own mortality."

"I was counting on that," said Laetícia. "Now sit down and eat your breakfast."

Chapter 33

Rescue Strategy

A few of the people at the table earlier had adjourned to Laetícia's study to brainstorm on ways to rescue Valentius. The late-morning sun was streaming in through tall windows. Laetícia shared details about Valentius, including everything Tembóku had told her. She reclined on a couch to listen to her guests' insights.

King Bjarni stood, his sword rattling against his wife's wooden chair. "The way I see it," said the king, "there are two main challenges—finding the Southern emperor's son and extracting him once you do."

"Without dying in the process," added Queen Signý.

"That goes without saying," said King Bjarni, nodding to his wife and the hooded, amber-robed figure behind her.

"I like to remind you to stay alive at frequent intervals," said Signý.

Sigrun and Rannveigr giggled. They were sitting on a thick carpet between Bjarni and Signý in colt-legged postures only girls about to become women could manage easily.

"I know, I know, sometimes I take too many chances," said King Bjarni.

"Sometimes?" asked Sigrun. She giggled again and was echoed by Rannveigr. Felix smiled at them and the girls giggled again, this time more self-consciously.

Bjarni moved his head slowly from side to side, showing an expression that was somewhere between a grimace and a smile. "Do you have daughters?" he asked Laetícia.

"Two," she replied.

"Then you understand what I have to deal with," said Bjarni, tossing his hands up theatrically.

"Whatever do you mean?" asked Laetícia. "Well-brought-up Roma girls are always models of decorum and obedience," she said, keeping her face completely neutral.

All the adults in the room erupted in laughter. Felix, Sigrun, and Rannveigr seemed puzzled, but they eventually joined in. Only the amber-robed wizard standing behind Queen Signý was silent.

"Sírénae's fleet should only be a day west of the Tempest Isles," said Grand Admiral Sónnel, attempting to get the meeting back on track. "It takes a long time to get that many ships under way."

"Could they be moving faster than we expect?" asked Inthíra. "Perhaps by raising their own wind with wizardry?"

"They don't have enough wizards to do that," said Mafuta. "Magister Callidus is a good man, but few truly talented wizards want to serve Sírénae voluntarily. The western empire has struggled to keep its ranks of wizards full ever since Sírénae achieved imperial status. I'm sure the shortages have become even worse since she was exiled."

"Except for positions with her spy network," said Laetícia. "Umbrose has no trouble attracting the sort of mages who enjoy meddling in other people's business and tracking citizens' comings and goings."

"Umbrose?" asked Inthíra.

"Sírénae's spymaster," said Laetícia. "He's all too competent in his role, too—blast him."

"Where would the empress keep Valentius?" asked Grand Admiral Sónnel. "Would she hold him on his own ship—the one she captured—or keep him close to her on her flagship?"

Laetícia turned to Mafuta. "What do you think?" she asked.

"You know my answer," said Mafuta.

"She'd keep him close," said Laetícia. "Close enough to snip off body parts personally, if it came to that."

"I don't think I like Sírénae," said Sigrun.

"I don't either," said Rannveigr.

"And neither of us has met her," added Sigrun.

"You've got plenty of company in that poor opinion," said Laetícia. "Do you think we need to check both places?" she asked Mafuta.

"Yes," said the older Roma wizard. "We really can't be confident we'll find Valentius either place," she continued. "Sírénae may have Umbrose and his people guarding Valentius, in which case he could be anywhere."

"That's not what I wanted to hear," said Laetícia. She sat up and rested her chin on top of her closed hand with her elbow on her knee, looking pensive.

Verro was holding hands with Fercha on another couch. He gestured to get Laetícia's attention. "You said the ship Valentius was taking had a hold full of magestones?"

"That's right," said Laetícia. "Obsidian from the largest of the Isles of Dogs."

"Shouldn't we be able to detect a large concentration of magestones from a distance?" asked Verro. "I'm sure *I* could."

"So could I," said Fercha.

"The best that would do for us is help locate the ship Valentius *had* been on," said Laetícia. "As we'd discussed, there's no guarantee he'd still be aboard."

"Would Sírénae want to keep the magestones close by, along with her captive?" asked Nûd. He was seated next to Bonnie in a large overstuffed chair big enough to hold them both. Neither one of them seemed to object to their forced proximity.

"Possibly," said Mafuta. "But the emperor wouldn't put a high value on the magestones. Magister Callidus would, though."

"And so would Magister Umbrose," said Laetícia.

"In other words," said Nûd, "detecting a large collection of raw magestones won't necessarily help us."

"Right," said Laetícia. She shook her head and the beads on her braids clacked.

"I may have a way to help us locate Valentius," suggested Inthíra.

"Oh?" asked Laetícia. "What are you thinking?"

"Do you have a picture of Valentius?" Inthíra asked. "That would be essential to my idea."

"Here," said Mafuta, removing a large silver coin from her pouch and tossing it to Inthíra. "One side shows Emperor Valens when he first took office," she said.

"And Valentius looks just like Valens did when he was younger," Laetícia exclaimed. She stood up, crossed to Inthíra, and stared down at the coin—a double denarius.

"Is it a good likeness?" asked Inthíra.

"It is," said Laetícia. "Valentius should be smiling, though. The engraver who carved the die made Valens too serious—which is only fitting for a sitting emperor. If you make him happier, the image would be accurate."

"Excellent," said Inthíra.

"What are you thinking?" asked Laetícia.

"I'm thinking of having an illusion of Valentius appear in the air above Sírénae's flagship," said Inthíra. "He could be riding on a wyvern or standing behind a wizard on a flying disk."

"Brilliant," said Grand Admiral Sónnel. "Guards would rush to where Valentius was being held to confirm he hadn't escaped."

"That helps identify where Valentius is being held," said Queen Signý. "It doesn't help us get him free, since he'll have twice as many guards around him as usual."

"You're not thinking big enough, my love," said King Bjarni. "Once we know where Valentius can be found, we'll need an even bigger distraction to rescue him."

"What do you have in mind?" asked Laetícia.

"Perhaps a kraken?" offered Grand Admiral Sónnel. "One as big as a dozen ships should do nicely."

"I like the idea," said Inthíra. "But I can only create something that *looks* like a giant kraken. My illusions can't actually toss vessels around. A kraken that appears and simply flails its arms around without causing any destruction is only a limited distraction."

"Could you hide a great dragon's presence with your illusions?" asked Sónnel. "Zûrafiérix could effectively mimic the damage caused by a kraken."

"I could," said Inthíra. "But it would be wise to have help. We should see if Merry can join us."

"I can assist," said the amber-robed wizard standing behind Queen Signý.

"Thank you for your offer, wise counselor," said King Bjarni. "You can form *ad hoc* gates, too. That means we can travel with a somewhat larger party..."

"...to check multiple locations for Valentius," said Mafuta.

"And still get everyone home safely," said Queen Signý.

"That's all well and good," said Laetícia. "But what if Zûrafiérix can't get there in time to be useful? We don't know how fast she can swim."

"Then I suggest we ask her," said Grand Admiral Sónnel.

Chapter 34

Dust in the Wind

Eynon bounded into the kitchen, preceded by a squawking raven on the wing. Corvi was indignant that Eynon hadn't stayed put and allowed her to fetch Rōlin and Peregrína to confirm he had recovered enough to be out of bed.

"I'm glad you're feeling better," said Peregrína from a counter on the far right, where she was nursing a dozen healing potions through the final steps until they were completed.

Rōlin was standing by the sink, washing fresh berries for dinner. "Are you hungry?" he asked.

"I'm starving," said Eynon. "You wouldn't have whole flathorn roasting in an oven somewhere, would you?"

"Just a wisent haunch for tomorrow," Rōlin replied. "Will that do?"

"What will you and Peregrína eat?" Eynon responded with a smile. He was pleased to feel well enough to joke.

"Let me see your wrist," said Peregrína as she left her rack of potions to lift Eynon's arm. She held his wrist up and inspected it closely. "The swelling is gone," she said. "Is it tender?" Peregrína pressed both her thumbs into Eynon's wrist.

"Careful," said Eynon. "I'd like to keep my hand attached to my arm."

"Your wrist doesn't hurt?" Peregrína asked.

"No," said Eynon. "But there's something strange about my vision. I'm seeing thousands of colored sparks drifting in the air." He rubbed his eyes and stared at Peregrína. "Your magestone is glowing like a wizard lamp, too."

"Caw!" said the raven.

"So are your feathers, Corvi," Eynon added.

"What about me?" asked Rōlin as he turned to face the young wizard.

"Your magestone is so bright it looks like you have a piece of the sun embedded in your chest," said Eynon.

Rōlin touched his magestone and smiled. "It's not warm enough for that."

"Don't tease the lad," said Peregrína. "It's not funny. Do you think it's a reaction to the megapede venom?"

"It could be," said Rōlin. "The sparkles in the air could be magestone dust blowing down from Melyncárreg."

"You did say there might be some odd effects from the venom," said Peregrína, looking fondly at her husband before turning to Eynon. "And *you* haven't seen magestones or magestone dust like this *before* you were bitten, have you?"

"I've seen magestones," said Eynon. "Or perhaps it's more like I've sensed them, really. They didn't shine like wizard lamps."

"Most wizards can sense other wizards' magestones," Peregrína replied. "It takes skill to hide them so they're *not* seen. But seeing magestone dust is something different."

"So I've gathered," said Eynon. "I'm not sure I like seeing it, either. Do you think the effect will wear off?"

"I don't know," said Rōlin. "My father's notes didn't say anything like this happened to the person who was bitten—but they weren't a mage. Can you do more than *see* magestones and magestone dust?"

"I'm not sure," Eynon replied. He tightened his jaw in concentration.

"Be careful," said Peregrína.

"Caw!" said Corvi. The raven retreated beneath the kitchen table.

Eynon stretched his arms and moved his hands in circles as if he was conducting a room full of musicians. The magestone dust in the kitchen coalesced into glowing polychromatic streams that flowed around the kitchen in interweaving strands so bright Rōlin and Peregrína had no trouble seeing them. The two older wizards felt their magestones growing warm and saw their usually soft glows expand like hot blue flames.

"Outside!" shouted Rōlin. Peregrína opened the kitchen door and Rōlin hurried Eynon through it. They watched the swirling multicolored strings of magestone dust surround the young wizard and lift him a dozen feet into the air without help from his flying disk, which was still inside. More magestone powder from the atmosphere around him seemed to seek out Eynon. Particles of blue and green and black and purple and red and amber added themselves to the ever-changing ripples of dust, making Eynon seem both taller and much more massive.

"What's happening?" Eynon exclaimed before the dust surrounded his head and neck. "How am I flying without my flying disk?" His arms kept circling involuntarily. They seemed to be drawing more and more sparkling dust to the glowing aura that surrounded Eynon. "I feel like I could defeat all the Emperor's forces single-handedly," he said. Eynon's voice seemed as distorted as his body looked through the haze of magestone dust. It felt like it was rising an octave. "The dust is full of power," he said quickly, "and so am I!"

"Careful," said Rōlin. "I thought you were trying to learn your limits, not become even more overconfident."

"It's not overconfidence when you really *do* have enough power to destroy armies," said Eynon. The dust started to circle his throat.

Peregrína thought Eynon's face looked both exultant *and* worried. "Channel the dust away from you," she said from her home's back porch. "You're not strong enough to control it." Peregrína watched Eynon's expression alternate through cycles of fear and exhilaration as he struggled to keep the crackling energy of the dust from over-whelming him.

"Direct the dust at the top of the mountains," said Rōlin. He pointed at the saw-toothed range of snow-covered peaks to the west. "Don't release it anywhere nearby, or you might kill us all."

Eynon closed his eyes, put his palms together in front of him, and directed a tremendous blast of magestone dust-fueled power at the distant serrated mountains. Like a blow from an immense sword, the blast carved a new indentation into the side of the tallest peak.

Peregrína's mouth opened, but no words came out. She saw clouds of new sparkling magestone dust rush in to replace what Eynon had released. "Don't give up," she said. "Find a way to master the dust."

"I'm trying," said Eynon. The syllables shot from his mouth like arrows from a fast archer's bow.

"It's not the dust itself that's causing the problem," Rōlin told Eynon. "Somehow you've triggered every grain of magestone dust to open a congruency to a source of magical energy."

"That feels right," Eynon replied. "But what can I do about it?"

"Displace it?" Peregrína suggested.

"Good idea," said Eynon. "Displace it where?"

Corvi chose that moment to fly out of the kitchen and perch on Peregrína's shoulder. "Caw!" said the raven insistently. "Ca-ca-ca-*caw!*" The bird raised one wing and pointed toward the east where a shape on the horizon was rapidly growing larger.

"Dragon!" exclaimed Rōlin.

"Kârk!" croaked the raven.

Seconds later, the huge rust-colored dragon was hovering above them. "Corvi said I was needed," Kârkingórēx told Eynon. "Let *me* share your power!"

Without questioning how the raven got word to the dragon almost instantaneously, Eynon balled his hands into fists and brought them to his sides, no longer drawing more dust toward him. He slowly descended until his feet touched the ground as he gained a measure of control over the cloud of magical particles around him. "Brace yourself," he said, directing a coherent stream of energized magestone dust at Kârkingórēx.

When the flow cut off, Kârkingórēx was sparkling like a rainbow of ice crystals. Eynon's glow was muted, except for a vivid purple emanating from his neck where the red and blue of his magestones combined.

Corvi launched herself toward the dragon and landed on his scaly head. Within seconds, the raven was also sparkling.

"Thank you, young mage," said Kârkingórēx. "You've given me and my weyr a great gift."

"Uh, you're welcome," said Eynon. He was able to control the much smaller cloud of magestone dust now surrounding him without much difficulty.

"Until we meet again," said the dragon. Kârkingórēx twisted until he faced northeast.

"Safe travels…" Eynon began to say, but Kârkingórēx and Corvi were already nothing but colorful specks in the distance.

"I've never seen Kârkingórēx move so fast," said Rōlin.

"He's never worn a cloud of magestone dust before," said Peregrína.

"What just happened?" asked Eynon.

"You've obviously unlocked new capabilities," said Rōlin.

"But I nearly had to die from megapede venom to do it," said Eynon. He stretched and blinked, then rubbed his eyes. "That was *very* strange. Can we go back to something ordinary, like learning more spells from *On Wizardry* now?"

"If that's truly what you want," said Peregrína. "Is your vision still compromised?"

"I can still see magestone dust in the air," said Eynon. "But it's much less noticeable than it was before."

"Good," said Rōlin. "Let's hope it doesn't distract you from learning the *Mule,* the *Locusts* and the *Hedgehog.*"

"Can we start with the *Skunk?*" asked Eynon. "I want to know how to counter dragons. I have a feeling I may be needing that knowledge in the very near future."

"Of course," said Peregrína. "So long as you don't try it indoors."

"I won't," said Eynon. He took a deep breath and savored the smell of roast wisent wafting from the kitchen. "Can we eat first?" Eynon asked.

"Certainly," said Rōlin. "You can set the table."

"And I can finish my healing potions," said Peregrína.

"The way things are going, I expect we'll need them," said Rōlin.

Eynon reluctantly nodded, acknowledging Rōlin was likely correct. He followed his hosts inside and put trenchers made from split loaves of day-old bread at three spots on the kitchen table. Eynon rubbed his forehead but didn't speak.

"What is it?" asked Peregrína as she turned away from putting corks in potion bottles.

"Ummm…" said Eynon.

"How many pronghorn sausages do you want?" asked Rōlin.

"Five or six, if there are enough," Eynon answered, glad to have the temporary distraction.

"The lad has a question for us," said Peregrína. "Stop serving sausages and listen."

"Yes, dear," said Rōlin.

"Now that I've had time to think about it, could we please explore my new abilities after dinner instead of learning spells from *On Wizardry*?" Eynon asked.

"I was hoping you'd say that," said Rōlin. He carried a platter of scrambled eggs with scallions to the table. "We don't want to wait before we investigate, since your remarkable new talents are nearly as rare as hen's teeth."

"Pass the eggs, please," said Peregrína.

"Yes, ma'am," Eynon replied. He followed Peregrína's instructions, passed the platter, and started buttering two thick slices of toasted bread to occupy his hands until the eggs came back to him. With his eyes sparkling, Eynon asked, "Are there any leftover apple-honey tarts for dessert?"

Chapter 35

Second Fleet

Admiral Pixo was pleased Sírénae had assigned Second Fleet twice its usual complement of wizards, despite the fact that many of them came from the barely competent thirteenth cohort. Even minimally-skilled wizards could generate wind to help his ships reach Moraría Bay in just over a day's sailing. He knew the bay was the gateway to the broad Moravon river and Tyford, the second city of Dâron.

Pixo completely approved of Sírénae's plan to strike deep inside Dâron and capture the stores, supplies, and slaves the emperor's forces would need until the fall crops could be harvested six months or more in the future. *I pulled all the illusionists I could find, too,* thought Pixo. *They'll keep our ships hidden.*

He remembered the emperor's words earlier in the day when she'd authorized the illusion mages and thirteenth cohort.

"Pixo," said Sírénae. "Stealth and speed will ensure the conquest of Tyford. More wizards will provide both. Use them wisely."

"Yes, my Emperor," Pixo had replied. "You can count on me."

"I hope so, for your sake," said Sírénae. She ruffled Thraxa's feathers and gave Pixo a hard look. "Just be victorious. I'd hate to have to break in a new admiral."

"Yes, my Emperor," said Pixo. When Sírénae was in that sort of mood—which was often—it paid to be deferential and say little.

* * * * *

Several hours later, Admiral Pixo and Lieutenant General Belisaria had seen to the transfer of the additional wizards to Second Fleet. Pixo knew these wizards were skilled in illusion magic and would help disguise the fleet's movements up the bay and the Moravon. Manipulating the winds was a common skill among Roma mages, even ones in the less-than-competent thirteenth cohort. They'd all be able to help the fleet make excellent time to the shores of Orluin.

Now they were sitting on either side of a wide chart table. Pixo's spacious cabin aboard the *Menodorus Maximus,* the flagship of Second Fleet, was designed for both comfort and utility. The admiral unrolled a map of Dâron on the chart table and moved brass weights into place to hold down the corners.

"You know the general outlines of our mission, don't you?" asked Pixo.

Belisaria leaned forward to review the map. "Of course," she said. "I understand the wisdom of taking Tyford, but why aren't we occupying the estates south of the city and seizing *their* supplies as well?"

"The emperor wants to travel disguised by illusion magic, so we're not seen, then take Tyford first," Pixo answered. "The warehouses there should be well-stocked, and once the city is taken, we can sail south again and gather supplies from much more lightly defended towns and villages. The emperor wants Tyford's fall to come as a complete surprise to our opponents."

"And if we pause to collect supplies farther south on the river, we won't be able prevent word of our arrival from preceding us," said Belisaria.

"Exactly," said Pixo.

"How effective is illusion magic at hiding ships?" asked Belisaria. "I've had wizards assigned to me use it to make my forces seem larger, and to disguise small ambush parties, but I've never seen it used for hiding anything as large as Second Fleet."

"Sírénae assures me we won't be seen," said Admiral Pixo. "It helps that we'll be sailing at night for most of the trip."

"Is that safe?" asked Belisaria.

"A few wizards with lenses that let them see in darkness will fly ahead of the fleet and warn us about shoals and islands," said Pixo. "We're fortunate that Moraría Bay and the Moravon are both well charted."

"If you say so," said Belisaria. "I'll still wait to have my soldiers put on their armor until we're nearly to our destination."

"That's your prerogative," said Pixo. "Just tell them to be quiet putting on their *loricas.* I don't want clanking plates or chiming mail echoing across the water to give us away."

"I'll pass the word to my commanders," said Belisaria.

"It probably won't matter that much, considering how lightly Tyford should be defended," said Pixo. "Even if they do hear us coming, there's not much they can do about it."

"True," said Lieutenant General Belisaria. "It sounds like my legionnaires won't have too much to do at this stage. From what we've heard from Umbrose's agents, most of Dâron's army is still in the east near Brendinas. Tyford's leaders will see they can't stand against us and should surrender the city."

"If they have any sense," added Admiral Pixo.

"Which is never assured with Orluin barbarians," said Belisaria. She smiled and Pixo could see why Machaera had selected her for her position. Belisaria's smile reminded him of a hungry wolf staring at a spotted fawn.

"We can hope they'll be sensible," the Lieutenant General continued. Belisaria rubbed her palms together. "If not," she said, "we'll have to *take* the city."

"We'll also have to load most of the supplies we capture on cargo vessels and transport them to Nova Eboracum," said Pixo. "Our forces occupying that city will need them. We can fend for ourselves by raiding up and down the Moravon and the farms along the bay."

"I expect we'll have to do that quickly, though," said Belisaria. "Before King Dârio can bring the army of Dâron west."

"True," said Pixo. "But Dârio isn't king of Dâron any longer. He's king of Tamloch."

"Really?" asked Belisaria. "There's no understanding these non-Roma. Who *is* king of Dâron, then?"

"Dârio's cousin, according to Umbrose," said Pixo. "A man named Nûd with no military experience."

"Better and better," said Belisaria. "We'll crush whatever ragtag resistance they muster to try and stop us."

"Don't get cocky," said Pixo. "No plan—"

"—of battle survives confrontation with the enemy," said Belisaria, finishing the maxim. "I understand," she said, "but this doesn't sound like it will come to battle. We'll just overwhelm them."

"I hope that's so," said Pixo. "All those extra mages assigned to us should help, too. Dâron's mages are far to the east with their army, so we will control the skies as well as the land and river."

"I doubt any mages will be necessary," said Belisaria. "My legions will occupy Tyford and seize all the warehouses in a few hours. Do we have them identified?"

"No," said Pixo. "We have an old map of the city, but it's two decades out of date. Our mages should be able to tag any new warehouses away from the river, and my sailors will mark new ones with access to the river, which should be most of them."

"Good," said Belisaria. "I will organize smaller squads that can hurry to warehouses as they're identified." She regarded Pixo and rubbed her chin with a calloused hand. "What about the locals?" she asked. "Do we kill them or capture them?"

"The emperor wants slaves to help build new fortifications," said Pixo. "She said we should work our captives but not waste much food on them, except the farmers."

"Right," said Belisaria. "Someone has to bring the crops in to keep the emperor's forces fed."

"Exactly," said Pixo. "But there's no need to feed most of the citizens of Tyford. The emperor said to consider them 'surplus population' and treat them accordingly."

"We'll take hostages to ensure the good behavior of the farmers," said Belisaria. "Keeping the hostages on short rations will stretch our supplies *and* make them less likely to cause trouble."

"Of course," said Pixo. "That's standard procedure." He noted the pragmatic brutality showing in Belisaria's face and posture. "Are you ready for guerrilla raids?" Pixo asked.

"I'm well prepared to follow Roma's standard procedure against such resistance," said Belisaria. "Start by executing one person in ten for each attack and hang their bodies from the city's walls."

"Let's hope that doesn't become necessary," said Pixo. "I'm glad you're prepared to take such action if it comes to that. I can see why Machaera thinks highly of you."

"The emperor wants results, not excuses," said Belisaria. "I deliver them."

"Here's our planned course," said Pixo. He used a small silver stylus to trace their route from south to north up Moraría Bay and the Moravon river.

"Ah," said Belisaria, noting their destination and stabbing the map with her finger. "And *here* is Tyford." She shared a feral smile with Pixo. "By this time tomorrow, the city—and all its supplies—will be ours."

"Barring any surprises," said Pixo. He remembered previous missions where bad weather or incorrect intelligence reports had forced him to improvise.

"I think we'll be the ones providing the surprises this time," said Belisaria.

"Hope for the best…" said Pixo.

"And plan for the worst," Belisaria completed. "Now let's figure out what could go wrong…"

"And how we'll respond if it does," said Pixo. He smiled at Belisaria and she smiled back. It was good to work with a fellow professional.

Chapter 36

Faster and Stronger

"Slow down," said Rōlin from his chair at the kitchen table. "I can't understand what you're saying."

"Move the dust away from your throat," urged Peregrína. "It's distorting your speech."

Eynon stood at the end of the long trestle table in his hosts' comfortable kitchen. He moved his arm almost faster than the eye could see and wiped away the polychromatic magestone dust glowing around his head and throat. "Is this better?" he asked.

"Much better," said Rōlin. "I think we've established that the dust can substantially speed you up..."

"But what else can it do?" asked Peregrína. She looked over Eynon's shoulder and feigned surprise, then tossed half a dozen apples from a basket on the table toward him while the young wizard was distracted. Peregrína wasn't surprised when Eynon turned around. His right arm blurred, and he caught each apple in mid-flight, directing them gently back into the basket in front of Peregrína.

"All my reflexes are accelerated," said Eynon.

"So I see," said Rōlin. "Are you stronger as well as faster?"

"How can I tell without breaking something?" asked Eynon.

"See if you can bend this," said Peregrína. She rose and handed Eynon a fireplace poker from the kitchen hearth. It was made from wrought iron and thicker than Eynon's thumb. Both of Eynon's arms glowed with sparkling dust from hand to shoulder. He held the ends of the poker and effortlessly curved it into a tight arc.

"The wrought iron must have grown soft from so much time in the fire," said Eynon. He looked at Peregrína apologetically, then straightened the curved poker and gave it back to her. "Sorry," he said.

"There's nothing to be sorry about," Peregrína replied. "I asked you to do it—and it's a brand-new poker," she added. "Nûd made it for me a few months ago."

"Nûd is a smith?" asked Eynon. His jaw dropped and his lips formed a circle.

"Nûd is a man of many talents," said Rōlin.

"So I'm learning," said Eynon. He shook his head slowly from side to side. "I wonder what else the dust can help me do?" Eynon asked.

"We know it can be passed along to others," said Peregrína.

"Kârkingórēx proved *that*," added Rōlin.

"I wonder how long the effect lasts?" mused Peregrína.

"And whether or not it can be shared more than once," said Rōlin.

"You mean, can Kârkingórēx pass it on to the other dragons back at Dragon's Tower?" asked Eynon.

"That thought did cross my mind," said Rōlin.

"Would you like me to share the magestone dust's magic with *you?*" Eynon asked his hosts.

Rōlin shared a glance with Peregrína. It reminded Eynon of the way his parents could communicate without using words. Peregrína nodded.

"I wouldn't mind," she said. "I'm starting to slow down these days, and it would be interesting to have the same energy I had when I was younger."

"Give it a try, lad," said Rōlin. "You can share dust with me, and I can try sharing it with Peregrína."

"If you'd like," said Eynon. He gathered more magestone dust to him. The valley south of Melyncárreg seemed to have plenty of dust suspended in the air for him to draw on. Eynon concentrated the extra dust into shimmering balls of powder around each of his hands. Rōlin stood and approached Eynon.

"I'm ready," said the older wizard.

Eynon put his hands on Rōlin's shoulders and willed the glowing dust to transfer. Soon Rōlin's body glowed from head to foot. "Try to transfer the dust now," said Eynon.

Rōlin replied, but he wasn't easy to understand. His voice sounded like a chipmunk chittering. Eynon extended his dust to cover his neck and head again so he could understand Rōlin.

Peregrína seemed to understand Rōlin without dust to speed up her senses. She embraced her husband and some of Rōlin's dust spread to cover her body. Her eyes grew wide and so did Rōlin's as the two of them felt the energizing effect of the magestone dust.

"I feel like I could fight a wyvern, a gryffon, and a basilisk simultaneously—and win," said Rōlin.

"I feel like I could toss in a couple of bears as well and match you blow for blow," said Peregrína. She tightened her embrace.

Rōlin sighed and increased the pressure of his own hug. "I think we've established that the magestone dust's magic can be transferred," he said.

"I think it's time for us to retire for the night," said Peregrína. "Would you be a dear and finish cleaning up the supper dishes please, Eynon."

"I'd be glad to," Eynon replied. He recognized the look in his hosts' eyes—he'd seen it often enough on his parents' faces when they wanted to spend time in bed together.

Rōlin and Peregrína left the kitchen hand in hand. Eynon cleared the supper dishes, thinking of Merry. *How am I going to face her when I get back?* he wondered. *And am I even ready to return? I still have so much to learn.*

Eynon busied himself with washing dishes. He built up the fire in the kitchen hearth, poured himself a mug of cider, heated the poker he'd bent earlier in the coals, and stuck the tip of the hot poker in the cider to warm it up. Then he pulled a chair closer to the fire and watched the flames dance, trying hard not to notice the sounds coming from down the hall in the direction of Rōlin and Peregrína's bedroom.

"I'll *have* to return soon," he said to himself and the crackling fire. "I won't be much good against the emperor's invasion fleet if I stay here."

The flames didn't answer and Eynon felt more and more like he wanted to be back with Merry and his friends in Nova Eboracum. Guilt over running away made him sad, but the thought of being back in Merry's arms—if she'd have him—filled his heart with joy.

Eynon wrote a note to Rōlin and Peregrína, stepped to an open spot in the center of the kitchen, and jumped to Melyncárreg by way of an *ad hoc* gate from one kitchen to another.

He walked upstairs to the castle's library and located all three volumes of *On Wizardry*. Leaving strips of paper noting he'd borrowed the books, he put them in his backpack, then returned to the kitchen. In one of the larders, he located a small flour sack filled with ground rye that had begun to spoil with some sort of rot or fungus. He emptied the sack and cleaned it as best he could. Then, with books and sack in hand, he *popped* to the battlements on the castle's western wall and began to call magestone dust from the dark sky around him.

Soon, he was surrounded by a cloud of sparkling dust even thicker than what had gathered around him in Rōlin and Peregrína's valley. It felt like the stars had descended to gyrate around him. Eynon wasn't overwhelmed by the dust this time and directed the multicolored specks into the flour sack, filling it and leaving some left over around his hands and wrists. He pulled the drawstring on the flour sack tight to seal it closed, put the sack in his backpack next to the books, and took a deep breath.

I hope Merry's not too *angry,* thought Eynon. *Here I go.*

The *pop* of his departure echoed in the still night air.

Chapter 37

Rescue Tactics

Laetícia, Quintillius, Fercha, Verro, Inthíra, Mafuta, Felix, Nûd, Bonnie, and the Bifurlanders were discussing next steps for rescuing Valentius in Laetícia's study at the top of her tower.

Bifurland's senior mage spoke to Nûd. "Your Majesty," said the amber-robed wizard. "I can transport us to Bucket Island, but I'm not sure how Viridáxés and Zûrafiérix would react to my sudden and unexpected appearance in their territory."

"Don't worry," Nûd replied. "I'll be glad to come with you and make the necessary introductions. Try to find Zûra first."

"That sounds sensible," said Bifurland's master mage. "We should leave immediately."

Nûd glanced to Bonnie. "Do you still want to join us?"

"I think I'll return to the Institute in Bhaile Pónaire instead," said Bonnie. "Along with finding candidates to help learn wide-gate magic, I know scholars there who are highly skilled in finding lost people and things. They may have suggestions on ways to locate Valentius."

"Understood," said Nûd. He smiled at Sigrun and Rannveigr. "I'm sure Rocky will be well cared for in my absence."

"Of course, Your Majesty," said Sigrun. She didn't stand, but she did offer a nod of respect in his direction.

"There's no need for fancy titles—just call me Nûd."

Bonnie grinned and squeezed Nûd's hand.

"Yes, Uncle Nûd," said Sigrun and Rannveigr in singsong voices.

"Better quit while you're ahead," said King Bjarni.

"Don't worry," said Rannveigr. "We'll take good care of Rocky."

"Thank you," said Nûd. He turned to Bonnie. "Do you think it would be wise to bring Dârio with us in case Viridáxés wants to attack the Roma immediately?"

"I wouldn't bother Dârio," said Bonnie. "We can make up a story about why we need Zûrafiérix."

"Like testing some boring new naval maneuver?" offered Grand Admiral Sónnel.

"Exactly," said Bonnie. "Dârio and Jenet are busy organizing the evacuation of Riyas. We don't want to slow down their work."

"Thank goodness Duke Háiddon is overseeing the evacuation of Brendinas for you," Bonnie told Nûd.

"And thank *you,* Fercha, for telling the duke about the extensive cave network west of the Moravon and in the mountains of the southern provinces," said Nûd. "There should be plenty of space for the people of Dâron to hide from the invaders."

"Wherever you find limestone, the odds are good you'll find caves," said Fercha. "I'll be busy creating gates for people and supplies from the mustering points to the refuges, or I'd be glad to come with you."

"Your talents can be put to a better use elsewhere," said Laetícia, smiling at Fercha. "Your husband, on the other hand, would be quite welcome to join the rescue attempt. Wizards who can form *ad hoc* gates would be particularly valuable team members."

"Now that I no longer need to transport Nûd to Bucket Island personally..." said Verro. He looked at Fercha and raised an eyebrow in a silent question.

"Go ahead, if it will help," she said. Then her voice turned stern. "But be careful, my love. I'd hate to lose you now that we're finally together."

"I will keep an eye on him for you," said Mafuta.

"You're coming?" asked Laetícia. "I thought you'd stay here and assist Quintillius."

"Quin is quite capable of looking after himself," said Mafuta. "There are more than a dozen competent wizards on my staff who will soon be able to help him with gates to speed the evacuation." The older wizard faced Laetícia. "Besides, I'm the only mage on this side of the Ocean who knows Umbrose and the way he thinks. I was a visiting instructor at the school in Lundinium in the Western Empire when the slimy toad of a man first poked his ugly head out of the mud. He showed his aptitude for deception and double-dealing even as a new apprentice."

"In that case, you're quite welcome to join our rescue expedition," said Laetícia.

"Does Umbrose *look* like a toad?" asked Sigrun.

"Only on the inside," replied Mafuta.

"Is he the one who...?" asked Felix.

"Not in front of the girls," said Mafuta.

Felix pressed his lips together and hoped Sigrun and Rannveigr wouldn't pester him for details after the meeting.

One corner of Laetícia's mouth turned up but she promptly turned serious again. "You and Nûd should head north immediately to confirm Zûrafiérix can reach the invasion fleet in time to be useful," she said to the amber-robed master mage from Bifurland. "We'll want to confirm that part of our plan will work before putting things in motion." Laetícia reached into a drawer and handed the amber-robed mage a gold ring. She whispered to the Bifurland wizard, who nodded.

"Understood," said the amber-robed mage. After putting the ring in a pouch, the mage turned to Nûd and helped him to his feet. Nûd bent down and kissed Bonnie, then stepped to the other wizard and boarded the Bifurlander's flying disk. The amber-robed mage put one hand on Nûd's arm and the pair of them disappeared in a single *pop*.

"Do you have another one of those coins with Valens' likeness?" Bonnie asked Mafuta.

"How many do you need?" asked the older wizard.

"One should be enough," Bonnie replied. "There's someone I know who might be able to help." Mafuta tossed her another double-denarius and the younger scholar-mage left a few moments later, presumably to consult the academic wizards at the Institute. Her travels were so much easier since Verro and Laetícia had authorized a gate between Nova Eboracum and Bhaile Pónaire.

Laetícia cleared her throat. "I think we'll need three teams," she said. "Verro, you can guard Inthíra and protect her if she's discovered."

Verro nodded, while Inthíra shrugged her shoulders. She knew offensive magic wasn't her strength.

"Verro," Laetícia continued. "You're also our reserve force in case anything goes wrong."

"Understood," said Verro. "But what could go wrong?"

Laetícia didn't dignify that with an answer. "Mafuta, you and Felix can watch for the ship Valentius was in when he was captured. Grand Admiral Sónnel should be able to tell you what it looks like in general terms, though it will be hard to pick out from a fleet of other Roma vessels."

"Don't worry about that," said Mafuta. "If it has a hold full of magestones, I'll be able to locate it." She smiled at Felix. "I'll teach you the trick of it too, former apprentice," she said. "Once you understand how it's done, that many magestones, even raw ones, will shine like a beacon."

"I look forward to additional instruction," said Felix. He glanced down at Mafuta and grinned. His mentor made a mock frown and gently swatted the tall young mage on the hip with the back of her hand.

"Pay close attention," said Mafuta. "Something useful might, just might, get through your thick skull," she teased.

"Yes, honored and ancient grandmother," said Felix in a similar tone.

"I'll *ancient* you, child," said Mafuta. "And you're not—unfortunately—my grandchild, more's the pity."

"I love you, too," said Felix.

Laetícia spoke. "If I might interrupt this charming display of affection to get back to planning a rescue?"

Felix bowed, which was impressive given his height. "Sorry," he said.

Laetícia faced King Bjarni and Queen Signý. "Your, um, master mage," she began.

"You can say *Amber*," said Bjarni.

"Our master mage answers to that name when necessary," said Signý.

"Which will be much more convenient," said Laetícia. "Especially in the middle of a rescue."

"Quite right," said King Bjarni. "How would you like Amber to assist you?"

"I'd like Amber to partner with me on infiltrating Sírénae's flagship," said Laetícia. "I still think that's the most likely place he's being held.

If either one of us finds Valentius, we can transport him back to Nova Eboracum in an instant with an *ad hoc* gate."

"I'm sure Amber would be glad to accompany you," said Bjarni. "Unfortunately, as an old raider, I see a major flaw in your plan."

"What's that?" asked Laetícia.

"You, Verro, and Amber can all form *ad hoc* gates and escape when necessary," said the king. "As I understand it, Mafuta and Inthíra cannot."

"That's true," said Mafuta. "At least for my part." She nodded at Inthíra. "But my emergency gate is not far from the city. I would be able to escape back to Occidens Province if threatened."

"My emergency gate is closer to Brendinas than Nova Eboracum," said Inthíra. "Though that shouldn't matter, since it's unlikely I'll be carrying Valentius out on my flying disk."

"My apologies, I was mistaken," said Bjarni. Signý patted his forearm and Laetícia hid a smile as she recognized a gesture she often used to let Quintillius know she approved of his actions.

"What about communications?" asked Grand Admiral Sónnel. "Trying to use rings will be much too cumbersome."

"I have an, um, *associate* who can help with that," said Laetícia.

"The Gray Lady?" asked Fercha.

"How *is* Tempora these days?" asked Verro.

"Wait," said Laetícia. "I understand how *you* know about Tempora, Fercha. You're your father's daughter. But how do *you* know about her, Verro?"

"A gentleman never tells," Verro replied.

Laetícia tossed up her hands. "Be that way," she said. She was smiling, not angry. Spymasters knew the lifespans of secrets were vanishingly short. "I'm just pleased she's skilled at crafting small artifacts that fit in our ears and can help small groups keep in touch."

"Umbrose has them as well," said Mafuta. "The little toad used something similar to blackmail fellow students two decades ago in Lundinium."

"O-o-o-oh," said Rannveigr. "I understand now."

Felix shook his head slowly, realizing there'd be no way he'd escape telling the golden-haired girls Mafuta's stories about Umbrose now.

"It will be dark when we attempt our rescue," said Laetícia. "Everyone should wear black clothing. If you don't have anything black to wear, let me know. My staff will be glad to provide something appropriate."

"I don't think Amber owns anything black," said Queen Signý.

"I don't either," said Inthíra.

"We'll remedy that lack shortly," said Laetícia.

"I have something black to wear," said Felix.

Mafuta put one hand to her forehead and sighed.

"What?" asked Felix.

"You've been hoping for a chance to wear that outfit since you had it commissioned a year ago," said his mentor.

"It's protective, useful offensively, and black," said Felix. "It's perfect."

"Wizards don't wear armor," said Mafuta.

"This one plans to," Felix insisted.

Mafuta sighed again.

"Why don't you put it on and let me see if it's appropriate," said Laetícia.

"Great!" said Felix. "I'm sure you'll love it."

"Perhaps," said Laetícia. "We'll depart in two hours. We've got a lot of flying to do."

Chapter 38

Zûrafiérix

Nûd and the amber-robed wizard were on a small sandy beach above the high tide line. It was overcast, with clouds blocking the sun, but it wasn't raining.

"Where are we?" Nûd whispered.

"On Bucket Island," said the wizard. "Where Bjarni and his crew put in for water and fresh meat on a raiding trip a few years ago."

Nûd could see a smile shining out from inside the wizard's amber hood. He was being teased.

"*Where* on Bucket Island are we?" said Nûd, trying a second time to get useful information.

"On the western side of a small harbor on the north shore," said the mage.

"Thank you, good wizard," said Nûd.

"Call me Amber," the wizard said.

"That's easier than saying *good wizard* all the time," said Nûd. "Are you a woman or a man?"

"You've asked an inappropriate and irrelevant question," said Amber. "The closest answer I can give is *Yes*, but that would be incomplete at best."

"I see," said Nûd. "My apologies if I've offended."

"You've actually been far more polite about it than most people who aren't from Bifurland and are ignorant of our ways," said Amber.

"I'll take that as a compliment," said Nûd.

"It was intended as such," Amber replied.

"The dragons are probably in the rocks toward the center of the island," said Nûd. "That's where Zûrafiérix said she'd planned to build her nest."

"I don't think we'll have any trouble finding her," said Amber. The wizard gestured upward.

Nûd's eyes followed and he saw that Bucket Island had grown a new spire at its highest point. It was a dragon, perched at the top of the modest stone hill that formed the island's center. "Take us up, please," he told Amber. "I think that's Zûrafiérix."

Seconds later the king and the wizard were hovering in front of a great dragon's head. The dragon's huge, whirling eyes circled with amusement.

"You *think* it's Zûrafiérix?" said the blue dragon. "I thought we knew each other better than that, King of Dâron."

"My apologies, Zûrafiérix," said Nûd. "Dragons have much better night vision than mere humans like myself. I can say that I certainly *hoped* you were atop the hill, not Viridáxés, since you're the dragon I wanted to see. This is my new friend Amber, by the way. Amber is the master mage of Bifurland."

"We've met already, at the treaty-signing ceremony," said Zûrafiérix. "At the time, however, I was unaware of Amber's formal role. This dragon is pleased to meet Bifurland's master mage."

"And *this* mage is pleased to meet the eminent and excellent dragon Zûrafiérix," said Amber.

Zûrafiérix beamed with pleasure, reconfirming for Nûd that the old stories about dragon's susceptibility to flattery must be true. Viridáxés liked to be flattered as well, even more than Zûrafiérix.

"Where is Viridáxés?" asked Nûd. "I expected him to be close by."

"The inconsiderate green wyrm is asleep on the far side of the island," said Zûrafiérix. "He captured a whale and swallowed it whole this morning, without bringing any back for me. I informed him of his discourtesy and sent him off to learn better manners and the wisdom of treating his mate properly."

"Are you hungry?" asked Amber. "I could find a small whale and retrieve it for you with magic if you'd like."

"No, I wasn't particularly hungry," said Zûrafiérix. "It was more about the principle of the thing. What kind of mate will Viridáxés be when it's time to feed starving hatchlings? I must teach him how to behave *before* I lay my first clutch."

"Best of luck with your challenges," said Nûd. "As it turns out, we are here to request *your* aid with challenges of our own. Only a dragon of your vast power and wisdom can truly assist us."

"What can I do to help?" asked Zûrafiérix. Her sparkling blue eyes grew brighter and the whirlpools inside them began to spin faster. "I assume it has something to do with the invasion?"

"It does indeed," said Nûd.

"If any degree if subtlety is needed, I can understand why you wanted to talk to me, not Viridáxés," said Zûrafiérix. "He's been consumed with the idea of setting the entire invasion fleet alight with his fire blasts and sinking them all. It's been a challenge to restrain him."

"The struggle is real, I'm sure," said Nûd. "Your efforts are greatly appreciated." He quickly sketched out the main points, noting the details Zûrafiérix hadn't heard yet, like the size of the emperor's fleet and Sírénae's ultimatum that all Orluin surrender to her authority.

"You didn't agree, did you?" asked Zûrafiérix. The spines along the dragon's back stuck out like the fur on an angry cat. "Viridáxés and I could destroy a thousand invading ships on our own."

"We did not," said Amber.

"Good," said Zûrafiérix. "To the depths of the Ocean with subtlety. If you'd like, I'll wake my foolish mate and together we can destroy half of this *Siren Hawk's* fleet before sunrise, when they're still hundreds of leagues from shore."

"That won't be necessary," said Nûd. "We considered that approach and decided on another option. None of us doubted your combined prowess, but such tactics would result in at least a hundred thousand deaths. It didn't seem right to kill so many soldiers and sailors whose only crime was to be under the command of a woman like Sírénae Accipiter."

"She wants to conquer a new continent," said Amber.

"Because she was exiled by the three other emperors of the Roma across the Ocean," added Nûd.

"Could Viridáxés and I drive her fleet back across the Ocean instead of sinking her ships?" asked Zûrafiérix.

"We're concerned about her wizards," said Amber. "As far as we know, you and Viridáxés are the last breeding pair of great dragons remaining on either side of the Ocean. Your species—and yourselves—can't be risked on a frontal attack. We don't yet know the extent of her wizards' skills."

"I can see the wisdom in that," said Zûrafiérix. She rubbed a front claw along the bony ridges of her lower jaw and focused her gaze on Nûd and Amber. "What's *your* plan?"

"We want to starve out Sírénae's forces, so they leave Orluin voluntarily," said Nûd. "You and Viridáxés can attack the boats they send out to fish," he continued. "If you rise from the depths, bash holes in their hulls, and dive immediately, you'll still keep your presence hidden and prevent the emperor's forces from being resupplied."

"We're arranging a mass evacuation of the people and stores from eastern Orluin," said Amber. "When the invasion fleet arrives, they'll find an empty land, with no crops planted and no livestock to slaughter."

"No citizens to enslave, too," said Nûd.

Zûrafiérix scratched her chin again and released a giant blast of steam from her nostrils after warning Amber and Nûd of her intentions first.

"Where will these invading Roma go when they're starving?" asked the great blue dragon.

"It matters not to the people of Bifurland so long as it's far away," said Amber.

"I've considered that," said Nûd. "I think there's a better answer than wishing them on some other settled land. There's an entire empty continent to the south of Orluin. Friends of mine are planning to map it soon. Sírénae's forces can go there if they wish."

"Clearly, the King of Dâron is wise beyond his years," said Zûrafiérix. "And merciful as well. Wouldn't you just be pushing an inevitable conflict off on your descendants, however?"

"Not necessarily," said Amber. "The study of our futures and fates holds a particular interest. There is wisdom in Nûd's plan. A generation would likely see Sírénae's death and opportunities for the people of both western continents to trade and grow closer, not necessarily make war on each other. It's a valid option."

Zûrafiérix nodded thoughtfully. "We're talking of what may happen months from now," she said. "Your arrival at night indicates a matter of particular urgency. What do you need me to do *now?*"

"You can start by telling us how long it would take you to fly from Bucket Island to Sírénae's fleet a hundred miles northwest of the Tempest Isles," said Nûd.

"You'd have to swim the last fifty miles to be sure you aren't seen," added Amber.

"Now I'm glad Viridáxés *didn't* share any of his whale with me," said Zûrafiérix. "I'm not sure how fast I can truly fly, but I could reach a hundred and fifty miles an hour before I was placed in the quarry." She opened her vast wings and stretched them out to their maximum extension. "Now I think I could be much faster."

"Excellent," said Nûd. He explained how Sírénae held Valentius captive and their plan to have Inthíra cast a giant kraken illusion.

"I *like* it," said Zûrafiérix. "It will be a pleasure to pretend to be a sea monster, since I was mistaken for one by the sailors with Tamloch's fleet."

"So long as you stay out of sight," said Amber. "Inthíra will help hide you."

"I'll do my part," said Zûrafiérix.

Nûd found a patch of sand a bit farther downslope. It was clearly new, and he assumed Zûrafiérix had moved it there for her future eggs. "Take us down, please," he said to Amber.

The wizard descended to the sandy spot and Nûd hopped down from Amber's flying disk. He found a stick and traced the relative locations of Bucket Island, the Tempest Islands, and the probable location of the emperor's fleet in the Ocean.

Amber located the gold ring from Laetícia and spoke a word of command with extra emphasis. The ring expanded until it was large enough to encircle one of the dragon's big external ears. "We can keep in touch with this ring," Amber told Zûrafiérix. "It will help us carefully coordinate our attack, since Laetícia has the ring's mate."

Zûrafiérix nodded.

"Speaking of mates," said Nûd. "Should we leave a message for Viridáxés, letting him know where you've gone? It could be a disaster if he appears above the invasion fleet."

"I wouldn't worry," said Zûrafiérix. "After eating that whale, Viridáxés couldn't fly to and from Fishhook Cape in under five hours. He'll be asleep until noon tomorrow."

"Safe flying," said Amber.

"And confusion to the enemy," said the dragon.

"I'll be happy if we can avoid too much of our own confusion," said Nûd. He stepped back onto Amber's flying disk and the two of them gated back to Nova Eboracum.

Chapter 39

Evacuation Challenges

Duke Háiddon wiped sweat from his forehead with the back of his sleeve. Dâron's earl marshal was standing under the hot noonday sun in a broad field south of Brendinas. Three wide gates had been built there, and long lines of families, carts, and wagons were passing through the gates in a mostly organized manner. Duke Háiddon had wanted to supervise the orderly evacuation of Dâron's capital in person, since everyone was willing to take his suggestions as commands. Conflicts in the queues vanished quickly when Háiddon became involved.

Duke Néillen, the disgraced former earl marshal of Tamloch, was standing beside Duke Háiddon. Néillen was an able administrator and skilled tactician, but Háiddon didn't trust him farther than he could throw a Bifurland mammoth—which is to say, not at all. In the spirit of keeping your friends close and your enemies closer, Duke Háiddon kept Duke Néillen within arm's reach on the mustering field as thousands of men, women, and children trudged through the wide gates.

"The portal to the caves in the southern mountains is flowing nicely," Duke Néillen remarked.

"They have no shortage of space in their caverns," said Duke Háiddon. "I wish I'd had time to inspect the southern caves personally," he added. "I've been told they're quite beautiful."

"If you say so," said Duke Néillen. "The center gate to the caves in the western marches of Dâron is only bunching up from time to time."

"That's because it doesn't lead directly to caverns," said Duke Háiddon. "It comes out at the Earl of the Rhuthro Valley's castle, and individual parties have to be led to a series of smaller caves as far as a day's march away." He summoned a soldier standing nearby and gave the woman a detailed message. "Go through the center gate and tell the earl to move newcomers away from the exit so they don't block future arrivals."

"Yes, Your Grace," said the soldier.

Duke Háiddon spoke softly to Duke Néillen, using a voice pitched so only Néillen could hear. "I'm going to need to promote Baron Derry to an official post like War Leader for the Rhuthro Valley and the Bordermarches. The earl needs someone close by he can learn from. Like many of us at his age, the earl is more interested in using his sword than his brain."

"I'm familiar with the problem," said Duke Néillen. "Is this baron—Derry, you called him—Salder's father?"

"Yes," said Háiddon. "And Merry's. He has a good head on his shoulders."

"It's unfortunate Túathal tended to remove wise heads, not promote them," said Néillen.

"Present company excepted?" asked Háiddon.

"Sometimes I'm not so sure about that," Néillen replied.

The third wide gate led to a pair of caverns in eastern Dâron. Duke Háiddon had it mostly populated by trained members of his infantry, thinking it would be easier to bring them together to fight if the emperor left herself vulnerable to an attack. His cavalry wings went through the southern and western gates where there was room for horses to be fed and exercised. Unfortunately, the eastern caverns were also the most likely refuges to be discovered. Soldiers destined to go through the eastern gate helped keep civilians moving smoothly through the other two gates.

For some time, the two dukes stood a few feet apart, watching the ebb and flow of the evacuation. At intervals, carts and wagons would bump into each other, leading to an argument at one of the gates. Duke Háiddon, with Duke Néillen a few paces behind, would step in to find a quick resolution and keep the processions moving.

When the sun was an hour past noon and tempers were more likely to fray, Duke Néillen noticed a high-spirited horse—probably a young stallion—pulling an overloaded cart nearly the size of a wagon. The horse was skittish, and Néillen walked toward the animal while Duke Háiddon was giving a message to another soldier.

A girl with short brown hair walked beside the horse and encouraged him to be calm and keep moving. She was doing well enough until a spotted dog with long floppy ears saw a rabbit munching grass near the stallion. The dog started barking and the horse reared, tugging his reins from the girl's fingers and getting ready to run. With the cart behind him, the galloping horse would strew belongings everywhere.

Néillen crossed the space between his position and the stallion's in three heartbeats. He clutched at the reins, holding them firmly in both hands, and leaned down so most of his weight pulled the stallion's head down. "Whoa there," said Néillen. "Nothing to be afraid of. Just a noisy dog. Whoa. Settle down, big fellow."

"Thank you," said the girl with short brown hair. She moved to stand next to Néillen.

"Glad to help," said Néillen. "What's his name?"

"Clatter," said the girl. "We named him that after the way he liked to walk on cobblestones after the first time he was shod."

"Hah!" said Duke Néillen. "He looks like a fine horse." Néillen patted the stallion's neck and handed the reins back to the girl. Together they continued to guide the cart toward the center wide gate.

"We got him for my brother," said the girl. "A challenging horse makes a skilled rider, my father always says."

"Where are your parents?" asked Néillen.

"Back at our townhouse with the other wagons and the money chests," said the girl. "Please don't tell them I couldn't handle Clatter."

"I won't," said Néillen. He promised himself he'd find out who the girl's parents were and share strong words with them. Néillen expected Duke Háiddon would be glad to assist. In a strange way, it felt good to know that Dâron had its share of rich fools, just like Tamloch. Néillen watched the girl get to the gate's interface. She turned and waved to him before she led the horse and cart through.

Néillen wondered how many people he'd need to ask to learn the identity of the family who owned a stallion named Clatter...

* * * * *

"Thank goodness Merry found that cavern system northwest of Riyas," said Jenet. "They say there are a dozen more caves beyond the one she found, and all the mushrooms in the complex will help stretch our supplies."

"It was a timely discovery," said Dârio. "I'm told the ones below and behind the Great Falls farther west are quite big as well. We can keep most of the population of Tamloch safely underground..." he continued.

"And the rest will retreat to beyond the Inland Seas where the invaders are unlikely to penetrate," said Jenet. "My big concern is having enough supplies to not only last until the Roma invaders depart, but until we can till and plant and sow again."

"That's my worry, too," said King Dârio. "It would be ironic for us to run out of food when we were trying to starve Sírénae's legions."

"Do you think we're doing the right thing by evacuating instead of fighting?" asked Jenet.

"You're my earl marshal," said Dârio. "Tell me what *you* think, and then I'll share my opinion."

Jenet put her chin on top of her fist as she stood next to Dârio in the command tent at the evacuation mustering field. The creaks and squeaks of the wagon wheels, along with the sounds of horses, oxen, drovers, and hundreds of excited and frightened children, provided a complex background to her cogitations.

"I think running away and hiding is the best of several bad options," she said. "Any direct confrontation is likely to result in tens of thousands of soldiers dead and the rest of the citizens of Tamloch—and Dâron—enslaved. Bifurland would eventually be conquered as well."

"What about the idea of assassinating the emperor?" asked Dârio.

Jenet grabbed Dârio's forearm and held it, her nails biting his flesh through his sleeve like a hawk's talons. "If we try to kill Sírénae, what's to prevent her from killing *you?*"

"Nothing, of course," said Dârio. "Though I doubt the emperor would have any moral compunctions about a few strategic royal assassinations if she thought they were in her best interest."

"All the more reason for our current course of action," said Jenet. "She can't have you killed if she can't find you."

"Yes, but I *hate* running away," said Dârio. He put his hand over Jenet's. "I want to *do* something, like release Viridáxés and watch him sink half the invasion fleet."

"If he can," said Jenet. "The emperor's wizards are reputedly quite skilled. They may be able to counter Viridáxés and Zûrafiérix combined, and then where would we be?"

"I know," said Dârio, "But I still want to slash or skewer something."

"Of course you do, my love," said Jenet. "You're eighteen and filled with the impetuous energy of youth. You need to listen to the older and wiser counsel of your earl marshal and hold back your temper."

Dârio laughed. "Older? Wiser? You need to recheck your birth records. You're five days *younger* than I am, not older."

"Perhaps where the mere count of days is concerned, my king," said Jenet. She turned to face Dârio and smiled. "But when it comes to wisdom, I must be wiser, for what sort of fool must a ruler be to appoint someone *less* wise than himself as a counselor?" Jenet wiggled her eyebrows at Dârio, then kissed him until they were both a bit short of breath.

"There's a logical fallacy in there somewhere, but my brain can't focus enough at the moment to find it," said Dârio.

"Don't think too hard about it," teased Jenet.

Normally, such conversations would end up with the two of them entertaining themselves horizontally, or in other interesting physical configurations, but this time Dârio pulled his shoulders back and paced around the confines of the tent, alert for any sounds from outside that would merit his attention. When he got back to Jenet he regarded her at arm's length.

"What about raiding concentrations of imperial forces once they arrive?" he asked. "We could strike by night and steal their food and wine? That might satisfy my urge to *do* something."

"It would also encourage Sírénae's generals to focus on finding us," said Jenet. "Remember one of Ealdamon's epigrams—*Out of sight, out of mind.*"

"Of course," said Dârio. "That's why I spent so much time away from court at your father's estates when I was growing up."

"Was that the only reason?" teased Jenet.

"Well," said Dârio. "Your younger sister was good company, at least."

"My younger sister loved you, and still loves you—like a puppy dog loves the person who feeds her," said Jenet. "I admired the fact that you never took advantage of her infatuation."

"I had other, more satisfying distractions," said Dârio with a twinkle in his eye. He took another deep breath. "Let's find another topic of conversation, or we may find ourselves putting knots in the tent closures and ignoring how thin the canvas is."

"Would that be so bad?" asked Jenet.

"Not for me," said Dârio. "But how would *you* ever keep quiet?"

"A royal counselor like a kingdom's earl marshal must be discreet about all things," said Jenet. "Try me, and you'll see I can keep silent."

"Where's the fun in that?" asked Dârio.

Jenet frowned at him, then both were distracted by a herald announcing herself just outside the entrance to the command tent. "Your Majesty. Earl Marshal. We need your help regarding a dispute over whose wagons should take precedence through the wide gate to the Great Falls' caves. The earl of Korq insists on moving to the head of the line."

"Saved from a fate worse than death," whispered Jenet.

"What do you mean?" asked Dârio in a matching volume. "I was about to go tie up the tent flaps."

"We'll be right out," said Jenet.

* * * * *

Quintillius was glad he had dependable deputies to help with the evacuation of Occidens Province. Several of the leading citizens in Nova Eboracum had wanted him to welcome Sírénae's invasion and join her legions in putting all of Orluin firmly under Roma rule. They didn't know Sírénae like he did. The odds were good those leading citizens would lose their lives and have their great estates along the Abbenoth given to Sírénae's supporters.

I wish Laetícia was here with me, Quin thought. *She's far better at managing wizards than I am.* "At least the wide gates are built," he said out loud.

"Governor-General?" asked a legionnaire attending Quin.

"I was saying I'm glad that the wide gates are built," said Quintillius.

The legionnaire smiled. "I'm glad they are, too," he said. "The supplies from the military and civilian warehouses are going through first, four wains abreast, and the quartermasters report they should all be transferred by mid-afternoon."

"And then the people can start crossing," said Quintillius, smiling back. "Won't that be a zoo?"

"Citizens of Nova Eboracum aren't known for waiting politely in line, Your Excellency," said the legionnaire.

"Make confident the centurions understand they and their troops are authorized to use their spears to keep order, if necessary," said Quintillius.

"I'm sure they're well aware they have that option," said the legionnaire. "Your instructions were quite explicit."

"Good," said the governor-general. "Once a few patricians and wealthy merchants shed a few drops of their own precious blood, the rest will get the message and behave themselves."

"We can hope, Your Excellency."

"Very well," said Quintillius. "Carry on."

The legionnaire nodded and stepped back two dozen paces. He was close enough to hear a summons but far enough away to give Quin a modicum of privacy. He liked the legionnaire—the man had an attitude that said he respected authority but didn't think any other Roma citizen was his better. Once this emergency situation was over, whenever that might be, Quin resolved to dig deeper into the legionnaire's record and see if it was time for him to be promoted.

"What's your name, soldier?" the governor-general called out.

"Gaius," said the legionnaire. When the man reduced the distance between himself and Quintillius, the governor-general could see curly blond hair that sparkled so brightly it might have been made from the Golden Fleece of the winged ram of Colchis.

"Take off your helmet, please," said Quintillius.

"As the Governor-General commands," said Gaius.

When his helmet was removed, Quin could see the man's hair was remarkably gold in color. *Its unusual shade must make him popular with potential bed partners,* thought Quintillius.

"Where are you from, Gaius?"

"Alexandria, Governor-General," Gaius replied. "I served under Valens in the upper Nile campaign before he was named to lead the Southern Empire."

"You don't look Egyptian," said Quin.

"I'm Thracian," said Gaius.

"An Athican, then," said Quin, nodding as the legionnaire's answer cleared up a mystery.

"And a proud Roma," added Gaius. He stood proudly in front of the governor-general as if daring Quin to doubt his loyalty to the province and the empire.

Quintillius looked at Gaius more closely. "You look familiar," he said. "Have you ever been assigned to my support staff before?"

"This is the first time," said Gaius. "But you might be thinking of my twin brother Aurelius. His hair is the same color and has the same curl. He's a wizard—one of the top qua-qua players for the Reds."

"That's where I know your face—and hair," said Quintillius. "I met Aurelius at a party six months ago in honor of his team's victory in the city championship."

"He told me about meeting you and Laetícia," said Gaius. "The two of you made an impression on him."

"And Aurelius made an impression on me," said Quintillius. "At least enough to remember his face."

"And hair, I expect," said Gaius. He shook his curls and both men laughed.

"You've given me an idea," said Quintillius. "I'm dismissing you for the rest of the afternoon. Tell your commander to send me a replacement aide."

"Have I failed you in some way, Governor-General?" asked Gaius.

"Not at all," said Quin. "Your very presence has been a boon to our efforts against the false-emperor's invasion. I want you to find your brother and the captains of all the qua-qua teams still in Nova Eboracum and have them—and you—join me and my wife in the royal palace for dinner. I expect we'll have a fascinating discussion."

Gaius looked simultaneously confused and elated, but he quickly snapped his expression back into a more neutral and professional demeanor, except for hints of a smile that kept breaking through. "As the Governor-General commands," he said.

"Tell your commander to give you entry tokens," shouted Quintillius to the legionnaire's rapidly departing back. Quin hoped he'd have time to run his idea past Laetícia before dinner. She'd need to brief him on the status of her plans to rescue Valentius, after all. Maybe his recent brainstorm could help *her* planned rescue of Valentius.

Chapter 40

Taverna

The taverna run by the dough-ring man's brother-in-law wasn't hard to find. Merry and Doethan had descended into the area frequented by Távi's gang and received directions to the establishment's location from Távi directly. To her surprise, it was a lot easier to give directions in a city laid out in a regular grid—except for the broad way cutting diagonally up the island that Távi told them had once been a deer trail. They offered to buy Távi lunch, but the youth declined their invitation. As they walked away from the leader of the band of young people, Doethan explained.

"We didn't invite everyone," he said. "Távi is a good leader and won't have a meal with us when the rest of the gang can't as well."

"I understand," said Merry. "My father told me he would often go hungry on campaign when his soldiers were on short rations."

"Derry was—and *is*—a good leader," Doethan replied.

"And I'd do well to emulate him, right?" asked Merry.

"The best lessons are the ones where students can draw their own conclusions," said Doethan. "You're doing a good job as a leader on your own."

"Thank you," said Merry. She hoped Doethan was correct in his assessment. Ace was walking next to Merry's heel in his dog form, and Chee sat on her shoulder watching everything—especially the food vendors—on the streets around them.

The taverna was on a corner a few blocks east of the former deer trail. It occupied the entire first floor of a six-story apartment block. Merry read the sign hanging above it: "Joseph's Food and Drink." A white arrow painted on the cobblestones pointed at the taverna's entrance and was accompanied by a short, clear message. "Eat at Joe's." Other arrows and messages were drawn on the pavement nearby. "For a good time, follow the pointing male member," read one. "Need help with your imperial taxes?" read another, written in green. A series of arrows the color of new grass led off down the block toward the tax expert.

"I'm impressed," said Merry.

"By the outside of the taverna?" asked Doethan.

"No," said Merry. "By the high rate of literacy implied by these signs painted on the pavement." Doethan turned his head quizzically and Merry continued. "You wouldn't have signs like these if most people couldn't read."

"I guess you're right," said Doethan. "Let's hope this taverna's food is as good as the dough rings we had earlier."

"The place seems busy enough, anyway," said Merry. People had been entering the taverna while they'd been talking. The cheerful hum of friendly conversations and the reassuring clacking of wooden spoons on wooden bowls echoed out onto the street. Chee chittered eagerly and Ace's tongue lolled out from the delicious smells wafting from the taverna.

"After you," said Doethan, gesturing with an extended hand.

Merry entered. She seemed surprised to see that the ground floor walls of the apartment building were six feet thick. The interior of the taverna was cool, even though the temperature outside was warm enough for people to put aside their heavy cloaks.

"Why are the walls so thick?" asked Merry.

"Because Roma Mater across the Ocean is prone to earthquakes," answered Doethan.

"That makes no sense," said Merry.

"It makes quite a bit of sense," said Doethan. "Have you ever seen any structures as tall as this apartment block in Dâron or Tamloch, except for castles or palaces?"

"No," said Merry. "We don't seem as fond of crowding together as the people of Nova Eboracum."

"The Roma *do* love their cities," said Doethan. "Over the centuries, they figured out what it took to build sturdy apartments six and even eight stories high."

"What does that have to do with thick walls and earthquakes?" asked Merry.

"The guidelines for building apartment blocks came from Roma Mater's engineers," said Doethan. He moved to the side to allow a man and a woman who smelled like tanners to step past them and shifted Merry to the left, so they didn't block the taverna's entrance. "They'd discovered that if you over-built the lower stories of apartment blocks—like we do when we're constructing castles—they were far less likely to collapse during earthquakes."

"I... see..." said Merry. "You're saying people do things a certain way because that's the way they've always done them, despite changing circumstances."

"Exactly," said Doethan.

"There's a lesson in there somewhere, but I'm too hungry to analyze it," said Merry. She pointed to a line of local tradespeople holding bowls and spoons, standing along the left side of the taverna. "Let's get some lunch."

Doethan and Merry joined the end of the line. Merry was surprised Chee and Ace hadn't already shot ahead to raid the stew pot.

A short woman with a broad smile who resembled the dough-ring man refused the coins Doethan offered.

"Your money's not good here," she said. "Not with all you've given us already." The woman waved toward the kitchen where Merry and Doethan saw the dough-ring man himself filling wooden bowls with a thick stew.

"I'm *so* glad to see you, good wizards," said the dough-ring man. "As you can see, our business is booming, thanks to the chilled wine we can now provide."

"Do you have any cold cider?" asked Merry hopefully.

"Of course," said the dough-ring man while still filling bowls. "We have a broad range of clientele here," he continued. "Some barbarians even prefer beer."

A dozen long-haired laborers with the calloused hands of shipwrights lifted foaming mugs and shouted, "Beer!"

The dough-ring man waved his arm and a girl younger than Eynon's sister Braith appeared from the kitchen pulling a small wheeled cart laden with two sturdy barrels on their sides. Both had taps. Additional mugs were on a shelf beneath the barrels.

"Which of you will be wanting cold beer and which warm?" she asked the men and women at the table. Merry laughed when the shipwrights who looked like Bifurlanders opted for cold beer while ones whose ancestors must have originally come from the White Isle uniformly wanted their beer warm.

The smiling woman personally escorted Doethan and Merry to a round table for four in the center of the establishment. "These are the best seats in the place," she said. "They usually go to guild masters or anyone buying drinks for the house, but today they're yours as our honored guests," the woman continued. Chee stood on one of the chairs and Ace hopped up on another. The woman rubbed both familiars under their chins and seemed to take the animals' presence in stride. A few other dogs took notice of Ace, but there weren't any growls from beneath nearby tables.

The dough-ring man brought three steaming bowls of stew to their table and a basket of fruit for Chee. He bent down and whispered in Doethan's ear. "I put extra meat in your bowls," he said conspiratorially.

"What sort of stew is it?" asked Merry.

"Wisent," called a voice from the kitchen. "Our legionnaires brought back quite a few of them from the south."

"Wonderful!" said Merry. "My lover is the one..." she began, then cut herself off when the side of Doethan's boot rapped her shin. "...who gave me my first taste of wisent," she completed, receiving Doethan's message. Now was not the time to share that she was a *very close friend* of the new Master Mage of Dâron.

Ace had his face in *his* stew, but Doethan sat before his portion with a fist on either side of his bowl.

"What a fool I am," said the dough-ring man. A tall bearded man came out from the kitchen and took over the dough-ring man's job of dishing out stew so the dough-ring man could fetch spoons for Merry and Doethan. "My apologies," he said. "You said you wanted cold cider, if I remember correctly, young wizard?"

"That's right," said Merry. "Cold cider would be wonderful."

"I'd like a chilled white wine," said Doethan.

"Of course, good wizards," the dough-ring man replied.

Before the girl pulling the cart with two barrels could make her way to the second table of beer drinkers, the dough-ring man had delivered a glass goblet of pale wine to Doethan and a much larger pewter mug of cider to Merry. The mug clinked as he put it on the table.

"I've put chunks of ice in your cider, good wizard," said the dough-ring man. "It sounded like that was something you'd like."

"I like it quite a bit," said Merry. "I hope your other patrons turn out to enjoy it as well."

He leaned close to Merry. "If you show that you really like it, I'm sure I'll sell a lot more iced ciders in the days ahead."

When he stood up and returned to dishing stew, Merry theatrically lifted her mug, took a long swallow, and banged the bottom of the mug on the round table. "Best cold cider I've ever had," she announced. The dough-ring man winked at her and smiled.

It didn't take long for Doethan and Merry to finish their bowls of stew. More stew was offered, but their first serving was filling, so they declined. Merry did take more cold cider, however, and Doethan had a second glass of chilled wine. They were sipping their respective drinks when the noisy taverna went quiet. Turning to face the taverna's entrance, they saw three legionnaires standing a few steps inside the room.

"Attention all citizens, slaves, and visitors in Nova Eboracum," began the legionnaire standing in the middle of the trio. He held a scroll sealed with purple wax and read from it. "His Excellency, Governor-General Quintillius Martius Africanus of Occidens Province, commands that the city must be evacuated immediately. Everyone between Via XII and XXV must gather up all their food, valuables, and family members and make their way to the staging point at the southern end of the Great Park by the third hour. You will receive further instructions there. Legionnaires will be positioned at intersections to assist you and answer questions.

This order is given in the name of the Senate and People of Roma."
The speaker looked over the lunch crowd in the taverna and offered
parting words of advice. "I'd get moving *now* if I were you." He struck
his fist on his breastplate, turned on his heel, and departed with his
subordinates trailing behind him.

The taverna remained quiet until the sound of the soldiers' footsteps
faded. Then it erupted into shouts and protests. Doethan looked
at Merry.

"I think we'd better get back to the palace," he said.

"I completely agree," said Merry.

Ace and Chee gladly accompanied them out of the taverna. The
two wizards didn't pause to thank their hosts as they left. They made
their way to the street, hopped on their flying disks, and flew off.

Chapter 41

Gate Hopping

Laetícia heard a firm knock on the door to her study. It was the distinctive rap of the senior guard on the landing outside, and she knew he wouldn't be bothering her if it wasn't important.

"What is it?" she asked when she opened the door.

"It's us," said Merry. She bustled past the door with Doethan behind her and stepped into Laetícia's sanctum. All the others had departed earlier, leaving Merry and Doethan alone with the unified person of the governor-general's wife and Occidens Province's spymaster.

Ace trotted over to one of Laetícia's thick carpets and settled in for a nap after his large bowl of stew. Chee jumped to a hanging wizard lamp and surveyed the office from above, looking for food. Laetícia tossed him a ripe pear from a bowl on her desk.

"Sorry for arriving unannounced," said Doethan.

"You didn't tell us you were going to start the evacuation *today!*" Merry interrupted. "You Roma work *fast!* We were in a taverna having lunch after practicing my line-of-sight gating in the park— I'm getting really good at it, by the way—and legionnaires came in and announced that everyone had to leave the city immediately. There was chaos everywhere, so we left and came here."

While Merry took a breath, Laetícia replied. "We need to move quickly," she said. "Sírénae will have no mercy on any stragglers, so the sooner we can get people out of the city, the sooner they'll be safe."

"That's sensible," said Doethan. "You've got a huge population to evacuate, and not much time to accomplish the move."

"What can we do to help?" asked Merry.

"I'd thought about asking you both to help with rescuing Valentius," said Laetícia. She summarized the plans to catch up with the emperor's fleet, find Valentius, and gate him safely back to Nova Eboracum.

"Are you sure using Zûrafiérix is a good idea?" asked Doethan.

"Inthíra and Amber assure me they can mask Zûra's presence," said Laetícia.

"I'd be good at that, too," said Merry.

"Amber is the Bifurland master mage?" asked Doethan.

"Yes," said Laetícia. "Amber and Nûd are on Bucket Island talking to Zûrafiérix right now." She smiled at Merry, enjoying the young woman's enthusiasm and appreciating the way it distracted her from worrying about the upcoming rescue attempt. "Can you get to Tyford within an hour?" she asked Doethan.

"I can use the new gate that's just been built from Nova Eboracum to Brendinas, then jump from my apartment there to my tower on the Rhuthro, then use my gate to Taffy's inn," Doethan replied. I could try to use the gate from the Conclave in Brendinas direct to Tyford, but it would probably take longer getting the appropriate authorizations." He paused and looked carefully at Laetícia. "Why do you ask?"

"Duke Háiddon just contacted me asking for help building gates from Tyford to caverns farther west," said Laetícia. "Fercha is pulled in all directions trying to help set up wide gates in Dâron, Tamloch, and Occidens Province. Her focus is on eastern Dâron, but Duke Háiddon says it's important that Tyford be evacuated, even if it is farther inland. He told me he sent someone senior to Taffaern's inn to coordinate Tyford's efforts. From what the duke didn't say, it sounded like the person wasn't a wizard and would need help with the magical side of the evacuation."

"I see," said Doethan. "And I'm one of several senior wizards Fercha's taught how to make wide gates, correct?" He regarded Laetícia. "Duke Háiddon needs wizards who can pop in quickly, establish wide gates to caverns in western Dâron, and then ensure they continue to function properly. I think I can—"

"Doethan knows those caves *and* Tyford," said Merry, jumping in. "He's perfect for that role."

"And he'll need help with creating the wide gates," said Laetícia. "Fercha's taught you the art as well."

"So you *don't* want me to help with the rescue?" asked Merry.

"I'm only taking a small team," said Laetícia.

"I... see..." said Merry. She looked down for a moment, then turned to Doethan wearing an obviously forced smile. "Let's be on our way then," she said. "Duke Háiddon needs us." Merry called to Ace and Chee. "Come along, boys. We've got to be going."

Merry bustled out the door to the landing outside Laetícia's study. Doethan smiled at Laetícia and shrugged. She replied with a shrug and a smile of her own. Doethan followed Merry out on the landing and the two of them swooped down from Laetícia's tower toward the building in the governor-general's palace complex that held the new permanent gate to Brendinas.

* * * * *

The new permanent gates set up connecting Nova Eboracum to Riyas, Bjarniston, and Brendinas were in hastily constructed, arched stone corridors twenty feet long in one of the palace court-yards. Armed legionnaires stood in each corridor, confirming that those crossing from one side to the other had approval to do so. Merry laughed when she saw the legionnaire assigned to guard the corridor to the gate leading to Brendinas. She nudged Doethan and he held back a grin.

"Stultio, my old friend," said Doethan. "So nice to see you. You're looking fit. Have you been exercising?"

"Go right through," said the once-haughty young legionnaire who had tried to block Merry and Doethan's entry into the palace more than seven days earlier. He wouldn't meet their eyes and pressed his body against the side of the corridor to give them room to pass.

"Aren't you going to ask us for our entry tokens?" teased Merry.

After Stultio had been rude to Merry and Doethan more than a week earlier, his commander had punished the soldier by making him run ten times around the palace in full armor. Stultio had absolutely no interest in earning another ten laps.

Merry sniffed. There was still a whiff of night soil lingering around the legionnaire from the punishment of cleaning privies, which he'd been assigned after completing his run. Ace sniffed the soldier and turned up his nose in disgust. Chee made faces at Stultio from the safety of Merry's shoulder.

"What's the trigger phrase for the gate, Stultio?" Doethan commanded.

The legionnaire muttered something too soft to hear.

"Speak up," said Doethan, "or I'll inform your commander you're being unhelpful."

"Azure Draco," said Stultio, reluctantly.

"Thank you," said Doethan. "If you would do the honors?" he asked Merry.

The young wizard spoke the words and the gate shimmered into existence. Ace, Chee, Merry, and Doethan stepped through without another thought for the once-arrogant legionnaire.

* * * * *

The other end of the gate in Brendinas was quite similar to the gate in Nova Eboracum, but the corridors were made of brick, not stone. The older man on guard wearing a Dâron-blue soldier's uniform recognized Doethan and waved them through.

"Now where?" asked Merry. "I don't know my way around Nûd's palace."

"I don't think *Nûd* knows his way around his palace yet, either," said Doethan.

Merry grinnws at the truth of Doethan's statement. "Are your apartments inside the grounds?" she asked.

"No, but they're not far."

Their light-blue wizards' robes were enough to allow them to leave the palace through the gate at the rose garden. Doethan led them up and down a maze of interlocking streets and alleys until they reached a narrow, whitewashed, frame structure in a row of similar buildings. A bookbinder's shop occupied the ground floor and Merry guessed there were private rooms on the upper two stories that extended out over the street in front.

"Which one is your apartment?" asked Merry, tugging on Doethan's robe and pointing up.

"They both are," said Doethan. "Come along," he said. Doethan opened the door of the bookbinder's shop and entered. Merry, Chee, and Ace followed. A tall, muscular man a bit older than Doethan was working at a bench near the back of the shop. The place smelled of old leather, glue, and solvents. Three bookcases stood on the left-hand wall and Merry was sorely tempted to see if they held any books she hadn't read. She hadn't seen books bound in purple bindings with gold-leaf titles before.

"Welcome back, Doethan," said the bookbinder. "Is Rowsch with you?"

"He's at my tower keeping watch, Jym," Doethan replied. "We can't stay to visit—we're headed straight there. This is Merry, one of my former apprentices. Merry, meet Jym. When he was younger, he was quite a soldier."

"Doethan likes to exaggerate," said Jym, giving Merry a nod. "You have unusual pets, Merry-former-apprentice." He took a closer look at Ace. "Is that even a dog?"

"It's a long story and we don't have time to tell it now," said Doethan. "I'll let Rowsch know you were asking after him."

"He's welcome to visit whenever he likes," said Jym. "I miss seeing the old hound."

"I'll try my best to bring him along next time I visit," said Doethan. He began to walk to the back of the shop. Merry could see a flight of stairs through an open door.

"Wait," said Merry. "Shouldn't we tell him?"

"Tell me what?" asked the bookbinder.

"About the invasion," Merry replied. "And the evacuation."

"That part of things is Duke Háiddon's problem," said Doethan. "You didn't hear it from me, but I'd be ready to leave Brendinas in twenty-four hours. Rent a wagon before they're all spoken for and fill it with every scrap of food, and every drop of drink you have. Bring your valuables, too."

"Like those beautiful books," said Merry.

"Duke Háiddon's soldiers will be around soon to tell you where to report to evacuate," Doethan continued. "Best of luck with it. We're going west to help Tyford."

"Thank you for the warning," said Jym. "I'll rent that wagon right now before rumors start to spread."

"I knew you were a wise man," said Doethan.

"Which way is the gate to your tower?" Merry asked Doethan.

"Upstairs," said Doethan.

"The third floor?" asked Merry.

"Of course," said Doethan. "Why would you expect anything else?"

When they reached the third-floor landing, Doethan took a key from his belt and unlocked the door. They entered a somewhat musty storeroom filled by odd shapes that Merry assumed must be furniture covered by old sheets. She saw footprints in the dust on the floor leading to one of the taller pieces of furniture. Ace stayed close to Merry, and Chee was holding her hair a bit too tightly.

"Is there something special about that one?" she asked, pointing at the piece.

"Yes," said Doethan. He seemed pleased Merry had deduced the location of the gate. "Help me take the cover off."

Merry stood opposite Doethan and helped remove the white linen sheet that protected a beautifully carved oak wardrobe. It had been stained a rich brown and was tall enough for Eynon to stand inside it without stooping.

"You built a gate inside a piece of furniture?" asked Merry.

"Lots of wizards do that," said Doethan. "It makes it easier if you change apartments."

"Huh," said Merry. "I have a lot to learn about being a wizard."

Doethan did not reply. He just opened the doors of the wardrobe, revealing a darker stain that seemed to fade away into blackness the more Merry stared at it.

"Keep Ace and Chee with you," said Doethan. "Here we go." He took a deep breath and recited a long string of syllables that ended in a sibilant, a buzz, and a nasal sound something like *Sssssuuu-zzzzz-nnnn.*

The back of the wardrobe formed the usual gate interface pattern and they crossed the barrier without a problem, emerging in Doethan's tower on the Rhuthro.

"RRRooofff!" barked Rowsch, Doethan's big canine familiar, when they stepped out.

Ace shifted to his flying carpet form, launched himself upward, and found purchase on the room's ceiling. Chee decided he wanted to pull Merry's hair out by the roots.

She yanked the raconette off her head and tossed him toward the wizard lamp hanging from a chain in the middle of the room.

"Who's a good boy?" said Doethan, who seemed oblivious to Chee and Ace's reactions to Rowsch. He was too busy hugging his hound and telling him how much he'd missed him.

"Where's your gate to Tyford?" Merry asked.

Doethan spared a moment from petting Rowsch to point at a fresco that looked like Taffaern's storeroom on the opposite wall.

Merry waited for at least a minute before she cleared her throat and spoke. "We have places to be," she said. "Let's get moving."

"RRRooofff!" Rowsch repeated.

Merry hoped the big dog wouldn't be coming along on the next leg of their trip. If he was, it would be quite a challenge pulling Ace and Chee from the ceiling.

Chapter 42

Tyford Surprise

Merry and Doethan emerged into a dim corner of a storeroom at Taffaern's inn hidden behind two huge barrels. The room smelled of apples, yeast, and spilled beer. From the markings burned into the bottom of the barrel facing Merry, she realized it was one of the tuns of Applegarth cider she had brought down the river on her trip with Eynon. She'd created the inscription with the tip of a hot poker and recognized her own careful printing. After comforting Chee on her shoulder and stroking the fur on Ace's back so he'd stay calm and not immediately wander off to start exploring, Merry gently tapped the end of the barrel with her knuckles.

Good. It's still full, or mostly full, she thought. "Where to now, Doethan?" she asked. Merry knew her way around Taffaern's inn and expected that Doethan did as well, but she was here to help him, not vice versa.

"The common room," Doethan answered. "Laetícia told us that Duke Háiddon said we should look for the person he'd put in charge of Tyford's evacuation there."

"Maybe I can get another mug of cider," said Merry.

"You had two mugs at the taverna," Doethan chided.

"Yes, but not *Applegarth* cider," said Merry. "There's no taste like home."

"It *is* the best cider in Dâron," said Doethan.

Merry moved in front of Doethan so he could see her mock glare.

"I'm sorry," he said. "I'm being disloyal to your father." Doethan lifted his eyebrows and smiled. "Applegarth cider is the best in Orluin."

"That's better," said Merry. She kissed his cheek, then herded Ace away from some interesting smells with the edge of her booted foot. "Lead on," she said.

Doethan stepped around the giant barrels and along a space between the operating ends of perhaps two dozen barrels where the taps were. Large ceramic bowls glazed in Dâron sky-blue caught any drips or overflow from the taps. Most barrels held beer and ale, but five were from Applegarth and filled with cider. Taffy's customers must have emptied the sixth one she'd brought down the river earlier. She was happy the enormous wooden tuns she'd started to take to Taffaern's inn had arrived safely. Merry reminded herself to thank Madollyn and Llyffan of Flying Frog Farms for their help as soon as she had a chance—which might be near her twenty-first birthday or even later, given how busy she'd be fighting the emperor's invasion.

With the sweep of an arm, Doethan opened the door from the storeroom to the common room, and the two wizards stepped into bright daylight. The common room was filled with an assortment of tables with tops cut in geometric shapes. There were circular and oval tables of various sizes, surrounded by sturdy wooden chairs. There were square tables, mostly for four, and long rectangular trestle tables with benches instead of chairs. A polished oak bar ran along the wall away from the windows that faced out onto the street. Tall stools, most of them occupied by men and women holding mugs, were at the bar where Taffy was filling orders for a trio of servers to distribute.

Merry recognized the small circular table where she used to read in the evenings. It was near one of the short walls and allowed her to face the inn's door, which was located in the center of the side with the windows. She was pleased to see her table wasn't being used at present. Chee hopped down from Merry's shoulder and began to dance from table to table, begging for treats. Ace slipped through the partially opened door back into the storeroom. Merry expected her familiar planned to lap up the beer, wine, and cider in the sky-blue bowls beneath the taps.

The common room was full, and the noise level inside was high. Taffy hadn't spotted them yet—a clear indication that things were busier than usual this afternoon. Merry noticed that a square table near the center had two occupants. One was a very old wizard she didn't recognize. His sky-blue robes were patched and faded and the long beard that disappeared into his lap was gray with a streak of white as wide as his chin running down its center. He was bald with a fringe of gray hair and wore a deep blue magestone the size of a robin's egg embedded in a silver circlet that ringed his head. He seemed even older than Ealdamon.

"Oh no," Doethan whispered.

"What?" asked Merry. "Do you know the old wizard?"

"Yes," said Doethan. "That's Merrillōn. I was his apprentice when I was your age."

"Really?" said Merry. "It's hard for me to imagine you ever being my age."

"Funny," said Doethan without any hint of a smile. "That's not what I mean. Do you see who Merrillōn is sitting with?"

Merry leaned into the room and stepped back into the shadows of the doorway quickly. Duke Néillen was the second man at the square table with the old bearded wizard. The former Tamloch earl marshal was sipping a mug of something foamy and making notes with a stylus on a wide wax tablet while Merrillōn spoke. The intricate tattoos on Néillen's arms and neck didn't seem out of place as she inspected the customers at other tables. Still, Néillen had an air of authority around him that could be seen in the way others around the room kept looking his way.

"What's *he* doing here?" Merry whispered to Doethan.

"I have no idea, but I think we need to find the person Duke Háiddon put in charge of the evacuation right away and have *that* person deal with Néillen," said Doethan.

"Let's talk to Taffy and find out who Duke Háiddon has appointed," Merry suggested. The innkeeper had been more like an uncle to her than a customer when she was growing up. She stepped over to the open end of the space behind the bar and saw Taffy was busy several feet away at the beer and ale taps, so she got mugs of cider for Doethan and herself. When Taffy handed the mugs of ale he'd pulled to a harried server, he finally noticed Merry.

"Welcome, welcome, Merry-dear-lass," he said. "I'd give you a hug, but I see your hands are occupied."

"That's easily remedied," Merry replied, handing the cider mugs to Doethan. She embraced Taffy and could tell he had massive muscles under his barrel-shaped form.

"What brings you and that poor excuse for a country hedge wizard to my inn?" asked Taffy.

"It's good to see you too, old friend," said Doethan, sidestepping the question for a moment. "I see you haven't lost an ounce."

"Hah!" said Taffy. "Pot, meet kettle," he said, pointing at Doethan's round middle and patting his own belly.

The two shook hands like the battle-tested comrades-in-arms that they were. Then they embraced and slapped each other's backs.

"We're here to assist with the evacuation," said Doethan quietly when the greeting rituals were complete. "We were told to help build the wide gates that people will use to get out."

"Aye," said Taffy. "Word's come here about the evacuation. I'm doing my best to make everyone take the threat seriously. I expect we will need the local city militia *and* regular troops from Brendinas before people will leave their homes, though."

"We heard Duke Háiddon appointed someone to be in charge of the evacuation of Tyford," said Merry impatiently. "We need to find him right away so we can get started."

"That won't be difficult," said Taffy, waving his hand toward the common room. "He's sitting right over there with old Merrillōn."

"Duke Háiddon made Duke Néillen responsible for the evacuation of Tyford?" said Merry in a voice so loud that the entire common room went quiet.

Duke Néillen stood and waved Merry and Doethan over to his table.

"There's got to be more to the story," Doethan whispered to Merry as they walked. "Maybe Duke Háiddon is giving Néillen a chance to prove himself?"

"He's already a proven traitor," Merry whispered back.

"Let's hear what he has to say," said Doethan.

Merry and Doethan didn't shake the duke's offered hand. They sat, regarding the other two warily.

Doethan and Merrillōn didn't seem happy to meet again. Their body language wasn't quite two-dogs-fighting-for-the-same-territory. Merry thought Doethan's expression was more like Távi's, wondering if a kick, a scream, or a pat on the head would be coming next. Merrillōn had a supercilious look that made Merry think the old wizard was sure he was better than everyone else in the city, not just at the table.

"Thanks for coming so fast," said Duke Néillen. "I didn't expect to get help so quickly, and such capable help at that."

"We came where we were needed," said Doethan, wary of Néillen's praise.

"I heard it took Damon's timely arrival to save you when you were about to lose a wizard's duel for leadership of Dâron's Conclave," said Merrillōn.

Merry expected Doethan to set the record straight, but instead he simply said, "What you heard is incorrect."

"Oh," said Merrillōn. The older wizard was clearly hoping for a different response.

Duke Néillen immediately jumped into the conversational impasse.

"The local militia captains here in Tyford, including the owner of this inn, have promised me their help," said Néillen. "Unfortunately, we don't really have firm destinations for the citizens of the city when they *do* evacuate." He turned his head to look at Merrillōn. "Merrillōn here had stayed in Tyford instead of going to Brendinas for the Conclave meeting," said Duke Néillen. "He's been telling me about caverns between Tyford and the Coombe that may serve as effective refuges. We just need to know where they are and how many people they'll hold."

"Then build gates to get evacuees there safely," said Merry.

"We will identify the caverns," said Doethan. "Once we find them, we'll need either six or fourteen wizards to help us build and stabilize the wide gates."

"I'll see to that," said Merrillōn. "There are quite a few of us free wizards near Tyford. We're mostly uninterested in kingdom affairs, but quite a few of us would like to learn the art of making wide gates."

"We're glad for any help you can give us," said Merry, when it was clear Doethan wouldn't comment.

"I'm sure I can find *five* more wizards in the area," said Merrillōn. "Fourteen may be more of a challenge."

Merry looked at Doethan. He remained stone-faced. "Do the best you can," she said.

"If you can get people organized into two lines and ready to go," Doethan told Néillen, "citizens can start to leave as soon as the gates are finished."

"Where do you want to build the gates?" asked Néillen.

Doethan thought for a moment. "Is Tyford's stadium available?" he asked the duke.

"If it isn't, it will be," Néillen replied.

Merry remembered the stories her father had shared at the dinner table about the stadium Doethan had referenced. It had been constructed for horse racing, a popular sport in Tyford, and was built of wood, imitating the giant multi-tiered stone arena for gladiatorial combat in Nova Eboracum. Tyford's stadium had been erected in a previous mayor's administration. The mayor at the time had an over-sized ego and friends who owned construction companies. When the project's finances were inspected after the racetrack was complete, the outgoing mayor was sent down the Moravon in a small boat without a paddle. Violations of the public trust were not taken lightly in Tyford or the Kingdom of Dâron.

"There are still wide arches at either end for spectators to leave and enter, aren't there?" asked Doethan.

Merrillōn nodded, and Taffy shouted, "That's right!" from behind the bar.

"We'll use those arches for the gates, then," said Doethan. "I'll also need every pot of glue in the city. Get more cooking in case we run out."

"What kind?" asked Merry, forgetting for a minute that she was already supposed to know what needed to be done.

"All kinds," said Doethan. "Mostly anything that will help rock dust stick to wood."

"Got it," said Duke Néillen. "I need to get everyone organized to use the racetrack's stadium as a departure point. The local militia will help me with that. Merrill will find more wizards to help build the gates, and you need huge quantities of glue."

"Merrillōn," said the old wizard. "Never Merrill."

"What will the two of you be doing?" asked Néillen.

"Confirming the locations and capacities of the caves," said Doethan. He looked over at Merry. "And gathering critical components of the spell for the wide gates."

Merry nodded. She understood. Doethan wanted her to get powdered magestones. The closest place to find that in large quantities was at the green magestone quarry where Viridáxés had been buried. It would be a challenging test of her new-found line-of-sight gating to see how fast she could jump there, collect the magestone dust, and return.

"It sounds like everyone knows their responsibilities," said Doethan. He stood and Merry followed his example.

"I will see that everything else is done," said Duke Néillen. He nodded at Doethan and made more notes on his wax tablet.

Merry's attitude toward Néillen softened by the width of her little finger.

"Could we use one of the rooms in your inn for a few hours?" Doethan asked Taffy. "I have work that requires privacy and I have to confirm a few details with Merry as well."

"Of course," said Taffy. "Follow me."

The innkeeper took a key down from a peg at one end of the bar and escorted Doethan and Merry up two floors to a spacious room with two beds and a balcony.

"Wizards like this room," said Taffy. "The balcony makes it easy for them to come and go on their flying disks. I make most of them pay in advance, however."

"Wise," said Merry with a smile. "It's too easy for them to depart without taking care of their bills first."

"I've got to get back to the bar," said Taffy. "Let me know if you need anything." The big man departed, closing the door behind him.

Doethan dropped a wide wooden bar into angled lengths of wrought iron on either side of the door to secure the room.

"You'd better get going," he said, gesturing toward the balcony.

"I thought you had more instructions for me?" said Merry. "How much magestone dust will you need?"

"Fifty pounds, at least," said Doethan. "A hundred would be better. I'm not as good at this as Fercha, so more is better than less. You can get some sacks to hold the dust from Eynon's parents in Haywall."

"Right," said Merry. "Do you need it to be fine dust, like sand?"

"That would be better than pebbles," he said. "Are your skills with solidified sound good enough to crush and sieve the pieces?"

"I'll manage," said Merry. She looked over at Doethan and saw he was nailing a bed sheet to one wall. "Taffy's not going to like that," she said sharply.

"He's going to like being enslaved by Sírénae's soldiers and sailors even less if I don't mark the locations of every cave in the vicinity," said Doethan. He pulled a pen and ink horn from his pouch.

"You're going to write on the sheet?" asked Merry.

"I am," said Doethan.

"Do you have the location of every cave in western Dâron memorized?" Merry asked.

"Of course not," said Doethan. "I'm just getting ready to draw everything out once I contact some friends of mine who've made an atlas. *They* know where every cave in western Dâron is located, along with its size, access to running water, and more."

"Oh," said Merry. "That would be quite useful." *Maybe she could find her emergency sanctum in one of the smaller caves?*

"See if you can be back in three hours or less," said Doethan. "I want to have at least the first wide gate constructed before dark."

"I'll try," said Merry. "I'm not sure how fast I can cover ground with line-of-sight gating."

"Try hard," said Doethan, looking over his shoulder at her and smiling. "And don't forget to pick up your menagerie."

Merry laughed, imagining the damage Chee and Ace could do if left unsupervised. She'd circle around to the front door and collect them on her way west. With a last wave to Doethan—who ignored her—she took her flying disk off her back and moved to the balcony door. When Merry stepped on her disk and was about to depart, she heard the three clear chimes of a communications ring being activated. Doethan must be contacting his friends with the atlas.

Chapter 43

At the Institute

Bonnie knew exactly who she'd talk to when she arrived back at the Institute in Bhaile Pónaire northeast of Riyas. Cúardaìgh was the Institute's foremost expert on finding things, be they treasures, lost children, or missing pets. She was older now, but her mind was still sharp, and her tongue was equally so. As a young scholar-mage, Bonnie had frequently felt the edge of Cúardaìgh's well-reasoned arguments shaping her own thinking and making it more rigorous in the process.

Cúardaìgh's primary mode of thinking was more intuitive than numeric, so Bonnie had been pleased to work with the older scholar-mage on refining the mathematical underpinnings of her insights. That's why Bonnie felt confident Cúardaìgh would at least hear her request for help locating Valentius.

"I have a challenge for you," said Bonnie when she reached her mentor's office and stuck her head inside the door.

"Your very existence is a challenge for me at times, Bonnie," said the older scholar. "Come in and sit down so I don't have to strain my neck to look up at you while you tell me what you need so urgently you've left your new swain."

"How did you know about Nûd?" asked Bonnie.

"Just because I prefer books and magical experimentation to most people's company doesn't mean I'm blind and deaf to what's going on around me," said Cúardaìgh. "Your relationship with the new-found king of Dâron has been a major topic of Institute gossip for days now." The older mage smiled at Bonnie. "There are several scholar-mages hoping to take your place in the Institute's hierarchy when you leave to become queen."

"What?" said Bonnie. "He hasn't even asked me yet, and I don't know if he ever intends to."

"The chair of Mathemagical Studies says she thinks the odds are over ninety-five percent you'll be queen of Dâron before Midsummer," said

Cúardaìgh. "Tell me, your soon-to-be-Majesty. What challenge requires my assistance? I have a lot on my plate preparing my papers before we evacuate. The deans insist we have to be gone before moonrise, and I still have hours of work to do in the library."

"We're trying to find Valentius, the son of the Southern Emperor of the Roma," said Bonnie. "Emperor Sírénae kidnapped him, and we don't know where he's being held."

"Did you bring me anything to help locate Valentius?" asked Cúardaìgh. "A lock of hair? Fingernail clippings? A few drops of blood?"

"All I've got is this coin with his father's likeness," said Bonnie. "It's said he resembles his father." She placed the double denarius she'd been given by Mafuta face up on Cúardaìgh's desk.

"How many tens of thousands of these coins are there?" asked Cúardaìgh when she'd picked up the shiny coin and turned it this way and that with her fingers, examining the image of Emperor Valens.

"Quite a few," said Bonnie. "Enough to support a substantial portion of the coinage requirements of the Southern Empire."

"That will make things harder," said Cúardaìgh. "It will be nearly impossible to use *similarity* to find the prince, because attempts to find him will be more likely to turn up other coins instead."

"Right," said Bonnie. "It was worth a try." She pressed her lips together unconsciously, considering various options in her quite capable mind. "You mentioned blood," she said. "Does it have to be *his* blood?"

"As opposed to what, the blood of a random squirrel from the quadrangle?" asked Cúardaìgh. "If you had a drop of blood from Valentius, finding him would be trivial."

"What about a relative's blood?" asked Bonnie.

"That depends on consanguinity," Cúardaìgh replied.

"That's a word I've seldom heard," said Bonnie.

"When you're a queen, you'll probably hear it more often," said Cúardaìgh.

"Let's not count any ducklings before they hatch," said Bonnie.

"From what I've heard at meals in the faculty refectory, those ducklings hatched some time ago and are already close to fully grown," teased Cúardaìgh.

Bonnie's face grew red, but she smiled at the fact that the rumors at the Institute were more likely right this time than not. "Enlighten me, O Great Scholar-Mage," she said. "What about consanguinity?"

"It's all a matter of how closely related the person whose blood you've sampled is to Valentius," said Cúardaìgh. "With blood from a parent or full sibling, it would only be a bit more complicated to find him than it would be if I had a sample of his own blood."

"What about a cousin?" asked Bonnie.

"There are cousins and *cousins*," said Cúardaìgh. "How *close* a cousin?"

"A first cousin," said Bonnie.

Cúardaìgh's eyes lit up. She tossed the double denarius in the air and caught it before it fell to her desk. "First cousins aren't a problem," said the scholar-mage. "I was afraid you were talking about a more distant relation."

"I'm thinking about Valens' niece," said Bonnie. "That would make her first cousin to Valentius, wouldn't it?"

"It would," said Cúardaìgh. "Do you know if this niece is the child of Valens' brother, or his sister?" she asked.

"I don't know," said Bonnie. "Does it matter?"

"I wouldn't have asked if it didn't matter," said Cúardaìgh. She frowned at Bonnie and wagged a finger on her left hand while her right hand still held the Roma coin. "Though come to think of it, that would really only make a difference if the sample came from a man, not a woman." Cúardaìgh rubbed her chin and apologized as much as she ever did. "Never mind," she said.

Bonnie sat up straight and tried not to show her amusement at her old mentor's familiar prickly behavior. "I'm sorry the niece wasn't a nephew," she said in mock contrition.

"See that it doesn't happen again," said Cúardaìgh. She winked at Bonnie.

Bonnie giggled like the schoolgirl she'd been when she'd first arrived at the Institute. She stood and bowed to Cúardaìgh. "I'd best go fetch the sample," said Bonnie. "I'll be back within an hour."

"Good," said Cúardaìgh. "I'll make preparations for the finding spell while you're gone. If the degree of consanguinity is what you say it is, I should have a magestone ready for you within thirty minutes of your return."

"But I already *have* a magestone," said Bonnie, touching the green gem in a gold setting at her throat.

"Not *that* kind of magestone," said Cúardaìgh. "This would be a finding stone. It will glow brighter the closer you get to the person you seek."

"Oh," said Bonnie. "That makes sense. It's not my field, so I didn't realize what was necessary."

"It is *my* field, however," said Cúardaìgh.

"Which is why I consulted you," said Bonnie. "You're the expert in such things."

"True," said Cúardaìgh. "Now get moving and hurry back with that sample. I don't want to be late for dinner and miss out on any news."

"Afraid you'll be a topic of conversation yourself if you're not present?" asked Bonnie.

"I'm sure I'll be thoroughly interrogated about your visit by other senior faculty as soon as they pour my berry wine," said Cúardaìgh.

"Please don't tell them how you're helping me," said Bonnie. "We need to keep things quiet, so we don't jeopardize the rescue."

"How unfortunate," said Cúardaìgh, turning up one corner of her mouth. "Nothing stays quiet for long at the Institute."

"Perhaps you'll all be too busy packing for the evacuation for word to spread too far," said Bonnie.

"Perhaps," said Cúardaìgh. She leaned back in her chair and her shoulders slumped. "There's so much to do before we leave, and I've got to find a suitable magestone to enchant into a finder's stone before I can get started.

"Don't worry about that," said Bonnie. "I'll bring back a nice piece of obsidian along with the blood sample."

"Obsidian?" said Cúardaìgh. "Of course. We're trying to find a Roma. That makes it perfectly appropriate."

"Valentius has a particular affinity for obsidian as well, I've been told," said Bonnie. "He was captured sailing home on a ship with a hold full of it."

"Why are you still here?" asked Cúardaìgh. She waved the hand not holding the coin at the door. "Go!" she said. "And hurry back!"

"I will," said Bonnie. She smiled, left Cúardaìgh's office, and ran down the Institute's hallowed stone halls to the gate back to Nova Eboracum.

Chapter 44

Merry and Braith

With Chee perched on her shoulder and Ace standing close by on her flying disk, Merry had nearly started to make line-of-sight gate jumps west from Tyford toward the Coombe and the green magestone quarry. Before she'd traveled more than a dozen feet from the balcony, she stopped and smacked herself in the middle of her forehead with the heel of her palm.

"I'm a fool," she announced to Ace and Chee. "Why travel the entire distance on my own when I can take a shortcut?"

Chee responded with an interrogative, "Chee?" and Ace rubbed his head against Merry's knee supportively.

"Back to the inn," Merry announced.

She turned her flying disk in a big arc that brought her to the inn's front door. A customer was just coming out, so Merry sailed through into the inn's large common room, heading for the storeroom. She waved to Duke Néillen as she skimmed along a few inches above the floorboards.

Taffy realized where Merry was heading and opened the stockroom door ahead of her.

She smiled at him, gave a small bow, and said, "Thank you!" Then she guided her flying disk behind the big barrel of Applegarth cider and found the outline of the fixed gate that led to Doethan's tower. With five quick syllables, she spoke the phrase that opened the gate and slid through the interface from Tyford to Doethan's residence on the Rhuthro.

"RRRooofff!" barked Rowsch, surprising them all.

"Blast!" said Merry as Ace and Chee both leapt for the ceiling. Chee had pulled her hair, quite painfully, when he'd departed for the safety of a wizard lamp hanging above. Ace was clutching the ceiling and trembling near Chee. Both of them were afraid of Doethan's big canine familiar.

The overly exuberant hound jumped up on Merry and put his massive front paws on her shoulders.

"Down, boy," said Merry as she fended off Rowsch's wet tongue that slurped at her face. "I've missed you, too." The two seemed to dance a few steps as Merry backed away, simultaneously moving to her right, while Rowsch circled with her. Merry laughed, thinking the two of them must look like an illustration she remembered from book she'd read years ago. *A Tale as Old as Time* was its title, she remembered. It was a traditional folk tale, but it stuck in Merry's head because the young woman featured in it was a bookworm like herself.

Rowsch shot his tongue out again, and this time Merry couldn't avoid an undesired bath as doggy saliva covered her face from chin to hairline. She laughed, being careful not to open her mouth too wide.

"That's enough, boy," she said. "I have to go now." Merry used her line-of-sight gating ability to bounce to the far side of the room. Rowsch's front paws no longer had Merry's shoulders to support them, and soon all four of the hound's feet were back on the floor.

Rowsch turned to see where Merry had gone. At her new location, Merry generated a solidified sound illusion to make herself invisible. Doethan's familiar jumped for her as if her illusion didn't exist.

Merry smacked her forehead again. "I'm still not thinking," she said. "Visual illusions don't work on scent hunters." She gated across the room again as Rowsch nearly reached her previous position.

"RRRrooofff!" barked Rowsch again. "RRRrooofff, RRRrooofff, RRRrooofff!"

"I get it," said Merry. "You want to play!" She gated to the other side of the room just ahead of the excited hound, who seemed to think chasing Merry was a game. "Unfortunately, I don't have the time, and you'll keep barking and jumping on me until I do".

"Arf arf arf!" proclaimed Ace. He'd released his hold on the ceiling and was spinning around above Rowsch's head, attempting to protect Merry. Chee joined in by screaming at Rowsch and swinging back and forth from the bottom of the hanging wizard lamp.

All the noise and motion brought Rowsch up short. He shook his shaggy head and stared at Merry, waiting for her to gate across the room again.

The momentary respite gave Merry time to come up with something that might distract Rowsch. "Where's your ball?" she asked in a sing-song voice, remembering that Doethan played ball with Rowsch *outside* his tower.

"RRRawlll?" the big dog exclaimed, reminding Merry that familiars were often smarter than most animals of their kind.

"Get your ball!" Merry commanded. She gestured toward the nearest of the three arched windows on the second floor of Doethan's tower and was pleased—and amused—when Rowsch launched himself through the window toward the grass below. The big dog's legs effortlessly absorbed his impact with the ground. Merry watched Rowsch run toward a leather ball the size of a blackseed melon near a pair of tall birch trees on the far edge of the clearing surrounding the tower.

"Come on, my friends," she called to Ace and Chee. The rockhound and raconette joined Merry on her flying disk. Merry eased her disk out of the same window Rowsch had used and quickly curved up hundreds of feet, leaving Doethan's familiar baying below. "I'll be back to play with you," she shouted. She wasn't sure *when* she'd be back, but she promised herself she would be. Merry extended her hand and sent five beams of tight light down to hit the ball and send it rolling down the hill toward the river. Rowsch's baying intensified, and he followed the ball downslope.

Merry continued to climb until she was a high as the tops of the mountains to the west. They were too far away to make out any details, so she started to plan a shorter jump then realized she could make distance-viewing lenses of solidified sound to sharpen her sight. With the lenses in place, she focused on three tall pines on top of one of the mountains and executed a line-of-sight gate. Merry hovered above the trees and put one hand on Ace's head, since the rockhound seemed ready to fly on his own. Chee was making soft *chee-chee-chee* sounds and Merry interpreted them as *That was fun, can we do it again?*

The Coombe is to the west, thought Merry. It was no problem finding landmarks for gating inside the bounds of the Coombe, and soon they were floating above the easy-to-spot milking barn in Haywall. Merry remembered where Eynon's family's cottage was located in relation to the barn and brought her flying disk in for a smooth landing in the flagstone courtyard shared by several cottages, including Eynon's. With her flying disk strapped to her back, Chee on her shoulder, and Ace trotting beside her, Merry stepped up to the door of Eynon's cottage. She heard someone singing inside and knocked loud enough to be sure the singer heard.

"Just a minute," said the sweet and familiar voice of the singer. "I'll be right there."

The door opened a moment later and Braith greeted Merry with a hug.

"Welcome to Haywall!" Braith took in Merry's companions. "Chee! What are you doing here without my brother?" She looked down at Ace, then up at Merry. "And who's this odd-looking fellow?"

"That's Ace," said Merry. "He's *my* familiar," she said with more than a touch of pride in her voice. "Eynon left Chee with me for a while. He's off on a secret mission." Merry didn't want to get into the details of Eynon's defeat against Sírénae's wizards and dragons. It would take too long to explain and Merry was in a hurry.

"Come in, come in," said Braith. "Are you hungry? Would you like a drink? There's fresh bread, butter, and ale."

"That would be great," said Merry. "But I'm really here for grain sacks."

"You can explain while I slice the bread," said Braith. "You're welcome to pour your own ale and spread your own butter." Braith gestured for Merry and her entourage to enter the cottage and take a seat at the kitchen table.

Chee made a beeline to the fruit basket at one end of the table to snag an apple, while Ace shifted form and flew up to sniff around the rafters.

"That's a very strange dog," said Braith. She watched Ace explore the ceiling of the cottage while she sliced fresh dark bread.

"He's not really a dog," said Merry. "I call him a rockhound, and I found him when I was exploring a cave in Tamloch, not far from Riyas. He eats bats."

"Not the good bats who eat bugs, I hope," said Braith as she brought the cutting board, the loaf, and several slices over to the table.

"I don't really know about that," said Merry. "I expect he'd eat any bat he caught. For that matter, he'd probably eat almost anything."

"Would he like a slice of bread?" asked Braith.

"You can offer him one," said Merry.

Braith buttered a slice and held it over her head. Ace swooped down from a rafter, caught the slice in his mouth, and returned to his previous perch to eat it. Chee held his apple in his mouth and clapped.

"That answers your question," said Merry.

"Why do you need grain sacks?" asked Braith.

"I need to collect magestone dust from the quarry," Merry replied.

"Why do you need magestone dust?"

"To help build wide gates so we can evacuate Tyford and Brendinas and hide everyone in Dâron."

"Why?" asked Braith.

"It's a long story," said Merry. "We're being invaded by the former emperor of Roma's Western Empire. You should tell everyone to get their families, food, and livestock underground as soon as you can. Messengers from the Crown should be here soon to inform the Coombe, but I'm ahead of them."

Braith shook her head. "Does Eynon have anything to do with this invasion?" she asked.

"He didn't cause it," said Merry. "But he is trying to stop it, somehow."

"Good," said Braith. "I don't want to hide in a cave."

"I'm afraid you'll have to, at least for now," said Merry. "Though it will likely be quite a while before the invaders get this far west."

"Maybe Eynon will stop them before they cross the Moravon?" offered Braith.

"We can hope," said Merry. "About those grain sacks?"

"There are two here in the cottage," said Braith. She found them folded over a split-log stool and handed them to Merry. "How many more do you need?"

"Four more should do it," said Merry. "I'd rather have too much dust than too little. We have lots of wide gates to build, and I don't think I can carry more than six sacks on my flying disk."

"That makes sense," said Braith. "How is that tall young Roma wizard doing? The one I met at the signing ceremony."

"Felix?" Merry responded, hiding a smile. "He's fine." She was glad Braith was over her crush on Nûd. Bonnie seemed like a better fit for Dâron's new and somewhat reluctant king.

Braith's mind seemed momentarily elsewhere.

Probably imagining kissing Felix, thought Merry. "Where can we get four more sacks?" she asked.

"There are plenty of empty feed sacks at the milking barn," said Braith. "Let's fly over there, and I'll get them for you and tell my parents I'll be gone for a few hours."

"What do you mean?" asked Merry.

"I'm coming with you," Braith answered. "You'll fill the sacks faster if I hold them open."

Merry laughed. "Come along if you want," she said, "but you'll have to walk home."

"That's not a problem," said Braith. She put on a sweater made from light-blue yarn and picked up an apple from the fruit bowl and another slice of bread from the cutting board. She waved the fruit and bread and walked out the kitchen door with Chee and Ace scampering and gliding behind her, respectively. Merry followed as well, closing the door as she went.

* * * * *

Braith stepped off Merry's flying disk at the quarry. Her cheeks were flushed with excitement after flying and line-of-sight gating from Haywall to Wherrel. Chee had decided to ride on Braith's shoulders, and Eynon's sister stroked the raconette's soft fur as she encouraged Chee to jump to the ground. Ace left his spot between Merry's feet and shot up to reconnoiter the quarry and its surroundings.

"It looks a lot different than I remember," said Braith.

"Viridáxés was somewhat *energetic* when he broke free," said Merry. "At least there are lots of chunks of magestones around to crush into dust."

"You just want the really green ones, right?" asked Braith.

"Correct," said Merry. "We can collect them together, then pile them up for me to pulverize."

"This will be *fun*," said Braith.

It didn't take long for the two young women to assemble a sizable stack of green rocks. Merry confirmed they had the glow of stones transformed by heat and pressure into magestones, though not of a quality that would serve as magestones for wizards. *It's more like limestone than marble,* Merry considered. *Wizard-quality magestones need a lot more heat and pressure. Still, this dust will work for constructing wide gates.*

"Should I get some hammers from the quarry workers to crush the rocks?" asked Braith.

"Just hold the first sack open," said Merry. She created a sphere of solidified sound big enough to hold one of the rocks and slowly compressed it, making it smaller and smaller until the rock inside fractured into tiny pieces.

Braith clapped her appreciation and watched, wide-eyed, as Merry compressed her sphere again until the pieces shattered into particles the size of grains of sand.

"Hold the sack under the sphere," said Merry.

"Gladly," said Braith.

Once the first sack was in position, Merry opened a small hole in the bottom of the sphere and dust sifted down like the contents of an hour-glass that had just been turned. Merry realized, too late, that she could have maneuvered the sacks into place using solidified sound. She wasn't as good at manipulating solidified sound as Eynon but would have been able to manage it on her own without assistance. Now that Braith was here and helping, however, it didn't seem like the right time to mention that fact.

Braith was enjoying the chance to contribute, and Merry was enjoying the chance to get to know Braith better. She loved the younger woman's joy-filled, innocent approach to life. Her attitude reminded Merry of Eynon and she resolved not to be too hard on her lover when he finally returned from Melyncárreg or wherever else he'd gone off to.

Another half an hour's work had filled all six sacks. Braith found cords in the quarry workers' supply shed and used them to lace the sacks closed with unnecessary assistance from Chee that only added a few extra minutes to her task.

"Thank you so much for your help," said Merry. "I couldn't have done it nearly as fast without you."

"It was my pleasure," said Braith. "Please say hello to Felix for me the next time you see him."

"I'll be glad to," said Merry.

They arranged the heavy sacks on either side of Merry on her flying disk. Chee hopped up to his usual spot on Merry's shoulder. Ace made a last-minute appearance, circling around Braith and dropping a large green lizard with a frilled neck ruff at Braith's feet. The lizard was stunned, but still breathing.

Braith looked at the lizard, then at Ace. "I will treasure it always," she told the rockhound.

Ace snapped his jaws twice and emitted a friendly, "Arf! Arf!"

"I think he wants you to eat it," said Merry.

"Maybe later," said Braith, smiling at Ace.

Ace found a space to stand on the back of Merry's flying disk and rubbed his nose against the back of her knee.

"Time to go," said Merry.

"Safe travels," said Braith. "And don't forget to give my best to Felix."

Merry disappeared with a *pop* and reappeared high above and far away, near the distant horizon. Braith waved until she couldn't see Merry, her cargo, and her companions any longer.

On the rocky floor below Braith, the lizard-offering Ace had presented to her got to its feet, shook its head, and shot off to hide under a nearby boulder.

"Just as well," said Braith to herself. She started to walk east from the quarry. "I'd better go alert my relatives in Wherrel about the evacuation."

Chapter 45

The Rescue Begins

Laetícia's little finger still hurt from where Bonnie had pricked it to gather a dozen drops of blood, but the black sphere she held in her hand was worth that small bit of pain and much more. The obsidian orb's smooth surface allowed a bright white glow to show through. The glow marked the direction they needed to travel to find Valentius. Bonnie's expert from the Institute had come through and had crafted a finder's stone attuned to the heir to Roma's Southern Empire, and more besides.

Mafuta shifted her flying disk until she was on Laetícia's right and their protective, streamlined wedges of solidified sound could temporarily merge. "How are you holding up?" the older wizard asked.

Laetícia shook her her head, making her beaded braids clack. The familiar sound centered her. "I'm worried," said Laetícia. "There are so many things that can go wrong, though this"—She gestured toward Mafuta with the dark glass finder's stone— "increases our odds of success quite a bit."

"You were right not to allow Bonnie to come with us," said Mafuta. "She's a scholar, not a warrior."

"I know," said Laetícia. "But her contribution will likely be key to us pulling this off."

"Agreed," said Mafuta, sparing a moment to glance over her shoulder at Inthíra, Felix, Verro, and Amber, the Bifurland master mage, flying single file behind them. It was dark, but their forms could still be made out in the moonlight. "I'm glad you *did* decide to bring Inthíra, though."

"She has the strongest skills in illusion magic of any mage I've seen," said Laetícia.

"Though Eynon and Merry are quite talented in that area, too," teased Mafuta.

"You know very well that Eynon is missing and Merry left for Tyford with Doethan," Laetícia replied. "Besides, I trust Inthíra to keep her head if things don't happen the way we expect."

"While the same can't be said about Eynon, at least," said Mafuta.

"Exactly," said Laetícia. "Look what happened the last time I brought him with me on a mission."

Mafuta put her hand over her mouth to hide a smile. "Quin's suggestion for a distraction was inspired, by the way," she said.

"My husband has a history of coming up with good ideas," said Laetícia.

"I almost hope we'll need that distraction," said Mafuta. "I want to see how Sírénae's wizards and dragons deal with Quin's plan."

"I'd prefer for us to slip in and out without being detected," said Laetícia.

Felix chose that moment to guide his flying disk to Laetícia's left and merge his wedge. He looked a bit absurd wearing black leather armor and a necklace of teeth extracted from large cats around his neck. "What new torments for Sírénae are the two of you plotting?" he asked.

"A major distraction if we're caught trying to free Valentius," said Laetícia.

"Another creative brainstorm from Quintillius," said Mafuta.

"Now I almost hope we *are* caught," said Felix.

"Don't," said Laetícia. "Sírénae is not kind to her captives."

Felix grinned. "I said I *almost* hope we're caught."

"I heard the caveat," said Laetícia.

"Good," said Felix. "While I have your attention, I have a question."

"Ask," Mafuta commanded, using the same tone of voice she'd employed with Felix back when he'd still been her apprentice.

"Why are we just trying to rescue Valentius?" he requested. "If we're already aboard the *Seahawk,* why don't we just kill Sírénae outright?" He nodded to Mafuta and Laetícia. "I'm ready to do what's necessary."

Mafuta gave Felix a stern glance. "I'm ashamed of you for even suggesting such a thing," she said. "Assassination is *not* the Roma way."

Laetícia, Felix, *and* Mafuta started to laugh. The first emperor of the Roma *had* been assassinated, after all, and many more had died at assassins' hands in the centuries since then.

"Thank you, Mafuta," said Laetícia. "I needed something to break my bleak mood. There are so many things that could go wrong."

"Glad to oblige, my friend," said Mafuta. "But why not focus on what could go right?" She reached up to put a hand on Laetícia's shoulder. "You've put an excellent team together. If five of the most powerful wizards in Orluin can't rescue Valentius, I don't see who could."

"Five?" asked Felix. He held up one hand and counted off its digits with the other, mouthing names as he went. "What about me?"

"You're just along for heavy lifting if we need to *carry* Valentius out of wherever he's being held," said Mafuta.

Felix flexed and sharp blades flicked out from bracers along his forearms. He clenched his fists and dagger-like claws shot from his gauntlets. "I can also handle guards *without* using magic, if need be."

"I'm sure you can," said Mafuta. "Let's hope you don't have to. And feel free to stick one of those claws of yours through Sírénae's heart if you come across her."

"Or that snow leopard of hers," said Felix. He sliced empty air a few times before retracting his claws and the blades on his bracers. "Die, Thraxa. Die!" he proclaimed, taking one last swipe.

"Do I want to know what *that* was all about?" came Verro's amplified voice from twenty feet behind.

"No," said Mafuta. "Felix was simply giving us a demonstration of his new armor."

"You should put some robes on over that," Verro shouted up to Felix. "It would be more effective as a surprise if your opponents think you're a wizard, not a warrior in a boiled-leather cat suit."

"I *am* a wizard," Felix called back. He slowed his progress until he flew next to Verro then spoke quietly to Tamloch's master mage. "You're probably right, though."

Verro nodded and shifted to fly closer to Felix so he could help the tall young wizard extract his robes from a canvas pack tied to the upper surface of his flying disk and help Felix get into them.

"That's better," said Verro. "Now there's more to you than meets the eye."

"Sírénae's guards won't expect *this*—" said Felix, letting the left sleeve of his purple robe slide back revealing the blades on the bracer on that arm, "—or *this,*" he continued, showing off the blades and small crossbow fitted into the bracer on his right arm.

"I like that crossbow," said Verro. "Fercha shot me in the calf with one not much larger a few weeks ago. I'll have to get one made for myself."

"I can recommend a skilled artisan for you," said Felix.

"Let's wait and see if we both live through this rescue first," said Verro.

"We will," said Felix. "I'm confident of my own immortality."

"I hope your confidence isn't misplaced," said Verro. He grinned at Felix and the two of them flew along in companionable silence.

After a few more hours of monotonous flight, Laetícia lifted her hand holding the finder's stone over her head. All the team members arrayed behind her could see that the bright light inside the obsidian orb was blinking.

"What does it mean?" Felix asked Verro.

"I think it means we're close to the invasion fleet and Valentius," Verro replied.

"Good," said Felix. He extended and retracted the blades on his bracers with a loud *snick-snick,* ripping the fabric of the sleeves of his wizard's robes in the process.

"Stop that," said Verro.

"Sorry," said Felix.

Verro glanced over to see an uncertain look on the younger wizard's face, as if he was simultaneously eager to attack someone and worried about how he'd measure up if he did.

Three chimes sounded ahead when Laetícia handed the finder's stone to Mafuta and opened a communications ring. Felix accelerated to parallel Laetícia so he could listen in. He ignored Mafuta's small smile at his curiosity.

"I'm glad you're here," Laetícia told Felix as she opened the ring. "Send a sphere of solidified sound twenty feet underwater, expand it, then dispel it," she commanded.

"I can do that," said Felix, doing as he'd been told.

"Did you hear that?" asked Laetícia. "Are you close by?"

The great blue dragon's head broke the surface beside them. "I did and I am," said Zûrafiérix after a few seconds.

Felix made night-seeing goggles from solidified sound and scanned the ocean below. He could just make out the streaming white of foaming waves where the dragon's wedge-shaped head cut through the water.

"The invasion fleet and Valentius aren't far," said Laetícia. "The finder's stone is blinking. Can you sense the fleet's hulls when you're underwater?"

"I can," said Zûrafiérix. "I will be in position when you're ready for me to support your distraction."

"Excellent," said Laetícia. "The emperor is in for a big surprise."

"I hope *we* aren't surprised as well," said Zûrafiérix. "You can count on me to do my part. It will be a pleasure for me to attack the Roma—Occidens Province Roma excepted, of course."

"Of course," said Laetícia. She smiled at the dragon through the ring's interface, which was only large enough for the huge whirling blue eye of Zûrafiérix to be visible. Laetícia nodded. "Thank you," she said.

Felix heard three tones chime and watched Zûrafiérix submerge. "Have you spotted the fleet?" he asked Laetícia.

Mafuta, not Laetícia, answered. "The finder's stone says they're off to our right," she said.

Felix added distance viewing lenses to his night vision goggles and saw thousands of white sails off in the distance in the direction Mafuta indicated.

"I see them," he said.

"So do I," said Verro.

"And I," added Inthíra.

Amber, as usual, said nothing. The Bifurlanders' master mage bowed slightly to indicate agreement.

Laetícia moved her arm in a circle, and the six wizards gathered around her for final instructions. "You'd better start hiding us now in case Sírénae has scouts deployed," Laetícia told Inthíra.

Inthíra crafted a pass-through illusion that surrounded them in a sphere of solidified sound and transferred the pattern of moon, stars and clouds in the night sky above them to the lower surface of the sphere. She inclined her chin to confirm they were hidden, and Laetícia reviewed the rest of their plan.

"You will open the distraction portal to the teams in Nova Eboracum," Laetícia indicated to Amber. "If Valentius is on Sírénae's flagship, bring them in above the ship Valentius brought from the Isles of Dogs. You should be able to detect all the magestones in its hold."

"And if Valentius is being held on his own ship, bring the distraction in above Sírénae's flagship. I understand," said Amber. "Then gate them home before they're overwhelmed by Sírénae's forces."

"Correct," said Laetícia. "Come back to assist us if you can."

"I *will* be back," said the Bifurland master mage.

"Verro, as we'd discussed, your mission is to protect Inthíra," said Laetícia.

"And act as your reserve if you run into trouble, I remember," said Tamloch's master mage. "Inthíra will keep up her illusions as long as possible, then use her emergency gate to escape if more wizards attack us than I can handle."

"Also correct. Don't be a hero, Inthíra," said Laetícia. "We need you for battles yet to come."

"Understood," said Inthíra. "Though I don't have to like it."

"If circumstances permit, you're welcome to go underwater with Zûrafiérix and maintain your kraken illusion," said Laetícia. "The more we can distract Sírénae's guards, the more time Mafuta and Felix and I will have to find and free Valentius."

Five heads nodded.

"It should be obvious which ship has Valentius when I start to dive," said Laetícia. "Trigger all the distractions then—and be careful."

"I will," said Felix, sounding much more serious than usual. "Careful is my new byname."

Everyone looked at him and grinned. He'd done them a favor by breaking their solemn mood.

"I'm counting on you to take risks and be unpredictable," said Laetícia. "Not to be careful." She leaned in and squeezed the young wizard's upper arm, feeling the leather armor he wore. "You also know Roma ships' below-decks design as well as Mafuta and I do. We're the ones most likely to find Valentius."

"Especially with this," said Mafuta, holding up the finder's stone.

"Are we ready?" asked Laetícia.

Five wizards nodded to signify their assent.

"Then let's be about it," said Laetícia.

The rescue team, hidden by Inthíra's magic, moved toward the fleet.

Chapter 46

The Rescue Proceeds

Magister Callidus had been exhausted after his long flight back to the fleet from Nova Eboracum. He hadn't done the hard work of flying, like Xaxidiánus, but even the best-padded saddle couldn't make riding a dragon's spine truly comfortable, and Callidus was a good deal older than he'd been the last time he'd ridden such a long distance roundtrip on dragonback.

Gates were so much easier and more convenient. He was enjoying his goose-feather mattress, resting his tired bones and sleeping soundly, when urgent knocking on his cabin door disturbed his slumber.

"What?" he shouted before he had a chance to fully wake.

"We're under attack," said a servant's voice. "Sírénae wants you on deck immediately."

Callidus shot out of bed, pulled robes over his head, stuck feet into boots, and slammed his cabin door open, knocking the servant to one side in the process. The emperor did *not* like to be kept waiting. He ran up two ladders and spotted Sírénae on the foredeck with one of the wizards Callidus had assigned to scout duty. A single lamp hung from a nearby stanchion, illuminating the pair.

"Where are they?" Sírénae asked the scout wizard.

"Coming in fast from the northwest," the wizard replied. "I sensed seven, maybe eight magestones and I think they're heading for the *Seahawk.*"

Sírénae noticed Callidus had arrived and acknowledged his presence with a command. "Gather your strongest mages and prepare to attack," she ordered. "I'll summon Xaxidiánus and the rest of the dragons."

"Why are they targeting the flagship?" asked Callidus.

"You're getting senile, old man," said Sírénae. "Senile or exceptionally stupid."

"Are they coming to kill you?" asked Callidus, ignoring the emperor's insult.

"Perhaps," said Sírénae. "But I think it far more likely that they intend to rescue Valentius."

Callidus was now completely awake and felt like Sírénae had thrown a bucket of cold seawater in his face. "Of course," he said. "You threatened to dismember the man, after all. I'll have a contingent of wizards surround the cabin where he's being held."

"Think in three dimensions, old man. Laetícia certainly will. Have guards above and below his cabin as well," Sírénae commanded. "If you're capable of the task."

"I'll do my best," said Callidus. He tilted his head and looked at the emperor's face, strangely distorted by the light and shadow from the nearby lamp. "Do you think Laetícia will be part of the rescue mission?"

"No, I think she'll be *leading* the mission," said Sírénae. "If we can capture *her,* she'll make an even better hostage than Valentius. Quintillius will change his mind and support my conquest of Orluin with Laetícia's life in the balance."

Callidus wasn't so sure, but he didn't want to contradict his empress. "I will instruct my battle mages to spare Laetícia if she is one of the attackers."

"Good," said Sírénae. "Be *very* clear. If she dies, so do you."

"Understood, Your Imperial Majesty," said Magister Callidus. He knew she wouldn't hear the defiance in his words.

Sírénae gave another order to a servant, and a trio of deep brass horns permanently mounted amidships on the *Seahawk* began to sound their low urgent call to Xaxidiánus and the other dragons on their flat-decked transports.

As he left Sírénae's presence, Magister Callidus knew his scaly friend would enjoy waking in the middle of the night every bit as much as he did—which is to say, not at all. Covering a yawn, Callidus went aft to give the necessary orders and deploy his wizards. He passed Thraxa, her claws clacking on the decking, as her keeper pulled the bloodthirsty snow-gryffon toward the prow to join the emperor. The hawk-feline's dark eyes regarded Callidus the way a hungry cat might gaze at an anxious chipmunk. *How long do I have before I lose Sírénae's favor and am fed to her pet?* mused the senior wizard. *Months? Days? Or only hours?*

* * * * *

Laetícia heard the brassy *basso* of the *būcina,* the ancient instruments once used by Roma's legions to announce the watches of the night and now largely dedicated to summoning and signaling dragons. "They know we're coming," she said, no longer worried about staying quiet. "Amber, fetch the players from Nova Eboracum to provide the first distraction."

Amber nodded, always a wizard of few words. "I sense a ship with a hold full of obsidian. I'll set up the distraction above it," said the Bifurlander.

"Good," said Laetícia. "Go!"

The Bifurland master mage created a disguise from solidified sound and set off for a point five hundred feet above the graceful vessel that still flew the black-eagle-on-gold banner of the Southern Empire. It was only five ships away from what was clearly Sírénae's flagship.

Felix stretched his muscles under his boiled leather armor and prepared a set of offensive spells, holding them at the ready for their impending attack.

Laetícia looked down and saw a distinctive long, narrow pattern of waves in the sea below her. Zûrafiérix was in position and ready. Occidens Province's spymaster shook her head. The beads on the ends of her long braids smacked together and sounded like slippery bits of talus sliding down a mountain at the beginning of an avalanche.

"Ready for me?" asked Inthíra.

Laetícia gave Inthíra a grim smile, then shared one with Verro, who stood beside the talented illusionist.

"It's time," said Laetícia. "Summon the kraken."

The sea began to boil for hundreds of yards around the ships nearest to the emperor's flagship, and the body of a great kraken, or what seemed to be a kraken, emerged from the depths. Gigantic tentacles stretched out to wrap around masts and gunwales. Inthíra's illusions, supported by calculated *nudges* by Zûrafiérix from below the waterline, created panic on the affected vessels. Some crew members threw themselves into the water and others ran below to warn their fellow sailors, still in their hammocks at this hour of the night.

Laetícia watched two dozen Roma wizards swarm off the flagship on their flying disks, heading for the kraken. *Inthíra is good,* Laetícia considered, *and Verro should be able to keep her alive even after she is discovered, but now is the the best time to board the flagship.* Off in the distance, Laetícia saw Amber had already accomplished the first part of Quin's plan. Flashes of colorful robes and balls of solidified sound high above the obsidian-laden vessel that had once belonged to Valentius made that clear. *The qua-qua players should keep Sírénae's dragons busy,* thought Laetícia.

Felix and Mafuta looked at Laetícia expectantly. Laetícia took the finder's stone from Mafuta and put it in a thin, translucent cloth bag she strapped around her forearm. They'd all need their hands free for what would come next. Laetícia would focus on asphyxiating enemies with spheres of solidified sound, while Mafuta would use tight light to hit multiple opponents at once and Felix would shoot low-level zaps of lightning or take direct physical action with his special armor as circumstances warranted.

"Let's go," said Laetícia, after confirming Mafuta and Felix were ready. "We've got to rescue my cousin."

* * * * *

Amber had strained to hold open the *ad hoc* gate long enough to allow sixteen Roma wizards through from Nova Eboracum. It helped that they sped through Amber's gate in close order, four at a time. Soon, they were all through and were beginning to set up a complex web of four square levels high above the ship with the obsidian in its hold. The levels were in four colors—black, green, blue, and gold from bottom to top, standing for earth, crops, sky, and sun. Pulsing congruencies the size of dinner plates were in the center of each level. They rotated like spinning dancers, throwing off sparks in the colors of their levels.

The new arrivals' robes began to glow as well, with patterns of bright lights radiating from the middle of their backs and chests and washing over their bodies in rhythmic waves.

"Dragons!" shouted Amber to the wizards. The Bifurland master mage rose until everything happening below was visible. It looked like the bright curtains of colored light that occurred in the skies of northern Bifurland at certain times of year, crossed with a speed round of shah-mat played by grandmasters, or clever, impulsive children.

Sírénae's seven dragons were drawn to the game of *quattuor quadratum—qua-qua*—like felines to catnip. They were nearly hypnotized by the shifting colored balls of solidified sound as they moved up the levels and the patterns on the robes of the players as they wove in and out of the playing field. Dragons were usually sent away on distant errands when qua-qua matches or practices were scheduled because they tended to circle the players and bellow advice on game strategy and tactics.

All dragons were convinced they knew everything about qua-qua and were not shy about sharing their expertise. Dragons would frequently quarrel over the progress of a game and nip or buffet other dragons who disagreed with them. Sometimes draconic debates escalated to the point where arguments were settled with blasts of dragonfire. Amber had heard Laetícia explain that over the centuries more than a few dragons had died from conflicts over qua-qua matches. Across the Ocean, where dragons were more common, an outer ring of scout wizards flew in wide circles around games of qua-qua to ensure dragons didn't invade the field and distract the players or injure each other.

The Bifurland master mage smiled, remembering how Laetícia had joked that qua-qua was not only known as the *duck game,* from qua-qua turning into *quack-quack,* but the *drake game,* from the way it fascinated dragons. Amber was glad the youngsters in Bifurland who rode small golden dragons hadn't shown any interest in qua-qua. At least not so far.

A large black—Xaxidiánus, thought Amber, recognizing the dragon who had traveled to Nova Eboracum with Magister Callidus on his back to deliver Sírénae's ultimatum—was the first to reach the game.

"No, no!" Xaxidiánus exclaimed. "You have to *pass* the sphere, not carry it if you want it to rise from the black level to the green!"

The qua-qua players from Nova Eboracum ignored the dragon and played on.

Two more black dragons, each somewhat smaller, joined their leader.

"Not an underhand pitch!" complained one of them.

"Bounce pass it, don't just *toss* it," said the other.

As more dragons arrived, their comments grew louder, and dragons began to snap at those who didn't share their opinions on how the game should proceed.

Amber was amused as well as concerned and kept watch to intercept any wizards sent up to attack the qua-qua players, since the dragons were more interested in offering advice than physically disrupting the game. *Quintillius was inspired,* thought the Bifurland mage. *Sírénae's dragons have been removed from the board by a qua-qua game. It* does *look interesting,* Amber mused. *Perhaps I'll have to try it myself.*

* * * * *

"Umbrose! Callidus!" shouted Sírénae as she watched her dragons' fascination with the qua-qua match in growing frustration. Unfortunately, neither her spymaster or master mage were close enough to hear her protests.

* * * * *

Magister Callidus saw that the two dozen Roma wizards who'd left the *Seahawk* to deal with the kraken were focused on stabilizing ships struck by tentacles and saving sailors tossed into the sea rather than attacking the kraken directly. He'd seen great krakens in the Middle Sea break galleys in half with their sucker-covered arms and had a lot of respect for the monsters' power. This kraken was even bigger than the ones he'd seen when he was younger. *The Ocean is far deeper and more vast,* thought Callidus. *It makes sense that it would be home to larger krakens—and the passage of all the ships in Sírénae's armada must have been quite a lure for the tentacled beast.*

Callidus lifted a pair of sailors from the water with beams of tight light radiating from each hand and deposited them gently near the rail of a ship just starboard of the *Seahawk*. Too many sailors and legionnaires were being knocked overboard by the kraken's shaking, however. Taking a deep breath and considering the consequences of crossing his own personal Rubicon with Sírénae, he decided that hundreds of men and women's lives were more important than his own. Stepping aft unsteadily, he reached a ladder and called down for half the wizards he'd assigned to guard Valentius to come up and join the two dozen steadying ships and saving sailors. Then he called again for the rest of the wizard guards he commanded. When they arrived on deck, Callidus told them to attack the kraken directly, to encourage the tentacled *thing* to return to the depths.

"It looks like I'll have to guard the prisoner myself," he said, to no one in particular.

* * * * *

Laetícia, Mafuta, and Felix flew to the aft end of the *Seahawk,* where several wide windows allowed Sírénae to watch the Ocean's waves from her spacious cabin. Screams, shouts, and splashes echoed around them as Zûrafiérix, playing the part of a kraken in the evening's performance, continued to make nearby ships toss, as if caught by massive sucker-covered arms.

"Should I break one?" whispered Felix as the trio hovered just below the windows.

"There might be an easier way," said Laetícia. She rose enough to peer into Sírénae's cabin, confirmed it was empty, and made a tiny *ad hoc* gate jump inside. A few seconds later she had unlatched one of the windows and helped Mafuta enter. Felix scrambled in behind her.

"Should I close it?" he asked.

"I would," said Mafuta. "There's no sense in leaving a big *Intruders Aboard* sign for the emperor."

"Right," said Felix. He turned the latch to lock the window. "Where to next?"

Laetícia consulted the finder's stone. It was pulsing rapidly and pointing forward and down.

Felix turned and looked out the window. "I guess it couldn't be farther aft," he said.

"Not unless they're holding him on a small boat they're dragging behind them," offered Laetícia.

"They can't afford the drag that would cost them," said Felix.

"You'd know better than I would about that," said Mafuta. "You grew up along the Ocean."

"Insula Longa Sound, actually," said Felix.

Laetícia shook her head. She adjusted her magically constructed night vision lenses to be particularly sensitive to human body heat and put her face close to the door. "There's only one guard outside," she said softly. "I'll get him." Laetícia inserted a tendril of transparent solidified sound under the door and directed it up until it reached the level of the guard's neck. The tendril expanded into a ball that surrounded the guard's head and stayed in place until he ran out of air and lost consciousness. Laetícia eased the guard to the floor and led the others outside the cabin. "This way," she said, pointing to a steep set of narrow treads a dozen feet ahead. "Down these stairs."

"Down that ladder, you mean," said Felix softly.

"I've sailed across the Ocean more than once," Laetícia whispered back. "I know they're ladders, but at this point I just want to find Valentius. Can you save the lectures on proper nautical nomenclature for later?"

Felix nodded and said nothing. *Laetícia must be more worried about this rescue than she seems,* he thought. Mafuta looked at him like she'd have words with him later. *Didn't she realize correcting terms was* his *way of coping with his own case of nerves?*

A thick oak door was set in the wall across from the bottom of the ladder.

"The finder's stone is vibrating as well as pulsing now," said Laetícia. "I think this is where Valentius is being held."

"I don't like this," said Mafuta. "Where are the guards? There ought to be guards."

The door in front of them slowly opened. Laetícia saw a man tied to a chair in the middle of the room and recognized him as her cousin Valentius. The door continued to swing wider. Felix gasped in surprise while Laetícia and Mafuta stood still as stone, as if a Medusa or basilisk had been revealed. They didn't expect Magister Umbrose, Sírénae's spymaster, himself. Four more wizards wearing plain gray and black robes stood guard near Umbrose inside the room.

"Don't bother, they're here," said Umbrose.

Laetícia found his twisted smile much more disconcerting than his words.

"And so are you, Laetícia," Umbrose continued. "Sírénae will be *so* glad you were able to join us."

Felix had heard enough. He hadn't recognized Umbrose and didn't realize who he was facing—not that he would have cared if he'd known. The blades and claws on his armor *snicked* out and he did a forward roll into the quartet of wizards next to Umbrose, knocking two of them over and leaving them with bloody cuts on their arms and faces.

Laetícia and Mafuta *did* know Umbrose and were well aware of his reputation as an interrogator and killer—though torturer and assassin might be more apt. They stood rooted in place and watched as Umbrose materialized a sphere of solidified sound around Felix's head. A few seconds later, the tall young mage suffered the same fate as the guard outside Sírénae's cabin and slumped to the deck. The two uninjured mages in gray and black ensured Felix couldn't summon a congruency to bring air into the sphere Umbrose had created.

"Don't hurt Felix," said Laetícia. "You have me, after all."

The four wizards stripped the purple wizards' robes from the young mage, revealing his black armor beneath. They found the triggers that retracted the blades and claws and looked at Umbrose.

"Felix is a cat, then," said Umbrose. "How appropriate. It's too bad he's not very effective as either a wizard *or* a warrior."

"Quintillius won't be happy if you harm him," said Laetícia.

"I don't think Quintillius is going to care about him in the least, when his wife's life is hostage for his good behavior," said Umbrose. He looked at Mafuta. "I wouldn't try using your emergency gate, if I were you," he said. "The walls of this cell beneath the paneling are steel, coated with magestone dust. There's no telling what would happen if you tried to gate out."

"I'm staying with Laetícia," said Mafuta, glaring at Umbrose.

"That's for the emperor to decide," said Umbrose.

Felix began to moan from his position on the floor.

Umbrose waved to the two of his wizards who'd been cut during the attack Felix had made. "Get him out of here and put him in the other gate-blocked cell," said the spymaster. "Remove his magestone before he recovers consciousness, then strip that suit off him and take it to the armorer. We might learn something from it. And get yourselves cleaned up. Don't waste a healing potion. The scars will look impressive."

"Yes, Magister," said one of the bleeding wizards. Together with his associate, they carried Felix from the room. Felix moaned when they contrived to drop his head on the floor as they left.

Umbrose crossed to Valentius, whose head had been hanging down with his chin on his chest. He slapped the young man, leaving a bright hand print on his cheek. "Wake up, sweet prince," said Umbrose. "There's someone here to see you."

Valentius slowly raised his head and focused his eyes. "Cousin Laetícia?" he said, his voice thick from disuse. "Are you here to rescue me?"

"I'm afraid she's not," said Umbrose. "She's another hostage to keep you company—and another bargaining chip for the emperor."

Umbrose watched the eyes of his original captive go wide as Valentius spotted something or someone behind him. The spymaster turned around quickly and was struck five solid blows to the forehead by a hand reaching around the door and releasing beams of tight light from long, slender fingers. The hand shifted and also knocked out the other wizards in quick succession before they could react and put up shields. They all slumped to the deck.

"Did someone say something about a rescue?" asked Magister Callidus from the doorway. "I've grown tired of working for Sírénae and could gladly trade getting you all out of here for a job working for someone who doesn't want to feed me to her snow-gryffon."

"I think that could be arranged," said Laetícia. "When can you start?"

Chapter 47

Doethan and Merrillōn

Merry and her sacks full of powdered magestone dust landed next to Doethan inside Tyford's racetrack stadium more than an hour before dark. Her old mentor was standing in front of the bedsheet he'd appropriated from the inn earlier. It was covered in lines that resembled a map and tacked to the wall separating the viewing stands from the track. Covered buckets holding something foul-smelling—glue, Merry assumed—were lined up against the wall near the sheet.

"Taffy said you'd be here," said Merry after giving Doethan a hug. "He said I should tell you that in recompense for ruining his bed linens, he wants something magical to keep his beer cold, for his patrons who prefer it that way."

"All five of them?" said Doethan with a wry smile. "Let's see how we manage evacuating ahead of Sírénae's invasion first, and then I'll worry about the temperature of his beer."

"That's between you and Taffy, then," said Merry. "Did you find out where the best caverns are located?"

"I did," said Doethan. "My friends were quite helpful. Take a look." He pointed at the bedsheet and Merry stepped closer to inspect it.

"Is that the Rhuthro?" she asked, pointing at a medium-sized blue line that intersected with a thick blue line near the middle of the sheet.

"It is," answered Doethan. "And these red circles mark the two biggest caverns in western Dâron." He waved an arm at the drawing. "My friends say there are cave complexes farther south that are much larger, but King Nûd and Duke Háiddon will be using them to hide the excess population in eastern Dâron who can't fit in ones that are closer."

"I hadn't realized there were so many caves in the kingdom," said Merry.

"Most of the land in Dâron rests on limestone," said Doethan. "Some of the academic wizards in the Valley of Towers say limestone is made from the shells of millions of sea creatures and Dâron was once under the Ocean."

"It seems odd that dry land like this could have once been underwater," said Merry. "How is limestone relevant to our present situation?" she asked.

"Where you have limestone, you get caves," Doethan replied. "Dâron has magnificent caves."

"So does Tamloch," Merry noted.

"Dârio and Jenet are quite pleased it does," said Doethan. "They need to hide their own population."

"I brought the magestone dust you requested," said Merry, trying to get a rather confusing conversation back on a path to somewhere she recognized. After Doethan's cryptic comments, she resolved to visit the Valley of Towers and learn more about Dâron being submerged long ago, once the invasion had been dealt with.

"I knew I could count on you," said Doethan. He pointed to his left toward two tall wooden frameworks at the far end of the stadium arrayed across two of the straightaways on the racetrack. "Duke Néillen has things organized to have everyone being evacuated come in through the other end of the stadium and follow the long tracks to the pair of wide gates. Each one goes to a different cavern."

"That makes sense," said Merry. "I saw wains filled with food, drovers leading livestock, and crowds of people headed this way when I flew here from the inn."

"Duke Néillen is surprisingly competent," said Doethan.

"He was Tamloch's earl marshal," said Merry. "It's not his competence that worries me."

"Agreed," said Doethan. He looked at Merry and smiled, realizing something was missing. "Where are your two familiar troublemakers?" he asked.

"Back at Taffy's," said Merry. "He wants to see how Chee behaves when he's drunk, so he's given him a full tankard of today's fresh ale."

"I suspect that won't end well," said Doethan.

"Chee was *chee-chee-chee-ing* along with the tavern's patrons singing a drinking song when I left him," said Merry. She grinned. "If Eynon is going to leave Chee with me, the least I can do is teach him a few bad habits."

"Sounds like Taffy is doing the teaching," teased Doethan. "What about your canine flying carpet?"

"Ace is helping Taffy get rid of the bats that manage to sneak into the tavern through holes under the eaves," said Merry. "I made sure he's giving Ace water, not beer. Two drunk familiars would be too much."

"A responsible wizard sees to the well-being of her familiar," said Doethan.

"Like you do, leaving Rowsch on his own for so long?" said Merry, her tone a touch reproachful.

"Rowsch likes running with the wolf packs near my tower," said Doethan. "He doesn't lack for company."

"He still misses you, I'm sure," said Merry.

"Maybe I'll take him east to Nova Eboracum where he can look after Távi's band of young thieves and cutpurses…"

"Hah!" said Merry, imagining the big hound in a city, not open country. "You don't want to do that," she said. "That's where Sírénae's fleet will probably land and you don't want him to be captured."

"True," said Doethan. He rubbed his chin.

Both of them looked up when ten wizards in motley robes flew in from the southeast and landed near them. One was Merrillōn, Doethan's old teacher. The other nine represented a range of ages and genders, united only in the fact that looked like they hadn't been living anywhere near barbers, tailors, or soap.

"Where did Merrillōn get *them?*" whispered Merry. "The southern Clan Lands?"

"I hope not," Doethan whispered back. "But wherever they come from, we need them. He already brought me six wizards in his first batch more than an hour ago. I sent them off to the destination caverns, along with city guards to build the wide gate frameworks at that end."

"Smart," said Merry. "That will save us time."

"I hope so," said Doethan. The old wizard stepped over to join him and stood next to Merry.

"Hello, my former apprentice. I've produced all the wizards you asked for and a few more besides," said Merrillōn, waving toward his companions. "Now let's get on with you teaching me how to make wide gates."

"I will," said Doethan. "The first thing is to make sure the gates are identical and covered top, sides, and bottom with magestone dust."

"Not that much different from smaller fixed gates, then," said Merrillōn.

"Correct," said Doethan. "The difference is in the way the links are established and triggered. Send your two fastest wizards off— one to each destination cavern—with a sack of magestone dust, brushes, and a couple of buckets of glue."

Doethan pointed out the sacks and buckets, while Merrillōn selected a pair of wizards—a middle-aged man and a woman a few years younger. The chosen wizards put a sack, a collection of brushes, and two buckets on their flying disks. Doethan gave each of the wizards a communications ring.

"I'll need these back when we're done," he said. "But we'll need to stay in touch in case any last-minute adjustments to the gates have to be made." He told each wizard the phrases needed to trigger their rings, then stepped back and nodded at his old mentor.

"Very good," said Merrillōn. "Be about it, then," he told the two wizards. "Fly fast and let us know when you arrive."

The pair launched themselves into the air and were soon dots on the northwestern horizon.

"If you and your associates could start gluing magestone dust to the frames at this end, that would be quite helpful," said Doethan.

Merrillōn promptly goaded his remaining mages into action and they skimmed along the track toward what would soon be wide gates.

"How can I assist?" asked Merry.

"You can go back to the inn and tell Duke Néillen the wide gates will likely be ready by dusk," said Doethan. "If all goes well, the city should be successfully evacuated several hours before dawn."

"I'm sure he'll be glad to hear that," said Merry. "He told me to mention that he'd sent instructions downriver for all holders to head west until we could organize caves for them as well."

"Good," said Doethan. "We may actually pull this off."

Chapter 48

Eynon Returns

Laetícia's study appeared empty when Eynon gated in. He looked for someone he could ask about Merry, since he *really* needed to make amends for his behavior and apologize. Just like he had at the Tempest Isles, he'd tried to be helpful, but had ended up failing miserably. He should have stayed and talked things over with Merry before leaving back in Verro's sanctum, instead of just disappearing while she was asleep.

The sun had just gone down, but several wizard lamps filled the room with light. Eynon was about to descend to the governor-general's palace to search for Quintillius, Laetícia, Mafuta, Felix, or any of the people he knew, for that matter, when he heard giggling from under a circular table in the middle of the study.

The table was covered with a purple linen cloth long enough to reach the floor. He walked over to stand beside it. "Hello?" said Eynon. "Is anyone here?"

The giggles under the table continued, accompanied by children's voices whispering. Eynon now had a good idea about the sources of the whispers and giggles. He remembered his own delight in the game of hide-and-seek when he was young and decided to play along.

"Fum, fie, foe, fee. I smell Roma children three!" said Eynon, augmenting his voice with magic to make it sound an octave deeper.

"I don't smell," said a tiny voice under the table. "I had a bath this morning."

"Shhhh!" said another voice. "Keep quiet. We don't want the giant to get us."

"I'm *hungry*," said Eynon, keeping his words in lower registers. "If I found a little girl, I could eat her all up!"

"Don't eat me, Mister Giant," said the tiny voice.

"I'll protect you," came a third, somewhat older voice from under the tablecloth. "I have a knife."

"I have a knife, too," said the tiny voice, now sounding quite fierce. "I'll stab the giant's toes."

Eynon quickly danced back from the edge of the table, held his flying disk over his head, and rose a few feet into the air.

"Don't hurt him," said the second voice Eynon had heard. "He's nice."

"I know," the tiny voice whispered, less fiercely. "But I like pretending."

"So do I," said the other voice.

"I don't see his feet anymore," said the older voice. "But I didn't hear him leave."

The hem of the tablecloth rose, and three young faces peered out. Eynon quickly shifted to hover over the center of the table.

"He must be gone," said the second voice.

"Giants are afraid of warriors," said the tiny voice.

"You're no warrior," said the older voice.

"I am, too!" insisted the tiny voice.

From his vantage point floating above, Eynon watched three children—ages four, six, and eight, he guessed—crawl out from under the table. Before they could stand, Eynon bellowed an augmented roar worthy of Viridáxés. He lifted the tablecloth and dropped it over the children. Shrieks and giggles followed, then pleas to be released from the linen cloth's captivity. Eynon let out another roar, but this one was much softer and ended in a rising interrogative. "RRRawrrr?" he said.

"Let us out, let us out," the children chortled.

"Of course," said Eynon. He lifted the tablecloth, revealing Primus, Seconda, and Tertia, Quintillius and Laetícia's children, rolling on the floor like playful kittens.

"You make a good giant," said Primus as he got to his feet.

"I wasn't scared a bit," asserted Tertia.

"Thanks for adding to our fun," said Seconda.

"Where are your parents?" asked Eynon as he descended, then centered the tablecloth back on the circular table.

"Our *mater* is on a secret rescue mission with Auntie Mafuta and Felix," said Seconda. "We're hiding from our nursemaid in here."

"She had three cups of unwatered wine on an empty stomach," said Primus. "We didn't have to hide very hard."

"I don't need a nursemaid," said Tertia when she stood.

"You're a big girl," Eynon confirmed, knowing the proper response from growing up with lots of younger cousins around.

"And I have a knife," said Tertia, pointing to a carved wooden knife with a gently rounded business end tucked into the belt of her tunic.

Eynon was pleased to see Quin and Laetícia didn't allow their younger daughter to carry a steel blade but suspected that wouldn't be true for much longer. Tertia had more of a warrior's heart than he did.

"Who are they rescuing?" asked Eynon.

"Valentius," said Primus. "He's our mother's first cousin and heir to the Southern Empire. Sírénae captured him."

"I see," said Eynon, though he was still confused. "Aren't Roma's emperors selected by the appropriate Senate?"

"You don't know much about politics, do you?" noted Primus.

The boy is right about that, thought Eynon. He tried asking the children a different question. "Where's your father?"

"He's in the city, organizing the evacuation," said Seconda.

"The evacuation?" asked Eynon.

"Uh huh," said Seconda. "The invasion fleet is too strong, so the leaders of Orluin decided to hide our people and our food, so the invaders could either leave or starve."

"Fascinating," said Eynon. He had a lot to catch up on, but first things first. "Do you know where my friend Merry is?" he asked.

"She left," said Tertia.

"Do you know where she went?" Eynon asked all three children, hoping for a useful answer.

"Our mater asked Doethan and Merry to go to Tyford to support the city and surrounding area's evacuation," Primus informed Eynon. "They left early this afternoon."

"Chee and Ace were with them," said Seconda.

"Who's Ace?" asked Eynon.

"You'll see," teased Tertia.

Eynon looked at the older children, hoping for more information, but they just smiled enigmatically. "All right, then," said Eynon. "I'm off to Tyford."

"Safe travels," said Primus.

"RRRawrrr!" said Tertia, making a face that was so cute Eynon was hard-pressed not to laugh.

As he gated out, Eynon saw Seconda patting her little sister on the head. He was gone before he could see what happened next, but he grinned as he imagined the consequences.

* * * * *

Eynon gated to the spot in Tyford he remembered best—the dock behind and below Taffaern's Inn. Everything was quiet along the river, but Eynon could hear the hustle and bustle of a busy tavern above him. He guided his flying disk up and around through the moonlit night to the inn's front door, then shrugged the disk onto his shoulders and entered. Several wizard lamps and light from a massive fireplace made the inn's common room bright, warm, and welcoming. Taffy, behind the bar, saw Eynon and waved to him.

As Eynon threaded through the tables to reach the innkeeper, a thick hand reached out and grabbed his upper arm.

"What brings *you* here?" asked Duke Néillen. "Did Nûd send you?"

Eynon pulled away and was deciding which sort of offensive magic would be most effective against the duke when Taffaern called out.

"Don't!" said Taffy. "He's here on the king's orders to coordinate the evacuation."

"Nûd put *you* in charge?" Eynon asked Néillen. "Has he lost his mind?"

"No, but you seem to have lost your manners, young wizard," said Duke Néillen. "For all my faults, I know how to organize men and resources. Nûd knows not many have that gift."

"If Taffaern vouches for you, I won't make trouble," said Eynon. "I'm looking for Merry—and Doethan."

"Doethan is off preparing wide gates for the evacuation," said Néillen. "He said he was reaching out to some friends of his who had an atlas showing the location of every decent-sized cavern in western Dâron. He's also got local wizards building frameworks for the wide gates."

Eynon smiled, feeling certain he knew who Doethan was contacting. "What about Merry?" he asked.

"Doethan sent her west to get magestone dust," said the duke.

"From the green magestone quarry?"

"I remember hearing them say *something* about a quarry," said Néillen.

"I'll find her there, then," said Eynon. He generated a sphere of solidified sound and used it to push the closer tables a few feet away from him before he gated out.

"Wait!" said Duke Néillen. "We need your..."

Eynon didn't hear the rest. He was already at the quarry.

* * * * *

The moon was bright enough to show the jagged floor of the green magestone quarry west of Wherrel. Eynon had gated in to the same point where Verro's raiders had come sweeping down to attack him on their quest for magestones earlier. The quarry's floor looked a lot different now. A green dragon breaking free from dozens of feet of rock tends to change things.

He lit a glow ball and tossed it high, pumping magical energy from his red magestone into it until it rivaled a small winter sun.

"Merry!" Eynon shouted. "Where are you?"

Echoes from the quarry's walls were the only reply. *Maybe someone in Wherrel saw her,* thought Eynon. *I have some cousins who won't be too unhappy if I wake them at this hour,* he rationalized. He dispelled the glow ball, brought his flying disk closer to the ground, and skimmed along. Using only moonlight, he followed the path through the cut in the quarry's walls that led to Wherrel, the town in the northwest corner of the Coombe best known for the green slate roofs on its cottages. Eynon was thinking about Merry and wasn't watching where he was going when he heard a familiar voice taking a familiar tone.

"Watch where you're going!" said Braith sharply as she ducked out of the way. She took a breath and realized she'd nearly been knocked over by a flying wizard. "Eynon, is that you?" Braith asked.

"It is," said Eynon. "I'm sorry. I didn't see you."

"I'll bet I know what—or should I say *who* you were thinking about," teased Eynon's sister.

"Have you seen Merry?" he asked, turning back and descending low enough for Braith to board his disk.

"I have," said Braith. "I'll tell you about it on our way home."

"Have I missed her by much?" asked Eynon as he steered his way toward Haywall. He could have made an *ad hoc* gate back to Haywall and just jumped there, but it wasn't far, and he wanted to hear what Braith had to say about Merry.

"I expect you've missed her quite a bit," said Braith. She stood on her toes and whispered in Eynon's ear. "Confidentially, I think she's missed you quite a bit, too."

Eynon's smile was bright enough to match the Moon's glow. "I was *so* foolish," he said.

"You often are," teased Braith. "But I think she's already *mostly* forgiven you for whatever it was you did."

Eynon let the air in his lungs out in a rush. "I'm so glad," he said.

"I said *mostly*," Braith reminded him. "The way I read things it would still make sense to grovel—at least a little."

"I'll be glad to," said Eynon. "She's even welcome to yell at me until she runs out of words."

"I don't think any of us have *that* much time, dear brother," said Braith. "The Coombe has to be warned about the Siren Hawk's invasion and we'll have a *lot* of work to do to get all the cows underground, along with all their fodder, to say nothing of all the people and *their* requirements."

"I wish I could stay and help," said Eynon.

"You can help by using your magic to fight off the invaders," said Braith.

"That's what I plan to do," said Eynon. He didn't say anything about his defeat by Sírénae's wizards and dragons.

"About Merry…" said Braith.

"Yes?" Eynon responded, inviting more.

"She stopped in Haywall to get half a dozen grain sacks for the magestone dust," said Braith.

"You helped her, I'm sure," said Eynon.

"I did," said Braith. "I found the bags and held them open while she filled them."

"Good," said Eynon. "Thank you for helping her. When did Merry leave?"

"Only a few minutes ago," said Braith. "Just enough time for me to walk from the quarry to where you found me."

"If you didn't dawdle, that means she's been gone for less than half an hour," said Eynon. "I should be able to catch up to her."

"She was moving pretty fast."

"I can move faster," said Eynon.

The farms between Wherrel and Haywall flew by beneath them. They were quiet for a few seconds, then Braith tapped Eynon on the shoulder.

"I don't understand why the Roma from across the Ocean want to conquer Dâron and Tamloch," she said. "The Roma I met in Nova Eboracum for the treaty-signing ceremony seemed very nice."

"The Roma of Occidens Province *are* nice," said Eynon. "They're our allies against the invaders."

"You mean the treaty is actually being honored?" asked Braith. "The old stories are full of alliances being broken."

"The alliance is firm," said Eynon. He rubbed his forehead. "There's something personal about the way *our* Roma hate Sírénae, the invader," he said. "Apparently Sírénae kidnapped Laetícia's cousin and Laetícia is leading a team of wizards to get him back."

"Who's on the team?" asked Braith, concern in her tone.

"Mafuta and Felix were the only other names I heard," Eynon answered.

"Felix," said Braith softly.

Eynon was about to tease his sister about her latest infatuation but thought better of it. "I'm sure he'll be fine," said Eynon.

"I hope so," said Braith. She squeezed Eynon's upper arms tightly from her position behind him. "Keep Felix safe, big brother."

"I'll do my best," said Eynon. "We're here."

Braith stepped down to the slate paving stones of the courtyard between the cottages in the center of Haywall and gave her brother a hug. "Take care of yourself," she said, releasing him from her embrace.

"You too," said Eynon. He rose skyward and disappeared with a familiar, echoing *pop*.

* * * * *

Eynon floated high above Applegarth, the home Merry said she greatly preferred to her father's castle several miles upstream. For the first time he could see rows and rows of what he assumed must be apple trees arrayed in neat lines upslope from the river. Applegarth was a good spot for him to wait to intercept Merry on her flight back to Tyford. Tempting as it was to stop in to visit with Merry's parents and enjoy a mug of cider, Eynon scanned the western horizon looking for Merry instead. *I don't even know if Derry and Mabli are home,* he realized. *Finding Merry is much more important.*

He constructed combined distance and night-vision lenses from solidified sound and resumed his search, then turned to look east in case Merry had already sped past Applegarth. Something tickled the back of his brain, then exploded like fireworks. "Why do *I* have to find *her?*" said Eynon to empty air. "Why can't I help *her* find *me?*" As he had in the quarry, he made a glow ball and sent it high in the air—much higher than he had previously. He used his red magestone to pump it up so the the land for ten miles around the glowing ball was as well lit as it would be at noon.

Merry's got to see that! thought Eynon. She could only fly so far if Braith had been at all accurate in her time estimate.

Time passed. With his lenses he could see people up and down the Rhuthro Valley emerge from their homes and shield their eyes from the strange evening sun. Merry, however, did not appear.

"Blast!" Eynon exclaimed. "Maybe she's back in Tyford already."

He extinguished his glow ball and took an *ad hoc* gate back to the docks beneath Taffaern's inn. When Eynon came through the inn's front door this time, he first noticed Chee sitting on the bar next to Taffy. The raconette was holding a pewter mug at least half his own size and Eynon smiled to realize his familiar had probably consumed most of its contents.

Then he shifted his glance and saw Merry at a table in the middle of the room, talking to someone who could only be Duke Néillen. Her back was to Eynon and she hadn't yet seen him, so he softly walked over to where she sat, knelt beside her, and extended one of the special pair of communications rings he'd crafted toward her.

Taffy noticed him, even if Merry didn't. He smiled at Eynon the way an affable uncle would indulge a niece's favored suitor. He rapped a pewter mug with a knife, drawing the attention of everyone in the common room, including Merry. "Merry Derrysdaughter," he said, glancing down. "There's someone here who'd like a word with you."

Merry followed Taffy's eyes and saw Eynon kneeling beside her. Without a moment's thought, she slid off the chair, put her arms around Eynon and hugged him so hard he nearly lost his balance and tipped both of them over to the floor.

Keeping a tight grip on the ring, Eynon hugged her back, enjoying their renewed connection, while thinking it strange to hear a dog barking in the rafters. After a few seconds, Merry stood, tugged Eynon to his feet, and pulled him in the direction of the stairs leading up to the inn's sleeping rooms.

"I need a key," she told Taffy. She didn't need to speak up because the common room had gone silent.

Taffy tossed a brass key the size of his massive index finger to Merry. "Room Seven. End of the hall on the right."

Merry plucked it out of the air and continued to guide Eynon to the stairs and up the first few treads.

"Don't be too long about it," called Duke Néillen. "There's work to be done."

Merry shot Néillen a look that spoke volumes, and soon the two young wizards were out of sight with only their footsteps echoing down to report their progress.

The common room erupted in raucous shouts of encouragement and advice.

Néillen looked across the room to Taffy standing behind the bar. The duke turned out his hands in a what-are-we-going-to-do gesture.

The big innkeeper, who had once been the Barrel Knight, just shrugged. Sometimes you simply got out of the way and let things happen.

Chapter 49

Up the Moravon

The ships of Second Fleet slipped softly up the wide Moravon heading for Tyford, propelled by wind generated by dozens of wizards. Still more mages hid the ships' passage with veils of illusion, their work made easier by traveling at night. Admiral Pixo, Lieutenant General Belisaria, and Náegosh, the mage Magister Callidus had assigned to manage the wizards assigned to Second Fleet, stood on the deck of Pixo's flagship, the *Menodorus Maximus,* watching the eastern shore. They were close together, speaking softly, since voices carried far too well over open water.

"I don't like it," said Belisaria. The expression on her face made it seem like she'd just spit out a rancid olive.

"Frankly, I don't either," said Pixo.

"Don't like what?" asked Náegosh. A short and wiry man of three decades, he'd worked with Belisaria before, but not with Pixo. In his time on this expedition, he was learning that the admiral's abrupt manner hid a quick mind and a sincere concern for the people under his command.

"It's too quiet," said the lieutenant general. "I haven't seen any sentries, or any lights in the small settlements we've passed, for that matter."

"Would you expect to this far inland in the wee hours of the night?" asked Náegosh. "Where I grew up in the mountains of Éberria, the only people up at this hour would be shepherds, and they'd rely on light from the moon and stars, not lanterns or wizard lamps."

"He may be right," said Pixo, his voice sounding less than confident. "Even if the farms and towns along the river received word of the invasion, they can't be expecting us to be here so soon. The main fleet is still at least a day's sail from Nova Eboracum."

"I still don't like it," said Belisaria. "Something seems off."

"Like mutton from an old ewe?" asked Náegosh.

Belisaria's lips tightened. "Perhaps," she said. "Now that you mention ewes, it's not just that I haven't seen any people; I haven't seen any livestock, either."

"Maybe they have problems with wolves and keep their flocks and herds inside at night?" suggested Pixo.

"These lands look too tame for that, even in moonlight," said Belisaria. "The towns we've seen heading upriver don't even have walls."

"Historically, walls haven't been effective forms of defense," said Pixo. "Not since wizards and fireballs, at least."

"They're not very helpful against dragons, either," said Náegosh. "Against big ones, anyway."

"You both have valid points," said Belisaria. She ran her calloused hands through the short brown curls on her head.

Náegosh thought her hair reminded him of the busts carved by Athicans from the days before the Roma first came and conquered, back when there was only *one* empire, not four-in-one. He was pulled away from his woolgathering when Belisaria tugged at the sleeve of his robes.

"Didn't you hear me?" she asked. "I wanted to know if the fleet's concealment spells your illusionists are casting might also muffle sounds from shore."

"They shouldn't," said Náegosh. "That's why the legionnaires aren't in armor, so the clanking of plates doesn't give us away."

"Not exactly," said Pixo. "There's also the matter of not drowning if a ship sinks or a soldier falls overboard."

"If nothing is keeping sounds from shore from reaching our ears, I stand by my original concern," said Belisaria. "There's something off. It's too quiet."

"Maybe my wizards are simply doing an excellent job of disguising our passage?" offered Náegosh.

"From human senses, perhaps," said Belisaria. "But what about dogs? I haven't heard a single dog barking on our entire trip."

"No one has ever tried to hide an entire fleet with magic before," said Pixo. "It's the emperor's idea, and so far, it seems to be working quite well."

"I'm still worried," said Belisaria. "My legionnaires can handle whatever military force these Dâroni barbarians array against us, to say nothing about local levies of peasants with pitchforks." She looked at Admiral Pixo and he nodded in agreement. "The problem is, I don't know what to think about things being *this* quiet. My instincts tell me this is a trap."

"Dâroni?" asked Náegosh. "I thought they were Dâroners."

"The precise demonym for citizens of the kingdom doesn't matter," said Pixo. "They could be Dâronians for all I care. From what I hear, they're not barbarians, either. They're a civilized people—much more civilized than the axe-wielding Nordlanders we had to endure across the Ocean. My briefings from Magister Umbrose note that the real barbarians in Orluin are known as Clan Landers and live in the mountains."

"My apologies," said Belisaria. "I hadn't been informed of their cultural sophistication. Just their military capabilities."

"Don't worry about it," said Pixo. "The important thing is planning for contingencies. If your instincts are telling you there's a problem, General, we'd be wise to investigate."

"Thank you, Admiral," said Belisaria. "I appreciate your support."

"I'm a bit uneasy myself, if the true story is told," said Pixo. He caught the mage's eye. "Do you have any wizards who could fly ahead of the fleet and scout out both shores?" Pixo asked. "That should relieve our concerns—or confirm them."

"The original plan was to have enough wizards to include a dozen forward scouts," said Náegosh. "Unfortunately, Magister Callidus had to reduce the number of wizards from the thirteenth cohort assigned to Second Fleet in order to increase the number of guards protecting an important prisoner."

"I *see...*" said Pixo, remembering Valentius. He hoped Sírénae wasn't being too smart for her own good by shortchanging Second Fleet on wizards. It wouldn't be the first time the emperor had done so—or the first time he'd figured out a path to victory, nonetheless.

"Couldn't *you* scout ahead?" Belisaria asked Náegosh. "You don't seem to be doing anything important at the moment."

Pixo made a mental note to tell General Machaera, the overall military commander of the invading forces, that Belisaria should be schooled in the wisdom of not giving offense to subordinates, especially ones in different chains of command—and that went double for wizards. He spoke up to distract Náegosh from Belisaria's offensive words.

"Might it be possible for *you* to help us, good wizard?" asked Pixo.

"I'm an administrator, not a scout or an illusionist," said Náegosh. "But under the circumstances, I can probably free up a scout-wizard—and Umbrose will want one of his spy-wizards along as well, I'm sure. When they report, you'll see we have nothing to worry about."

Chapter 50

Eynon and Merry

When the door closed behind them, Merry threw the bolt, dropped the heavy key on the floor, and hugged Eynon hard enough to force most of the air out of his lungs. Eynon hugged Merry back tightly, but not quite as fiercely. After a dozen shared heartbeats, Eynon took a deep breath.

"I'm glad to see you, too," he said.

Merry rose up on her toes and whispered in Eynon's ear. "You're an idiot, but I still love you."

"Agreed, and reciprocated—the I love you part, I mean," Eynon replied. "I'm sorry I left without talking to you first."

"Where have you *been?*" asked Merry. She pushed Eynon back to arms length and stared up at him. Eynon began to explain, but Merry put her hand over his lips and turned her head in the direct of the large bed that nearly filled the small room. "Tell me later," she said. "After." Merry pulled her hand away, revealing Eynon's broad smile. She smiled back. "It's easier to talk horizontally—when we're both the same height."

"This is for you," said Eynon when they were both sitting on the bed's thick quilt, about to take their boots off. He extended the gold ring he'd been holding and presented it to Merry.

"I told you I didn't want to get married yet," she said.

"No," said Eynon. "It's not a wedding ring. It's a communications ring so we can always stay in touch when we're apart."

"In that case," said Merry. She grinned and held out a hand.

Eynon rotated Merry's wrist and put the gold band in the center of her palm, not on her finger.

"I like the apples around the band," said Merry. "Were those for me?"

"Of course," said Eynon. "This is a very special communications ring. I made it myself."

Merry held the ring between her thumb and forefinger and was about to put it on so they could return to what they'd planned to do, when Eynon stopped her.

"You really need to try it out."

"Now?" asked Merry. She gave Eynon a look that made it clear she thought they were both wearing too many clothes.

"I think so," said Eynon. "I'm hoping it will make you happy enough to forgive me, or at least reduce the time you spend being mad at me."

"This must be some ring," said Merry. "I'll try it if we have to," she grumbled. "Show me—then we can get naked."

"Yes, my love."

Eynon removed the mate to Merry's ring from his own left hand. *"Síarad â chi!"* he commanded.

Merry laughed as three chimes sounded and both rings began to expand until the two sat side by side on the edge of the bed, each holding a thin circle of gold in which the other's face appeared. "This is wonderful," said Merry. "Now we'll always be able to talk to each other, even when we're apart." It was a bit strange to hear her words from her own lips *and* from Eynon's ring.

"There's more," said Eynon. "We'll need to stand up for me to show you." He stood, holding his ring's two-foot circle in front of him like a precious, well-polished silver platter. Eynon tugged gently on Merry's elbow and she rose as well, staring at Eynon's face through the ring while sensing him only a foot or two away.

"I'm on my feet," said Merry. "Hurry up and show me, so I can show you how much I've missed you."

"Wait right where you are for a minute," said Eynon. "I need to move to the other side of the bed."

Merry saw him smiling but didn't hear his stockinged feet on the floorboards.

"I'm on the other side now," he said. "I'm going to tug on my ring to expand it. The circle may get bigger than you can hold with both hands, so be sure to grip at least part of it."

"If you say so," said Merry. She could hear Eynon's voice coming from across the room *and* directly in front of her. Then Merry felt—and saw—her ring grow wider until its diameter stretched from floor to ceiling. She could see Eynon's entire body on the other side, not just his head and shoulders.

"Coming through," said Eynon.

Merry jumped and lost her hold on her ring when Eynon stepped through her ring's interface and stood beside her.

Eynon grabbed her ring's thin edge, shrank his own ring, and pulled it through. For a few seconds he held a larger ring and a somewhat smaller ring, then both gold circles shrank down small enough for Eynon to hold in his palm. "Your ring, my lady," he said. He bowed and gave Merry one of the rings. She slid it on her left hand as if she was afraid it might disappear if she didn't.

"That was amazing!" she said, loud enough to be heard down in the common room. Merry and Eynon ignored shouts of approval and clapping from below. She hugged Eynon after he'd put his ring back on his finger.

Bowing again, Eynon beamed at Merry's praise.

"Do you realize what you've done?" she said, still excited. "You've created a mobile fixed gate."

"I understand what you mean," said Eynon, "but we'll have to find a better name for it. *Mobile fixed gate* sounds like an oxymoron."

"We can just call it a mobile gate," said Merry. "But whatever we call it, it's something that's never been done before."

"How do you know?"

"Because anything as amazing as *this*"—said Merry, holding up her ring— "would be featured in a story *somewhere*. Who could resist including such a thing in a tale if one existed?"

"You may be right," said Eynon. "Does this mean you won't be mad at me quite as long?"

"Probably," teased Merry. "Ask me again after we've spent time horizontally." She lifted his flying disk from his shoulders and slid it under the bed, then loosened his belt and let it—and the dagger and pouch attached to it—thunk to the wooden floor.

Eynon tried to remove Merry's flying disk, but she kept her arms by her sides, and he ended up lifting her until their mouths were at the same level. Merry kissed Eynon, then raised her arms and slipped through the straps until she was standing again. She undid her own belt, which landed near Eynon's. With the grace of a dancer, she shifted behind Eynon and pulled his backpack down until its straps had trapped his elbows. She leaned on the backpack and Eynon fell to his knees. Merry continued to circle Eynon and when she was in front of him again, she leaned down and kissed him hard.

"It's only fair that you should have to look up to kiss *me* from time to time," she teased.

Eynon tilted back until his knuckles brushed the floorboards and his backpack slid down his arms. He straightened, leaving his pack behind, and attempted to throw his arms around Merry's waist. She tried to disengage and step out of reach, but Eynon caught the hem of her robes and tugged her closer. Merry did a pirouette to spin away, but since Eynon still held her hem, it only managed to wrap her tighter in her robes. She put her arms around his neck and shoulders and allowed herself to be lifted and tossed on the bed. Both their robes and small clothes were off shortly thereafter.

They managed to delightfully reconnect for some time, despite more cheers, shouts, and applause from the common room. The distraction of constant cries of *Chee! Chee!* and a strange-sounding dog's howling just outside their door did nothing to reduce their enthusiasm.

Chapter 51

The Great Escape

Laetícia considered the possibility that Magister Callidus was trying to trick her but discounted it. *What other option do I have than to trust him?* she considered.

"This way," said Callidus, indicating the other side of the doorway where he stood.

"Grab their magestones," Laetícia ordered Mafuta, pointing at the unconscious spy-mages.

"There's no time," said Callidus. "My mages will deal with the kraken and be back to capture us if we don't move quickly."

Laetícia and Mafuta freed Valentius and helped him to his feet. The three of them followed Callidus out of the compartment and watched him seal it shut from the outside with a length of heavy chain. "It won't slow them down for long," said Callidus, "but they can't *gate* out now."

"Good," said Laetícia after she scanned the corridor. "Where do you think they've taken Felix? We're not going to leave here without him."

"We may not have much choice in the matter if we want to escape," said Callidus.

As if to underscore his words, dozens of booted feet pounded on the deck above them, headed their way.

"Follow me," said Callidus. "You can rescue the young man later. But you won't be any use to him if you're captured."

"But Felix," said Mafuta, as she reluctantly followed Callidus, Laetícia and Valentius.

"Where are we going?" asked Laetícia. She was worried about what Sírénae might do to Felix, but reluctantly agreed with the logic of the magister's words.

Callidus led them ten paces to starboard, then down another ladder to a long straight passageway leading forward.

Valentius moved stiffly at first, then more smoothly as his muscles recovered their range of motion after being tied to a chair for far too long. He caught up to Laetícia as they sped along and whispered to her. "Your friend isn't the only one we still need to save," he said. "My key advisers—and Aleña—are being held on *Cloud Dancer*. We have to rescue them, too."

"Cloud Dancer?" asked Mafuta and they sped down the passageway.

"My ship," said Valentius.

"Aleña?" asked Laetícia.

"My wife," Valentius whispered. "My very *new* wife—from the Isles of Dogs."

"Congratulations, cousin," said Laetícia. "It's about time you settled down."

"Thank you," said Valentius softly. "Sírénae has no idea who Aleña is and thinks she's just another member of my entourage."

"Say no more or Sírénae soon *will* know," said Magister Callidus. He put a finger to his lips. "Umbrose has ears everywhere."

"Umbrose is unconscious in a compartment on the brig deck with two of his spy-mages," said Mafuta.

"But for how long?" asked Valentius. "We have to save my advisers—my entire ship and crew, if possible."

"And my former apprentice," added Mafuta. "Are we nearly to wherever it is we're going?"

"We are," said Callidus. "In here," he said, opening a door marked *Mess,* then locking and barring it from the inside once they'd all entered.

Valentius and the wizards were standing in a narrow room holding a dozen long tables and twice that many benches. There was a pass-through counter leading from the mess hall to the galley. The hall was empty, given the time. Had they been making their escape an hour later, there would have been cooks soaking hardtack for the crew's breakfast. The place smelled of grease and the ubiquitous *garum* sauce made from fermented fish intestines that the Roma poured on everything. Together, the four of them crossed into the compact galley.

Valentius sniffed and sighed. "Is there anything here I can eat?" he asked. "The smells are making me salivate. I haven't had anything for a week except stale bread and watered wine that was nearly vinegar."

"You shouldn't eat anything heavy after fasting for so long," said Callidus. He found a barrel marked with a circle, grabbed a mug from a rack, and filled the mug for Valentius. "Drink this," he said, handing the mug to the other man. "It's lime juice and honey."

"That will help," said Valentius. "Down the hatchway." He tossed back the mug, wiped his mouth with the back of his hand, and smiled. "When we get to the *Cloud Dancer,* you can have a taste from a barrel made from sweet *naranges,* not sour limes."

"You two can discuss recipes later," said Laetícia. "How are we getting out of here?"

"Can you all swim?" asked Magister Callidus as he stepped into the small galley.

"Why?" asked Mafuta, looking at Callidus as if he'd next want to know if she could dive for squid at the bottom of the Ocean like one of the great toothed cetaceans.

"You may have to, before you can fly," said Callidus. "Here's our way out." He pointed to a half circle cut into the galley's outer wall near the deck. It was the size of a bisected flying disk and he could feel a breeze blowing into the galley from below.

"Is that where the cooks toss the slops?" asked Laetícia.

"It is," said Callidus. "You first, then Valentius. He can stand on your flying disk while you hover. Be careful, you'll only be a few feet above the waves."

"Right," said Laetícia. She took her flying disk off her shoulders, put her feet in its leather thongs, and sat down, scooting herself forward until the disk was through the hole.

Valentius helped Laetícia slide the rest of the way. He looked back at Magister Callidus before exiting.

"Don't worry, I'll help Mafuta get through," said Callidus.

Valentius nodded. "Good luck," he said, and followed Laetícia to stand with her on her flying disk outside the *Seahawk.*

"I don't know if I can *fit* through something that size," said Mafuta, eying the narrow half-circle cut in the ship's wooden hull. She knew it would be a challenge, given her generous body shape.

"That's why I'll stay to assist you," said Callidus. "You can start by doing what Laetícia did."

Mafuta gave Callidus an uncertain smile, then stood on her flying disk and allowed Callidus to hold her arms and help her sit. To her surprise, instead of trying to slide her out through the hole, Callidus surrounded her with a form-fitting envelope of solidified sound and guided her through the hole, using his construct to help her passage by compressing sections of the envelope as necessary. Two seconds later, Mafuta was floating ten feet above the waves beside Laetícia and Valentius. Despite being older than Mafuta, Magister Callidus was able to bend his thin frame and exit through the hole to join them without any difficulty.

"There's *Cloud Dancer*," said Valentius, pointing at the vessel still flying the black-eagle-on-gold banner of the Southern Empire five ships away. It was hard to miss with sixteen wizards playing qua-qua five hundred feet above it and seven dragons flapping about providing commentary.

"How many people are aboard?" asked Laetícia.

"Perhaps a hundred," said Valentius. "My advisers, the ship's crew, other passengers headed from the Isles of Dogs to Alexandria, and Aleña."

"That's far too many to gate out, even with three master mages who can form *ad hoc* gates," said Laetícia.

"I can transport some with my emergency gate," offered Mafuta.

"I could *ad hoc* gate ten or twelve to the governor-general's palace in Nova Eboracum, if that would help," said Magister Callidus.

"It's still not enough," said Laetícia.

"And it would be nice if we could save the obsidian magestones in the hold, too," said Valentius, "though they're far less important than the people aboard."

Laetícia was silent for a moment. She balanced on her flying disk with her chin resting on one hand.

"I know that look," said Mafuta. "What are you thinking?"

Two heartbeats later, Laetícia allowed herself to smile. Then she outlined her plan.

Magister Callidus was delighted when he heard the details. "You have a dragon larger than Xaxidiánus?"

"We do," Laetícia confirmed, remembering not to mention they had *two* giant dragons, not just one. Magister Callidus was gaining her trust more and more by the minute, but she still wasn't sure he was completely on their side and didn't want to give him more information than absolutely necessary. "Can you help us generate a large protective construct of solidified sound?" she asked.

"Can I?" Callidus exclaimed. "It's one of my specialties!"

"You'll have several powerful mages to assist you," said Laetícia.

Callidus smiled. "Their help would be quite welcome."

"Good," said Laetícia. "I'll brief the others." In the relative calm of the port side of the *Seahawk,* with the illusion of a kraken attack taking place nearby, she used a handful of communications rings to speak with Amber, Verro, and Zûrafiérix. Verro was able to confirm that Inthíra could do what was needed to adjust her kraken illusion and Zûrafiérix nodded underwater, her huge whirling blue eyes signaling her amusement and appreciation for Laetícia's plan.

"They all know what to do," said Laetícia. "Cousin, you should ride with Mafuta when you head over to the *Cloud Dancer.* With help from Callidus and Mafuta you should be able to deal with any guards aboard."

"If you say so," said Valentius, stepping from one flying disk to the other. "Where will *you* be?"

"Rescuing Felix," said Laetícia. She saw Mafuta smile and Callidus and Valentius frown.

"Why risk being captured yourself?" asked Magister Callidus. "Sírénae wants you as much or more than she wants Valentius."

"I know why," said Valentius. He pressed his lips together. "Laetícia is a leader."

"And leaders don't leave team members behind," said Mafuta. She held Laetícia's hands in hers. "Good luck, my friend," she said. "Save Felix."

"Save *Cloud Dancer*," said Laetícia. She smiled at Valentius. "And Aleña." Laetícia watched her three companions skim along just above the waves. She was pleased they were very hard to see, especially with all the chaos caused by Inthíra's illusions and Zûrafiérix using her body to batter ships that were supposedly in the grasp of the simulated kraken. Laetícia squared her shoulders, shook her head to hear the reassuring clack of the beads in her braids, and began to work her way aft along the *Seahawk's* hull in search of Felix.

* * * * *

When Laetícia determined she'd gone nearly far enough, she tried to sense magestones inside Sírénae's flagship. It seemed like most of the battle mages assigned to Callidus were no longer aboard, being busy fighting the kraken and rescuing sailors instead. That meant any magestones on the *Seahawk's* lower decks should belong to Umbrose and his furtive minions. Perhaps, with luck, one would still be with Felix.

Laetícia's purple magestone was a faceted amethyst as big as a red-breasted thrush's egg embedded in a small rectangular gold plate she wore suspended around her neck on a fine chain. She used her stone to reach out to find other magestones and slowly proceeded farther along the hull, straining to detect what she was seeking. *There they are!* she thought. *Three magestones and a distorting fuzz of interference with my attempts at detection, which is probably caused by the magestone dust on the walls, ceiling, and floor of the cell where they were holding Valentius.*

Using hot beams of tight light, Laetícia created a circular opening in the ship's oak hull that intersected with the passageway running from port to starboard outside the cell. Laetícia slipped inside and stowed her flying disk on her back. Down the passage, she saw two spy-wizards in black and gray standing in front of the cell door where she'd left Umbrose, trying to remove the heavy chain Magister Callidus had used to seal it shut. They were so focused on their task,

Laetícia was able to pop bubbles of solidified sound around their heads and knock them out before they noticed her presence.

She walked to the cell door and knelt to check the two wizards' pulses. They'd be out for some time. Laetícia searched their necks and wrists for magestones but didn't find them. She didn't have time for a more detailed search.

Laetícia looked at the chain across the cell door and decided it wasn't worth worrying about. She didn't really need to interrogate Umbrose to determine where Felix had been taken. *It can't be that far. This seems to be the level for prison cells—or the brig deck as Felix would insist.*

Laetícia moved along the passageway and saw the ladder Callidus had led them down earlier. She kept going and saw another door that resembled the one to the cell holding Valentius farther on. Laetícia tried to identify magestones inside and sensed four. She gently pushed on the door. It opened with an ominous creak of hinges that clearly hadn't been oiled in far too long.

As the interior of the cell was revealed, a plane of solidified sound slapped Laetícia on the back and pushed her inside. Before she could put up a shield, tight bands of solidified sound slapped painfully around her wrists and ankles, immobilizing her. The door slammed shut behind her like the closing of a treasure room's vault, it's steel and magestone-dust-lined walls, floor, and ceiling blocking any possibility of escape by gating away. Laetícia wasn't happy about who was waiting for her.

"Hello, Laetícia," said Sírénae Accipiter. "Or should I say, 'Fly, meet Spider?'"

Sírénae sat on a tall, ornately carved and gilded chair with a thick purple cushion. Umbrose was on her right, smiling at Laetícia like a pleased jackal. On the emperor's left, Thraxa stood eagerly, waiting to see if Sírénae would make *this* captive one of her treats. A pair of Umbrose's spy-wizards stood on either side of the door, controlling the bands that held Laetícia locked in place. They were the same two who'd been in the room with Valentius and didn't have cuts from Felix's blades and claws.

Laetícia was in shock, afraid of what Sírénae would do with her. She was even more fearful about how she might be used to blackmail her husband into surrendering Occidens Province without a battle. Laetícia decided she wouldn't give Sírénae the satisfaction of thinking she was defeated, however. Instead, she stood as tall as her bonds allowed and smiled at the emperor, ignoring Umbrose on one side and Thraxa on the other.

"Your hospitality leaves much to be desired," said Laetícia.

"Hospitality is reserved for *invited* guests," Sírénae replied.

"I thought telling me you held Valentius was *meant* as an invitation."

"Perhaps it was," said Sírénae. "We'll recover Valentius and the others in your so-called rescue party shortly, and then we'll have you both as hostages."

"Don't count your eggs before they're back in your basket, Sírénae."

"I suppose not," said the emperor. "I do have *you* however," she said. "Perhaps I could send Quintillius your right hand? Do you think that would get his attention?"

"A hand is rather extreme," said Laetícia. "One of my braids should be enough."

"Enough for him, but not for me," said Sírénae. The emperor stared at Laetícia and rested her chin on her fist before continuing. "You might change my mind if you answered a question," said Sírénae. "Summoning a great kraken from the depths of the Ocean to attack my fleet was powerful wizardry. How did you do it?"

Laetícia didn't reply.

"Come now," said Sírénae. "You know you'll tell me eventually. There are things I could do to cause you a great deal of pain, even before I have Umbrose cut off your hand. It would be a pleasure watching you suffer."

"You won't have to rip off my fingernails," said Laetícia. "It wasn't complicated. All we had to do was ask the beast nicely. It didn't want you crossing the Ocean either."

The emperor glared at Laetícia, unamused by her prisoner's defiance. Sírénae pressed her lips together until they formed a tight, angry line and rubbed the feathers on Thraxa's head hard enough to make the snow-gryffon snap her beak.

"We should thank you for forcing Callidus to show his lack of loyalty," said Umbrose, interrupting the silence.

Sírénae turned to look at her spymaster. "The old mage may still have his uses, even now that he's revealed as a traitor."

Umbrose gave the emperor a small bow, acknowledging her words, even if he clearly did not agree with them. "As you say, Your Imperial Majesty," he replied.

"Where's Felix?" asked Laetícia.

"The wizard in the black cat-armor?" asked Sírénae. "He proved more resourceful than expected, didn't he, Umbrose?"

"Yes, blast him," said Umbrose. "He had more breath in his lungs than I thought."

"Cats *do* have nine lives, Umbrose," said Sírénae. "You may have to kill him ten times."

"Once should be enough if I do it personally," said Umbrose.

"After you find him again," said Sírénae.

"He can't be far," said Umbrose. "I took his magestone." The spymaster held up a disk of silver holding a round magestone of deep purple chalcedony on a heavy silver chain. After walking over to Laetícia and letting it dangle in front of her eyes for a moment, he stuck the chain through his belt and returned to stand next to the emperor.

Sírénae stood up from her throne-like chair and slowly walked over to Laetícia, regarding her like a horse to be purchased. Next to her paced Thraxa, her claws clicking on the cell's steel floor. The fierce beast looked at Laetícia like she was meat hanging from a hook in a butcher's shop, then rubbed her head against Sírénae's hip.

"No," said the emperor. "Not for you—at least not yet. But I do want to show our captive you're not the only one with claws, my pretty girl." Sírénae drew a jewel-hilted dagger from her belt and put the edge of the blade to Laetícia's throat. "You and Quintillius *will* bow to me and accept me as your emperor," Sírénae whispered, her mouth inches from Laetícia's ear. "You wouldn't want your children to become orphans, would you?"

Laetícia froze, not wanting to provoke Sírénae by an errant word or motion.

Sírénae slid her blade across Laetícia's throat, barely breaking the skin and leaving a thin trail of blood drops like small sanguine pearls. After the space of a breath, the emperor surprised Laetícia by stretching out three of her beaded braids and cutting them off close to Laetícia's scalp. "These should be useful," said Sírénae. "They will help Quintillius know what's at stake." The empress lowered her knife and stepped back. "Just a taste," she told her snow-gryffon.

Thraxa put her front claws on Laetícia's shoulders and licked the blood from the captive wizard's throat with her long rough tongue. The snow-gryffon turned to look at Sírénae, asking with her eyes if more was permitted. Sírénae shook her head from side to side, so Thraxa retreated to rejoin the emperor, who had returned to her gilded and cushioned chair.

Laetícia felt like her audience with the emperor was over. She waited for Sírénae to leave or have her taken to one cell or another, but instead the emperor just *looked* at her, smiling in a way that made Laetícia feel like she'd just jumped into the frigid waters of the Abbenoth in late January. She closed her eyes for a moment and centered her mind, wrapping herself in a cloak of courage and determination.

Behind her, the door to the cell crashed open. Like a battering ram, it slammed into the spy-wizard holding her left side captive, and suddenly her left arm and leg were free. Two small black pebbles—obsidian magestones—Laetícia realized, bounced into the center of the cell in front of Sírénae, Umbrose, and Thraxa. They began to strobe beams of polychromatic light in all directions. Laetícia saw a tall figure in black enter the room.

"On his belt," she shouted.

Felix grabbed his magestone from Umbrose's belt and placed its chain around his neck. Then he slashed at the spymaster's robes with his claws so the shredded fabric tangled Umbrose in its folds while the two magestones Felix must have taken from the wizards Laetícia had encountered out in the hall continued to strobe. Thraxa leapt at

Felix, but the tall young mage caught her in mid-flight, twisted, and tossed her into the second wizard who'd been restraining Laetícia. That hapless mage went down as well, completely freeing Laetícia. With all his youthful strength, Felix dragged Laetícia from the cell while Sírénae screamed, "Stop them!"

When they were outside the gate-blocking cell, Laetícia put her arms around Felix and gated them both five hundred feet in the air. They struggled to mount their flying disks as they fell.

* * * * *

On a prearranged signal from Amber, the qua-qua teams abandoned their colorful game and gated back to Nova Eboracum through an *ad hoc* gate Amber created. The observing dragons were unhappy when the game abruptly ended. They took out their displeasure on Xaxidiánus, who—as their chief—was always the first to receive complaints. While Sírénae's seven black dragons milled about above, Callidus, Mafuta, and Valentius made their way to the *Cloud Dancer* and dealt with the guards aboard the ship. Verro and Inthíra soon joined them.

Inthíra waited until Verro, Callidus, and Amber surrounded *Cloud Dancer* with solidified sound and bands of crystallized vibrations that bound the ship to Zûrafiérix, who was swimming beneath them. Once she'd confirmed the shields and bindings were in place and Zûrafiérix was in position, Inthíra adjusted her kraken illusion so the monster appeared to be sinking back beneath the Ocean's surface. As it slowly disappeared, the great beast extended two massive tentacled arms and seized *Cloud Dancer,* pulling it down as well.

Verro watched for Laetícia and Felix and opened a small hole in the sphere around the ship when they appeared. Above, Xaxidiánus noticed the kraken's ship-taking and saw Magister Callidus on *Cloud Dancer's* deck. Callidus realized that the dragon had seen him and knew he couldn't disappoint his scaly friend by seeming to switch loyalties—at least not now. There would be time to convince Xaxidiánus to do the same and leave with him in the future.

"I've got to go," he told Verro, who was standing nearby. "Tell Laetícia I'll look for her in Nova Eboracum."

That said, Callidus climbed up the stern mast until he was above the protective bubble being maintained by the other wizards. Surrounded by his own wrapper of solidified sound, he waited.

Xaxidiánus dove, beating his wings rapidly in hopes of saving his friend, but it was almost too late. *Cloud Dancer* was fully submerged. That didn't matter to Xaxidiánus, however. He swam down to follow the sinking ship and saw his friend clinging to a mast and waving to catch his attention. The big black dragon reached out a claw, found Callidus, pulled him from the mast, and lifted him up into fresh air.

The Ocean was dark, and the black dragon was concentrating so greatly on his friend that he didn't see Zûrafiérix or took her scaled back to be part of the retreating kraken.

"Are you well?" Xaxidiánus asked Magister Callidus. "Do you need a healing potion?"

"I'm well enough, old friend," said Callidus. "Or at least I will be until Sírénae catches up with me."

* * * * *

To the northwest, a hundred feet beneath the surface, Zûrafiérix swam quickly, carrying the *Cloud Dancer* and her passengers toward safety.

Chapter 52

An Efficient Evacuation

The racetrack stadium was lit by dozens of wizard lamps driving back the dark night as thousands of people and hundreds of carts and wagons made their way through the pair of wide gates at one end of the oval structure. Duke Néillen had proved remarkably effective in getting the people of Tyford to evacuate. Taffaern helped as well, since he knew everyone who was anyone in the city. His inn was popular, and his reputation as the Barrel Knight from the war with Occidens Province a generation earlier had made him a local hero, so he could smooth over problems caused by the duke's evacuation edicts.

Many still dragged their feet, unwilling to leave their homes until Eynon projected a three-dimensional illusion of the imposing invasion fleet above the top of the city's great domed market so that everyone could see the overwhelming might arrayed against Dâron and all of Orluin.

"I know we need to evacuate soon," complained one merchant impatiently standing in line to gate out to the caves. She had three oxcarts piled high with valuables and only one of food. "What I don't understand," she said, "is why do we have to leave *now?*"

Taffaern nodded to Néillen to indicate he'd handle the question, since he knew the merchant and had once served with her on the city council.

"We're leaving now, because we're not sure when Sírénae's invading legions will reach the Moravon valley," said Taffaern. "As you know," he continued, "the lands along the river are highly productive. Tyford's warehouses are full of grain, fruit, and vegetables. Our cold houses are stocked with pork, beef, and venison. We're a tempting target when Sírénae is ready to search for supplies to feed her legions."

"Yes, but her fleet hasn't even reached Nova Eboracum," said the merchant. "At least not according to the young wizard."

Taffaern sighed, but only on the inside. Merry had indeed shared that news about the timing of the emperor's arrival while at his inn. His patrons had doubtless spread that news to half the city.

"Do you want to risk all your goods being seized and yourself enslaved by waiting a few more days before you leave?" asked Taffaern.

"No, of course not," said the merchant. "But..."

Néillen cut the merchant off. "King Nûd charged me with seeing that everyone in the city and the surrounding countryside is safely evacuated tonight," said the duke. "Would you have me go against the king's commands?"

"King Nûd," muttered the merchant. "Where's King Dârio, ruling Tamloch now, I hear? And an invasion is coming from the Roma across the Ocean, and great dragons are in the sky? Why can't a woman have peace and quiet to make an honest living..."

"I know you," said Taffaern to the merchant. "You'll find a way to prosper even in the caves. Besides, you're a natural leader. Your wisdom will be needed from the very beginning to help the people of the city adapt to life underground."

"Thank you for the new perspective," said the merchant. "I can see now that it's far better to be in the caverns earlier than later."

Taffaern turned back to Duke Néillen, but the merchant tapped Taffaern's arm before he could go far.

"Do you think there's any way you could move me and my carts ahead in the queue?" she asked. "The sooner I'm there, the sooner I can help."

Putting a hand over his mouth to hide a smile, Taffaern answered. "I'm sorry but moving you farther ahead in the line would cause a great many people to resent you for receiving special treatment. You wouldn't want that, would you?"

"I suppose not," said the merchant. "Carry on, then. Keep up the good work."

Taffaern nodded and watched the merchant move back to stand beside her oxcarts, then chide her servants to close up the distance between her carts and the wagons of the family ahead. He returned to Duke Néillen and stood beside him. Once they were both facing away from the merchant, the two rolled their eyes and grinned.

"Merchants in Dâron are as arrogant as nobles in Tamloch," said the duke softly. "They behave like they own the kingdom."

"Some of them *are* quite wealthy," Taffaern responded, keeping a straight face. "But not that woman," he added. "Let's see how the wizards are faring."

"An excellent idea," said Duke Néillen. The duke heard a noise overhead and looked up to see Chee riding on Ace's back as the pair of familiars circled the grandstands.

Néillen smiled, remembering Eynon's reaction when he'd first been introduced to Ace in the common room at Taffaern's tavern. Ace had jumped into Eynon's arms in his dog form, then immediately shifted to his gray rock form. Eynon had said, "Huh?" then looked completely disconcerted when a long, wet tongue slid out from the 'rock' and licked his face. Merry and most of the remaining patrons in the tavern laughed until Taffy threatened to close the bar if they didn't stop. Eynon had kept Ace cradled in the crook of his arm, stroking the rockhound and crooning until Merry reclaimed her familiar and hugged Eynon.

Young love is grand, thought Néillen. *Perhaps I'll find someone worth spending horizontal time with in the caverns. There'll be precious little else to do.*

Pushing his reverie aside, Néillen snapped back into the present. He matched Taffaern stride for stride as the two of them sought out Eynon, Merry, Doethan, and Merrillōn. The four wizards were conversing not far away, inside the fence that formed the inner boundary of the racetrack. Taffaern hailed them and complimented Doethan.

"Your wide gates are working perfectly," said the innkeeper. "And aside from the usual grumbling, the evacuation is proceeding quite well."

"Let's hope that continues," said Doethan. "I keep waiting for something to go wrong."

"So do I, frankly," said Duke Néillen. "Though that could simply be because I'm used to dealing with Túathal. He could find a way to snatch defeat from any victory."

"Túathal is dead," said Merry. "And we're ahead of schedule, aren't we, Néillen?"

"A few hours ahead of schedule, yes," said the duke. He nodded at Eynon, who was standing close to Merry, holding her hand. "Your illusion scene showing everyone the size of the emperor's fleet helped instill a sense of urgency, young wizard."

"Thank you," said Eynon. "The evacuation *should* be urgent."

"True enough," said Taffaern. "I'm impressed with the caverns you helped identify as well, old friend," he told Doethan. "They're large enough so that we haven't had to worry about capacity bottlenecks."

Doethan put his hand on his old mentor's arm. "The wizards Merrillōn sent to the caverns did an excellent job at enlarging entrances and smoothing interior pathways so the carts and wagons could reach the deeper chambers easily," he said. "It's been a team effort."

Merrillōn beamed at Doethan's praise.

"Since we're ahead of schedule," said Duke Néillen to the quartet of wizards. "Could you spare anyone to notify the farmers and townsfolk south of Tyford to come forward now, instead of staying back from the river and coming up to gate out later?"

"We can do it," said Merry. She pulled her flying disk off her shoulders and stepped on it, motioning Eynon to do the same.

"Don't go farther south than the Rose Towns' Road," said Taffaern. "It's marked by docks where travelers can take ferries across the Moravon."

"I know," said Merry. "We won't go farther south than the road from Redrose to Whiterose." She tugged at Eynon's hand. "Come on, let's go."

Eynon waved at the others and followed Merry into the air. "Why the big hurry?" he asked once they were a few hundred feet up.

"I want to show off my new line-of-sight gating," she replied. "Catch me if you can!"

With a *pop*, Merry disappeared and reappeared a mile ahead. Eynon drew on his own new abilities gained from the megapede venom and sped up to catch her.

Chapter 53

Aboard the Cloud Dancer

Laetícia wasn't able to accept the hug Valentius wanted to offer. Instead, she was concentrating on helping the other wizards maintain the bubble of solidified sound around *Cloud Dancer* that protected the ship from the waters of the Ocean surrounding it. Verro, Amber, Mafuta, and Felix were all on the ship's foredeck, working hard to keep the bubble in place against the pressure a hundred feet below the surface. Inthíra was the only wizard not contributing to the ship's protective shell or the bands of solidified sound connecting that shell to Zûrafiérix. She was sending up subtle constructs to sense pursuit by the emperor's minions.

"Do you think we're being followed?" Valentius asked Inthíra.

"I don't think so," said the illusionist. "The large black dragon grabbed Magister Callidus but didn't pursue us."

"I was surprised when none of the other dragons dove to follow the ship," said Valentius. "So many dragons love to swim."

"Maybe they didn't want to deal with a giant kraken," said Inthíra. "My illusion did its job well."

"The kraken was your creation, then?" asked Valentius. "It was truly impressive."

"Thank you," said Inthíra. "Did all your friends escape with the ship?"

"They did," said Valentius. "Aleña just confirmed all of Sírénae's guards have been disarmed and locked in the smaller hold."

"Aleña?" asked Inthíra.

"My wife," said Valentius.

"I look forward to meeting her," said Inthíra.

He saw a pack of black-and-white-patterned wolf whales speed by to port, pursuing a pod of dolphins, and Inthíra watched his eyes go wide in amazement. "How long will we be traveling underwater?" Valentius asked. "And what is carrying *Cloud Dancer?* Are we riding on the back of a whale or some other monster of the depths?"

"I expect we'll surface when my fellow wizards grow tired of keeping the sphere and bands of solidified sound in place. We should be far enough from the fleet to be safe, so judging from their faces, I don't think it will be much longer."

"Good," said Valentius. "What about my remaining question?"

"That, good sir," said Inthíra, "will be easier to show you than to describe. I can assure you we're not on the back of a kraken *or* a whale. Zûrafiérix will be glad to introduce herself when we surface."

"Zûrafiérix sounds like a name for a dragon," said Valentius, "but I don't see how any dragon could bear a ship the size of *Cloud Dancer* on its back."

"Wait and see," said Inthíra. "You'll be impressed."

The mage and the emperor's son stopped conversing when they felt the ship start to rise. Several minutes later, it emerged from the Ocean with sheets of seawater sliding off the protective sphere around it. Inthíra watched her colleagues ease *Cloud Dancer* free and finally cancel both the bands and the bubble keeping the ship safe. Above them, the moon and stars were visible in the dark sky as wispy clouds sped by, propelled by a gentle west wind. The body of Zûrafiérix, beside them and visible for only a breath before she descended again, looked more like an island than anything alive.

Laetícia stretched her arms wide, and Verro rolled his head around in a circle, making the vertebrae in his neck crack. Mafuta and Amber rotated their upper torsos around where their spines joined their hips. Felix lunged with his left leg, then his right, extending the claws on his gauntlets to increase his already formidable reach.

"That's better," said Felix after he'd executed a few more standard attack-and-defend moves. "My muscles get stiff when I have to hold spells in place for a long time."

The other mages responsible for the protective bubble and connecting bands nodded their agreement.

"Thank you for helping," said Verro.

"I'm glad you and Laetícia were able to escape," said Mafuta. "I was worried."

"I was worried, too," said Laetícia. "I set off to rescue Felix and he ended up saving me. That was quick thinking," she said, extending a hand to the tall young wizard.

Felix retracted the claws on his gauntlets and shook with Laetícia. Mafuta joined her friends and wrapped them both in her arms, hugging them as tight as if *she* were a giant kraken.

"Don't scare me like that again," said Mafuta when she finally relaxed her grip.

"Laetícia faced down Sírénae, her snow-gryffon, *and* Umbrose," said Felix.

"But it was your timely intervention that saved me from losing a hand..." began Laetícia.

"And probably your head, if I know Sírénae," added Valentius. He stepped in and managed to disentangle Laetícia enough to finally give her a hug of his own. "Thank you for saving my life," he said. "And the lives of my retainers."

"Don't forget your wife," said a short woman with intelligent eyes and long, dark hair that fell unbound to her waist. She wore an embroidered white silk tunic and moved to stand beside Valentius and take his hand.

"Good cousin," said Valentius, nodding to Laetícia. "And honored wizards," he continued. "This is Aleña, my new wife."

"Pleased to meet you all," said Aleña. She turned to look up at her husband's face, at least a foot above her own. "I'd better not find out you have any old wives, either," she said, squeezing his hand.

"I can assure you that you're my first and only wife," said Valentius. He smiled down at Aleña, then lifted his head to address the others. "I was sailing back to Alexandria to introduce her to my father when a trio of ships from Sírénae's fleet captured us outside the entrance to the Middle Sea."

"It was my fault," said Aleña. "Two wizards in black and gray—"

"From Umbrose," inserted Laetícia.

"Two wizards captured me and threatened to kill me if Valentius didn't surrender," completed Aleña.

"I had no choice," said Valentius. "I owe you a debt I can't repay."

"Don't speak of debts," said Laetícia. "We're family."

"Where's Magister Callidus?" asked Mafuta, as if she'd just noticed his absence.

"A black dragon snatched him from the stern mast as we went under," said Inthíra.

"Xaxidiánus," said Laetícia. "The dragon who flew Callidus to Nova Eboracum. I met him at the palace."

"Does this mean we'll need to mount a new expedition to rescue the magister?" asked Verro. "If so, I'm going to need a night's sleep before making the attempt."

"We can probably wait a day before we try," said Laetícia. "Callidus told me he can make *ad hoc* gates. Perhaps he will be waiting for us in Nova Eboracum when we return."

"Or perhaps he'll be held in one of Sírénae's gate-proof cells," grumbled Felix softly.

"Magister Callidus has been dealing with Sírénae since before you were born," said Laetícia. "He'll survive for at least one more day."

"Callidus is a survivor," said Valentius. "I'm more worried about what new traps Umbrose might have waiting for any returning rescue party."

"Good point," said Verro.

"Besides," said Valentius. "I have to get word to my father, so he knows I'm safe."

"Valens isn't well, cousin," said Laetícia. "When I spoke with Tembóku recently, she told me he'd been poisoned—probably by Sírénae. That was the last straw and the reason Sírénae was exiled."

"Will my father live?" asked Valentius.

Aleña put a comforting arm around his waist.

"Tembóku seems to think so," said Laetícia. "They've given him several healing potions and put him in a protective coma while he heals. Old General Sénnex commands as interim emperor of the Southern Empire until your father recovers."

"Sénnex is a good man, and reliable," said Valentius. "He's served my father well, but I have to get to Alexandria to be by Valens' side. You gate back to Nova Eboracum—I'll sail for Alexandria immediately."

"I wouldn't recommend that," said Laetícia. "We need to check in with Tembóku and find out if your father's status has changed first. You also don't want to be recaptured by outliers from Sírénae's fleet."

Valentius sighed and his shoulders slumped. "Yes. You're right of course, cousin," he said. "Can you gate me and Aleña to Nova Eboracum?" He let more air out of his lungs in a slow exhalation. "It would probably be wise to confer with Quintillius first, anyway."

"Very wise," said Laetícia. "Let's prepare to gate out. Can you carry Mafuta and Felix, Verro?"

"Gladly," said Tamloch's master mage.

"I will carry Inthíra," said Amber. "I assume you plan to transport your cousin and his wife yourself?"

Laetícia nodded. She looked like she was trying to remember something important, but her concern for Valentius was driving whatever it was from her head. After putting her hand to her chin and giving her head a shake to rattle the beads on her braids, she remembered.

"We have to make sure *Cloud Dancer* gets to Nova Eboracum safely as well," said Laetícia.

Slowly, to reduce waves from her movements, Zûrafiérix lifted her great blue-scaled head up until it was even with the foredeck. One of her huge sapphire eyes spun slowly, observing the wizards and non-wizards gathered there. "I can assist with that," said the dragon.

Members of the crew of *Cloud Dancer* screamed from amidships and farther aft. Mafuta plucked a crew member out of the air with solidified sound as he tried to jump overboard.

"She's as big as Old Black," whispered Aleña.

Laetícia filed Aleña's comment away for future reference and promised to follow up with her cousin's new wife soon. "Tell them the dragon is on their side," she told Valentius.

"The dragon is on our side," her cousin repeated, loud enough for the entire crew to hear it over the screams.

"Her name is Zûrafiérix and she will guide you safely to Nova Eboracum harbor," Laetícia told her cousin softly.

Valentius repeated the phrase. It took several repetitions before the screaming stopped. Laetícia introduced Zûrafiérix to *Cloud Dancer's* captain and the captain's relative calm went a long way toward reducing the crew's anxiety.

Laetícia noted the positions of the stars. "With help from the dragon, *Cloud Dancer* should arrive in Nova Eboracum a few hours before dawn," she told Valentius. "Sírénae's fleet will be right behind and should reach the city at sunrise. We'll send your ship to hide somewhere along Insula Longa Sound, so it won't be trapped by the invaders."

"If you say so," said her cousin. He and Aleña stepped on Laetícia's flying disk. Everyone gating back to Nova Eboracum rose and popped out.

Zûrafiérix turned her massive head to face *Cloud Dancer's* captain. "You should tell your crew to secure themselves," she said. "Your ship will soon be moving rather quickly."

The captain nodded. "All secure," he said after a few minutes.

"Good," said Zûrafiérix.

The great blue dragon set the ship's stern into the angle formed by the front edge of her right wing and her torso. Then she swam at high speed, turning *Cloud Dancer* into a ship that danced atop the waves at least, if not the clouds, as they sped toward the city.

Chapter 54

Sírénae's Cabin

Magister Callidus tried to convince the emperor that his apparent betrayal was inspired by one of her own suggestions a few days earlier.

"Your plan worked well, Your Imperial Majesty," said the magister as he sat across from Sírénae and Thraxa in the emperor's cabin. "I'm sorry we lost Valentius, but there's not much he can do to harm us from the western side of the Ocean, and Laetícia did reveal information that will be important for the invasion."

"Excellent," said Sírénae. "What did Laetícia let slip?"

"She said the combined fleets of Occidens Province, Tamloch, and Bifurland would be waiting for us when we arrived at Nova Eboracum harbor," Callidus replied. "There will even be a few Dâron warships rapidly refitted back from merchant vessels."

A voice spoke from a shadowy corner of the cabin.

"I thought the provincial fleet was busy at the upper reaches of the Abbenoth, supporting the legions Quintillius assigned to fight the Northern Clan Landers," said Umbrose.

"What did your scouts tell you about things upriver?" asked Sírénae.

"Not much, unfortunately," said Umbrose. "The ones I sent north haven't reported back yet, and they're not answering when I contact their communications rings."

"Perhaps they've been captured?" suggested Callidus.

"Or killed," said Sírénae. "I like the Clan Landers, north *and* south. They're not afraid to spill blood, are completely ruthless, and prefer direct action to stealth."

"Admirable qualities," said Umbrose. He smiled at Sírénae. "It's almost as if they've modeled themselves on your career."

"You can kiss my nether cheeks later," Sírénae told her spymaster. "Did you learn anything from that pair of wizards your agents found in a tavern in Riyas?" she asked. "The ones with a ring that connects to a clan chief in the southern Clan Lands?"

"I did," said Umbrose. "Southern Clan Landers are gathering in Dâron's western marches, ready to attack when I give them the word."

"That's excellent news," said Sírénae. "The Orluin allies will be surprised to have the *southern* Clan Landers attack as well. You serve me well, Umbrose.

"Thank you, my emperor," Umbrose replied.

Sírénae shifted her attention to her senior mage. "Tell me, Callidus," she said. "What more did Laetícia tell you about the provincial fleet?"

"She said Quintillius arranged for a large bribe for the Northern Clan Landers so his legions could sail south soon enough to meet your ships," said the magister. "Apparently some of the Northern Clan Landers are coming south as well, aboard a flotilla of flat-bottomed barges. Quintillius promised them a share of whatever treasure they could take from us."

"Did he now?" asked Sírénae. "That's unexpected. Quintillius is becoming more pragmatic as he grows older, it seems, if he's setting his enemies against *us*." She turned her piercing, hawk-like glance at her two senior subordinates in turn. "As they say in the Eastern Empire..." she began.

"The enemy of my enemy is my friend," the three completed in unison.

"Unfortunately," said Magister Callidus. "It may be too late to turn the Northern Clan Landers back against the Occidens Province forces. Laetícia said the province's ships are already in motion, sailing for the city."

"Blast," said Sírénae. "I'd hate to fight a full-scale naval battle without Pixo."

"That's wise, my emperor," said Umbrose. "Shall I check with my assets embedded with Second Fleet to see how he and Belisaria are faring with their mission?"

"There's no need for that," said Sírénae. "Reports through formal channels say the only thing unusual is that their journey up the Moravon is a bit *too* quiet. Given how far Tyford is from the Ocean, it's no surprise that people in that rather sleepy part of Dâron wouldn't expect Second Fleet's arrival."

"Bifurland dragonships *did* raid up the Moravon in living memory," Magister Callidus reminded them.

"People who are up before the dawn to milk cows will not be awake and watching the riverbanks past midnight," said Sírénae.

Callidus thought it wise not to contradict his emperor.

"Do you think Laetícia and the others are truly dead?" asked Sírénae, changing the subject.

"I don't," said Umbrose. "I think it was a trick."

"I don't either," said Magister Callidus. "I was pulled below the water with them, and saw the shields protecting them. There was some sort of great beast, like a sea snake, pulling the ship along."

"A tame sea snake could be a problem for us," said Umbrose.

"Not now that we know they have one," said Sírénae. "Xaxidiánus and the rest of my dragons could eliminate a sea snake, even underwater."

"Perhaps," said Umbrose.

Callidus was surprised by the spymaster's equivocation. Usually Umbrose agreed with everything the emperor said, to the point of being obsequious. "It was a very big sea snake," said Callidus. The magister wished Admiral Pixo was here to caution Sírénae about overconfidence. *Then again, it may be better that she remains over-confident,* he thought. *She'll be more likely to make mistakes.*

Sírénae's demeanor changed abruptly, as if she sensed her magister's unease. "Your wizards were remarkably ineffective against the kraken attack," she said. The emperor stroked Thraxa's feathers and the fur along the snow-gryffon's back while feeding her a strip of raw meat from a covered brass bowl.

"It's not every day that a kraken three times as big as the *Seahawk* attacks in the middle of the night," said Magister Callidus. "My wizards couldn't exactly *practice* against such a threat."

"They should be trained to expect anything," said Sírénae. "I don't want excuses, I want results."

"Yes, Your Imperial Majesty," said Callidus. *My wizards would be more successful if Sírénae didn't keep assigning my best talents to Umbrose.*

Sírénae glared at him, recognizing the phrase Callidus used to indicate he thought the emperor was wrong. "What?" she barked.

"My wizards did a good job rescuing sailors and helping ships escape from the kraken's tentacles," he said. "You and Umbrose wanted the prisoner to appear lightly guarded to draw in Laetícia."

"True," said the emperor. "And we gained valuable insights into our opponents' plans when you gained their confidence."

Callidus formed a thin-lipped smile on his face.

"But we lost Laetícia *and* Valentius in the process," protested Umbrose. "Along with the master mages of Tamloch and Bifurland. They would have been valuable hostages as well."

"Capturing a skilled mage is one thing—holding them quite another," said Magister Callidus.

"I could do it," said Umbrose.

"You couldn't even keep the young mage wearing cat armor in a cell for long," said Sírénae. "I'm not that concerned about losing Laetícia and Valentius, either. They'd have limited value as hostages, since Quintillius is so stiff-necked and honor-bound that he'd never negotiate, no matter how much I threatened."

"Honor is overrated," grumbled Umbrose.

"You're a fool if you believe everyone thinks that," said Sírénae. "Some people are unbending—but I'd hoped to have the chance to see if that would be true for Quintillius." She frowned at Umbrose. "How much success did you have getting Valentius to switch sides and serve me?" she asked her spymaster.

"None," said Umbrose. He shook his head slowly. "No matter how much pain I put him through."

Sírénae nodded. "The three of us are much more flexible than Valentius," she said. "We're willing to do what's necessary to achieve our desired ends, just like Thraxa here"—she ruffled the snow-gryffon's feathered head— "is willing to eat whatever meat I offer, be it fish or goat or human flesh."

Magister Callidus shuddered inside his head, though he didn't allow his feelings to show on his face. *Is Sírénae trying to send me a message?*

Of course she is. She often sends such messages. The question is whether or not she knows my thoughts.

"Learn to recognize those who won't bend," Sírénae told Umbrose. "Then break them. It's your only option."

"As you say," said Umbrose. "In the future, I'll enjoy torturing such captives until they break."

"You're missing the point," said the emperor. "Explain it to him, Callidus."

"Yes, Emperor," Callidus replied. "The best way to torture people like Quintillius, Laetícia, and Valentius is to get them to trust you—then betray them."

Sírénae smiled and clapped her hands like she was applauding an actor on stage in an Athican amphitheater. "Precisely," she said. "Just like you convinced Laetícia you'd switched sides and gained her trust, so she told you about their fleets' movements."

"Indeed," said Callidus.

Sírénae yawned and so did Thraxa, revealing the razor-sharp edges of her beak.

"We should arrive at Nova Eboracum harbor at sunrise," said the emperor. "I'm getting some sleep in the meantime." She yawned again, then squared her shoulders and beckoned Callidus to lean closer. "Send six scout-wizards on dragonback to Brendinas and Riyas," Sírénae said conspiratorially. "The dragons should overawe the locals and convince them of our power. Xaxidiánus is our fastest dragon, so have him fly high over Nova Eboracum and up the Abbenoth valley carrying one of Umbrose's best agents as my emissary. Between the two of them, perhaps they can entice at least some of the Northern Clan Landers into attacking the provincials' legions from the rear. Promise them anything. We can worry about paying them later."

"Yes, my emperor," said Umbrose.

"Sleep well," said Callidus. He stood, and so did the spymaster.

Sírénae tugged Thraxa and handed the snow-gryffon's chain to Umbrose. "Take her to her keeper," the emperor commanded. "Thraxa isn't safe to sleep with," the emperor added, with an expression that made Callidus decidedly uneasy. He'd sooner sleep beside Thraxa than Sírénae. Umbrose and Callidus waited for any additional orders. Two were given. "Get out," said Sírénae. "And tell my steward to wake me an hour before dawn."

Magister Callidus nodded and left. He passed the word to the emperor's steward and was glad he didn't have to pull Thraxa's chain. It was a duty Sírénae often gave to her spymaster. Callidus was confident Sírénae didn't trust him, and he knew the feeling was mutual. He hoped Umbrose didn't have sources of information that proved Callidus had been lying about the disposition of the Orluin allies' ships.

I had no choice but to brazen it out when Xaxidiánus retrieved me, thought Callidus. *And I'll* ad hoc *gate to Nova Eboracum after I've sent the scouts on their way. It would be wise to be out of Sírénae's reach before my subterfuge is detected,* he decided. *Very wise.* Then he thought again. *It would be even better if I told Laetícia what I've learned and return here to retain Sírénae's confidence. Laetícia might be particularly interested to know that the dragons will not be with the emperor's fleet when it arrives. The Orluin allies will need every advantage to survive the emperor's invasion.*

Chapter 55

Down the Moravon

Eynon was pleased when he caught up with Merry—or more precisely, when she allowed him to catch up with her. They had flown, or in Merry's case, gated, at least five miles south of Tyford, following the course of the broad, fast-flowing Moravon. The banks of the river were dark and only faintly outlined by moonlight and starlight. They hadn't spotted a single torch or wizard lamp illuminating a dock or manor house.

"Thanks for waiting for me," said Eynon as his flying disk came even with Merry's. He slid his disk partway over hers so he could put his arm around her waist.

Ace shifted away from the encroaching edge of Eynon's disk and curled up around Merry's ankles in his canine form. Chee jumped from Eynon's shoulder and capered over to find a comfortable resting spot beside Ace.

Merry smiled down at the two familiars, then up at Eynon. "I wasn't waiting for you," she said. "I stopped to figure out the best way to do what Duke Néillen requested and inform farmers and townsfolk they can head north and evacuate tonight."

"What's the problem?" Eynon asked. "You can just knock on the door of the largest house or cottage at each farmstead or manor and let them know."

"I *could* do that," said Merry, "but it's dark, and I don't want to wake anyone up. With no lamps or torches burning, I can't tell who's asleep and who's not, and I don't want to risk getting a not-so-friendly crossbow bolt in my chest for my trouble."

"Didn't Duke Néillen send word south for everyone to prepare for the evacuation and keep lights hidden from any of the emperor's spies who might be scouting things out?" asked Eynon.

"No," said Merry. "His instructions were for people downriver to head west, toward the caverns."

"Oh," said Eynon. "I guess that's right. My brain was still spinning with joy from seeing you again and spending time together upstairs at Taffaern's inn." Eynon intentionally put on what Merry called his *lovesick puppy* expression.

Merry looked at him and frowned, then couldn't help smiling when he let his tongue loll out and panted.

"If you lick me, you'll be sorry," she teased, snuggling closer.

Eynon leaned in, pretending to continue his exuberant pup impression, but Merry held a hand up to protect her face, and Eynon refrained from licking her palm. He erased his sappy look and stood straight. "If everyone was sent west, why did Néillen want us to go south?" he asked.

"Maybe to tell folks on the eastern side of the Moravon that they should come to Tyford to gate directly to the caverns?" offered Merry.

"I doubt it," said Eynon. "Look at the docks we can see on either bank."

Using combination lenses of solidified sound designed for far-seeing and night vision, Merry joined Eynon in counting rafts and boats. "All the boats are on the west bank," she said.

"That's what I noticed, too," said Eynon. "Everyone on the east bank seems to have crossed over and headed west."

"That's strange," said Merry. "Why would Duke Néillen send us south if there wouldn't be anyone around for us to notify?"

"To round up stragglers?" Eynon suggested.

"I don't think so," said Merry.

"To get us out of the way so he can execute some devious plot because he's secretly an agent of the emperor?" asked Eynon, not believing it as he said it.

"That's not outside the realm of possibility," said Merry. "Unfortunately, it doesn't make sense. If that were the case, why would he warn us of the invasion fleet in the first place?"

"And why would he betray us now when he's worked so hard to regain our trust?" Eynon replied. "I can't see Dârio, Nûd, Quintillius, or Bjarni sending him back into exile on the Tempest Isles."

"Neither can I," said Merry. "I just can't figure out his angle."

"Maybe he forgot the exact wording of the message he'd sent south?"

"Could you see Duke Háiddon or Jenet forgetting?" said Merry. Eynon shook his head side to side.

"Duke Néillen is almost as competent as they are," Merry continued. "My understanding is that Néillen has an excellent strategic mind. Unfortunately, Túathal seldom loosened the reins enough to allow him to use it."

"Maybe that's it," said Eynon. "Néillen could have sent us south because he suspected something about the emperor's strategy that involved the Moravon."

"Like a strike force of battle mages?" said Merry. "Attacking out of the eastern sky at dawn?"

"That sounds a bit melodramatic, but sure," said Eynon. "Something like that. Verro and his wizards attacked the quarry in Wherrel at dawn."

"I doubt that was Néillen's idea," said Merry. "Verro probably figured the quarry attack out on his own."

"I was just using it as an example," said Eynon.

"I think you may be on to something," said Merry. "I just can't understand why Duke Néillen wouldn't have just told us to scout downriver and search for threats."

"Because it's ludicrous to think any of the emperor's forces could be this far inland before her invasion fleet has reached Nova Eboracum," said Eynon.

"How do you know it hasn't?" asked Merry.

"Doethan would have told us," responded Eynon. "After Laetícia told *him*."

"Laetícia could have been tied up elsewhere and unable to contact Doethan," said Merry.

"Then Mafuta would have told him," said Eynon. "Or Felix."

"I don't think they have rings to contact Doethan," said Merry.

"I love arguing with you," said Eynon, "but about ideas, not Duke Néillen's motivations."

"I love arguing with you, too," said Merry. She pulled Eynon's head down and kissed him. Then she kissed him again. "There's an easy way to find out what Duke Néillen meant."

"What is it?" asked Eynon. He seemed so happy to be kissing Merry that he no longer had attention to spare for her answer.

"You could *ad hoc* gate back and ask him," said Merry. "I'll wait here for you."

"No," said Eynon. "I don't want to."

"Why not?" asked Merry. "It's better than spinning theories that may or may not have any basis in fact."

"Because I've missed you," said Eynon. "I'm really enjoying spending time alone with you—even if we're vertical, not horizontal."

"It's nice to be alone with you, too," said Merry. "No matter our orientation."

They hugged for a moment, then released their tight embrace and held each other at arm's length, their flying disks still overlapping slightly.

"I think we should fly another ten miles south," said Eynon. "If we see any signs of life on either bank, we can notify people to head for Tyford. If not, I could *ad hoc* gate us both back to the racetrack and we could let Duke Néillen know we've done what he requested."

"I can go for that," said Merry. "It's a good solution. When you make that *lovesick puppy* face, I sometimes forget you have a brain at all, so it's surprising when you show me otherwise."

"I love you, too," said Eynon.

Merry's reply was postponed when they saw several hundred black-necked geese heading up the river. The flock was traveling at the same altitude the two young wizards were flying, so the pair rose fifty feet to get out of their way. Only a few *honks* marred the night's silence as they passed below.

"Why are they flying at *this* hour?" asked Merry.

"Are there foxes along this stretch of the Moravon?" said Eynon, offering a question as a potential answer.

"There are foxes everywhere geese can be found," said Merry. "Given Duke Néillen's concerns, though, we should be alert for two-legged foxes, not just the four-footed variety."

"Duly noted," said Eynon. He leaned down and Merry shifted her head for another kiss that lasted until the last stray goose from the flock went by with a *wait-for-me* honk.

Ace was about to shift his form and fly after the goose, but Merry wagged her finger at her familiar and he stayed put. Merry squeezed Eynon's fingers.

"Ready?" she asked.

"I think so," said Eynon. "Can we stay together instead of you doing line-of-sight gating?"

"Of course," said Merry. "As long as you keep your arm around me."

"That shouldn't be a problem," said Eynon.

Chee yawned, closed his big round eyes, and put his head back on Ace's furry shoulder.

Merry allowed Eynon to provide most of the energy for their flight. The wind whipped at their hair as they followed the curves of the Moravon at a velocity twice as fast as Eynon's previous cruising speed. Strands of Merry's auburn hair blew up into Eynon's mouth, so he formed a wedge-shaped shield of solidified sound around them both and began to move even faster. Soon they'd covered close to ten miles.

"Is this one of the side effects of the megapede venom?" Merry asked.

"Yes," said Eynon. "I'm hoping it will help me in battle."

"I'm glad you're not faster at *everything,*" Merry teased.

"Ummm..." said Eynon. He saw a narrow island in the river below and changed the subject. "What are those three tall structures like big beehives?" Eynon asked. "There's smoke rising from them."

"My father says they make steel south of Tyford," replied Merry. "Those may be stone-charcoal ovens."

"I didn't know you could make charcoal in stone ovens," said Eynon. "It would take a lot of wood to fill them."

"No," said Merry. "They're ovens for baking stone charcoal. People east of the Moravon call it coke. It's made from the black rocks mined in the mountains at the northern reaches of the Brenavon. The hardest black rocks are from there, anyway. There are seams of softer black rocks a lot closer."

"If you say so," said Eynon. "No one is tending them now—at least not anyone I can see—but they're still smoking. It must take a long time for them to burn out."

"I think you're right," said Merry. Then she gripped Eynon's arm like a gryffon's talons. He stopped and sensed that Merry had surrounded them with an illusion, making them look like a fluffy cloud reflecting moonlight.

"What is it?" Eynon whispered.

"Scout wizards," said Merry softly. "I think they're wearing purple robes."

It wasn't easy to distinguish fabric colors when wearing lenses for seeing at night, but Eynon followed Merry's pointing finger and spotted the pair of wizards. "You're right," he said. "Do you think they're from Nova Eboracum?"

"I doubt it," she replied.

"I wonder what they're scouting *for?*" said Eynon. He shifted his gaze to stare farther downriver. "I'm sensing *something*. Do you see anything?"

"It's not what I see, it's what I perceive," said Merry. "There are a lot of wizards on the river south of us. I can feel their magestones."

"That's what it is?" asked Eynon. "There are a *lot* of magestones, which probably means a lot of enemy wizards. I'll gate down there and see what they're trying to hide."

Before Eynon could do anything, Merry grabbed the fabric at the neck of his robes. "Eynon of Haywall, if you run off and leave me here, I'm going to have Rocky and Viridáxes play catch with your head."

"Still attached, or severed?" asked Eynon.

"Severed," said Merry. "Definitely severed." She released her grip and gave Eynon a stern look. "You should have learned this lesson," she said. "Think first, *then* act."

"Right," said Eynon. "What do you *think* we should do?"

"If you were casting an illusion around some ships—and that pretty much *has* to be what they are, since they're coming up the river—what would your illusion include?"

"Something to hide the ships from the front, back, sides and top," said Eynon.

"Exactly," said Merry. "That's why we're going to start at the bottom."

* * * * *

Eynon maintained the streamlined construct of solidified sound around them while Merry counted keels from below.

"Help me remember," said Merry. "I just got to three hundred, with that hull with all the barnacles."

"I don't think a precise count is all that useful at this point," said Eynon.

"Won't Duke Néillen want to know?" asked Merry.

"Remember, our strategy is to hide, not fight," said Eynon. "We can hide from five hundred ships as easily as five in the caverns. We can *ad hoc* gate back to the stadium and warn Néillen, Doethan, Taffaern and the others to get the last of the stragglers through, then destroy the wide gates and run for it."

Merry took Eynon's advice and gave up on counting. "I wish we could wide-gate the Bifurlanders' dragonships in to attack these Roma ships from the rear," she said. "That would really be something to see."

"The emperor's ships are more than twice the size of the Bifurlanders' vessels," said Eynon. "King Bjarni's warriors are fierce, but I'm not sure how they'd fare against all the legionnaires on the imperial vessels."

"You may be right," said Merry. "I know *I* wouldn't want to fight them."

"Me neither," said Eynon.

Merry turned to look at Eynon's face and saw him seem to disappear into his own head, his gaze unfocused and his expression one of concentration. She didn't say anything, since she'd seen Eynon look like this in the past. Usually it meant he was coming up with an impressive—or foolhardy—plan. After a few seconds, Eynon smiled.

"What is it?" asked Merry.

"What's what?" asked Eynon.

"Your idea," said Merry.

"Hold on tight," said Eynon. "I'll tell you after we've gated back and warned our friends in Tyford—and I've had a chance to see just how big that pair of communications rings I made can grow."

"Oh," said Merry, sounding disappointed. Then she thought for a few heartbeats. "Oh!" she said again, but this time with a much more optimistic tone. "What are we waiting for? Let's go!"

Chapter 56

Laetícia's Study

"Father! Father! They're back! They're back!"

Primus, Seconda, and even little Tertia, ran into the palace courtyard where wizard lamps blazed. Quintillius was there reviewing the progress of the city's evacuation with a pair of wizards and three senior legion commanders. The children bustled past the bodyguards protecting the governor-general and wrapped themselves around their father's legs with all the enthusiasm of a litter of kittens.

"Who's back? And what are the three of you doing up at this hour?" asked Quin.

"Mater and Mafuta and Felix and Inthíra..." began Tertia, enunciating each name carefully.

"And cousin Valentius!" said Seconda.

"Plus our cousin's new wife," added Primus.

Quin's eyes grew wide at their news. The pair of wizards, one nearly as tall as the governor-general and the other not much taller than Primus, slapped Quintillius on the back and gripped his forearm respectively. Each of the legion commanders smacked the armored plates on their chests with their arms and fists.

"Congratulations," said one commander.

Quintillius was surprised that any news about the capture of Valentius had gotten out. He'd have words with certain palace slaves and servants later. Now, however, he needed to find his wife, the rescue party, and the rescued parties. "I won't be angry about the three of you staying up past your bedtimes if you tell me where your mother and the others *are*," said Quintillius.

Primus was about to answer when Tertia beat him to it.

"They're all at the top of mother's tower," she said.

"The three of us couldn't sleep," said Primus. "We eventually nodded off on cushions I arranged on the floor underneath a table. We were pretending we'd made camp on a march."

"I did the same thing when I was your age," said Quintillius. He turned to the wizards he'd been consulting. "Could the two of you fly us up to Laetícia's study?"

"Gladly," said the tall wizard. "Hop on—then hang on. I'll fly like I have a gryffon on my tail." She waved Quintillius on behind her.

"You can ride with me, children," said the short wizard. "The bigger children can hold on to my belt and the littlest one can hold my hand."

"I'm not little," said Tertia.

"You're like me," said the short wizard. "Small, but mighty."

Tertia smiled and took his hand while her siblings climbed onto the back of the short wizard's flying disk. "I want to be a wizard someday," Tertia told him.

Seconds later they were hovering above the landing outside Laetícia's study.

* * * * *

Quintillius, a general who could direct tens of thousands of legionnaires on a battlefield, was overwhelmed by the chaos his own children generated as they bounced from person to person in Laetícia's study, inundating the new arrivals with questions. He moved to stand by his wife and leaned down until his mouth was close to her ear.

"Have the children been drinking maple syrup?" Quintillius asked. "Could their nurse have given them too many honey cakes?"

"I don't know why they're like this," Laetícia replied. "I think the most likely answer is that they're glad to see us home safely."

"You're probably right," said Quin. "Primus told me they did get *some* sleep, under that round table." He pointed at a table that Laetícia's servants had justed topped with several trays of bread, cheese, and olives. "The boy was wise enough to put cushions on the floor so his sisters would get some rest."

"Judging from his eyes, I think Primus slept as well," said Laetícia. "Did you?"

"Not a wink," said Quintillius. "I've been coordinating the effort to evacuate the city before Sírénae's fleet arrives. How much time do you think we have?"

"Not long," said Laetícia. "If the wind holds, I'd expect the lead ships to get to the harbor shortly before dawn. Is the evacuation going well?"

"Quite well," said Quintillius. "Nearly everyone is out, and all the stored supplies as well. We still have to move the last of the food and the staff from the palace, but now that you're home, we can move forward with that as well."

"Good," said Laetícia. She hugged her husband and welcomed Valentius to join their conversation, since he'd been standing close at hand and obviously waiting to speak with them. Aleña was by his side. There was as much difference in height between Valentius and Aleña as there was between Quintillius and Laetícia.

Valentius made the introductions.

"My husband told me your husband would be someone I could look up to," Aleña told Laetícia.

"While the two of us are the perfect height to converse as equals," Laetícia replied with a grin. "Now that we aren't in imminent danger of death or capture, welcome to the family."

"Thank you," said Aleña. "You also have my thanks for your timely rescue."

"And mine," said Valentius. "When will you be able to contact Tembóku and find out how my father is doing?"

"We can do it now if you'd like," said Laetícia. "I'm exhausted, but I don't want to make you wait any longer than necessary."

"You're the best, cousin," said Valentius.

"Don't push yourself *too* hard," said Quintillius.

"Look who's talking," teased Laetícia. She glanced around her study and confirmed that the others were standing in small clumps around the room, reviewing the recent rescue or answering her children's questions. "This way," she said. Laetícia opened the door to an inner, private meeting room filled with shelves lined with books. Quintillius, Valentius, and Aleña followed.

Inside, Laetícia looked longingly at the well-padded couch along one wall and wished she had the luxury of napping on it. Instead, she stood in the middle of the room and opened one of her communications rings with a short command phrase. Three chimes sounded, and as the circle of gold expanded, Tembóku's face materialized on the other side of the interface. It was nearly noon in Alexandria, the capital of the Southern Empire, and Tembóku looked far more awake than Laetícia felt.

"I have good news for you," said Laetícia before Tembóku could do more than smile. "We've rescued Valentius."

"What?" said Tembóku. "Rescued him? I don't understand. He was sailing home to be with his father."

Valentius stepped into view. "Hello, old friend," he said to Tembóku. "Three of Sírénae's ships captured *Cloud Dancer* when I was sailing back. I'd still be held if Laetícia and her friends hadn't rescued me from a cell on the emperor's flagship *and* liberated *Cloud Dancer*."

"My former student always was a resourceful wizard," said Tembóku. "If I had to learn about you being imprisoned, it's good to hear you've already been freed."

"Valentius has more good news to share," said Laetícia.

"Oh?" said Tembóku. Both of her eyebrows went up. She shifted her head slightly, moving it from side to side in a habit that remained from when *she* had worn beaded braids.

"Before I tell you," said Valentius. "I need to know. How is my father?"

"Valens woke last night," said Tembóku. "His body is healing, and his mind doesn't seem to be damaged—but he was so angry about Sírénae poisoning him, I had to give him a sleeping potion before he set back his recovery. He was shouting like an *optio* training raw recruits and ready to order every legionnaire in the Southern Empire to take ship for Orluin immediately."

"Not a bad idea," said Laetícia quietly.

"But not a practical one," said Tembóku. "Sírénae commandeered most of the Southern Empire's transport ships on the western Middle Sea when she departed."

"I may have a solution to that problem," said Laetícia. "I'll keep you posted and may need help from you and a few more wizards on your staff."

"Let me know," said Tembóku. "Does this relate to those wide gates you told me about?"

"It does," said Laetícia. "Things have been hectic here, but I hope to be able to consult with the wizard who knows wide gates best soon. We can test whether or not they'll work across the Ocean."

"After we've safely evacuated," said Quintillius. "You're the one who said we should expect Sírénae's fleet in the harbor just before dawn."

Laetícia turned to face her husband, who was just out of sight of Tembóku to one side of the interface. "Speaking of evacuating," she said. "Why aren't our children and servants out of the city and safely in a cavern?"

"Because I wanted to wait until you were back?" asked Quintillius.

"Try again," Laetícia replied.

Tembóku started to chuckle. She'd heard Laetícia and Quintillius have conversations like this before.

"Because I thought the palace slaves and servants would handle it?" Quintillius offered.

"Not without your explicit orders," said Laetícia. She glared up at Quin's face, a smile hiding close to the surface.

"Because I forgot?" Quin said at last.

"There you have it," teased Laetícia. She shook her head and the beads on her braids clacked reassuringly. "Why is it the tailors' children go naked?"

"Uh..." said Quintillius, starting to answer.

"It's a rhetorical question," said Laetícia. "I know you were organizing the evacuation of the entire city, and I'm sorry I wasn't there to help manage moving everyone from the palace."

"She had better things to do, for which I'm quite grateful," said Valentius. "Now it's past time to let you know *my* good news," he said. "This is my wife, Aleña."

The short, slim, dark-haired young woman standing nearby stepped into view. She moved close to Valentius, took his hand, and smiled at Tembóku through the ring's interface. "I look forward to meeting you face to face soon, honored wizard," said Aleña. "Valentius has told me so much about you."

"Has he now," said Tembóku. "It's all true, or most of it, anyway. I look forward to meeting you face to face as well, though as for *soon,* who knows."

"Agreed," said Valentius. "It's less urgent that I return to Alexandria, now that I know my father is recovering. I think I'll stay here and help fight Sírénae from this side of the Ocean."

"Thank you," said Quintillius. "We're glad to have you."

"I will tell Valens you're safe—and married—when he wakes," said Tembóku. "You have a lot left to do and I'll leave you to it."

"I'll be in touch when we're settled in a cave somewhere," said Laetícia. "Keep us posted on Valens' health."

"I will," said Tembóku. Laetícia cut the interface.

Quin nodded to his wife. "I've got to get back to my duties," he said. "The palace must be evacuated."

"I'll take care of that," said Laetícia. "You can worry about the rest of the city. How are things going in Tamloch and Dâron?"

"Dârio and Jenet told me the people of Riyas and the towns and cities along their coast have been gated to safety," said Quintillius. "The scholars at Bhaile Pónaire were reluctant to leave without their slates and books, but we got everything moved for them and they seem happy."

Laetícia looked thoughtful.

"What?" asked Quintillius.

"I was thinking about Tembóku," his wife replied. "Scholars and scholar-wizards are alike the world over. Imagine what it would take to move the Great Library."

"I certainly hope the Great Library of Alexandria is never threatened with invasion," said Quintillius.

"At least spells protect it from fire," said Aleña.

"What about Dâron?" Laetícia asked, trying to get things back on track.

Quintillius replied. "Nûd and Duke Háiddon have most of the population in the eastern part of the kingdom evacuated to huge cave complexes in the mountains of the southern provinces. The hardest challenge, according to Nûd, was getting most of the wisents back to

Melyncárreg. It wouldn't do to have tens of thousands of the shaggy beasts milling about near Brendinas if we're trying to starve the emperor's troops, would it?"

"No indeed," said Laetícia.

"You may also find it interesting that Duke Néillen has been put in charge of evacuating Tyford and the Moravon valley," said Quintillius. "He's apparently doing a good job of it, too."

"Néillen is probably trying to avoid being exiled again when all this is over," said Laetícia.

"Can you blame him?" asked Quintillius.

"Who are you talking about?" asked Valentius.

"It's a long story," said Quin. "I'll tell you when we've moved to safety. We should have plenty of time to talk then."

"Fine," said Valentius. "Can I borrow a sword and some armor? I want to be properly outfitted if I have to fight."

"Of course," said Quintillius. "Though we plan to do more raiding than fighting." Quin led Valentius out into the larger room, leaving Laetícia and Aleña alone.

"Do you need help moving your library?" asked Aleña. "I'm not a wizard—just a silk-farmer's daughter—but books are my passion, along with Valentius." She smiled shyly at Laetícia.

"If you could help take them off the shelves and put them in crates, that would be wonderful," said Laetícia. "I can *ad hoc* gate the crates to a cavern—once my husband tells me where to go."

"Good," said Aleña. "Packing up books is hard for me."

"Why so?" asked Laetícia.

"Because I keep reading them when I should be packing them, of course."

Chapter 57

Puzzled Waters

"Your scouts saw what?" asked Admiral Pixo from behind the desk in his spacious cabin aboard the *Menodorus Maximus.* Papers sat in stacks on the desk alongside a bowl of fruit.

"Smoking stone coal ovens a few miles upriver," said Náegosh, the senior wizard with Second Fleet. He sat on a thick cushion on a stool positioned across from the admiral.

"But no people?" asked Belisaria. She leaned on a comfortable couch near the wizard, swaying with the ship as it sailed up the Moravon.

"They said they didn't see anyone," Náegosh reported. "No one was tending the ovens."

"Uh huh," said Belisaria. "Once they've started burning, ovens like that just keep smoking until all the impurities are gone. I once captured ovens like that when I put down a rebellion in Macedóna."

"I've seen such ovens, too," said Admiral Pixo. "At least we can be sure there were people around recently to light the ovens. It's not like a plague killed everyone."

"What if there *was* a plague, but all the victims stayed indoors?" asked Belisaria.

"Then they won't be able to cause us much trouble, will they?" asked Pixo.

"Unless they infect us," said Belisaria.

"If sick people emerge from their halls and houses and try to give us whatever they've got, my wizards will blast them with fireballs," said Náegosh.

"Good," said Belisaria. "They're welcome to blast away. I'm not usually this fearful, but not having any foes visible makes me nervous."

"I'll admit I'm uneasy, too," said Admiral Pixo. "If we still don't spot anyone by the time we get to Tyford, I'd advise you to have your legionnaires ready to go ashore and commandeer all the supplies they can find before any surprise attack is launched against us."

"I'd already given orders to that effect," said Belisaria.

Pixo's respect for the lieutenant general went up a notch.

"The river charts say the channel narrows north of here," said Pixo. "It's only wide enough for three or four ships at a time."

"Making it an excellent spot for an ambush?" offered Náegosh.

"That's my concern," said the admiral. "I'd appreciate it if your scouts could be extra-attentive."

"Believe me, they are," said Náegosh. "The current situation has everyone on high alert."

"Hah!" said Pixo. "Good joke."

"What did I say?" asked Náegosh.

"You haven't spent much time on ships, have you?" said Pixo. "*Current* situation?"

"Oh, I get it now," said Náegosh with a grim grin. "We'll just have to go with the flow, I suppose."

Pixo shook his head and turned to Belisaria. "How are your legionnaires holding up?" asked the admiral.

"They're nervous," said the lieutenant general. "They want tangible enemies to poke with a *pilum* or gut with a *gladius*."

"It won't be much longer until we're in Tyford," said Admiral Pixo, facing Belisaria and Náegosh in turn. "I have a theory about what's going on."

Belisaria and Náegosh watched the admiral. When Pixo didn't speak after a few moments, Náegosh said, "Tell us!"

"I think they've pulled out and taken all their supplies with them," said Pixo. "They mean to starve us out, and hope we'll go back across the Ocean."

"Not much chance of *that*," said Belisaria. "This is rich countryside."

"But crops won't be ready to harvest until fall," said Pixo. "And all the livestock that might tide us over until then is missing, too."

"What about deer and game birds?" asked Náegosh.

"It will take a lot of venison and pheasant meat to keep my legionnaires and Pixo's sailors fed for six months," said Belisaria.

"How long will our existing stores last us?" asked Náegosh.

"No more than a month, and that at half rations," said Pixo.

"I wonder what kinds of fish are in the river?" asked Belisaria.

"Who knows?" replied Pixo. "I imagine we'll find out soon enough if Tyford's been stripped of food and drink."

"Let's think of something less depressing," said Náegosh. He pulled a fig from a bowl on Pixo's desk and began to eat it in delicate bites.

"Toss me one of those," said Belisaria. Náegosh tilted his head and raised an eyebrow. *"If you please,* good wizard," Belisaria added.

"Certainly," said Náegosh. He snagged another fig with his free hand and flipped the small fruit to his colleague.

"I have a cheerful question," said Belisaria. "Do we have any idea whether or not Dâron has any ships on the river to block our progress?"

"You haven't heard the story about Princess Gwýnnett and the Dâron navy?" asked Pixo.

"The one about the princess selling the kingdom's fleet to merchants to pay for her personal extravagances?" asked Náegosh. "That tale's been told—and inspired laughter—even on the other side of the Ocean. Is it true?"

"It is," said Pixo. "We're not likely to encounter any resistance from *Dâron's* fleet."

"It sounds like there's more you want to say," said Belisaria. "Is it something we need to worry about?"

"Maybe," said Pixo. "Dâron's fleet isn't an issue, but Dâron and Tamloch are allies now, and Tamloch still has a fleet. It's unlikely, but they could be waiting for us upriver."

"Are the Tamloch ships like the Nordland raiding vessels?" asked Nágosh. "Long and close to the water, with high-pointed prows and square sails?"

"No," said Pixo. "They've copied their ships' designs from ours."

"How far up the Moravon can ships with that draft go?" asked Belisaria.

"Twenty-five miles above Tyford," said Pixo.

"I'll be sure to send scout-wizards north to look for a Tamloch fleet once we get to Tyford," said Nágosh.

"It's not likely we'll find one," said Pixo. "There's a chance we'll see warships Dâron managed to convert back from commandeered merchant vessels, but that's unlikely. I'm more worried about what we *won't* find than what we will."

"No people? No supplies?" asked Belisaria.

"Exactly," said the admiral. "Warn your legionnaires and wizards we should be arriving at Tyford just before dawn. They should be ready for anything."

"I'll tell my commanders," said Belisaria. She stood and took another fig from the bowl on Pixo's desk before she left the admiral's cabin.

"I have a bad feeling about this," said Nágosh as he rose and moved to the cabin's door.

"So do I," said Admiral Pixo, considering a fig and thinking better of it. "So do I."

Chapter 58

Golden Gate

Eynon and Merry touched down at the far end of Tyford's racetrack stadium, next to where Duke Néillen, Taffaern, and a few of the disreputable-looking mages Merrillōn had supplied were watching the last three wagons loaded with supplies go through the left-hand gate. To the right, Doethan and Merrillōn were shepherding an oxcart through the other interface. The cart creaked under the weight of a huge wine cask but crossed through without incident.

Néillen was facing the left-hand gate and hadn't noticed the new arrivals until Eynon tapped him on the shoulder and tugged hard enough to spin the duke halfway around.

"How did you know?" asked Eynon, close to shouting. Merry put a hand on his arm but Eynon shrugged it off.

"How did I know what?" asked Néillen with a phlegmatic calm that was part personal style and part exhaustion.

Before Eynon could respond, Merry tried to cool down his temper. She hadn't realized her lover *blamed* Duke Néillen for what they'd seen.

"There's an invasion fleet sailing up the Moravon," said Merry. "They're hidden by illusion magic, but they have to be from the emperor."

Duke Néillen tilted his head back and laughed until his upper body started shaking.

The strange sound startled Ace and Chee awake. The rockhound shifted form and took off into the night sky to search for bugs and bats with the raconette riding on his back.

"Are you well?" asked Eynon, his thoughts quickly shifting from anger to concern.

"I'm... I'm... fine," gasped out Néillen between bouts of laughter. "The emperor really did send an invasion fleet to Tyford?" he asked Merry, trying to confirm what she'd said. "How many ships?"

"I counted over three hundred," she said. "But there were more behind them. We were counting keels underwater and it was difficult to see."

"I'd estimate five hundred," said Eynon. "I assume you *weren't* aware of the invaders?"

"Of course not," snapped Duke Néillen.

"Then why did you send us south?" Eynon asked.

Merry smiled when she saw Néillen smile like a wolf contemplating a rabbit.

"Because that's what *he* would have done if he was in command of Sírénae's forces," said Merry. "You were right, Eynon. He *does* have an excellent strategic mind."

"He said that?" asked Néillen.

Merry nodded and grinned. "Uh huh," she replied. "Now what do we do?"

"Stick to the plan," said Duke Néillen. "Let them come. We've almost finished the evacuation. They're welcome to an empty city with stripped warehouses."

"How much time do we have until they get here?" asked Taffaern.

"A couple of hours, at most," said Eynon.

"Maybe a bit longer than that," said Taffaern. "Their progress will slow when they get to the Narrows."

"I know about that," said Merry. "Ships have to go four or five abreast there, instead of spreading out from shore to shore. That's even better for Eynon's plan."

"Eynon has a plan?" asked Néillen. "Please run it past my *excellent strategic mind.*"

Before Eynon could share what he intended, Doethan and Merrillōn joined them from the other gate. The remaining hastily recruited wizards, the ones who'd helped them build the pair of gates, either walked through a gate or rose on their flying disks and headed off. Some went north, more went west, and several flew off southwest in the direction of the southern Clan Lands.

Doethan shook his head and frowned at Merrillōn. "I hope we haven't just taught wide-gate making to southern Clan Lands' wizards," said Doethan.

"It couldn't be helped if we wanted everyone out of Tyford quickly," said Merrillōn. The older wizard tugged at his beard. "One problem at a time, eh, youngster?"

"You're the only one who calls *me* a youngster," said Doethan.

"We can worry about southern Clan Landers *after* the fleet Sírénae's sent to seize Tyford," said the duke. He summarized what Eynon and Merry had reported for the newcomers.

"Another invasion fleet," Merrillōn began. "I remember when Bifurlanders' dragonships attacked up the Moravon."

"You can tell us that tale when we need to pass the time while hiding in caves," said Néillen. "What's your plan, Eynon?"

Eynon walked Néillen through the details and soon everyone gathered around was smiling and complimenting Eynon on what he intended.

"Show us the communications rings you made," said Doethan. "I'm quite experienced making them and nothing like you've described has ever happened to me."

"Of course," said Eynon. He rose a hundred feet on his flying disk and waited until Merry had reached the same altitude. Ace and his raconette passenger flew around the two wizards in a gentle figure eight until Merry's familiar spied a dozen bats below, feeding on a cloud of insects surrounding the wizard lamps in the stadium. The rockhound dove for the bats, and Merry waved to Eynon.

"I'm ready," she said.

Eynon took the special communications ring he'd made off his finger and spoke its trigger phrase, "*Síarad â chi!*" Three chimes sounded and his ring opened to a typical diameter of two feet. Merry's ring opened as well.

"Bigger is better," said Eynon. He started stretching his ring out by pulling on its edges and soon the interface was ten feet, not two feet across. Merry's ring matched the growth of Eynon's inch for inch.

"Bigger!" said Merry.

"How?" asked Eynon. "My arms can't go wide enough to make it stretch more."

"You're a wizard, silly," said Merry. "Use a sphere of solidified sound."

Eynon slapped his forehead with an open palm and started inflating his ring again, this time making the gold band as thin as a human hair, using the technique Merry recommended. He kept going until the material of the ring was so thin it was practically invisible, and the bottom of the arc touched the ground.

"That should work," said Duke Néillen. "You can cover a circle two hundred feet across."

"The Narrows are about that size," said Taffaern.

"And I can't even see the gold forming the ring's perimeter," said Merrillōn.

"Your eyes have been failing for decades now, old friend," teased Doethan. He called up to Eynon. "Will they still work as gates at that size?"

Eynon was about to step through his end of the gate when Ace and Chee entered the interface formed by Merry's ring, chasing a particularly fast insectivorous bat. Instantaneously, the bat and the two familiars flashed out through the gate Eynon held.

"Well," said Doethan. "It's clear they *do* work as gates!"

Eynon and Merry allowed their rings to shrink down until they fit on their fingers and landed next to the others below. Ace and Chee, munching on a not-quite-fast-enough bat and a beetle that looked like an oversized ladybug with odd, colorful markings, respectively, found a comfortable spot for an early breakfast on Merry's flying disk.

"I'm impressed," said Doethan. "I've been making communications rings for longer than you've been alive, and I've never made gates out of them."

"Beginner's luck?" suggested Eynon. "I'll be glad to help walk you through the exact steps I took when I made them."

"Peregrína will remember what you did as well," Doethan replied.

"You two can swap magical recipes later," said Duke Néillen. "Eynon and Merry have to get moving..."

"...if they want to catch the invading fleet before they enter the Narrows," Taffaern completed. "Before you go, would you like a bit of advice from an old river man?"

"Of course," said Merry.

"Think about what happens when warm air meets cold water," said Taffaern.

"The fog of war," said Eynon with a smile.

"Take me with you," said Doethan. "I can help you make fog. You'll need a lot of it I expect."

"If you'd like," said Eynon. "Is that the only reason you want to come along?" he teased.

Doethan laughed. "You have me there," he said. "I can gate to Riyas from Nova Eboracum. From Tamloch's capital, I can find Princess Rúth and join her in whatever cavern she's found as a refuge."

"That makes sense," said Eynon.

"Take me, too," said Merrillōn. "Someone has to guard Merry in case any wizards from the invading fleet discover her."

"You're most welcome to help protect me," said Merry. "I hadn't even thought that I might be attacked."

"I was young and foolish once, too," Merrillōn replied.

Merry rolled her eyes and the four wizards, representing three generations, slipped through the *ad hoc* gate Eynon generated and prepared their surprise for the emperor's fleet.

They had arrived before the invaders' ships reached the Narrows. Merry rose high enough so the interface on her ring would cover the entrance to the Narrows from side to side. Merrillōn stayed at a lower altitude and began to heat the air. Soon, tendrils of fog started to rise from the surface of the cold river.

Eynon formed a new *ad hoc* gate to Nova Eboracum and disappeared along with Doethan. Merry waited patiently for the three chimes that signaled her ring was triggered. She scanned downriver and saw the Roma ships in the distance.

Come on, she thought, mentally encouraging her lover to work faster. *You've got to open the gate soon.*

Merry was timing the progress of the ships upriver when a tremendous bolt of lightning flashed below her, striking Merrillōn. She watched as the old wizard fell into the Moravon, his robes smoking. Before Merry could do anything to help her would-be protector, he sank into the dark water and didn't resurface.

Blast! thought Merry. *I can't take time to help him until I've dealt with his attackers.* Her eyes tracked back along the path of the bolt, and after blinking away an afterimage, she saw the scout-wizard in purple robes who'd blasted Merrillōn floating on her flying disk next to another wizard wearing black and gray. Merry triggered the listening spell she'd taught Eynon a few weeks ago.

"Got him," Merry heard the woman in purple robes say. "He was trying to raise fog to hide the entrance to the Narrows so our ships would run aground."

Merry also heard the black and gray-robed wizard's reply. "I will tell Náegosh about your initiative. I expect you'll be rewarded."

She didn't understand what the color schemes for the two wizards' robes signified, but it sounded like black-and-gray-robes was there to observe purple-robes. The invaders' wizards were keeping watch just north of the entrance to the Narrows. Merry's ring would soon be making three chimes, which would draw attention and probably result in a blast of lightning hurled her way as well. She nudged Ace with her foot. Her rockhound stood and looked up at Merry. Something unsaid passed between wizard and familiar and Ace launched himself off the side of Merry's flying disk and down toward the two invading wizards.

Ace softly landed on one of the flying disks, slipped his head under the black and gray robes, and sank his teeth into the unprotected flesh of the man's calf. The wizard's scream drowned out the three chimes as Merry's ring was triggered. The wizard in purple turned to see what was wrong with her companion. He was hopping on one foot, clutching his other leg. A solid shove from Ace sent the injured wizard off his flying disk and into the water below, two hundred feet upstream from the entrance to the Narrows. Ace stayed on the man's flying disk, but had assumed his round, rocky form, looking like a small boulder.

The wizard in purple robes wasn't sure what had happened. She turned her focus toward the other wizard bobbing in the river and didn't see Ace transform from boulder to flying carpet form. The rockhound's weight struck her in the middle of her back and tipped her off her flying disk. Ace soared up, but the wizard in purple robes fell, landing close to the wizard in black and gray. She formed a shield of solidified sound around them both and spun a cloud-illusion around her shield.

Merry opened her ring until it was wide enough to cover the entire entrance to the Narrows. She smiled and rotated her ring so the sphere around the two wizards floated through the ring gate and into the far-distant spot where Eynon's ring gate had been established. Then Merry quickly spun her ring back and watched the lead ships of the fleet invading Tyford cross its interface. She hoped the connection lasted long enough for every ship in the fleet to complete the transition.

I can't spare the time to search for Merrillōn now, she thought. *But I'll come back to find his body as soon as the invading fleet downriver has been handled.*

Ace landed next to Merry, his tongue lolling. He barked twice and Merry smiled.

"You're *such* a good boy!" she told her familiar.

Chee climbed up on Merry's shoulder and uttered an interrogative *Chee?*

"You're a good boy, too," said Merry. "Now don't distract me. I've got work to do."

Chapter 59

The Fog of War

Eynon appeared in Laetícia's study after *ad hoc* gating from the Moravon valley, and Doethan stepped through right behind him. They startled Laetícia, Mafuta, Felix, Inthíra, Amber, and Verro, who'd been conferring a few feet away.

"Oh good!" said Eynon. "I'd hoped there'd be somebody here. We need your help."

Laetícia looked at her fellow wizards, then back to Eynon. "What do you want us to do?" she responded.

"We all need to get to the harbor before the emperor's fleet arrives," said Eynon. He described his plan in a few quick sentences.

"It's a good thing the emperor's dragons won't be with her fleet," said Laetícia. "She's sent them off to intimidate and spy on other parts of Orluin."

"Oops!" said Eynon. "I'd forgotten about Sírénae's dragons."

"That's never wise," said Laetícia. She wiggled her eyebrows.

Mafuta and Felix grinned. Laetícia turned her head so the beads on her braids clacked in delight. Inthíra extended her fingers and wiggled them, preparing to generate illusions as if stretching before playing a harp. Amber said nothing. The Bifurland wizard disappeared and reappeared moments later with two nearly identical companions, also in amber robes and hoods, with yellow magestones glinting at their throats.

Felix clapped his hands. "More mages to share our fun."

Amber and the other two Bifurland wizards bowed. It seemed like they were attuned to Amber and already knew what was expected of them.

"I'm impressed, Eynon," said Verro. "I was afraid you were going to tell me you were sending another stampede of wisents, but this is much better."

"He wouldn't be using wisents if one of our goals is starving the invaders, now, would he?" teased Doethan. "I'll do my part to heat things up."

"Can wisents swim?" asked Inthíra. She didn't look like she expected to get an answer.

Eynon smiled but tried to hurry things along. He knew Merry was waiting for her ring to start expanding. "We have to go," he said. "It will take us some time to fly to the center of the harbor."

"Not if you follow me through an *ad hoc* gate to the New Colossus lighthouse," said Laetícia. "It marks the entrance to the harbor and should save us a lot of flying time."

"That sounds great," said Eynon. "Lead the way!"

"I'll meet you there," said Verro. "I need to get Fercha from Riyas. She won't want to miss this."

Verro winked out and the rest of them followed Laetícia through an *ad hoc* gate that came out on the beach at the base of the copper statue. The area was lit by the giant wizard-lamp torch held high above them. All the wizards hovered over the sand on the beach while Eynon spoke to Laetícia.

"We need to get away from the lighthouse," he said. "The statue's torch is too bright and might make our deception too easy to spot."

"Don't worry about that," said Laetícia. "I'll turn the torch off. The rest of you can get started."

Eynon, Doethan, Mafuta, Felix, Inthíra, and Amber flew west, into the center of the entrance to Nova Eboracum wide harbor. The other two Bifurlander wizards flew southeast at high speed. By the time Eynon was in position and his companions were heating the air, Amber reported the other two wizards from Bifurland had seen the sails of the emperor's main fleet approaching.

Here goes, thought Eynon. He triggered his ring and expanded it to a two-hundred-foot diameter. Seconds later, four ships from the fleet on the Moravon were sailing through his ring's wide interface and into the fog-shrouded waters of the harbor.

While Eynon held the ring-gate in place, Inthíra draped the lead ships with illusory green Tamloch pennants. Eynon was impressed by the giant reflective gold quatrefoils she added to the center of their white sails. The contrast between white and gold wasn't great, but the reflectivity would make the symbols stand out in the moonlight and the glow from the statue's wizard lamp.

Like a stately royal parade of the sort Eynon had only read about, not seen, the ships continued to pour through the interface. They didn't stop when they encountered fog but kept moving forward so the ships behind them wouldn't collide with the lead ships, given the limited visibility. When all of the ships from the Moravon had passed through into the harbor, Eynon, wearing his night-vision lenses, watched them form up into a broader formation, making more of a box than a line.

The forward units of Sírénae's main fleet were entering the harbor from the southeast. Eynon smiled when he saw that Amber's two fellow wizards from Bifurland had created illusions of pennants in Dâron-blue, Tamloch-green, and Occidens Province scarlet hanging from the rigging on the ships of the main fleet. In the diffuse glow from the lighthouse, the pennants were easy to spot with distance and night-vision lenses. Eynon assumed advance scouts for both fleets could see them before the great torch of the New Colossus suddenly winked out.

Eynon wondered if Laetícia would help things along with a few carefully placed fireballs or wait to see if the two formations attacked each other without her assistance. His question was answered when Laetícia guided her flying disk to float beside him.

"You can close your ring-gate," she told Eynon. "The ships from the Moravon are all here. I don't know how I undercounted the size of Sírénae's forces by so much?"

Verro and Fercha flew up in time to hear Laetícia's question. "That's been puzzling me, too," he said. "I wonder if the fleet that planned to raid Tyford started to cross the Ocean before the main fleet and missed the storm."

"That might explain it," said Fercha as Eynon shrank his ring-gate back into a ring. "But I have an alternative to offer."

"Tell me," said Laetícia. "Will it make me feel less foolish?"

"I hope so," said Fercha. "There's a framed map of the Tempest Isles hanging on a wall at the home of some friends of mine."

"Rōlin and Peregrína?" asked Eynon.

"Yes," said Fercha. "The Tempest Isles have *two* good harbors—the Great Harbor and a smaller one at the eastern end of the islands."

"So that's why I missed a second fleet?" said Laetícia. "Blast!"

"It might be for the best, if things work out the way we hope," said Eynon.

Doethan rose from a lower altitude to join them. He nodded to Verro and Fercha, then tilted his head to give Eynon a questioning look. "Aren't you going to get Merry?" he asked.

"Merry!" said Eynon. "I've got to get Merry!"

"See if Merrillōn wants to join us, too," called Doethan, but Eynon had already gated out.

* * * * *

Admiral Pixo felt the nervous exhilaration he always felt before battle. He'd already planned for this contingency and his captains knew their jobs well. Náegosh's wizards had been deployed in their attack and defend positions and Náegosh himself, wearing solidified sound lenses for night vision, was spotting for the admiral through the fog. The admiral's distance vision had declined since he'd reached his sixties.

"They're closing on us," said the wizard. "I see Dâron-blue pennants and Tamloch-green."

"How many ships?" asked Pixo. "Do we outnumber them?"

"I don't know," said Náegosh. "It's hard to tell in this blasted fog, even with my lenses."

"My legionnaires are ready for boarding," said Belisaria.

"Good," said Admiral Pixo curtly. Belisaria should have known not to interrupt him before they engaged the enemy, but he chalked it up to nerves. There was something that didn't feel right. The Moravon was a wide river, particularly just upstream from the Narrows, but the current had slowed to almost nothing and the smells around him had changed. He sensed salt spray and heard seabirds crying, as lost in the fog as his fleet was.

Pixo thought about his plan of attack. Battles at sea usually followed one of three patterns. He'd learned his craft and gained experience with the first pattern as a young officer on the Middle Sea where low-slung Roma galleys with banks of oars and sharp, reinforced prows would try to ram each other. The lightly-built ships often sank quickly when their hulls were damaged, but the warm waters where they fought often meant crews could be rescued to fight another day. The same was seldom true in the cold Ocean.

The second pattern featured far larger ships with multiple decks, masts, and sails. They sat high out of the water, exchanging thick iron ballista bolts or tossing great pots of oil with long-armed onagers at each other. At closer range, sailors working bellows would pump Greek fire through yard-long metal nozzles called brass dragons. If missiles or flames didn't serve, legionnaires would toss grapples and board. The goal was to overcome opposing ships and claim them as prizes—or burn them to the waterline. Pixo had advanced from captain to admiral in such battles.

The third pattern added wizards to naval encounters. As a professional who understood wind and wave, Pixo preferred battles based on sailing skill alone, without mages throwing fireballs or lightning blasts from well beyond ballista range. Still, like an expert *shah mat* player, he'd learned how to combine wizards' talents with ships' maneuvers to earn victories. This time, thanks to Sírénae's generosity, he had more wizards to deploy than in any previous battle.

Admiral Pixo's flagship, the *Menodorus Maximus,* was four rows back from the leading edge of his fleet. He'd assigned many of his wizards to the ships in front and instructed them to attack as soon as they could identify suitable targets. Groups of five mages would fly ahead of the fleet, with three of them launching fireballs or lightning blasts and two of them producing defensive shields. For the ten-thousandth time, Pixo wished he could control his forces directly, like moving pieces on a *shah mat* board, but he knew that conflicts at sea were more a matter of training sailors well and relying on the skills and common sense of his captains.

"Fireballs!" reported Náegosh. A moment later, a dozen blasts of flame exploded off the shields around the lead rank of ships. A pair of lightning strikes zigzagged through the air. One of them slipped through a crack in the lead ships' defenses and set a vessel's mainsail on fire.

"Wind!" Pixo commanded. "Give me wind so we can close with them faster and drive off some of this fog!"

"Yes, Admiral," said Náegosh. "The mages in our vanguard have hit them back hard. Two of their ships are burning."

"Well done," said Pixo. "Press the attack. Let's show them they can't stop us from taking Tyford!"

* * * * *

Merry was skimming along the surface of the Moravon when Eynon *ad hoc* gated back to find her. He dove to join her and was pleased when Chee jumped from Merry's flying disk to his own. The raconette scampered up Eynon's torso and put his arms— and prehensile tail—around Eynon's neck, chittering so quickly it sounded like *Ch-ch-ch-ch-ch-ch-CHEE!*

"I've missed you, too, my friend," said Eynon. He was puzzled over the fact that Merry hadn't greeted him. She kept her eyes focused on the river instead. "What's wrong?" he asked.

"Merrillōn was hit by a lightning bolt," Merry replied, her voice flat. "He fell in the river and went under. I think he's dead."

"Oh!" said Eynon. "That's terrible. I'll help you look. Are you trying to sense his magestone?" He flew closer to Merry and tried to put his arm around her shoulder, but she shifted away.

"Of course I'm trying to sense his magestone," Merry snapped. "I'm also looking for his body. I've been a mile downstream and back and there's no trace of him."

"That's *good* news, isn't it?" asked Eynon. "I just met Merrillōn, but he's been a wizard for long time and must know a lot of tricks."

"Maybe so," said Merry. "But if he *did* survive a blast from a lightning bolt and a fall into the river, I wish he'd show himself."

"He could be hurt," said Eynon. "Or unconscious."

"You're not helping," said Merry. She frowned at Eynon and returned to staring at the river and the closer eastern bank as she flew downstream.

Eynon tried to figure out something to say that might help. "The current on the Moravon may have been disrupted by the ring-gate," he said. "Maybe Merrillōn grabbed on to a ship and passed through."

Merry faced Eynon. "You're right," she said. "That could have happened. The river looked quite strange while the ring-gate was open. I'm glad the fleet passed through quickly and the gate only covered part of the channel because the salt from the harbor could make things hard for the fish and the farmers downstream."

"I don't know about the fish," said Eynon, "but I'd bet the farmers would rather deal with a few hours of extra-salty river water instead of an invasion fleet."

"You're probably right," said Merry. "How are things going on the other side?"

"When I left, it looked like there was a good chance the two fleets would attack each other," said Eynon. "If they didn't start soon, our wizards were going to *encourage* them."

"I'd like to see that," said Merry.

"Arf!" said Ace. The rockhound's tail was wagging as he stood beside Merry on her flying disk, ready for anything.

"Chee?" asked Eynon's familiar.

"Right, little one," said Eynon.

Merry reluctantly gave the river one last look and joined Eynon as he created an *ad hoc* gate to a spot high above Nova Eboracum harbor.

* * * * *

"What's going on!" shouted Emperor Sírénae from her cabin when she heard fireballs booming detonations overhead. "Umbrose! Callidus! Attend me!"

Sírénae had been asleep, dreaming of her triumphal entrance into Nova Eboracum, when the noise woke her. She was far from happy.

"I'm here, Your Imperial Majesty," said Umbrose as the spymaster stuck his head into Sírénae's private bedchamber.

"What's going on?" asked the emperor. "Are we under attack?"

"Apparently so," said Umbrose, entering completely. "It looks like the entire Tamloch fleet and most of the ships in the Occidens Province navy are waiting for us in the harbor."

"Callidus told us about that," said Sírénae. She slid her feet into boots, stood up, and pulled a heavy purple tunic worked with gold thread over her head. "I thought *you* told me he'd made it up." She glared at her spymaster. "Maybe *you're* the one making things up."

"My agents told me the Tamloch fleet was north of Fishhook Cape with the Bifurlanders' longships," said Umbrose. "They can't be here!"

"Sadly, there *is* a fleet blocking our way, no matter where they come from," said Magister Callidus from outside Sírénae's bedchamber. "Come on deck and see."

"Get out of my way," said Sírénae as she pushed Umbrose to one side. Callidus slid the bedchamber door open ahead of her, then followed the emperor as she stomped out of her cabin and up the ladders to the *Seahawk's* stern. Umbrose joined them a few moments later. Fireballs were exploding overhead, and bolts of lightning cracked across a dark sky that would soon be turning orange and red as the sun rose behind them. "I can't see a thing through all this fog," complained the emperor.

"Let me assist you," said Magister Callidus. He swiftly created a set of night-vision and distance-vision lenses for Sírénae and himself.

"That's better," she said, "but it's still hard to see who's attacking us."

"My advance scouts report seeing pennants with Occidens Province eagles and Tamloch quatrefoils," said Callidus.

"I'm sorry I doubted you," said Sírénae.

"I live to serve my emperor," said Callidus. He kept his face impassive, but inside he wondered how the lies he'd made up about the ships defending Nova Eboracum had suddenly managed to come true.

A series of bursting fireballs and massive lightning bolts discharged against the shields on the lead ships in Sírénae's fleet. Rolling booms of thunder pealed above them, and the air was tinged with the sharp smell of sulphur and the tang that came after lightning.

"Attack them! Board them! Send them to the bottom of the Ocean!" shouted Sírénae.

Callidus had seen his emperor like this before—she wanted nothing except the destruction of her enemies. He watched her eyes light up as his battle mages turned two of the opposing ships into torches. The two fleets were closing rapidly, and the level of damage each inflicted increased as the distance between them shrank.

"I wish Pixo was here," Sírénae told Callidus. "He would *love* this."

Callidus nodded. He'd found that the less you said to Sírénae when her blood lust was up, the better. The senior magister was contemplating flying up to have a better view, but he wasn't sure how the emperor would react to his absence. Before he could ask her permission, the *Seahawk* shuddered as if it had hit a reef below the surface. He fell to his knees on the deck, and Sírénae lost her balance and tipped over, landing on Umbrose, who'd gone down hard.

"What was *that?*" spat the emperor in a tone that sounded like *how dare you get in my way, whatever you are?*

Nearby ships were also being knocked about by something beneath the waves. Magister Callidus could hear sailors on those ships screaming, then realized some of the screams were echoing up from the lower decks of the *Seahawk*. As he listened, another explosion rocked the ship from above. A fireball had slipped through the flagship's shields and the foresail was burning. Callidus lifted a huge hemisphere of seawater and dispelled the construct of solidified sound above the burning sail, dowsing it before the flames could spread.

He turned to check on Sírénae and saw the sky turn red to their stern. *More fireballs?* he wondered. *Are we being attacked from the rear as well? Could it be the Bifurlanders and their dragonships?* Then a sliver of the sun emerged from the eastern horizon and Callidus knew dawn had arrived. He heard cheers from the sailors around him.

"Pixo! Pixo! Pixo!"

The sun was burning away the fog and the attackers were revealed as their own Second Fleet, not ships from Tamloch or Occidens Province. Wizards stopped attacking and started assisting damaged vessels. Magister Callidus watched dozens of ships nearby tilt and shift as if they were toys for giants, then they resumed floating calmly in the harbor. *Had the Orluin wizards tamed great whales to attack the emperor's fleet?* Callidus considered.

"What just happened?" asked Sírénae using her *heads will roll* voice.

"We attacked our own vessels," said Umbrose. "And they attacked us."

"How did Second Fleet get to Nova Eboracum harbor?" demanded the emperor.

"I suppose we'll have to ask Admiral Pixo," said Callidus.

"Then send a wizard to fetch him," said Sírénae. "When he's here, all three of you can join me in my cabin."

"Yes, Your Imperial Majesty," said Callidus.

Umbrose said nothing. He just nodded and gave a small bow.

Magister Callidus ordered one of his wizards to fetch the admiral. Then he waited and watched while the sun rose higher. Its rays lit a path for the emperor's ships to follow as they limped toward Nova Eboracum.

Chapter 60

Parting Words

"That. Was. Impressive!" said Merry as she flew next to Eynon and the other Orluin wizards far above where the sea battle had been fought. "Your plan worked."

"It did, didn't it?" Eynon replied. He seemed to be as happy about being with Merry as he was about everything coming off as planned. Ace was napping by Merry's feet in his flying-carpet form, digesting the bat he'd recently consumed. To Eynon's amusement, Chee had deserted him to snooze on top of Merry's familiar, occasionally waking long enough to groom Ace in search of small bugs to crunch on.

Felix didn't notice the familiar fauna. "Too bad your plan didn't do more damage, though," he said. "It would have been really great if the two fleets sank each other, instead of only losing a few vessels."

"That wasn't the point," said Mafuta. "Our intent was never to sink ships and drown Roma sailors—they're our people, after all, even if they're under Sírénae's command."

"Then why do it?" asked Felix.

"To stop the fleet sailing up the Moravon from sacking Tyford, for one," said Doethan.

"To keep Sírénae off balance, for another," added Laetícia.

"Moving forward, the emperor will think twice, or even three times before taking action," said Verro. His flying disk was close to Fercha's, and the two wizards were holding hands.

"And if Sírénae needs to take swift, decisive action against us in the future, this should make her hesitate," noted Fercha, waving to the ships milling about in the entrance to the harbor.

"I'd certainly stop and think before I acted if I were her," said Inthíra. "Sírénae won't know whether or not to trust her own eyes." Inthíra rubbed her palms together and furrowed her brow in thought before speaking. "We're good with illusions, but from what you said about how the ships headed for Tyford were disguised, we'd be wise to double and triple check things ourselves before we're caught in traps of Sírénae's devising." Inthíra was pleased to see the other wizards nod, except for the Bifurlanders. Their heads were hidden in deep amber-dyed hoods, but their shoulders leaned forward, confirming their agreement.

Inthíra and Merry were maintaining an illusion that the Orluin mages were a fluffy cloud, but that wouldn't fool anyone for long because their cloud didn't move with the wind.

"I'm so sorry about Merrillōn," Merry told Doethan.

"That's the seventh time you've said that since you joined us," said Doethan. "What have I told you the other six times?"

"Not to worry about it," said Merry. "You said he probably used his emergency gate to escape and you wouldn't believe Merrillōn was dead until you saw his body and confirmed he wasn't breathing for yourself."

"Even then, I wouldn't be in a hurry to bury him," teased Doethan. "He'll probably come strolling into one of the sanctuary caverns west of Tyford in a week and ask for dinner."

"If you say so," said Merry.

Doethan guided his flying disk close enough for him to give Merry a hug. Merry held him close for a few seconds before Doethan moved back to arm's length. "Even if Merrillōn *did* die, he led a long life and would have given it to protect Dâron," said Doethan. "Death is part of life and he wouldn't want *your* life diminished by his death."

Merry put on a brave face. "I wish I'd known him better," she said.

"You'll just have to settle for knowing *me* better," said Doethan. "But not right now. I have to get to the governor-general's palace to take a gate to Riyas and find Princess Rúth. I expect she's been worried about me."

"She has," said Verro. "There's no need for you to go to Nova Eboracum, however. I can take you directly to the caves where she's located with an *ad hoc* gate. Fercha and I are headed there as well."

"I appreciate the offer," said Doethan, "but there's someone I have to see in the city before I leave."

"But everyone is evacuated," said Felix.

"Not everyone," said Doethan.

Laetícia caught Doethan's eye and smiled. "Give Távi my best," she said.

Amber instructed one of the other Bifurland mages to accompany Doethan and keep him hidden in flight. Then Doethan waved, turned, and sped north toward the city with his new companion.

"We'd best be going, too," said Mafuta. She tugged the sleeve of Felix's robes and looked to Laetícia for confirmation.

"You two go ahead," said Laetícia. "I have to consult with Fercha for a few minutes."

"Keep your guard—and your camouflage up," said Mafuta. "You don't want Sírénae's wizards to spot you."

"I can stay and protect you," said Felix. He snapped the claws on his gauntlets out and in a few times.

Laetícia hid a smile. "Please protect Mafuta instead," she told the tall young Roma wizard.

Mafuta raised an eyebrow on the side of her face away from Felix so Laetícia could see her response, but Felix couldn't. Another Bifurland wizard joined her, and all three mages directed their flying disks toward Nova Eboracum. Felix practiced his attack and defense moves as he flew.

"Farewell for now," said Amber. "Let me know if you need Bifurland's aid in the future."

"How do we contact you..." Laetícia began, then stopped when she realized Amber was gone.

Laetícia beckoned the others to come closer. The remaining Orluin wizards moved their flying disks into a tight formation so they could speak in soft voices. Inthíra continued to maintain the cloud illusion around them. Laetícia made sure she was floating next to Fercha.

"Yes, I think I can do it," Fercha told Laetícia before the Roma wizard had a chance to speak.

"You can build a wide gate across the Ocean?" Laetícia responded, seeking confirmation. "We've had trouble constructing standard fixed gates between Nova Eboracum and the Southern Empire in Afarika. More often than not, whatever we try to send through a transoceanic gate is never received at all, so we've been reluctant to build them."

"My father had the same problem getting supplies from Brendinas to his refuge far to the west," said Fercha. "He was eventually able to make his gates work across long distances by adjusting the bindings between each end to account for a curved, not a straight path."

"Because the world is a sphere," said Eynon, pleased that he'd figured it out.

"Exactly," said Fercha. "That's how your wisent stampede could arrive safely on the battlefield in Dâron."

"So you think it's possible we can quickly get reinforcements from Valens and the other emperors in our fight against Sírénae?" asked Laetícia.

"Not just possible, probable," Fercha answered.

"Wouldn't it be wiser to test things out before giving odds of success?" asked Verro.

"Don't pour vinegar in my honey, my love," said Fercha. She made a face at Verro, then smiled and kissed him.

Verro laughed. "If there's any way I can assist you in your experiments, please let me know."

"I'm counting on your help," said Fercha. "And yours," she told Laetícia.

"Once we've confirmed we can construct reliable fixed gates, we can send Valentius and Aleña through to Alexandria, so Valentius can work with Valens to assemble an army," said Laetícia. "I'm sure Flavia and Phraátēs will contribute legions as well."

"Flavia and Phraátēs?" asked Eynon.

"The emperors of the Northern and Eastern Empires," said Merry. Eynon gave Merry a surprised look.

"I read about them in a book I found in Tyford," said Merry.

"What are those black specks on the horizon?" asked Fercha.

"Dragons, I think," said Eynon. "They're probably returning to report to Sírénae."

"Then it's past time for us to go," said Verro.

"Agreed," said Laetícia. Air rushed in to fill the space she'd formerly occupied when she *ad hoc* gated out.

"Stay safe," said Fercha.

"And stay out of trouble," Verro told Eynon and Merry with a grin that confirmed he knew that wouldn't be likely. He *ad hoc* gated out with Fercha.

Only Eynon, Merry, and Inthíra were left floating lonely as a cloud, high above the now-united invasion fleets.

Eynon could now detect beating wings on the seven black specks headed their way. "Would you like me to transport you somewhere?" he asked Inthíra. "I'd be glad to."

"Don't worry about me," Inthíra replied. "My emergency gate brings me out in Dâron, not far from my preferred evacuation location." She noticed the rapidly approaching dragons and knew it was time to go. "Goodbye for now," she said. "I'll give Nûd, Bonnie, and Duke Háiddon your best."

"Thank you," said Merry, but she spoke to empty air.

"Where shall *we* go?" asked Eynon. "We never did learn where all the refuges for Dâron's people were located."

"Let's return to Freeholder Farnam's cabin on the Rhuthro," suggested Merry. "It will take a long time for Sírénae's scouts to get that far west, and we can figure out a better place later."

"What will we do for food and drink?" asked Eynon. "Everything has been taken to the caves."

"We can stop at Fercha's tower first," said Merry. "She hasn't had a chance to get her stores to a cavern."

"Thinking about the gate to Melyncárreg in Fercha's tower gives me a better idea," said Eynon.

"How much better?" she asked. Eynon could tell Merry was thinking about the time they'd spent together in front of the fire in Farnam's cabin.

"Well," he said, smiling. "Maybe not *better*, but different. Hang on tight. I have some new friends I want you to meet."

They disappeared, and even the sensitive ears of the returning dragons didn't hear the soft pop when Eynon and Merry gated out.

Chapter 61

Conquest Unsatisfactory

"Status report," barked Sírénae to Admiral Pixo. Beside her, Thraxa screeched with a sound so painfully penetrating it made a tutor's chalk scratchings on slate seem like a musician's sweet strumming on the strings of a lyre.

Magister Callidus watched Pixo consciously refrain from covering his ears. He had reflexively covered his own ears with protective baffles of solidified sound.

"I'm pleased to note that very few ships were lost, and none of our people were killed," said Pixo, accentuating the positive. "The good magister's mages did an excellent job of retrieving sailors and legionnaires who went overboard or were trapped on sinking ships." Pixo smiled at Callidus.

Callidus didn't do more than return a thin-lipped nod. He knew Sírénae would soon be shouting. Pixo, General Machaera, himself, and Umbrose—all the members of the emperor's senior team gathered in her cabin—were bracing for an angry tirade. It didn't come now, however. Sírénae's voice was calm.

"How did it happen, Admiral?" the emperor asked. "I sent you to Tyford and found you in Nova Eboracum harbor attacking me."

"I don't have an answer for you, Your Imperial Majesty," said Pixo. "One minute we were sailing up the Moravon, the next we were in the harbor."

"Ships don't just fly across hundreds of miles!" said Sírénae.

"Most excellent Emperor," said Umbrose obsequiously. "Weeks ago, my agents shared rumors of a fleet of Bifurland dragonships that had been on the Brenavon south of Brendinas suddenly appearing in Nova Eboracum harbor. I'd thought they'd had too much ale and discarded their report, but perhaps it *wasn't* a drink-inspired delusion."

"You tell me this *now*, Umbrose?" said Sírénae. "Had you informed us about this when it happened, we could have determined whether their report was correct or not and started developing counter-measures—since this morning's events make it clear that the Orluin wizards *have* perfected a new sort of gate." She glared at her spymaster and Callidus watched his rival sink even deeper into the cabin's shadowed corner where he sat.

Callidus wasn't pleased when Sírénae shifted her gaze to him. "Do *you* know how to make gates that could transport a fleet, Senior Magister?"

"I do not, Your Imperial Majesty," said Callidus. "If I did know such techniques, or was acquainted with anyone who could make them, I would have told you."

"Yes, yes," said Sírénae brusquely. "I think you would have." She rubbed the feathers on Thraxa's head for a moment. "Do you have any wizards interested in magical theory, not just practice?" she asked. "We'll need to have the same gate skills the Orluin wizards have if we want to conquer the continent quickly."

"None of the academic wizards left with Your Imperial Majesty," said Magister Callidus. "The only ones who joined us were mages with a talent for battle—"

"—or spycraft," added Umbrose. "The closest I have to gate experts are the ones who make fixed gates for their own use between cities in Orluin."

"Then it will fall to you, Umbrose," said Sírénae. "You'll have to kidnap experts in this new gate-building technique. Then we can interrogate them together."

"Yes, Emperor," said Umbrose. The glance Umbrose shared with Sírénae made Callidus feel uneasy. He hoped he'd never be the object of such an interrogation.

"If the Orluin wizards can gate legions from place to place as well as fleets, it will make *my* job ten times more difficult," said General Machaera.

"I'm sure you'll be up to the task," said Sírénae.

Callidus mentally translated the emperor's stern look toward Machaera as meaning, *or I'll find someone who is.*

"Umbrose!" said Sírénae. "Make finding experts in these new kinds of gates a top priority once we land," said Sírénae.

"Yes, Emperor," Umbrose replied. He lowered his head, temporarily removing himself as a target for Sírénae's wrath.

"What did my dragons find when they flew to Brendinas and Riyas?" Sírénae asked Callidus, shifting to a new topic.

"The wizards aboard your dragons report both capitals are deserted," said Callidus. "They fear you, Emperor."

"As well they should," said Sírénae. "They've run away and hidden like mice—and taken all their food with them, I'm sure." The emperor turned to Pixo. "That's why taking Tyford was so important."

"I'm sorry I failed you," said the admiral.

"As am I," said Sírénae. "We'll have to see if General Machaera can do better."

Machaera wisely sat silent, holding the emperor's gaze for a long breath before looking away.

"What do your spies in Dâron, Tamloch, and Nova Eboracum say about where everyone has gone, Umbrose?" asked Sírénae.

"They walked through gates wide enough for five wagons side by side and found themselves in caverns," said the spymaster.

"So they can tell us where they are?" asked Sírénae.

"Sadly no, Your Imperial Majesty," Umbrose replied. "Unfortunately, all they can tell us is that they're deep underground, but they don't know where."

"Blast!" Sírénae exclaimed, shocking the others and startling Thraxa into another ear-splitting screech. "We'll have to find those caverns and the supplies stored in them."

"Agreed, my Emperor," said Umbrose. "Once we land, we can start searching for them."

"Did your wizards on dragonback spot the Tamloch fleet or the Bifurland dragonships?" Sírénae asked Callidus.

"They did not," said Magister Callidus. "One dragon and her rider went north of Fishhook Cape and past Bhaile Pónaire, but they saw nothing more than fishing boats."

"Thoughts?" asked Sírénae. "Speculations?"

"If I commanded those fleets, I'd withdraw to the north and wait to see where we position our ships," said Admiral Pixo.

"Then, if they can truly gate fleets around, I'd send fifty of their vessels against twenty of ours, whenever they could manage such unfavorable odds for us."

"What do *you* plan to do to counter our opponents at sea then, Admiral?" asked Sírénae.

"That will depend, in part, on how you intend to deploy your legions," said Pixo, looking at Sírénae and General Machaera. "If you intend to spread your forces across Nova Eboracum, Brendinas, and Riyas, I'd keep half the fleet here in Nova Eboracum and a quarter of my ships in each of the other two locations. That way, forces from here can sail north or south to reinforce ships in Riyas and Brendinas in case of attack by sea. Where will you position your legions, Emperor?"

"I need to hear what the emissary Umbrose sent to the Northern Clan Lands with Xaxidiánus learned first, Admiral," said Sírénae.

Callidus hadn't had a chance to talk to Xaxidiánus before Sírénae had insisted on this meeting, so he'd be hearing the news for the first time as well.

"Unfortunately," Umbrose began, "the chief of chiefs of the Northern Clan Landers didn't welcome our proposal for her people to join us against Quintillius and his allies. According to my agent, she wasn't particularly polite about saying so."

"Oh?" said Sírénae, arching one eyebrow. "What did she say, exactly?"

"She wrote you a letter," said Umbrose. He removed a folded missive from his black and gray robes. "Shall I read it to you?"

"Why not?" said Sírénae. She hadn't dealt with Northern Clan Landers before and expected blunt, uncouth words. She also loved to make her opponents eat them.

"Unto the banished former ruler of the Western Empire and would-be emperor of Orluin comes this courteous greeting from Arminta, chief-of-chiefs of the Northern Clan Lands. Be it known that we have five eagle standards on display in our halls from previous battles with the Roma. We would welcome a chance to collect forty more." Umbrose refolded the letter and handed it to Sírénae.

"That sounds like a *No,*" said General Machaera. "Let's retrieve those five eagles."

"We will," said Sírénae. "If we have to burn down their homes and forests to do it."

Machaera slapped her fist and forearm across her breastplate in support of Sírénae's affirmation.

"Do you have a reply?" asked Umbrose.

"Yes," said Sírénae. "But not in writing. Chief Armina asked for forty legions. We'll see how she deals with five of them marching on her mountain strongholds once we get settled in."

"Very good," said Umbrose.

"As for troop dispositions, I like your idea, Pixo—provided General Machaera agrees. Half our forces in Nova Eboracum, with a quarter each in Riyas and Brendinas," said Sírénae. "We can shift legions later, however. This morning, I'm landing in Nova Eboracum with my full strength behind me."

"I'll see you have an honor guard of wizards shielding you from assassins," said Magister Callidus. That was standard procedure for victors entering conquered cities.

Sírénae nodded and turned her head to face Pixo. "When do we reach the city docks?" she asked.

"In less than an hour," said Pixo.

"Get to your preparations, everyone," said Sírénae, clapping her hands. "I need my slaves and servants to get me into my imperial finery."

"I'm sure you'll make quite an impression on everyone there," said Callidus.

As he left, the magister heard Sírénae calling after General Machaera. "Don't forget my elephants! I *must* have my elephants when I enter the city."

"Yes, Majesty," said Machaera.

Callidus and the general walked down the corridor away from Sírénae's cabin side by side. Both of them were muttering too softly for the other to hear.

* * * * *

Drums the size of cauldrons sounded deep resonant notes that echoed across the streets of Nova Eboracum. Four wizards' flying disks overlapped and supported a platform holding Sírénae Accipiter, Emperor of Orluin, six feet above the cobblestones. A dozen more wizards surrounded Sírénae, maintaining transparent shields around her and watching for would-be assassins.

Behind the emperor, four abreast, walked two hundred elephants. The massive beasts' heavy treads shook the buildings on either side of the broad avenue leading from the docks to the governor-general's palace. In the sky, high enough so as not to frighten the elephants, seven black dragons wheeled and roared.

Callidus stood beside the emperor, a step down from her raised position on the platform. He watched a slight wind blow small clouds of dust and dried dung down the empty street. Every taverna stood shuttered. Every merchant's stall was closed. Even the usual stray cats and dogs were missing.

"Where *is* everybody?" asked Sírénae. "They couldn't have evacuated everyone!"

"It seems they have," said Callidus. "Quintillius and Laetícia are known for their efficiency."

"I won't have it," said Sírénae. "We'll have to do this again."

"Do what again?" asked Callidus.

"Have my victory parade, of course," Sírénae insisted. "Once more legions have landed, we can have their soldiers line the streets and cheer."

"How nice, Your Imperial Majesty," said Callidus.

"Don't be that way," Sírénae chided. "It's not like it's a full triumph. I'll save that until after I've conquered the entire continent."

"Of course," said Callidus. He didn't sigh, at least not out loud, but thought he'd better leave Sírénae's side before he said something he shouldn't. "I'm going to scout ahead and see if I can spot anyone still left in the city," he said. "If I find any stragglers, maybe we can get some information out of them."

"Go," said Sírénae, waving Callidus away with one hand. "You're not helping my mood."

Callidus rose a dozen feet and sped far ahead of Sírénae's entourage and the elephants. The main gate to the governor-general's palace was not far ahead. He saw no signs that anyone from Occidens Province was left in the city. Callidus lowered his head and shook it slowly, wondering how many days he would wait things out with Sírénae before leaving and seeking out Laetícia. He knew it would take a long time to gain her trust but was confident he could do it. *Perhaps Xaxidiánus might even join me?* thought the magister in a rare moment of optimism.

He glanced up at the circling dragons, then lowered his gaze and scanned the street ahead of him. Something was odd, but he wasn't sure what. Callidus abruptly slowed and brought his flying disk lower until it floated only inches above the cobblestones. He saw a dirty young face peer up from a storm sewer. The face smiled at Callidus and winked at him before disappearing. Callidus decided to say nothing to the emperor and determined to wait and see what happened next.

Continued in the fifth book
of the Congruent Mage series:

The Congruent King

Appendix

The Empires of the Roma

Excerpts from *A History of Roma's Imperium* by Magister Herodotius Scribonia Peripatetica, written in celebration of the four hundredth anniversary of the establishment of the Northern Empire and dedicated, with great appreciation, to my patron, the esteemed Allorénzo Floréntinus, First Citizen of Roma and governor-general of Italia Province.

The Founding of Roma

The history of the Imperium properly starts with the founding of the city of Roma nearly twenty-eight centuries ago, for that is when dates in imperial reckoning begin. Earlier tales and legends tell of a time generations before Roma was established, when Aeneas, a prince of Troy, fled that city as it fell to its perfidious Athican besiegers. After facing great perils at sea and gathering companions from all the corners of the World on his voyage, Aeneas and his crew finally settled in the west of the Apennine peninsula north of the river Tiber. It was said that because the men and women of his crew accepted Aeneas as their captain, one day all the world would be joined under the leadership of his descendants.

Aeneas and his people prospered, for the land around them produced abundant harvests. Many generations passed for the Aeneans in their new home, and their territory expanded until they encountered and warred with nearby barbarians, the Truscans, who defeated them in battle after battle. Following one such conflict, Lupa, a fierce warrior called *The Wolf,* fled to the south and sought refuge in a sheltered region of seven hills.

Lupa's husband had been killed in battle, but Lupa was pregnant and months later gave birth to boy-girl twins, Romulus and Romula. It was said a she-wolf guarded the infant twins when Lupa left them to hunt and trade for food, though responsible historians consider this unlikely. Some scholar-mages speculate that Lupa was a wizard and the she-wolf her familiar, which is even less likely, given that wizardry itself had not yet been discovered. We can assume the *she-wolf-as-familiar* story is an attempt to backdate the beginning of wizardry and provide it with a Roma, rather than an Athican origin.

Returning to better-documented history, records note others descended from Aeneas or members of his crew soon joined Lupa and several small villages grew up around the seven hills. Two decades later a formal charter was established, uniting the villages into a new city, Roma, named for the twins, who had now grown wise and tall. Lupa marked Roma's founding with an heirloom, a stone from the walls of Troy, handed down the generations from Aeneas. Romulus, Romula, and Lupa placed the stone atop the tallest hill and vowed to build a palace worthy of an emperor around it.

Romulus and Romula, with Lupa's guidance, ruled Roma side by side and helped the city prosper. After their deaths, six strong and just kings ruled Roma, expanding its territory and bringing neighboring barbarian tribes like the Truscans and Sabynes under Roma's benevolent rule. The kingship ended when a cruel seventh king, Tarquinius Superbus, was overthrown and the citizens of Roma established the Roma Republic, which continues to this day under the four emperors. For additional details about the structure of Roma's government, please read my book *The Senate and People of Roma and the Four Empires.*

Magic and Magestones

Roma's expansion and growth owes much to the discovery of magestones and magic by the Athicans some four centuries after Roma's founding. Philosophers in Athenos, during the administration of Pericles, observed that some of their number, using bits of polished obsidian, were able to generate localized areas of heat and cold, create small flames, and form sparks that would jump between their fingertips. For several centuries such phenomena were considered mere amusements for children. Alexander the Great didn't see any use for philosophers of wizardry, as they were called, except for a single wizard included in his entourage specifically to chill his wine.

In the four hundred and fifty-fourth year since the founding of the city of Roma, Consul Gnaeus Fulvius Centumalus, commanding a fleet of triremes, rescued a dozen wizards from Athenos who had been captured by Illyrian pirates. The consul saw potential in the wizards' simple manipulations and promised them fortunes if they could scale up their flames and sparks into fireballs and blasts of lightning. All twelve wizards succeeded and joined Gnaeus Fulvius in ridding the Adriatic and Ionian Seas of pirates. Later, a Roma expeditionary force seized Athenos, primarily to gain control of the wizards at the various academies in the city.

While most philosophers of wizardry were taken to Roma and pressed into service with Roma's legions, a small number of wizards in Athenos escaped and made their way west by sea to sanctuaries in the White and Green Isles, where they established independent schools of magic. Wizards from other city-states such as Corinth and Sparta left Athica before Roma's armies could capture them and settled in Ctesiphon, the Parthian capital to the east. Eastern mages, or *magi,* were less interested in military uses of magic than they were in the mathematical study of the movements of the stars. Their research into the esoteric nature of mathemagic led to the development of Parthian numbers and the concept of *zero,* which was inspired by the apparent *nothingness* of circular congruencies.

Most wizards taken to Roma learned how to generate fireballs and lightning blasts. Adding their powerful offensive magic to Roma's disciplined legions made Roma's armies and fleets nearly unstoppable. Wind magic was harnessed to drive sailing vessels faster and blow volleys of arrows off target. Cold magic demoralized enemy soldiers and coated opponents' equipment with ice. Military magic was a potent tool for Roma's generals and admirals in their conquests.

Concerning Dragons

Roma's wizards found the first dragon's eggs in and near active volcanoes in Italia and Sicily. Strange, gray, ash-covered rocks tossed up by the eruption of Vesuvius that buried Pompeii turned out to be dragons' eggs. Nurtured by wizards, they hatched as small black beasts that escaped and went on to terrify survivors of the destruction. Successive groups of more cautious wizards raised dragons more carefully, enlisting them to fight with Roma's legions. It was several centuries later when wizards in the Kingdom of Nordland found gold dragon eggs on the northern coast of the Isle of Fire in the middle of the Ocean, but the golden dragons hatching from those eggs never reached the size of Roma's blacks. Tales have reached the wise of mages from the barbarian kingdoms or Orluin liberating dragon eggs from volcanoes on the southern coast of the Isle of Fire, but only sporadic reports of dragons in the far west have been recorded.

Early Roma Expansion

Seven hundred years from the founding of the city, Roma's territory had grown to surround the Middle Sea, from the Ocean's Gates to Byzantium and Alexandria. This was, in part, because Roma emerged triumphant in three Punic Wars against Carthage, using lightning, ice, and fireballs to defeat General Hannibal and his elephants, earning a decisive victory for Roma. Shortly thereafter, a huge fleet of Roma ships crammed with soldiers sailed south from Roma to Carthage. Presented with the Roman fleet and a dozen legions camped outside the walls of their eponymous capital, the Carthaginian empire decided to become a Roma client state rather than have Carthage torn down stone by stone and its fields sown with salt.

Many years later, Pompey the Great conquered Syria and Judea, adding to Roma's lands in the East and greatly enriching Roma's coffers. Gaius Julius Caesar, who would later become the first Imperator, extended Roma's reach north and west by subduing Gaul and the White and Green Isles. It was later learned that wizards and barbarians from those isles took ship to sail west ahead of Caesar's forces and established a pair of petty kingdoms in Orluin. When Gaius Julius returned to Roma with his victorious legions, he was hailed as Imperator and given power to manage Roma's vast lands with the help of wise counsel from Roma's Senate.

Caesar ruled wisely, avoiding several assassination attempts thanks to the diligence of his personal wizard, Aurelianus, who was the first to develop shields of solidified sound. Sadly, one attempt *did* succeed and the mantle of imperator passed to Caesar's nephew, Octavian. Octavian's senior general, Marcus Antonius, added the wheat and wealth of Egypt to what was now known as the Roma Empire. Later, in the north, an important victory was delivered by General Publius Quinctilius Varus, further extending Roma's dominions. Varus and his legions, supported by forty-two wizards and eight black dragons, defeated an alliance of Germanic tribes at the Battle of the Teutoburg Forest and opened the lands east of the Rhine to Roma expansion. Varus later served as governor of the new province of Germania.

The Study of Magic

Aurelius, the personal wizard serving Imperator Julius, was a particularly powerful mage. Few other wizards could master solidified sound like Aurelius, however, and wizards who *could* generate shields were required to give thirty years of service to the legions. Many mages decided not to admit they could generate shields, which slowed further development of defensive magic for several generations. Solidified sound constructs continued to be researched on a limited basis, but only shields in classical Platonic solids were perfected.

During the time of the first two imperators, the study of magic continued in academies in major cities around the empire. Many simple spells and devices that are now the province of hedge wizards, like crafting fertility-control charms, drying clothes, and summoning fresh water, were discovered in this period. The distinction between wizards, who could cast fireballs and throw lightning bolts, and hedge wizards, who dealt in lesser magics, began shortly after this period and was formalized during Imperator Nero's term as First Man of the Senate, as the imperators were also known.

Once of the most valuable and lasting contributions of Imperator Octavian was the establishment of a professional training program for imperator candidates, the School of Good Governance. Promising young men and women from leading families, including possible future emperors, generals, and provincial governors, were given rigorous training in law, politics, history, military strategy, tactics, logistics, and leadership by scholars and experts with extensive practical experience. The program encouraged working together and forming alliances over backstabbing and intrigue. Candidates who were not chosen for the purple were given responsibilities in the imperial administration commensurate with their character. Likewise, the rigorous elimination of candidates who put their own ambitions over the good of the state had the salutary effect of producing a long succession of wise emperors.

One such candidate, the son of General Germanicus and the husband of the granddaughter of Imperator Augustus, went by the nickname Caligula. This young man had the bad judgment to be overheard saying that when he became imperator, he'd show his disdain for Roma's Senate by naming his horse a consul. Caligula found himself rapidly assigned to be governor-general of the newly discovered Isles of Dogs, the Canariae Insulae or Canary Islands. Shortly after arriving on Nivaria—the province's largest island— Caligula fell to his death while ascending Old Man Mountain, a twelve-thousand-foot active volcano. The exact circumstances of Caligula's passing remain unclear to this day.

Continued Growth

One substantial expansion of Roma's territory happened in lands to the east. Under the military leadership of Imperator Vespasian, the king of Parthia found his army, a handful of magi, and a wing of mountain gryffons faced with sure destruction by Roma's overwhelming array of legions, wizards, and dragons. Choosing to retain his throne and his head, the king begged Vespasian's permission for his realm to join Roma's empire as a semi-autonomous client-state. A massive initial payment in gold and gems cemented the new relationship, and ongoing taxes on Parthian trade helped fund more legions and conquests to the north and south of Roma.

Roma's northward expansion reached the shore of the Baltican Sea, except for the Daneland, a peninsula controlled by the Kingdom of Nordland, a territory filled with undisciplined ax-wielding wildlings. Several emperors determined that it wasn't worth the effort for Roma to waste resources on such a cold and unproductive land. Nordland negotiated with Imperator Trajan and promised to give Roma tribute of fish, furs, slaves, and warriors to serve in the imperial guard in return for their continued autonomy.

In the south, Roma's conquests were blocked by the Great Desert, except in the Nile Valley, where General Antonia Camela Ferox traveled up the Nile and beyond with seven legions and five dragons to add Kush and Ethiopia to the empire. Improved shields against clouds of biting flies and midges and the first attempts at healing potions helped the legionnaires avoid diseases that had prevented previous armies from pressing farther south. With the help of wizardry and spells for producing streams of water from empty air, communities of Roma farmers began to plant crops and fruit trees on the edges of the Great Desert, reclaiming a tiny fraction of that vast emptiness for the empire and over time creating what is now the thriving province of Nova Aqua.

Three Empires

Following her conquest, Antonia Ferox returned to the city of Roma and was named imperator. She had two children, Diocletius and Constantia. The former Parthian empire had become thoroughly integrated into Roma's dominions by this time and had extended its territory to include Persia as well. Its eastern borders were the mountains of Bactria and the Indus River, and its lands were populous and wealthy. When her children were twenty-five, Antonia divided Roma into eastern and western administrative spheres under co-emperors, with Diocletius governing the West from Narbo and his sister Constantia governing the East from Antioch, the city that served as the gateway linking the former Parthian empire to the Middle Sea. Antonia served as high emperor above her children from Roma until her death.

When Antonia died, Diocletius and Constantia resolved to continue ruling as co-emperors, with neither of them residing in Roma. Every other year they would meet in Roma to ensure the smooth coordination of the halves of the empire. Constantia gave her oldest son, Antonius, control of Egypt and the valley of the Nile. Diocletius gave his daughter, Dído, rule over western North Afarika. When Antonius and Dído wed, the Southern Empire was created, with the new couple ruling it jointly.

The barbarians who had escaped the arrival of the legions of Imperator Julius in the White and Green Isles several centuries earlier had established two squabbling petty kingdoms, Dâron and Tamloch, on the far western continent of Orluin across the Ocean. Reports from scribes in the court of Diocletius note that emissaries from both kingdoms came to Narbo to ask for Roma's aid against the other. Diocletius responded by assembling a fleet and seven legions under the command of general Publius Cambrensis. The general's forces landed at the mouth of the Abbenoth river and established the garrison city of Nova Eboracum. Publius led his legions in battles against Dâron, Tamloch, and even more barbarous inhabitants known as Clan Landers before conquering the lands on either side of the river and providing them as farms for retiring legion veterans. The new Occidens Province thereby formed a buffer between the squabbling barbarian kingdoms, bringing Roma's rule and order to Orluin.

Three administrative empires, all part of what became known as the united Roma Imperium, proved to be a great benefit for the people who lived within the Imperium's boundaries. Geographic expansion began to slow, but wealth from trade increased imperial revenues and bound the disparate parts of the Imperium into a unified whole. Corps of imperial auditors, originally chartered by Imperator Antonia, reviewed expenditures, ensuring administrative transparency and integrity. Joint edicts by Diocletius, Constantia, Antonius, and Dído guaranteed that anyone in the Imperium could earn Roma citizenship by honorably serving thirty years in the legions. Commerce in silk and spices with kingdoms far to the east grew.

Roma of all ranks could safely walk from Hispania to the Indus on fine roads, built to speed the march of Roma's armies.

Correspondence traveled even faster than trade goods and made managing Roma's vast territories possible. The Imperial Dragon Express carried official letters and parcels between major cities quickly, and the Wizard Post, a network of wizards transporting letters from one end of the Imperium to the other on flying disks, was available to anyone able to pay the price.

Threats from the East and a Fourth Empire

The Imperium prospered for several generations with only minor external threats until the Eastern Empire was invaded by a confederation of hundreds of thousands of horse archers known as Huns. They were fierce warriors and their mobility allowed them to avoid or outmaneuver Roma's legions. Not even Roma's cavalry could keep pace with the Huns' small, fast horses. In addition, Roma did not have enough wizards able to generate shields of solidified sound to protect their legions and dragons from the waves upon waves of arrows the Huns could loose from their powerful bows.

Hun raiding parties attacked Parthian cities. Some even reached eastern Syria. Septimius Severus, Constantia's successor as imperator in the East, realized that Roma needed allies better suited to fighting the Huns than Roma's legions. He looked to the north, to the men and women of the Kingdom of Nordland. The Nordlanders had developed their own rapid attack techniques, using frameworks of struts to extend wizards' flying disks so a single wizard could carry a dozen warriors if necessary. Hundreds of small gold dragons, when fully grown, could transport individual warriors as well. Nordlanders also developed roundshields made from multiple plies of leather, horn, birchwood, and steel that could block the Huns' arrows. The northerners, in self-defense, became adept at devising traps that would stop Hun charges and send horses and their riders into pits lined with sharpened stakes.

With their new Nordland allies—who had already been expanding down the Dneiper, the Don, and the Volga searching for furs—

the Roma were able to hold off the Huns and establish an uneasy truce that reduced the Huns to an annoyance rather than a major threat. Imperator Septimius Severus encouraged more and more Nordlanders to settle in eastern lands and form a buffer protecting Persia, Parthia, Syria, and Anatolia from Hun incursions. Soon, furs, amber, gold, and timber began flooding into Byzantium, the gateway to the Sable Sea and the riches of the north. Former Nordlanders were fighting side by side with legionnaires and becoming thoroughly Roma in the process.

Imperator Constantius of the Eastern Empire, after consulting with the imperators of the West and South, named Haakon One-Eye as the first imperator of the North, with his territory extending from the Vistula to the Ural Mountains. The capital of the Northern Empire was, of course, Byzantium. Haakon immediately set wizards to build a canal from the Sable Sea to the Danube so he could connect the North more closely to the West. Ties were already strong to the Eastern Empire, and the fact that three of the four imperial capitals were situated on the eastern end of the Middle Sea would lead to problems in the future, until new magical discoveries changed travel and communications across the Imperium.

Rings and Gates

The first of those new discoveries was made by a young mage named Tintinabula, who taught at a wizards' academy in Alexandria. Tintinabula wanted to make her fiancé a gold ring so he would remember her when he was away on campaign in distant west Afarika. Working in front of a window so she could enjoy the gentle breeze off the Middle Sea and the tinkling of wind chimes above her, Tintinabula cast her ring with great care. It was twice as thick as a normal ring, but she planned to cut it in half with a jeweler's saw so the two separated rings—one for her fiancé and one for her—would retain a deeper connection.

The fact of the matter was that Tintinabula didn't trust her fiancé. She not only wanted the ring she gave him to remind him of her—she wanted to use the ring to keep track of him and learn whether or not he remained true. That meant she had a listening spell with a tiny congruency prepared, ready to add it to her fiancé's ring once it was ready.

Tintinabula had nearly finished cutting through the soft metal when the delicate chimes suspended above her head were caught by a vigorous gust of wind and emitted their trio of tones much louder than usual. The young wizard was startled and lost control of the tiny congruency for the listening spell. It fell inside the rings just as Tintinabula finished sawing all the way through. *No matter,* she thought. *I can generate a new listening spell easily.* Tintinabula held her lover's ring up to her eye to inspect it and saw there was something purple inside its circumference. The purple was the exact same shade as her wizard robes. She picked up the other ring from where it had fallen onto her lap and held it up to see if it had a purple center as well. Instead, she saw her own eye staring back.

Further experiments proved that sounds as well as sight could be transmitted between the rings, which only made sense given that the congruency used had started out as a listening spell. Trial and error helped Tintinabula refine paired rings so they could expand large enough to show speakers' heads, not just their eyes. Not wanting to lose control of her invention to the Roma state or have it restricted as a military secret, Tintinabula hired dozens of wizards and turned out several thousand pairs of rings, which she then sold to merchants, becoming one of the wealthiest women in the Imperium. Roma's military, aware that the horses had already left the stables, licensed Tintinabula's methods instead of holding her captive and insisting she make rings only for them.

A decade later, nearly every merchant house and officer in Roma's legions had at least one ring, knitting the four empires of the Imperium more tightly together. The eastern border of the Northern Empire became more secure, since Hun incursions could be quickly reported and flying squads of wizards, legionnaires, former Nord-land auxiliaries, and dragons could be dispatched without delay. Even Occidens Province in the far west across the Ocean could stay in touch with the rest of the Imperium more easily.

The development of gates also came about by accident, though several generations later. It started with Eilmer, an absent-minded cat-loving mage in Londinium, who was enjoying a cup of steeped mint leaves in a pleasant tea room near his favorite theatre on the South Bank. He was focused on reading a thick book on math-emagical geometries when he heard a cat meow. Thinking it was his own long-haired white Persian, Snowball, he reached out to rub the cat under the chin in the exact place she liked most. Snowball purred and rubbed back against Eilmer's hand. He thought nothing of it and, still stroking Snowball, went back to reading his book, oblivious to the stares of the wizards and non-wizards around him.

As eyewitness reports relate, Eilmer had opened a freestanding circular congruency as big as a dinner plate, reached his hand through, and found his cat sitting on a cushion in his apartment three miles away near the docks on the *north* bank of the river. After a few minutes, Snowball roused herself, walked across the interface, and settled on top of Eilmer's book, demanding more attention. In the way of cat owners everywhere, Eilmer shifted Snowball from atop his book to a position on his lap, a solution acceptable to all.

Snowball was far from happy when three wizards rushed forward and explained what they'd seen to Eilmer. He stood up, dislodging Snowball unexpectedly and earning—as I understand—a hairball waiting in his slipper the next morning. Eilmer, to his own surprise, was able to create a second *gate* back to his apartment and encouraged Snowball to return through it. He walked the three wizards through the steps he'd taken to construct the new *gate,* but none of them could replicate his creation. Tired of talking, and interested in researching what had happened in private, Eilmer used his purple magestone to summon a round congruency six feet across and stepped through it into his apartment. He stuck his hand back across the interface to grab his mug of tea, then disappeared.

It was later determined that Eilmer was one of a select group of wizards able to generate *ad hoc* gates. Wizard researchers now realized that gates were *possible* and set about determining how they could be constructed. The techniques needed to build fixed gates were determined, with the first two cities to be linked by such a gate being Londinium and Narbo in the Western Empire. Within a decade, thousands of gates were in place, connecting the major cities of the Imperium. Most were created by wizards working for the tetrarchs, as the four emperors were known collectively. Gates were created to serve private interests as well, including merchant families, bankers, and several new delivery services. These services focused on transporting documents, since most verbal messages could be handled via communications rings.

Gates and communications rings transformed the Imperium's administration, and not completely for the better. Where before the bureaucrats at Caesar's Palace in Roma would issue general guidelines to provincial governor-generals, now—thanks to communications rings—they would provide detailed instructions to dictate every aspect of the governor-generals' actions. Since the provincial governors were physically *in* the provinces they administered, while the bureaucrats were not, dissatisfaction with Roma's rule grew in the provinces. Some provinces were so unhappy they threatened to rebel unless they were given more autonomy over their own internal governance.

The members of the Tetrarchy also grew weary of the centralized tax collection function provided by the Roma bureaucrats. The tax collectors treated every part of the Imperium uniformly, without regard to regional customs and traditions. This led to particular problems in client states like Parthia and Persia, where taxes had traditionally been paid to local officials, who would keep a percentage and forward the balance up through several layers to the king or the shah.

With gates and communications rings, centralized tax collectors thought they could sidestep the traditional approach and collect imperial taxes first, without any intervening *deductions.* Imperator Carloman of the Eastern Empire, originally from Germania, initially supported the bureaucrats, but rapidly learned the importance of respecting local customs after a delegation of fifty thousand Parthian and Persian troops decided to camp outside the walls of Antioch to *encourage* him to reconsider. Responsibility for collecting taxes was promptly shifted from Caesar's Palace in Roma to the individual emperors of the Tetrarchy.

Following what was known as the Tax Revolt of Carloman, a new policy for selecting emperors was established. Earlier, emperors were selected from outside the regions they ruled, so they would have a more nuanced perspective on the issues affecting their citizens. Henceforward, most emperors would be chosen from a pool of candidates who were either born in the territory they served or had lived there for much of their lives. Officers and administrators at lower levels were rotated around the four empires to gain experience and help ensure the Imperium did not fracture. Entire legions were also shifted from empire to empire to instill loyalty to the Imperium, not any individual tetrarch or empire.

Concerning the First Citizens

For many centuries, the city of Roma was the center of the unified empire. After the death of Antonia Ferox, her children, Diocletius and Constantia, emperors of the Western and Eastern Empires, kept their capitals at Narbo and Antioch. The city of Roma continued to house much of the Imperium's bureaucracy in the great domed palace of the Caesars, but it was no longer the permanent home of either imperator. The twin emperors realized that whichever imperator controlled the center of the Imperium would automatically have more power than the other. Therefore, they decided that the city of Roma and the province of Italia would never be under the jurisdiction of any individual emperor but would henceforward be neutral territory under a governor-general selected by both imperators. When leadership of the new Southern Empire was given to Antonius and Dído, the children of Diocletius and Constantia, the custom of Roma and Italia's neutrality was continued and expanded under three empires, then four after Haakon One-Eye was named as emperor of the North.

The individual selected to manage the affairs of Italia and the city of Roma on behalf of the Tetrarchy took the ancient title of First Citizen. The position was typically filled by a seasoned administrator who was acceptable to all four tetrarchs. Sylvania Craton, the first person to hold the office, set the tone for her successors by choosing to live in a simple home with few servants, instead of a villa rivaling the ones belonging to the emperors. The emperors encouraged this modest behavior because they realized First Citizens would be well-positioned to expand their authority and rival them if they decided to do so. Accepting an appointment as First Citizen meant losing all eligibility to be named as an emperor.

To constrain their temporal resources, First Citizens were only given control of three legions—one each in northern Italia, southern Italia, and Sicily—along with troops of city guards to keep order in Roma and the larger cities of the Apennine peninsula. Even though their direct military strength was limited, First Citizens exercised power through controlling bureaucratic appointments in Roma and offering wise counsel to the tetrarchs. Because the First Citizens were acceptable to all four emperors, they frequently served as judges, arbitrating disagreements between various factions. By tradition, First Citizens preside over the quarterly meetings of the Tetrarchy in Roma. As the learned wizard Magister Giovanni di Bernardone famously said, "First Citizens have no formal power, but infinite influence. Cross them at your peril."

Concerning Slaves and Slave Revolts

Members of the patrician class know that not all threats to the Imperium came from outside its borders. Prior to the development and military use of wizardry, slave revolts were frequent, and legions were often deployed to crush them. After wizardry filled more functions in Imperial society, slaves' lives became easier, since the most difficult jobs, like deep mining, replaced slave power with magic. Likewise, slaves' roles in planting, weeding, and reaping crops on patrician's estates became less onerous as wizards found ways to accomplish those tasks with magic rather than physical labor. The development of listening spells made it much harder for slaves to plot against their masters in secret, as well.

New policies also served to reduce the frequency of slave rebellions, especially the edicts of the first Tetrarchy, Diocletius, Constantia,

Antonius, and Dído, granting citizenship in the Imperium to any slave who volunteered to serve in Roma's legions for thirty years. Slaves completing such service received a plot of land and the tools to work it as well, usually in the distant hinterlands of the Northern or Southern Empires. Not all slaves sought such honorable work, however. Many slaves assigned to hard labor in the mines and fields were manumitted by their masters when their services were no longer needed, thanks to the transformations brought about by magic. These newly-freed slaves moved to cities such as Roma and Narbo, creating crowded slums filled with vice and depravity, and living off the beneficence of the Imperium. The merchants and manufacturing concerns of the Imperium have absorbed a large fraction of these new arrivals, but there are still lazy and malcontented former slaves who insist on increasing the dole and expanding the entertainments staged by rising government officials.

Slaves' lives are so much better today than they were in the early years of the Imperium that any current slaves ungrateful enough to rebel or former slaves inclined to complain should count themselves lucky to be alive in the present age.

The Future of the Imperium

Roma's Imperium is a colossus, stretching from the ice of the North to the deserts of the South, encompassing lands west of the Ocean to the mountains beyond the Indus that form the Roof of the World. It is axiomatic that no foe can defeat her. Soon, Roma's legions will conquer the kingdoms of west Afarika and expand her control of the lands where the horses of the Huns once rode. And what then? The rich Silk Realm lies even farther to the east, ripe to fall to Roma's scythe. Territories beyond the Great Desert, in the far south of Afarika, await Roma's civilizing legions. Nordland in the north is already a client state in all but name, and her colony of Bifurland across the Ocean, along with the petty kingdoms of Tamloch and Dâron in Orluin, are sure to fall to Roma within a few generations. Sarluin, an entire empty continent south of Occidens Province, awaits settlement by our citizens.

The future of the Imperium is bright, but we must heed the lessons of history and guard against *hubris*. Roma stands impregnable against external threats but must be ever vigilant against threats from inside our borders. We continue to focus on good governance, but a government is only as good as its leaders, and we are only one bad emperor away from chaos. Gates and communications rings make it easier to bind the Imperium together, but they also make it easier for self-aggrandizing emperors to move troops and coordinate their efforts against other parts of the Imperium. New advances in wizardry, such as the illusion magic taught in Byzantium and Numidian Caesaria, may lead to further disruptive changes in imperial society.

Still, with the wise leadership of my esteemed patron, Allorénzo Floréntinus, First Citizen of Roma, and our honored tetrarchs, we can look to the future with confidence.

There is no better time to be a citizen of the Imperium.

MAPS

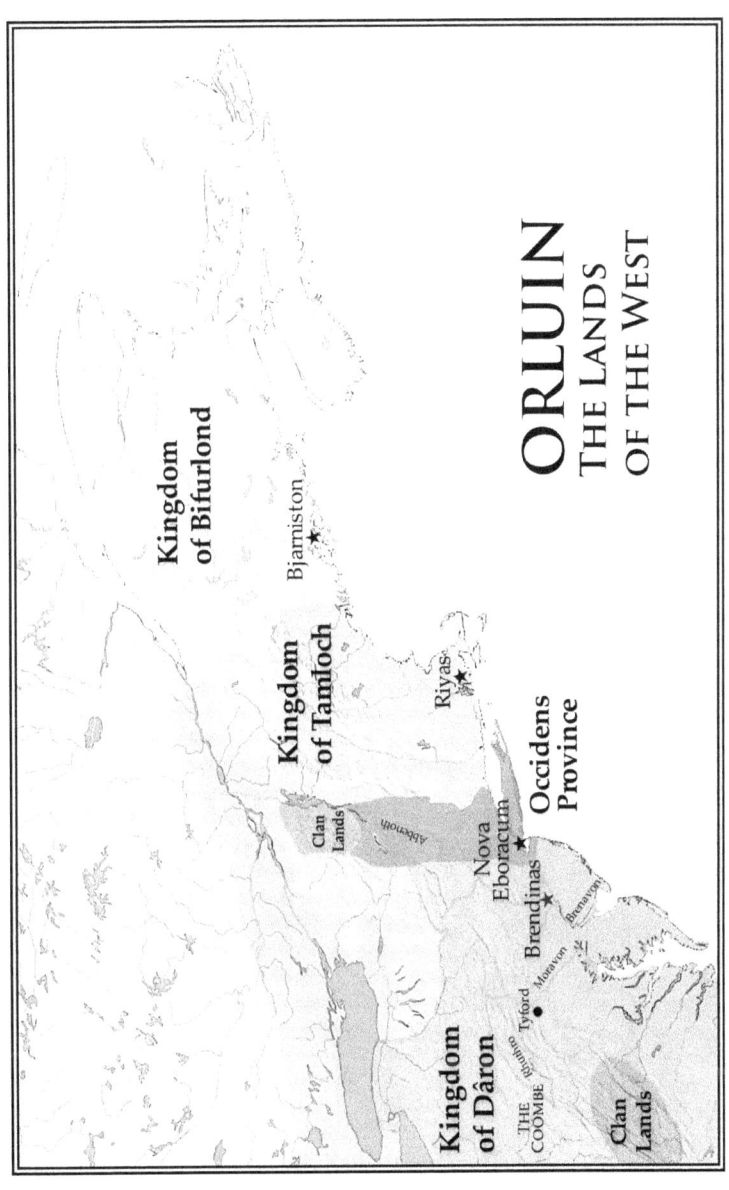

Larger color Orluin and Imperium maps are available at:

CongruentMage.com/maps.html

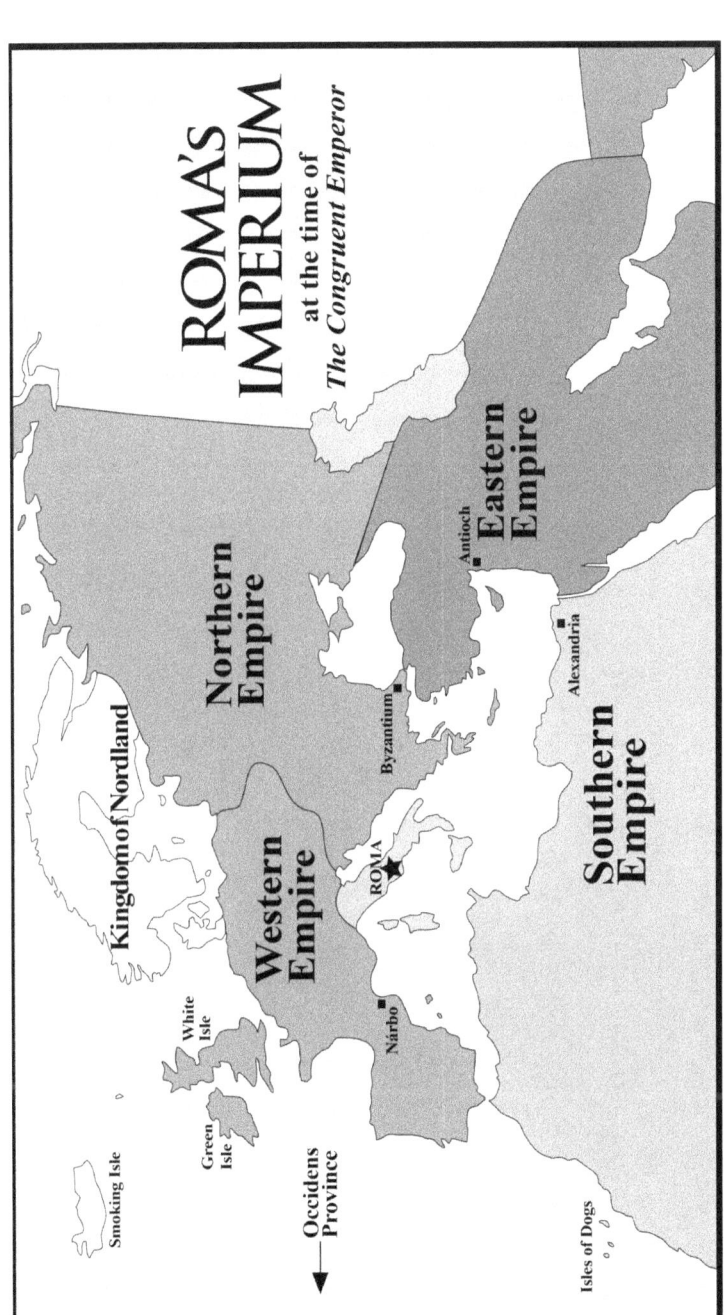

ROMA'S
IMPERIUM
at the time of
The Congruent Emperor

Northern
Empire

Eastern
Empire

Western
Empire

Southern
Empire

Kingdom of Nordland

Occidens
Province

Smoking Isle

White
Isle

Green
Isle

ROMA

Nárbo

Byzantium

Antioch

Alexandria

Isles of Dogs